Praise for The Poison Garden

'Highly imaginative, yet consistently belie... this wonderful dystopian novel is both terrif... ... as if a harbinger for our ti... ...illing read'

'Marwood is one ... the superstars of UK crime fiction and this pitch-black novel, which tackles the fallout from a mass suicide, is one of her best'
i newspaper

'This superbly eerie psychological thriller confirms Alex Marwood's reputation as the Queen of Unease'
Francis Wheen

'I devoured *The Poison Garden* ... Gripping and utterly convincing, it's Alex Marwood at the top of her (already impressive) game'
Jojo Moyes

'Highly imaginative, full of pace and appealing characters, *The Poison Garden* is one of the cleverest and most chilling thrillers of recent years'
Literary Review

'Suspenseful and distinctive, *The Poison Garden* is a powerful and character-driven study of obsession'
Martin Edwards

'Absolutely chilling. Alex Marwood's characters are hauntingly real – evil is always just below the surface. Another brilliant, shockingly dark book from a master storyteller'
Sam Blake

'Dark and shocking, this will chill you to the bone'
Heat Magazine

Alex Marwood is the pseudonym of a journalist who has worked extensively across the British press. She is the author of the word-of-mouth sensation *The Wicked Girls*, which won a prestigious Edgar Award; *The Killer Next Door*, which won the coveted Macavity Award, and most recently *The Darkest Secret*. She has also been shortlisted for numerous other crime writing awards and her first two novels have been optioned for the screen. Alex lives in south London.

THE
POISON
GARDEN

ALEX
MARWOOD

sphere

SPHERE

First published in Great Britain in 2019 by Sphere
This paperback edition first published in 2020 by Sphere

1 3 5 7 9 10 8 6 4 2

A CIP catalogue record for this book
is available from the British Library.

ISBN 978-0-7515-6598-0

Typeset in Sabon by M Rules
Printed and bound in Great Britain by Clays Ltd, Elcograf S.p.A.

Papers used by Sphere are from well-managed forests
and other responsible sources.

Sphere
An imprint of
Little, Brown Book Group
Carmelite House
50 Victoria Embankment
London EC4Y 0DZ

An Hachette UK Company
www.hachette.co.uk

www.littlebrown.co.uk

For Erin Mitchell, who is amazing

I am in blood
Stepped in so far that, should I wade no more,
Returning were as tedious as go o'er.

William Shakespeare, *Macbeth*

Give me the child until he is seven years old
and I will show you the man.

St Ignatius of Loyola

Prologue

Kill me now.

Police Constable Nita Bevan has realised that her partner, Martin Coles, is a windbag. Three weeks together in the car and he's barely drawn breath. He's pretty good when they're handling a shout, but the rest of the time it's babble, babble, babble. And once he's on a topic, there's no escaping it. No matter how tepid her responses, no matter how inconsequential the subject matter, you can guarantee that when he gets back into the squad car and says, 'Now, where was I? Oh, yes,' he will literally pick up in the middle of the sentence he was speaking when the radio call came in. As though he's stuck a bookmark in his brain.

He's at it again as they drive along the Dolgellau road. Subject of the day: cheese toasties and who does the best ones. He's hoping they'll get done with this shout in time to get to the café in Fairbourne, which he recommends even above the Old Station Café in Bala and the Sea View in Barmouth.

'Lovely bit of Caerphilly,' he says, 'and a spot of onion chutney. They do a good Welsh cake, too. Like Welsh cakes, do you?'
Kill me now.

'Not sure I've had one,' she says. She's only been in Wales a month, after all. They're not a foodstuff that's common in Essex.

'Never had a Welsh cake?' he cries. 'Well, you haven't *lived*!', and to her intense relief they round the corner and see the Land Rover they've been looking for, its owner standing beside it in his hill farmer uniform of checked shirt, wellington boots and binder twine.

'Here we are,' she says, and pulls onto the side of the road.

The hill folk tend to divide into two types: the garrulous, like her partner, and the taciturn. To her relief, Gavin Rees turns out to be closer to taciturn. Certainly not interested in bothering with local niceties. They'd be here all day before they got to the actual call, otherwise.

'Thanks for coming,' he says. 'I don't like to go up there by myself, you see. Trespassing.'

'But you're a neighbour, right?' she asks.

'Yes. Next farm over the hill. But they're not very neighbourly, like. They don't like visitors. I've barely been up there more than a handful of times, and then only by arrangement.'

They're five miles inland, beside lush deciduous woodland in the Snowdonia foothills, but the air is filled with the cries of seagulls. Seagulls and crows. If she didn't know better, she would suspect, from that and the smell that hangs in the air, that someone had started a clandestine landfill behind the trees. She eyes the little lodge house, the high metal gates, the wall that surrounds the woods. They're closed, and the lodge shows no sign of occupancy.

'And you think something's wrong because ...?'

Martin has shut up, and is listening intently. A strange mix of a man. You'd think from meeting him that he wouldn't notice a thing around him, but he has a memory like a steel trap when it comes to interactions with members of the public.

2

'Well, it's the smell, you see,' says the farmer.

'Oh, okay,' says Nita. 'So this isn't normal?'

'Does it smell normal to you?' asks Rees.

She pulls a non-committal face in response. No, it doesn't, but smells have many sources. She's been in enough farmyards that she doesn't immediately jump to conclusions any more.

This smell is something else, though. It's pervasive, nauseating. Sewage and ripe cheese and rot. The air is thick with it; so thick that it feels as though it will stick to her clothes. Martin won't be wanting his toastie once they've dealt with whatever's behind those gates.

'And the cattle,' says Rees. 'They've been lowing up in the high pasture for days now. Like they're in distress. I don't think they've been milked.'

'Okay,' she says. 'And the owners?'

'They're a ...' he considers his next words '... bunch of oddballs. Survivalist hippy types. Been up there thirty years preparing for the apocalypse.'

'The apocalypse?'

He nods. 'Years' worth of food they've got stored up there.'

'How many of them are there?'

He takes off his flat cap and scratches the back of his head. 'Hard to tell, really. You know, if you don't go in and they never go out ... Quite a few.'

'Right,' she says. 'Okay, well, I'll just report in to base and we'll get those gates open, eh?'

They find the first body halfway up the hill. A man, thin and shaved bald, face-down on the one-track road. They pull up the squad car behind Rees's Land Rover and get out, stand and stare at him in silence. No need to check his pulse. He's purple, and bluebottles fly busily in and out of his open mouth.

3

'Any idea who this is?' she asks. Rees shakes his head. The taciturn has kicked full-in now. He blinks and blinks.

She radios in to base, to order back-up. Dead bodies are above her pay grade. The two men stand by the corpse and gaze wall-eyed up the road ahead. Nita realises that she's the calmest of the three of them. But that's why I came here, she thinks. After her burnout in London, constantly on guard for terrorists and stabby teens, the prospect of a rural life of farm thefts and the occasional pub fight had been very appealing.

But she's clammy inside her hi-vis jacket. This body isn't making her optimistic about what's further up the hill.

'I think we'd better walk from here,' she says, eventually. 'We'll need to leave this guy as he is, for forensics.'

The birds are the first, the most obvious sign. The seagulls she noticed before, and the big black bodies of carrion crows. There are crowds – clouds – of them, wheeling and plummeting, over the land enclosed by a high wall on the far side of the orchard, where the chimneys of some grand old house soar up into the sky. The air rings with their cries. I had no idea all this was up here, she thinks. It looks like nothing from the road. Laundry – linen – hangs on cords strung between the apple trees, though it's been drizzling the past two days. I don't like this, Nita thinks. I don't like it at all. There should be people. There should be people everywhere.

'Do seagulls eat carrion too?' she asks.

'I think so,' says Martin, finally finding his voice again. 'I think they'll eat anything."

There's something behind that wall, she thinks, and I think it might change us all for life. She glances at her companions and sees that they are thinking the same thing.

*

The gateway is elegant, topped with pineapple finials. But someone has beaten out a message in metal letters and attached them in an arch over the top. She has to squint to read the words against the bright grey sky. *Everybody is a nobody*, reads the outer layer; *Everyone is a someone*, slightly smaller, inside. Not a good place, she thinks. It might have been once, but this is not a good place.

And then she sees the foot. Right there, in the gateway: bare, pointing upwards and black on the heel, the body to which it is attached hidden by the wall. It is only eight inches long.

'Oh, God,' she says. 'Are there children?'

None of us will be the same, by tomorrow, she thinks.

It's a boy. Nine, ten years old, long hair tangled into fingers, face creamy-white beneath its healthy outdoor tan. His mouth is open, and so are his cloudy eyes, and flies rise from the folds of the loose pyjamas in which he's dressed. One foot – the foot that was hidden as they approached the gate – still has a canvas shoe on: rubber sole, elastic across the top. The other lies sole-up in a puddle three feet away.

And beyond him, among lush beds of summer vegetables, lies hell.

They look like a river. Scattering out of the doorways, down the steps of the house, like a host of tributaries, joining together on the paths. More and more of them the closer they come to the gate. Piled on top of each other, frozen where they have fallen. As Nita, Martin and Rees step into the courtyard and the foetid, faecal smell overwhelms them, a tornado of gulls shrieks its way into the air.

The faces are blue, and green, and black. Mouths gape at falling rain. Fingers claw the empty space around them. Many eyes are open and many, she sees, are missing. Carrion birds love eyes. So tender.

Crawling, she thinks. They were crawling. Clambering over each other, trying to get to the gate. Trying to get out.

She gropes for the radio attached to her jacket as Martin bends at the waist to vomit.

They look for all the world like human jackstraws.

Among the Dead

September 2016

1 | Romy

Where I grew up, when someone died, we never spoke of them again.

Out here, among the Dead, it's not so easy. I'm the only adult still alive, and all *anyone* wants to talk about is the bodies left behind.

One more day, they say, and I would have been among them. Another statistic. As it is, this leg is never going to be what it was. They kept me for two weeks in the hospital. Then four days in a police station. They couldn't think of anything to charge me with, but they didn't want to lose me, either. Only Surviving Adult is, it seems, a status that makes you indispensable: a higher status than I've ever held in my life. Then they sectioned me, which meant that they could shut me away on mental health grounds in a thing called a 'facility' and ask me questions every day, and I couldn't run away unless I *literally* ran away. And, to be fair, I *was* quite mad when they let me out. In the two days of silence after the screaming was done, I had begun to think that the world had ended while I lay on my sickbed.

So I lived alone in a cell, like a monk, but not without luxury – my own toilet in the corner and three meals a day and access to the showers – hot showers – whenever I asked.

They were kind to me, on the whole. Brought extra bedding and a television, and a pleasant young family liaison officer took me out for slow, recuperative hobbles on my crutches between interrogations. I saw streets and shops and a small park filled with trees, children running and shrieking beneath a blue sky. There was a canal, an artificial river built before the railways to connect the cities. Little painted boats lined the banks, tin pots full of geraniums on their roofs and bicycles chained to their sides. People live on them. I like that. I would like to live on a boat, if I could. Cast the ropes off and float to the middle of the water. It would be like having a moat.

Every day someone would come and ask if I had remembered any more, and every day I would give the same answer: I was full of morphine. I was on morphine until everyone died, and after that was nothing but white-hot pain. And they would bring photographs of people they thought might have been among those livid blue corpses. Everyone changed their names to join the Ark, which has made identification a difficult process. I've seen so many young people in these photos. People with hair, people with families, teenagers with garish blue eyeshadow, smiling young adults in black cloaks and square-topped black hats clutching certificates. I saw Luz on a horse, in a tweed jacket and a hard hat, and Siraj with thick green hair gelled up into spikes and a tight sleeveless T-shirt emblazoned with the words 'Never Mind the Bollocks'. And there were others I didn't recognise: lost young people of the 1980s, the 1990s, the ones who vanished and left their families wondering. So many, so many, lost for the first time long ago. I would nod when the faces were familiar, and shake my head with the regret I suspected was appropriate when I didn't.

Sometimes the interrogator would tell me who they were in the photos. That way, I learned that Father's real name was Damian Blatchford, and Ursola was a Michelle. My own mother's name was Alison Maxwell, last definitely seen in Finbrough, Berkshire, at the age of eighteen, living in a caravan with a baby who was me, but I knew that. She was thirty-eight when she died at Plas Golau, which makes me almost twenty-one. It turns out that I have a birth certificate, which they say is a lucky break as it will make my life out here among the Dead less complicated.

They told me that Damian-pre-Lucien taught philosophy and politics at a thing called a plate-glass university on the south coast of England. He gathered a small group around him in the early 80s – most of them long gone, left or banished; one or two, I know, long buried in the chapel graveyard – and from there the Ark was born. With Vita – beautiful Vita – things are murkier. She was American, which makes it harder. They know she was in the country by 1986, because apostates from the early days have come forward and mentioned her as a driving force even then. You know how many Americans passed through the country in the decade before 1986? Literally millions, they tell me, and nobody really knows how many actually left. Somewhere in the big box wastelands of Ohio or Oregon or Tennessee, a family has probably thought her dead for decades.

I wonder if anyone has mourned me.

After a month they moved me here, to a place called a Halfway House. It's a large house in a town by the sea called Weston. It's mostly full of philosophical junkies and humorous alcoholics, but there are a few 'vulnerable adults' like me. Most of my peers in this category spend their time crying in corners, or smoking with intense concentration on the steps outside, so I don't feel particularly vulnerable by comparison. I, at least, am prepared for the disasters to come and stand some chance of surviving them.

We do group therapy once a day, and twice a week I see a counsellor. I have been designated 'disabled' because, I think, they don't know what else to call me, and so every two weeks I can go to a machine in a wall and insert a plastic card, and it will give me £110 from a bank account they've set up in my name. I don't really know what to spend it on – they give us two meals a day here and I was given an assortment of trousers, T-shirts and underpants while I was in the station. The Infirmary clothes they found me in were bagged up and taken away as 'evidence'. So I bought a pair of stout boots and a waterproof jacket at a hiking shop in Weston, and I buy tobacco for my new friend Spencer, because he likes it and says he has few pleasures left to him now that heroin is off the table.

My therapist is called Melanie. I'm not sure why I need to see her, and assumed at first that it was some sort of surveillance thing. But everyone has assured me over and over that I'm not under suspicion. Melanie says that there is something called survivor's guilt, and something else called PTSD, and I am a prime candidate for both. As such, I have a high chance of suicide, depression and 'social disability'. She believes in these things, has spent years studying them, the way I spent years learning to butcher animals and build shelters from sticks. Horses for courses, I guess. 'I'm not sure you're right about this "survivor's guilt" thing,' I told her once. 'I've spent my entire life being trained for survival. Surviving the Apocalypse was all we ever thought about. It was our purpose and our identity. Being a survivor is something to celebrate, not feel guilty about. I've done exactly what I was meant to do.'

'Yes,' she said, 'but this is the *real* world.' And then she went a bit pink and clammed up, because I guess that wasn't the sort of thing she was supposed to say.

Melanie isn't a specialist in cults. There aren't many to hand in Weston, I suspect. She does her best. I don't mind. I enjoy the opportunity for conversation. Everyone I used to know is dead, and I am invisible.

I quite like the Halfway. I grew up communally, after all, and I'm used to having people around me. What terrifies me is emptiness. The silence that would descend in the police station in the small hours once the drunks had passed out. The sound of the spyhole sliding back for the hourly suicide check was an intense relief because then I would know, just for a moment, that the world had not ended. Here, though, in these plasterboard cubbyholes, I can hear the creak of bedsprings and the coughs and sobs of my housemates, smell cigarette smoke combining with the salty murk of seaside air, and feel comforted in the knowledge that they're all still alive for now.

Melanie says that I must make myself go out every day. An hour a day at first, then more, then more, until I can leave my four safe walls all day, if I want. 'You can build yourself up,' she said. 'It's like a muscle. It gets stronger every time you use it. Think of it as physiotherapy for your brain.'

I nod and frown. I have learned that this is a good way to make them stop explaining stuff. If you smile, they know you're not listening. I hope that if I look as though I am, if I convince them I have improved, they will let me go. That they will think I'm safe to leave before they spot that my growing belly is more than just the sedative carbohydrate diet they serve us. The Outside fills me with fear, but I must achieve living there.

So I do what she says, and make myself go out into the streets every day, limp down to the seafront to savour the crash of

13

the waves and the cries of the gulls and the scattered litter and dropped ice cream cones, but oh, the fear I have to fight to do it. Every day at Plas Golau we would hear another tale of slaughter among the Dead: the knives and the guns and the lead in the water, the trucks driven into crowds, the women sold for sex, the glittering silver towers of Mammon plunging to the ground. You don't forget those tales, if you've heard them every day for almost twenty years.

Mostly what Melanie does is sit in her padded office chair and write notes, and say, 'And how did that make you feel?' And I will think up some words – *sad, lonely, isolated, afraid, angry, resentful,* though I will throw in the odd *hopeful* to encourage her – and she will write another note and nod. When they noticed that I was throwing up, it seemed to make her happy. She called it 'a symptom of emotional turmoil'. 'It's quite common, when people are experiencing powerful negative emotions,' she said.

'It happened this morning when I was deciding between tea and coffee,' I told her. 'And again when I was reading the newspaper. An article about how they train monkeys to look after blind people.'

'Well, we'll talk about those issues another time, perhaps,' she said, and wrote another note. I've noticed that you don't have to do much to divert people's attention. Once they've assumed something, most things they see or hear will confirm it. All you have to do is not point out the obvious, though most times even doing that won't make much difference. It's fine by me if she wants to think I'm throwing up because I can't handle the sight of a few dead bodies. I'm naïve in many ways, baby, but I'm not so clueless I don't know that your existence will complicate things. Much better to let Melanie think she's helped my neurosis by making me vomit.

'Let's talk about your family,' she says. 'How do you feel about them? Your brother and sister. Do you miss them?'

'I ...' How do you explain, to someone who didn't live it? 'Not particularly.'

She makes another note.

'No, look. We weren't, you know, a *family* family, the way you'd think of it. *All* of us were family to each other, whether we were related by blood or not. We were a ...'

I search for the words. I know she's waiting for me to say 'cult', but I'm damned if I'm going to. I hate this, more than I hate anything about my life now. The fact that our vocabulary was so different from their vocabulary, so I have to hunt for the words that they would use instead of the ones I've used every day of my life. No one ever gives me credit for this; they just assume that because we spoke English the problem must be that my vocabulary is lacking. If I were Syrian, they'd be offering translation services. But then, who could translate for me? They're all dead, or disappeared. I might as well be speaking Mayan.

'I suppose you'd call it a commune. It was communal,' I tell her for the umpteenth time. 'Because we were all raised together and the adults took turns to care for us.'

The Pigshed. That's what it was called, the schoolroom where we did our learning while the adults worked the fields. I tend to avoid using the name with Melanie.

She extrapolates. 'Ah, a sort of kibbutz?'

'If you say so. And besides, Eden's only fifteen and Ilo is thirteen. I was out training most of the day by the time they were out of nappies.'

'Training?'

'*Everybody has a function,*' I recite. '*Everybody is a nobody, and everyone is a someone.*'

She looks impressed. 'Is that something you came up with?'

15

I look back at her with my 'oh, please' look. I'm quite pleased with this look. I learned it in group therapy. And then I start feeling sick again, and have to excuse myself to run to the toilet. Which uses up another few minutes before I come back to Melanie and her own trademark look: 'you see?'.

'And how *is* the anxiety?' she asks, pointedly, when I return.

I get out my NHS-issue notebook and read out my homework. Over the last seven days my anxiety levels, on a scale of one to ten, have been eight, eight, six, ten, nine, nine, eight. The first nine was the day I nearly got mown down by a bus on the seafront. There are skills I have yet to fully master, and it seems that crossing the road is one. I rarely get down below eight even now, breathing exercises and mindfulness notwithstanding. I love beta blockers, though. The wonderful slow, calm beating of my heart after I take one.

She isn't delighted, I can tell from her face. Then she brightens, because optimism is Melanie's default, just as expecting the bombs to start dropping at any moment is mine. 'Well!' she says. 'Friday looks like an improvement! What did you get up to on Friday?'

I consult my diary. 'That was the day I stayed in and cleaned my room. I think it would have been lower, actually, except that I started worrying about the chemicals in the cleaning products. They won't harm me, will they?'

The ten, the next day, was when I thought I saw Uri down on the seafront, buying an ice cream from a van covered in cartoons of dancing confectionery. And my heart started thumping until he turned full-on to me and I saw that he was just a random man with a shaved head and a thick neck.

'Oh,' she says. I must be a frustrating patient. I must start lying in the notebook, or I'll never get out of here. And I need to get out of here, soon. If I register a few threes and fives, it'll make

16

her happy. Last week I had a bout of paranoia that chemicals from laundry detergent could leach from my clothes through my skin, and ended up rinsing everything I own in the bath. It's a shame, as I am still amazed by how easy cleaning is when you use chemicals. And how good the food tastes. But you can never be too careful.

Chemicals are one of the ways that the human race will end, Father said. Chemicals, plague, war, famine, nuclear winter, endless summer, economic collapse, devolution. 'All-natural is the way we live,' he would intone from his podium on the Great House steps as the Launderers scrubbed and squeezed at our clothing in bath-sized laundry coppers filled with soapwort. 'All-natural is the future. All-natural is life itself.' Our clothes were all-natural grey because bleach is a chemical, too, but it was convenient that they were, because soapwort, like feverfew, is not all that effective.

'Will they?' I ask.

'I don't think so,' she says. 'There are lots of laws about chemicals. They have to test them a *lot* before they start selling them.'

You say, I think.

Of course, what I really mean is whether they will harm *you*, but I can't tell her that, because she doesn't know you exist. But I can't kill my baby. Not now. You're the future.

I don't know why I'm worrying so much about the chemicals. After all, everyone at Plas Golau died an all-natural death.

17

2 | Sarah

Next of kin.

Sarah Byrne last saw her sister twenty-one years ago. She left when Sarah was ten, and their parents never spoke of her again. And, because she had never liked Alison much, Sarah just went along with it. She remembers her more as a looming presence, a whirlwind of rage ready to go off and destroy the world, than as a sister. Seven years is a big gap to bridge when you're children, and by the time Sarah was old enough to form solid memories and opinions Alison had been consumed by hormonal rage. In a way, her leaving was a relief. Sarah had just dismissed her from her mind as their parents had dismissed her from their lives. She'd felt the death of their old tuxedo cat, Mimi, two years later, more than she ever felt Alison's absence. It's been twenty-one years and she doesn't remember thinking about her in a decade. And now ...

Helen is looking at the centre-spread of the *Mail on Sunday* where Sarah first found her sister. One of these multi-page spreads with which the papers fill the space between ads in the silly seasons, while signalling that they *care*. There have been three this year already. At New Year, a round-up of every woman killed by her partner in the UK in 2015. At Easter, a year's worth of London's knife crime. And now, the holidays under way, every one of the identified dead of Plas Golau, in full colour.

NOT JUST A CROWD, reads the headline. Beneath, across sixteen full pages, a yearbook layout of the dead, a pious little editorial about how 'we' forget that behind the headlines and the body counts are real people. People whose lives fit neatly, with mugshots, eight to the tabloid page. And there was Alison, in among them, and Sarah's world imploded.

Helen looks up. She's on Sarah's great-grandfather's high-backed sofa, pretending she's comfortable. The fact is, there isn't a comfortable seat in this house. Just formal furniture for people who took pride in discomfort, and Sarah has been too sad, too demoralised by life, to do anything about it since she moved back in.

'So how does it make you feel?' asks Helen. She's the counsellor at the school where Sarah is administrator, and a lot of her conversation consists of questions like this. A professional tic, like always having a Kleenex pocket-pack about her person.

'I ... awful. Guilty.'

'Guilty? Why guilty? You were only ten when she left, you said?'

'Yes, but I'm not ten now, am I? I'm thirty-one. I've been an adult for over a decade.'

'And?'

Sarah swings her hands out, wildly. 'I should have ... I could have done something. I could have tried to find her.'

'Really?' Helen picks up her wine glass and takes a sip. So

kind. She could be home now with her two kids and her quiet husband, but instead she's taken time out to come and look after Sarah. I guess she probably thought I'd feel bereaved, Sarah thinks. I mean, you would, wouldn't you, if someone told you their sister had died? But she's grateful, whatever. She's felt very alone in the three years since her divorce, knocking about in her dead parents' museum of a house the past two. To find out that she has even one friend prepared to drop stuff for her is a pleasant surprise.

'You said you didn't know where she was,' says Helen. 'You know that's more down to her than it is to you, right? I think in the end, given that there was always someone here to contact, you can fairly safely assume that Alison didn't want to be found.'

Sarah finds herself tearing up for a moment. She doesn't know why. It's not as if she missed her sister when she was alive. She picks up the *Mail* and looks at Alison's pitiful biography.

Alison as she remembers her. A photo taken at school, in her dark blue uniform cardi. Alison at fourteen, fifteen, hair still unembellished blonde – it went every colour in the rainbow once she entered the sixth form – and cut to the shoulders with her mother's kitchen scissors. Glaring at the camera as though she wanted to blow up the world.

Sarah puts her wine down, feels slightly sick all over again, though she's read it and read it until she should be immune, really. She stares at all the other faces on the page. Young ones, thin ones, sad ones, ones that smile dutifully for the camera – decades-old photos donated by long-abandoned families. She still doesn't know where they got this photo. They certainly didn't contact the school; it would have been Sarah who would have answered the phone if they had. One of her sister's former friends, she guesses.

She reads again, though she remembers the words by heart:

Alison Maxwell, 38. Born Finbrough, Berks, a member of the Finbrough Congregation evangelical church. Having developed a reputation in the town as a 'wild child', she left the family home at 17 when she fell pregnant. Last seen in Finbrough in the winter of 1995. Spotted a handful of times with her baby, working stalls on the music festival circuit the following spring and early summer, then vanished from sight. Two further children, born at the compound in 2001 and 2003. 'She was lovely,' said an old schoolfriend. 'She was a rebel, but anyone would be, coming from that set-up: it was stifling. I can't believe this was what happened to her. But I can see, if you're all alone with a baby and you're looking for something better, how easy it would be to catch you.' The Finbrough congregation apparently disbanded some time ago, and her family are uncontactable.

Sarah sighs. Drinks. Puts her glass down. So much for the press's fierce reputation for tracking down their targets. Though to be fair they will have had enough easy pickings available that they'd not have needed to spend much time on the dead ends.

'So, what do you think?' asks Helen. 'About the kids?'

'I don't know,' she says. 'I don't, Helen. Social Services are all over my arse about taking them, but I don't know anything about children.'

Helen makes a pfft noise. 'You deal with them literally every day.'

'No, but ... that's shouting at them about lunch money and telling them not to run in corridors. It's not ... it's other people's kids. Not my own.'

Helen wrinkles her nose. 'Nobody knows anything till they have them. The global population was still growing last time I looked.'

They fall silent. She knows Helen is waiting, like the therapist she is, for her to say something, but she doesn't know what to say. Looks around her gloomy parochial home, all dark wood and ancestral portraits, and listens to the sound of the grandfather clock clearing its throat in preparation for striking. All those nights lying awake in the dark, feeling its malevolence as it waited to count off another hour of life with nothing achieved.

How can I provide a happy home for another generation here? she thinks. This place I was so keen to leave that I married the second I got the chance? I'm so stupid, coming back here when there was literally a whole world out there to move to after my marriage broke down. I should have sold it straight away. The only use for a house you hate is to get the money to buy a house you don't.

She especially hates that clock. Hates the sound of it, the tick, tick, tick, the whirring strike mechanism. Hates the sound of all clocks striking. She wanted no clocks, she stipulated, in her marital house in Reading, and Liam went along with that. They timed everything by mobile phone. Yet now, every Saturday night, she dutifully winds the evil thing, like her father and his father before him.

'I'm going to meet them on Saturday,' she says, eventually. 'It's the right thing to do. I'll put faces to the names, at least.'

'Okay,' says Helen. 'But that doesn't commit you to anything, just remember that . . . What *are* their names?'

'Eden,' Sarah says, 'and Ilo. Fifteen and thirteen. And there's a girl – woman, she must be twenty or so by now – called Romy. She's the one they found in the Infirmary. The sole survivor. Adult survivor.'

'Oh, God, I remember the photo,' says Helen. Sarah does too. A skeletal form that looked dead itself, oxygen mask strapped to her face, body strapped to a stretcher, snapped by a thousand

22

lenses as they carried her past the piled-up corpses to an ambulance. 'I didn't realise she was ... another of yours ...'

'Yes. She was the reason Ali left home in the first place. Well, I say "left". She wasn't exactly given a choice in the matter.'

Wow, I sound bitter. Well, I am, I am. They kicked her out, and now she's dead, and I have to make a decision and I don't know ...

The clock strikes, and she jumps. It's literally hard-wired into her, now. Pavlovian. I'll sell the bloody thing, she thinks, whatever else I do. Get an antique dealer round and flog him the lot. And then I'll sell the house. I don't have to put my life on hold for people I didn't even know existed until yesterday.

'I was going to go travelling,' she says, mournfully.

'I know,' says Helen, 'it's a bugger. Life does have a few curveballs up its sleeve.'

'Can't I just ... I don't know. Put money in trust for them when they're adults or something? You know – give them what would have been Ali's share of the house? That would be fair, wouldn't it?'

'If you can be okay about leaving them in care, I guess.'

'I can't do it, Helen. Except – God, I don't know how I'm meant to do this. They're going to be a mess. They saw everybody they've ever known *die*, for God's sake ... and a cult! The closest I've ever come to knowing about kids and cults is maintaining the anti-radicalisation staff training spreadsheet.'

'Well, you wouldn't be doing it alone,' says Helen. 'If they come to the school, there'll be me, for a start.'

'But they ... they need someone who knows them. Someone who knows how to comfort children. Look at me. It's not just them who'll be a mess. *I'm* a mess.'

'I wouldn't say so,' says Helen. 'No more than half the parents I come across.'

'I am! Come on – who would live in a place like this if they weren't a mess? I need to sort myself out before I can be any use to anyone else. What if I screw it up?'

'That's fear talking,' says Helen. 'Which is perfectly under-standable. You *don't have to do this*, Sarah.'

But it's not their fault, Sarah thinks, and feels the guilt all over again. They're orphans of a storm created by other people's wicked choices.

3 | Sarah

They enter the room on light feet, smiling, the taller one leading and the shorter – not much shorter, just a couple of inches – following behind.

They're extraordinary. They look like space aliens. Not of this world, certainly. Long and thin, with delicate wrists and long fingers and big blue eyes with eyebrows dark and arched. Small noses, flared nostrils. And hair so fair it's as though the sun comes out as they come through the door, curling close around elegant skulls like lambswool. They have got that, at least, from their mother, and the startling eyebrow colouring; little else reminds her.

The hair has grown in from near-total baldness, she knows from the reports she read in the papers. They shaved their heads once a month, men and women – and children as well, once they reached puberty. A gesture of equality or something: everyone reduced to the same androgyny, no one able to flaunt a crowning glory. Whatever; an upmarket wig supplier came forward and claimed that it had been a regular customer for their shorn hair, which fetches a surprising amount on the open market. Nothing gone to waste, then.

'Hello,' says Sarah.

It's hard to tell which is which, to tell boy from girl. They're both wearing jeans, loose-cut, and striped T-shirts that were clearly bought to be grown into. They're thin, and Eden, the girl, is small-breasted even for her age. It's only when they speak that she identifies who is who, for Ilo's voice has started to break and he speaks in a rusty, uncertain tenor. He's the shorter of the two, the best part of two years between them.

'Hello,' they say, both at the same moment. Same accent, same intonation. Surprisingly posh, though she's not sure what she'd been expecting. Some sort of deep Welsh accent, probably, given where they were born.

'Are you our aunt?' asks Eden.

'Yes,' she replies. Awkwardly, for despite the fact that she's been one for twenty-one years, she's never thought of herself in that role. 'I'm your Aunt Sarah. Sarah Byrne.'

'Sarah Byrne,' says Ilo. Considers it for a moment. 'That's a nice name,' he says. 'Did you choose it yourself?'

An odd question. But she'll be getting odd questions; she's been prepared for that. These two strange children have grown up away from the world. They've been in this care home in Barmouth for three months, but you can hardly expect the ferals they're sharing their space with to have educated them in the ways of the outside world. 'No,' she replies. 'Byrne was my husband's name.' She's considered reverting to her maiden name since Liam turned out to be a cheater, but on balance going back to being a Maxwell feels even more like regression. If there's one thing Liam has given her, it's that she doesn't have to walk round Finbrough with the burden of that surname, everyone wondering, just vaguely wondering, if she was related to that weird church on the High Street. As a Byrne, even though she lives in a house that belonged to the Congregation, sits on furniture it paid for, is gazed down on from the walls by generations of pastors, she is, at least, anonymous when she walks out of the door. Not an obvious target for press looking for relatives of the dead.

'How interesting,' says Eden. 'We're all called Blake. We were born Blake, but there were lots of adults who didn't start off that way, like you. We were named after our Father.'

Sarah doesn't know what to say to that. What strange little creatures. 'I thought you had different fathers,' she says, confused.

'Yes,' says Ilo. 'That's right.' Then 'Oh! I understand! Yes. We had different conception fathers. But Lucien Blake was Father to all of us.'

'And my *actual* father,' adds Eden, proudly.

'Yes,' says Ilo. 'Have you come to take us home?'

Sarah starts. Another question she hadn't expected. 'I—' she stumbles '—it's not that simple, I'm afraid.'

Their smiles never falter. Haven't left their lips since they entered the room. She looks imploringly at the social workers for back-up and receives nothing in return. Hell, she thinks, I should have paid more attention to the hints they've been dropping about the strain on Social Services. These children aren't really people to them, they're just the remnant of a massively increased workload in a system that's already creaking. Christ, they'd be encouraging me to take them if my surname were Hindley.

'Look,' she says, 'I came to meet you, and see that you were all right. I only found out you existed a few days ago.'

'I understand,' says Ilo. There's something eerie about that smile. She can't put her finger on it. Maybe it's just its constancy, or the fact that it's another thing that makes it so hard to distinguish him from his sister. 'Our mother told us about her parents.'

Silence. Of course she did, thinks Sarah. Bruce and Barbara Maxwell and the Little Baby Jebus. I made a joke of them at university, still share eye-rolling laughs about the Congregation with the staff at the school, though they haven't had any pupils from there in years. Turning them into a joke made it easier to live with. I should think Alison must have made them monsters, to her children.

She attempts to move the subject on. 'So, how are you both doing?'

'Oh. We're well,' he says.

'Everyone's been very kind,' says Eden.

She doubts that. But then, she doesn't really know much about their previous lives. Maybe life in a council care facility is a breeze by comparison. 'I'm so sorry about what's happened to you,' she says. Has to cut herself short, for she's shocked to find her eyes filling with tears. What for? My sister? The thought of their loss, the things they've seen, the mark it will leave on their life? She blinks them hurriedly back.

'Thank you,' says Ilo again. He seems amazingly composed. Shock, probably, she thinks.

Eden breaks the uncomfortable silence. 'It's nice to meet you,' she says, and gives her the brightest of smiles. 'Our mother always said that the one thing she regretted was not knowing you. I hope we'll get the chance.'

4 | Sarah

The hush just before the bell goes is like the calm before the end of the world. Every day, at 12.25 and 3.40, the school enters the eye of the storm, the silence palpable as the students listen for the bell, the teachers' voices suddenly audible above the shifting hubbub.

Sarah, behind her desk in the administration office, has become so accustomed to it that she no longer needs to look at the clock. As the sound drops, she picks up her keys, locks the office and hurries down the raised corridor by the dining hall to stand on the doors. The last thing she anticipated when she left the Wellesley Academy – Finbrough Church of England School, as it was then – was that she would one day return to work there. But there's barely a thing about her life now that she would have predicted three years ago.

Helen Brown is waiting in her usual spot. They team up for this duty every day, since these supervisory roles are often handed out to the people who won't be shut in a classroom when the bell goes. It was how they became friends in the first place;

two-minute chats before the dam breaks, just short enough that Sarah didn't get nervous, didn't get shy, didn't worry that she was boring Helen the way Liam said she bored him.

She smiles as Sarah approaches. 'Afternoon,' she says. 'How did it go?'

'Um,' says Sarah, 'it was … interesting.'

'Nice to hear some enthusiasm.'

'Yeah, maybe I need a while for it all to sink in?'

'I should think so.'

'Social Services seem to have practically decided I'm going to take them whether I like it or not.'

Helen frowns. 'Maybe we should talk about this in my office?'

Am I a client now? she wonders. I thought we were friends. 'No, it's okay,' she says. 'I think I'd rather have a friend's opinion than a therapist's.'

Helen nods. 'Okay. Friend's advice: you don't have to do anything, Sarah. I know you probably feel like you don't have a choice, but you do. I think you need to think hard about whether you're up to the job.'

'Surely nothing can be worse than the care system?'

A little twitch of the eyebrows. 'Why do you think the care system exists, if that's really true?'

'Okay, fair point.'

'Look,' says Helen, 'devil's advocate. They're going to be a massive mess, you said it yourself. I mean, the stuff they've seen, by itself … there's going to be trauma, and PTSD, and God knows what cognitive dissonances, and brainwashing, and survivor's guilt, and … you don't *know* them, Sarah. It's not like taking on a *real* niece and nephew. It's not going to be, you know, Little Orphan Annie.'

'They *are* a real niece and nephew, though,' says Sarah. 'They're the only family I've got left.'

30

Helen glances at the clock. Two minutes till the barrage breaks. She glances around in case an early bird has broken loose to overhear, then steps over to stand beside Sarah and lowers her voice. 'But you've never met them before yesterday. And a cult, Sarah. A *cult*. And they've not left it, you know, *voluntarily*. They'll not be looking for ways to liberate themselves from their beliefs.'

'I don't know,' says Sarah. 'Don't you think a mass suicide might straighten your head out a bit?'

'I've no idea. Seriously, this is well out of my zone of expertise. I mean, if they come to Wellesley Academy they'll most likely be passing through my office, but I can't say I feel confident about helping them. I'm more handsy dads and boozy mums, you know?'

'But surely Social Services ...'

'I wouldn't count on it. They're buried under piles of shaken babies. You'll be on waiting lists all over the place. Sorry. I know I sound pessimistic, but you need to know what you'd be getting yourself into. How did they seem, to you?'

'Polite,' says Sarah.

'Polite?'

She shrugs. 'They said Alison talked about me,' she tells her, and is surprised to feel that swell of grief again. How can I be grieving for someone I've not thought of for years? she wonders. Maybe it's the other stuff I'm grieving. That my life has ended up so empty that Helen is the closest thing to a confidante I've found since I came back here and all the old friends somehow melted away with my husband. Alison was the only person who knew what it was like, in our family. If things had been different, we might have been friends. Might have been each other's armour against the world.

'Did they?' asks Helen. 'Do you know what she said?'

'She said I was her one regret,' says Sarah. 'That she left me behind.'

'So you think that makes you responsible for her kids?'

'Well, at least I have a house,' she says, lamely.

'Which you were going to sell,' says Helen.

'I know,' she says, and the sense that the prison bars are closing around her once again is almost overwhelming. 'But you know, by rights half of it should have been their mother's ... '

'You don't even know them,' says Helen. 'You didn't even know they existed till last week.'

'I knew about the older one.'

'It's not the older one they want you to take. Have they given you any sort of timeframe for this?'

'I've not said I'll do it yet.'

'Mm,' says Helen. 'Look, do you know anything more about the sister? How about her? They *know* her.'

'Yeah, not really,' says Sarah. 'She's in a facility at the moment, apparently.'

Facility. Oh, the lengths we'll go to, to avoid saying 'mental hospital'.

'Sarah,' says Helen, 'it sounds as if you're talking yourself into it, honestly.'

The bell goes.

'Oh, hell, here we go,' says Helen, and goes back to her post. 'Brace!'

An escalating rumble, a salvo of slamming doors and the rumble becomes a thunder. Children tumble from the classrooms like water over rocks, ignoring raised voices begging them *not to run*. The big ones toss the littlies aside like flotsam; thousands of words burst from hundreds of mouths as though their owners have been in solitary confinement for days rather than the hour and a half since morning break. Sarah stands her ground as the

32

wave breaks. The rebels first: big boots, greasy unisex hair, girls pouting and boys with ties at half-mast. Tuesday is chip day in the canteen – the only prospect that will make the rebels break into a run. Then, once they're safely out of the way, the normal kids, the ones who have friends to walk with, the ones who have nothing either to fear or to prove. And finally, blinking into the light like dormice emerging from hibernation, the kids who want to avoid the attention of the ones in the front: the undersized, the ones with the cumbersome musical instruments, the geeks and the uncool and the socially awkward. And, hanging over it all, the scent of body odour.

And then here comes Marie Spence. Always the last to appear and always, nonetheless, at the head of the queue. Every school has one, at any given time, and the moment one melts away to join the real world, another springs up in her place. At her shoulders, inevitably, following in her wake like Secret Service agents, Lindsay and Mika and Ben McArdle, this year's court favourites. Sarah can't stop a wry smile rushing across her lips when she sees that they have taken to sporting white earbuds dangling from a single ear. It'll be Ray-Bans next, and grey suits. And even from this distance she can smell Victoria's Secret body spray.

Marie swanks up the hall past the staff room, and the smaller children – the less privileged children, children who don't want trouble – part before her like the Red Sea.

She reaches the queue, walks past as though it doesn't exist.

'There's a queue, Marie,' says Sarah.

'Someone's saving my place, miss,' says Marie. Tosses her hair over her shoulder like a shampoo ad. 'She's got my purse.' And she walks on past, her sentinels in step behind her.

Sarah looks up and catches Helen's eye.

Helen winks. 'God, I hate that girl,' Sarah says, as they

33

count up the lunch tickets, and Helen doesn't even bother to ask who. The entire faculty hates Marie Spence and her Jaguar-driving parents.

'The curse of entitlement,' says Helen.

'A curse on who?'

Helen laughs. 'God, on everyone. Like the universal quest for victimhood. It's a zero-sum game, in the end.'

'I can't wait for GCSEs,' she says. The school doesn't have a sixth form. They go to college in Newbury, or one of the big schools in Reading, if they want to go on to A-levels.

'The sister,' says Helen ten minutes later, picking up their earlier conversation. 'Can you maybe track her down and get in touch, at least?'

'I'm not sure how.'

'Ask someone?'

'I suppose.'

'It might give you some sorts of clues, at least. See what she's like? I mean, she might well be fine.'

'She's in a loony bin, Helen.'

'We don't say loony bin these days,' says Helen, all professional offence.

'Okay, sorry. I mean yes, if I could. It would be helpful to meet someone who's got some knowledge, but I don't think that's particularly an option.'

'Well, just think about it a bit more, then, Sarah. Don't take this decision in a rush, please. If you really are the last resort, and it sounds as though you are, they'll still be there.'

5 | Romy

The circumference of the Earth is 24,901 miles. There are 123 billion acres on its surface, of which just 37 billion acres are land. The Plas Golau estate was 487 of those. I knew the size of the Earth – for knowledge, as Lucien has told us many times, is the key to our survival – but the gulf between knowing something and understanding it is vast. I used to look at Cader Idris, towering above our farmland, and believe it to be a behemoth. Now I know that its 2,929 feet are just a pimple on the surface. The world is huge, and that scares and excites me all at once.

I was so frightened when they brought me from Wales to the Halfway House – across a river so wide that the far shore was lost in mist, over a bridge where juggernauts roared like dragons on a six-lane road – that I hid my face in the hood of my top and didn't look up until my police driver assured me we had arrived.

It's 129 miles from Weston-super-Mare, on the Bristol Channel, to Hounslow, on the outskirts of London. I am, at least, prepared this time. But my case worker's little car feels like a rabbit overtaken by stampeding horses as we race up slopes towards the horizon. Great tracts of green land, majestic trees, briefly glimpsed houses lost among them, and, in the far distance, the sea. Then a river, then cranes and ships and buildings so large that, even in the distance, I can see that their cavernous interiors would swallow Plas Golau whole. Strange names on signs. Ancient, I know, but a different order of ancient from the jumbles of consonants where I grew up. Portishead. Avonmouth. Bristol. A tangle of roads so fast and so convoluted it makes me nauseous with terror. But Janet switches through the maze of lanes with ease. More signs: *London 110*, *Newbury 65*, *Finbrough 71*, *Reading 78*. My skin prickles when I see the sign for Finbrough. I glance at the speedometer. She is sticking to a lawful seventy-two, which has already started to feel normal to me, until I try to focus on a detail at the side of the road only to see it shoot past in a blur of speed. In an hour, we will pass the place where I was born. If she stopped the car now, I could walk there in three days. From my new home, it would only take a day and a half. But maybe I'll take the bus. They taught me how to take a bus in Weston, as part of my life-skills training, along with buying things in shops and registering with a doctor and how to use a money card and how to look things up on the internet at the library. I like buses. Janet, the case worker, says that where I'm going there's an underground railway that goes all the way into the centre of London. The very thought makes me cold.

'It's a start,' says Janet. 'That's the thing. Nobody's saying you have to stay in Hounslow for the rest of your life. But it's as good a place as any to find your feet. Not too busy, not too rough, but handy for London, when you've got your nerve up. You've actually fallen on your feet, when you think of the places you could have been housed. The hard-to-let lottery can be very unforgiving.'

I can't imagine I shall ever want to go into London. It's dangerous in so many ways. As it is, if a nuclear bomb drops on Westminster, Hounslow will be flattened. I will most likely die in a collapsing building rather than a firestorm, and if I survive there will be no avoiding the fallout.

We turn off the motorway, turn left at a roundabout and then left at another. Street after street of square, squat houses, yellow bricks, car parks, a couple of gloomy towers. People live in those, Janet says. They're a bit of an eyesore, all that concrete. Building was like that in the 1970s. But they're not bad inside, and the new cladding has made quite a difference, and the views are great. I squeeze my eyelids together to help me focus and see that all the way up there in the sky there are washing lines, shirts and trousers and bedclothes, drooping forlornly against the grey sky. I wonder what it would be like to be in one of those if it caught on fire.

It takes ten minutes to reach our destination from the motorway. 'Write it down, Romy,' says Janet. 'Here: use a page out of my notebook. Keep it in your bra till you're sure you remember the address.' And I suppress a smile, because, rather than a bra, I have my breasts strapped down with a bandage from the chemist's shop, to stop their burgeoning growth showing. There's no room for *anything* in there.

'136b Bath Road, Hounslow. That's your home. It's near the station. You can ask people where that is, if you get lost. You won't need to tell people your actual address. Best not to.'

I stare and stare, try to memorise some landmarks, but everything looks like everything else. Roads, houses, yellow bricks, red bricks, cul-de-sacs, street signs. Just a blur of sameness. And then a huge aeroplane passes over us, so close that my hands fly to my head because I think we are about to die.

'Oh, yes,' says Janet, 'it's on the flight path for Heathrow.

37

That's one of the reasons there are flats available around here. Don't worry. You'll get used to it.'

Easy for you to say.

Looking out at the wide street, I feel as though the Apocalypse has already been and gone. It's lined with shops, but half of them have boards across their windows. And not new boards, as though they're expecting a riot, but old boards, boards that are rotting at the edges, boards that have had posters stuck on, layer after layer, peeled off again, re-pasted. Hounslow West Underground station looms out of the dusk.

'I know,' Janet breaks into my thoughts. 'It *does* look a bit run-down. You'll be surprised, though. There's most things you need, at least for now.'

Mainly, I can see a giant car park.

She pulls up in front of a launderette and a grubby little shop that calls itself Bath Road Foods and Off-Sales, a hundred yards down from the station. 'Here we are,' she says.

There's a blank door to the left of the launderette, with the number 136b in metal letters screwed to the front. I guess we're here.

Inside, it's warm, and smells of soap. After the sour pong of the Halfway House, it's pleasant for a moment, until the underlying scent of damp kicks in and I see from the light filtering through the windows that they are steamed up. Through the floorboards I hear the rumble of the machines below, turning over and over, beating out dirt, tumbling out steam. It's so warm I long to take my coat off, but I've got this far without anyone finding out about you, and all it would take would be for her to see me at the wrong angle and my liberty would be lost.

Janet switches on the light. I see a space that's large, after what I've been used to. Maybe twenty feet by twelve, with kitchen cupboards at one end and a couch and a little low table under the window. The walls are covered in flowered wallpaper – small pink roses on grey trellis, ivy leaves between – and the couch is covered in a shiny fabric that almost, but doesn't quite, match it. Clean patches on the wallpaper show where other furniture has stood, where pictures have hung. A low ceiling is lined with plasticky tiles that would melt and drip on your head if there were a fire.

We had plain whitewashed walls at Plas Golau. Nothing to divert our attention from the end of the world.

'Oh, my goodness!' she says. 'They've left the telly! Lucky you. I'm surprised the house-clearance didn't take it, but it's very old-school. I don't suppose it's worth anything. That'll be company for you.'

I guess it will be a good distraction, while I build up my courage. I like the channels with nothing but people selling things. The astonishment and enthusiasm about gadgets that solve problems you never knew you had, and clothes that even I can see are guaranteed to make you sweat.

'Come on,' she says. 'Let's go and get the boxes and we can get you settled in.'

I have three boxes and a suitcase, and I don't really know what they contain. I packed the suitcase myself, but the boxes came in the back of Janet's car with her. She said that it was 'bits and bobs we've all collected', and I know I should be grateful. No, I *am* grateful. I've met extraordinary kindness: kindness that's at odds with what I was told about the Dead. All the people I've met, even the junkies and the alkies, have rushed to press things into my hands, to think of things I might need. I left the police station with three dresses, two skirts, two pairs of jeans and five T-shirts, some of them brand new. At our parting session, Melanie gave me two sets of sheets and pillowcases, and a boxed set of plates and bowls and mugs. 'This probably counts as getting too involved with a client,' she said, 'but there you go. Four of everything. Start your own home.'

By the time we've got everything up the stairs, I'm puffed out and red in the face and the scar on my leg is throbbing. I've got so unfit, in only three months. Physiotherapy hurt, but it was hardly a comprehensive fitness regime. I must restart my training. Father would be ashamed of me. 'You never know when you may need to run,' he used to say. It was the basis of everything we did. Run, fight, hide, farm. But we had Plas Golau then, so we had somewhere to run *to*. I don't know what I'm supposed to do now or where I'm supposed to go. I need to work out the back exit from this place. There must be one. And then I need to work out the fastest route to open countryside.

Janet plods up behind me, a canvas carrier in one hand and a duvet, wrapped in plastic, brand new, white, unsullied, under the other arm. 'Here,' she says. 'Here's your bedclothes. You want a hand putting them on the bed?'

'Thank you,' I say. 'I'll be okay.'

'Okay,' she says. 'Time for your first cup of tea in your new home, eh? There's a kettle in that box. Only a basic one from Asda. But you have to have a kettle.'

'Oh,' I say. 'Tea.' I don't understand tea, or why it's so important to the Dead.

'In the box,' she says. 'And a pint of milk.'

A whole pint of milk, all to myself. I still haven't got used to the luxury they all take for granted. I guess this is what I'll use Melanie's mugs for.

'There's chocolate digestives, too,' she says proudly. 'I did you a little box of staples, so you won't starve while you're settling in. Pasta. Bread. Marge. Some apples. A few tomatoes. A bit of cheese. That sort of thing.'

'Thank you,' I say. They like their pleases and thank yous.

'And in here,' she says, opening the canvas carrier, 'I've got something I think you might be happy to see. I had a word. With CID. I've got a friend, comes in useful. It's not orthodox, but she could see my point. They've been through it, obviously. But it's not like you're a suspect, and they've got a whole warehouse full of evidence. Here.'

In the carrier, down at the bottom, is a box. My box. The one I made myself, as part of my training. We all made our own, when we did our Carpentry apprenticeship. I made it from a lovely piece of beech from a tree that came down the winter before. A tiny bit of privacy in a world where everything, everything, was in the open. 'Oh.' For a moment I feel tearful. Here it is, the whole of my past. 'Thank you,' I say, and this time I mean it.

Janet touches my shoulder, and I do my best not to flinch. 'I thought you'd like it,' she says, kindly.

'I do,' I say. 'I mean, what you've done. Thank you.'

She stays until she's sure I'm not going to burn myself to death. She shows me how to work the gas cooker, how to turn on the TV and where the meters are for the payment keys, and advises me to clean the fridge before I put anything into it. 'It will have been off for months,' she says, 'and when they're off they're like little bacteria farms.' I suspect she thinks I've not actually seen one before. As we've driven along she's explained windscreen wipers, traffic lights, and the purpose of the windmill that towers over the road at Reading. Like most people, she seems not to fully grasp what 'off the grid' means. Not that I myself knew the phrase, until I saw it in the *Daily Mail* in a long article about us, most of it wrong. We weren't a free-love organisation, for a start; the complete opposite, as anyone with half a brain would be able to tell from our birth rate. And our expectation

41

of the coming Apocalypse had nothing to do with God. And it wasn't that we had no power. We had solar panels and a small, well-hidden bio-gas plant. We just didn't squander energy. We rose with the sun and, in summer at least, went to bed with it, too. We weren't medieval and we weren't ignorant, but my vocabulary is cut off some time around 1984, when Plas Golau was bought and the library stocked. We shared the classics – the war poets, Shakespeare, Asimov, Dickens – in groups, on long winter evenings, but there was nothing modern, nothing the Dead would call *current*.

'Are you going to be okay?' she asks. A silly question, really, for what's she going to do if I say I won't be? Take me back?

'Of course.'

'Right,' she says. 'I'll be off, then.'

'You don't *smell* off,' I say, then have to give her another grin. Everyone who comes into contact with me, who knows my history, seems to expect me to be earnest, serious, rocking in a corner. It will be a relief to be able to make a joke without someone taking mental notes. Though I'm not sure who I'll be able to make a joke *to*. Eilidh was my joke buddy, and Ilo, sometimes, when he could be persuaded to take the world lightly. Lord, I miss them. I still find it hard, after all these years, to believe I'll never see Eilidh again.

She laughs, eventually. 'Good luck,' she says.

'Thank you,' I say, and edge her towards the door. 'I'll need it.'

'Oh, I'm sure you won't,' she says.

And then she's gone, and I am alone in my little kingdom. I draw the curtains and strip off my clothes; release the strapping and liberate my poor crushed breasts. I put a hand on my stomach and stroke it with my thumb, and relish the fact that I no longer have to hide you away. So far so good, baby. Three months out of Plas Golau, and we're still alive.

6 | Sarah

She stays sitting after she's finished her ready-meal lasagne, finishes her glass and pours another, looks at her dining room with a social worker's eyes for the first time in her life, with the home visit a few days away. 'Christ,' she says.

Clutter has built up, and she's never noticed it. She's never had a reason to eat a meal at the table, or to feed anyone else, so she's been using the table as a filing system since she moved back in. It's elbow-deep in paper and the floor's not much better. The paintings have collected cobwebs and the furniture that lines the walls is grey with dust. Miss Havisham hoping to find herself an Estella, that's what I'll look like, she thinks. This is what happens if you hardly ever have guests.

She walks through the house with the same eye. On the wall in the hall, an oil painting of a warty old woman in a black dress and white lace bonnet. Hester Lacey, founder of the Finbrough Congregation. She saw Jesus down by the river and dedicated her life to making a nice house for him to come back to. The antique shops of the M4 corridor have filled with portraits of her as the Carpenter's Estate houses have been sold off. They're so commonplace now that even the charity shops are turning them away. She's imitating a look of benevolence in this picture, but you can see that she had a heart of steel.

So many things she's not opened, not looked in, in the two years since she inherited. She walks through to the kitchen – memories of ham salads made up and sitting beneath fly-screens on the table for silent post-church meals. Always a pan of brown soup waiting on an unlit burner 'to warm us up', brown earthenware bowls on the side. Oxtail. Almost always tinned oxtail, the smell a mix of abattoirs and laundry baskets. Sarah longs to be free of all of it. Dreams of a place as far from Finbrough as she can get, of open skies and open windows with no hum from the motorway, and a new beginning. A sense of purpose, she thinks, that's what I need. Not to just be drifting through life doing a nothing job just to pay the heating bill.

I'll get a skip, she thinks. I shall get a skip and just dump the contents of every drawer I haven't opened since I've been back straight into it. That's one of the main decluttering tips, isn't it? That if you've not needed it in the past year, you don't need it at all? I've been paralysed all this time, but I can't go on living like this. Even if I wanted to, I can't bring children – my own or anyone else's – into this.

She gathers up an armful of papers and goes up to her father's office in the attic. Out of sight, out of mind, and she needs to find the birth certificates – her own and Alison's – to show the case worker when she brings the kids for their visit. Belatedly, it's occurred to someone to ask her to prove that she's who she says she is.

More dust. She feels ashamed. The room is lined with filing cabinets and the boxy old desktop computer sits on a big wooden desk. Otherwise, there's nothing on show. No family photos, no paper clips, no paper. Everything put away, as though he knew he wouldn't be coming back. He liked his secrets, Bruce Maxwell. Kept things separate – records here, the cash in the safe at the church – so that only he could really make it all add up.

She tries the drawers, looking for the folder she found it all in, two years ago. She opens the desk drawers first – a jumble of office-related bits and pieces, a whole drawer of blank paper. Another of paper that's printed on one side, a single line drawn across the print with a pen. Her parents never recycled. Thought of it as a socialist concept. But they were thrifty.

Leaflets. The ones she handed out on the High Street every Saturday from when she was baptised at five to when she left for university. 'THE WAGES OF SIN'. 'WHO WAS HESTER LACEY?' 'YOUR BLESSED WATER: HOW TO USE IT'. In the bottom drawer, the Congregation's own special brand of greeting-and-damnation cards.

It's all well labelled, at least. He might not have wanted his congregation to know what he was up to, but he liked to be able to lay his hand on anything in a moment. *Church accounts. Church history. Correspondence.* The latter turns out to be a collection of yellowing letters from people responding to Blessed Water ads, and a folder of receipts from newspaper ad sales departments. The *Membership* drawer is poignantly sparse. She leafs through a couple of files. Copies of will bequests, details of addresses and phone numbers, little else. The occasional folder is stamped with the word DECEASED. After a point he must not have been able to bear to throw any more away, as the membership counted down to zero. The day he collapsed and died at the lectern in the Lord's House Chapel, he was preaching to a congregation of thirteen. And only two of them were below retirement age.

I'll take the lot down there, she thinks, and leave them in the office. She still has a key, of course; several. But she's not set foot in the place since her father's funeral and has only the vaguest idea if anyone is there at all any more. It always looks shuttered and neglected when she walks past on market days. Maybe they realised it was all over, and sold up and cleared out the safe and got the hell out of Dodge, and the Lord's House is just going to rot there until the resurrection. She hopes so, for their sakes.

Property. A whole drawer. A collection of folders containing lease agreements for all the church's long-sold houses. *'The tenant agrees that this agreement will terminate with one calendar month's notice on the return of Our Lord Saviour Jesus Christ,'* they begin. Maybe I should frame one of these, she thinks, and put it in the downstairs loo. They're curios now, souvenirs of a flock that genuinely believed they were maintaining property for the return of the Lord. Nothing more.

And then she spots the drawer marked *Personal*, right down at the bottom in the corner, and her attention slides away.

Here they are. Her family, in paper and cardboard. A dozen folders. *House* (she puts the deeds away safely, at last). *Insurance. Health* (they had, it seems, private health insurance, despite the NHS and the protection of God). *Car* – spare keys, ownership documents, service record. Their old Volvo still sits in the garage, untried, untaxed and unloved. She doubts it would even start without help; she's never needed to use it as she has a car of her own.

A folder with plans for their funerals makes her blush with guilt. It would stand to reason that they would leave these things, and she never even looked. They're stark, and brief. Her father organised her mother's funeral and spoke there about death and unending hellfire. But it looks as though he did consult her file, for she remembers well the moment when the Congregation started marching on the spot while singing 'Onward Christian Soldiers'. She looks at her father's file. He wanted 'Amazing

Grace' and an oration from a man who she knows to have been dead for the past four years. Ah, well.

And then she finds the name files. *Barbara. Bruce. Sarah. Alison.*

She checks her own first. It's old stuff. Exam certificates, a confirmation photo, a birth certificate. School reports, for God's sake. And a photograph of her wedding to Liam, the bride looking both in love and terrified, and Liam looking – oh, God, why didn't she see it then? – sly. Nothing after. Sarah's record-worthy life ended, as far as the Maxwells were concerned, with her wedding to a heathen. She wasn't thrown into the outer darkness like her sister, but they clearly didn't think anything would be worth recording afterwards. They didn't even have this photo out on display, as normal people would. She takes her birth certificate and puts it on top of the cabinet.

She opens Alison's. It's thin. So thin she thinks for a moment that it is empty. But no: there are three things inside. Her birth certificate. Her GCSE certificate. Her first passport, bought for a school trip to Flanders when she was fifteen. The tales of dormitory shenanigans that leaked back to her parents were so scandalous that Sarah was never allowed to go anywhere overnight when it got to be her turn.

She runs her thumb over Alison's face, remembers the pudding-basin haircuts, the snaggly teeth because the Maxwells didn't believe in orthodontics or other types of 'playing God'. Which is worse, she wonders, being the elder and having to forge your own way blind, or being the younger one, who catches the flak for their predecessor's mistakes?

Well, I suppose only one of us is dead.

And then she feels guilty again, because nobody deserves death just for being foolish.

And those kids don't deserve to be left hanging because of the circumstances of their births, Sarah.

47

Stop it.

She bends to slip the file back into the drawer and her eye is caught by something lying on the bottom. The corner of a photograph. She pulls it out. A little shot taken in one of those passport booths in the post office, just the one, cut off the end of one of those strips of four. Alison and her baby. That's Romy. She recognises the wrinkled skin, the tuft of black hair, the almond eyes. A little bigger than that one time she saw her, when Alison brought her home for a failed thirty-second visit, but undoubtedly her.

It's a terrible photo. They both look unwashed and ungroomed and cold and wet.

She moves the files aside to see if there are any more. There are envelopes. A dozen, two dozen, her sister's handwriting. They hang open, the letters visible inside.

She takes one out, unfolds the letter. It's been torn from a spiral-bound book and written with a pen that's caught and blotted on the paper. The handwriting is kiddish, with circles over the 'i's and multiple underlinings and exclamation marks.

7 May 1996

Dear Mother——

This letter is to wish you a <u>happy birthday</u>!!!. I know the chances are that you won't read this, but I'm sending it anyway. I <u>do</u> wish you a happy, <u>happy</u> day, whatever you do, and send my love to Father and Sarah as well. I'm so sorry about the window. It was a <u>stupid</u> thing to do! I promise to pay you back and hope you will forgive me one day.

I'm enclosing a photo of me and Romy, your

granddaughter. She was born on November 11th and she's _nearly six months old._ We took this in the photo booth in Reading when we went up to register her birth, so it's quite out of date now. I wish you could see her. She's so sweet. She rolls over all by herself and drags herself over to her toys, and she's such a sunny little soul. She smiles at _everybody_. She's on purayed food now and she loves carrot and potato and chicken and rice especially. She sends her love to her nana and her grandpa and her Auntie Sarah, and wishes she could meet you all.

We're living at Riverside Caravans off the London Road. We'll have to move on when the summer season begins in June, though, as the rent will go up then. Social Services say they are looking for somewhere for us to go, but it will probably have to be a bed and breakfast as the waiting list is really long. But my neighbur Magda says I can work on her Chai Tea stall at the festivals in the summer, so that might work as she says I can take Romy with me and lots of people do. Anyway, we will be here till the end of May and would love to hear from you. Caravan 23. I don't have a phone, but you can call reception and leave a message.

With lots and lots of love,

Your daughter,

Alison

She slips it back into the envelope, looks at the others, some browned and faded and some, God knows, practically brand new, the handwriting maturing but still familiar. She was *writing* to them. All these years, she was writing to them, and one or other of them was just slinging them out of view into this drawer. Why didn't they just throw them away? Did they want me to find them one day, now it's too late to do anything? Subconsciously, at least? Or maybe they just didn't care. Were keeping them for themselves, as souvenirs of their righteousness, or as some sort of twisted gesture of contempt.

She reaches back into the drawers and gathers them all up, counts them. Seventeen. So if they came annually, on Barbara's birthday, she must only have given up shortly before Barbara's death. As she stands up, the interior of the room, the view of the garden below through the dormer window, suddenly swim, and she has to reach out and grab the cabinet for support. Adrenaline. Cortisol. Some change in her blood pressure, because as she was standing her mood changed from sadness to absolute rage, and that rage has made her giddy.

She died. My sister died in slow terror on a summer's day in Wales. I will blame them for this for the rest of my life. Wicked, wicked old people, to do this to their child. To all the children. Their hearts are made of granite and they deserve to burn.

She takes the letters downstairs to read, because she needs a glass of wine. She knows, now, what she will do, however much she fears it.

Before the End

2001–2002

7 | Romy

June 2001

'Cyanide.'

'Cyanide?'

Somer laughs. 'Not enough to kill you. Just the grass in the middle of the circle. You really wouldn't bother to try to poison people with fairy-ring champignons. They'd have to eat half a ton to get a proper dose.'

'Ohhh-kay,' says Romy.

'There are loads of more effective ways,' says Somer.

'Yew berries,' says Romy. She studies the pharmacopoeia every day, what she can understand of it. She's only five, after all, and, though the Plas Golau children are quite advanced in their reading, there are limits. But she wants to be a Healer, like her mother.

Some poisons are useful, in smaller doses, as medicines. Like digitalis, from foxgloves, for failing hearts. And for its own dark ends? Well, you never know when you might need poison.

When the hordes come over the hill, poison might be their only salvation.

'Belladonna.'

'Deadly nightshade.'

'That's right. Don't ever eat a berry unless you're sure what it is,' says Somer.

'I *know*,' says Romy, and rolls her eyes. Grown-ups repeat themselves, constantly.

'The largest organism in the world is a fungus,' says Somer. 'In Oregon. It's two and a half miles across.'

'No!'

'Yes!'

That's bigger than the whole of Plas Golau, with its woods and fields and little reservoir, its house, its kitchen gardens, the rough-grazing pasture where the altitude gets higher and the soil gets thinner, its patch of open moorland. Further across than Romy's entire world. 'A honey fungus,' says Somer. 'We have to root them up the second we see them. They kill trees.'

Romy stares at the fairy-ring, thinks about the thing growing beneath. Quietly, creeping outwards, root by root by root, taking over the world, killing it off.

'Come on,' says Somer. 'Time's a-wasting.'

She loves these afternoons with her mother. Knows they won't last forever – adulthood comes early here. And it will come earlier for Romy, because Somer has been blessed with a second child. And not just any child: Father's child. Of all the women at Plas Golau, he has chosen to make her the latest mother of his offspring. Romy is proud. So proud. It's rare to have a brother or a sister, and a brother or sister who could turn out to be the One is so special that sometimes she has to squeeze herself in bed at night to control her excitement.

It's nice to escape the summer heat, but Romy's glad they don't have to go deep into the woods. They've shared so many ghost stories, hunkered down beneath their blankets while storms howled around the dormitory rafters, that she's nervous of the outer edges of the estate, the band of tangled wildness that's been left to grow around its walls. Deep below them runs a peat-rich stream, the outlet from the reservoir, tumbling on down the hill over boulders deposited in the Ice Age, its rocks slippery. And the woods are full of bracken, and bracken means adders, everyone knows that.

'So remind me,' she asks as they clamber on, 'who is Jesus again?' She likes to cross-question her mother about the world into which she was born. She likes to tease herself with detail of the lives the Dead lead. Make herself horripilate with fear or howl with laughter. Make herself feel lucky.

'He's the son of God.'

Romy frowns. 'But I thought God didn't exist?'

'That's right.'

'So how ... ?'

'By making it up,' says Somer. Having left religion behind her, she has left it completely. The only thing that matters to them is survival. When the end comes, they carry the future of the human race. There is nothing more important.

'Mm.' Romy thinks of her new sibling, conceived not only with the Leader's blessing but with his seed as well, and shakes her head wonderingly. She doesn't know who her own father is, of course, but it doesn't matter, really. How people were on the Outside is not how they are here, and as he didn't come with them he'll be lost to them anyway when the End comes.

'So basically,' she asks, 'they thought Jesus was the One?'

Somer pauses and lays a hand on her swollen abdomen. Smiles a smile that gazes into the future, a modern madonna in a flaxen tunic. 'I suppose,' she says. 'Of course, the difference is that the One is real.'

'And our baby could be the One, couldn't he?' Romy asks proudly, though of course she knows the answer. The baby is Lucien's, and only one of Lucien's children can be the One. Everyone knows that; it's the Prophecy. But to be related even to a could-be-the-One is madly exciting.

'*Could* be,' says Somer, with false modesty. 'But let's not get ahead of ourselves.'

Romy spots a clump of saffron chanterelles clustered around the roots of a noble beech tree. Cries out and points.

'Oh, well *done*,' says Somer.

'So your mother and father think Jesus is going to come back?' continues Romy. 'Like a zombie?'

'Haha. Yes, I suppose so.'

'That's mad,' says Romy.

'Right?' says Somer. 'And they think when he does he's going to want to live in Finbrough. They built a house for him in the centre of town, and a model village for his most loyal followers. Everyone lives in the little ones and keeps the big one nice for him, with a church built in for convenience. But then they built a motorway – a great big road – right bang smack between the two, which was sort of funny.'

'What's Finbrough like?' she asks. She knows she was born there. Wants a picture in her head, for most of her peers in the Pigshed can point to the actual literal spot where their mother pushed them out.

'It's . . . not much, really. It's a small town on the road from London to Wales. People mostly go there to sleep, 'cos there's not a lot to do. But it's handy if you want to get to other places, and that's why they live there, I think.'

*

56

They finish gathering the chanterelles – a tenth left behind, always, so that there will always be more – and move on through the dappled shade. Somer is awkward, her movements clumsy with her big belly hanging off her bony frame. Pregnant women get an extra pint of milk a day from their small dairy herd, but any further level of gorging is frowned on. You still need to stay agile, Father says, still need to stay on your feet, because, when the worst thing of all happens, you will need to be able to run. But with no weight on the back to balance her she often looks as though she's going to tip right over. She's pink about the face, though her great thick blanket of shiny golden hair is plaited carelessly to get it off her neck in the summer heat. Their hair is a burden in the summer, for they all wear it long, getting it cut every three years. The Dead buy hair. Imagine. And blonde hair is the most highly prized of all. Romy holds her hand, and for the first time she's aware that it's she who's offering the protection, not Somer, and she feels proud again. Everything will change in three months, she knows that.

'Are you looking forward to it?' she asks. 'To meeting him?'

'Or her,' corrects Somer. 'Yes. I can't tell you. It's so different, this time. It's amazing, the way everyone is so happy.'

'Not like with me,' Romy says, sadly.

Somer looks down and squeezes her hand. 'We were in the wrong world, baby. I wanted you. I wanted you from the moment I knew you were there. You know that, don't you?'

She feels mollified. 'I just wish,' she says, 'that I belonged.'

Somer looks shocked. Drops to her knees in front of her daughter and squeezes her upper arms. 'Oh, Romy, but you do. You *do*. Don't you know? Vita chose *both* of us to come here, not just me. You were so wanted that you were *chosen*. We're the most important people in the world, Romy. You know that.

57

The Ark will be the survival of the human race. We'll be the fathers and mothers of the future. It's just that nobody knows it, apart from us.'

'Everybody is a nobody,' recites Romy. 'Everyone is a someone.'

'Precisely.'

'But this ...' She lays her palm flat on her mother's swollen abdomen. 'This could be the One. I'll never be the One.'

Somer lumbers back to her feet. 'No. But that doesn't mean the things you do won't matter. You'll need to look after your brother or sister. When they come. You'll need to take care of them and watch out for them, because they could save the world entire.'

'How will we know?' she asks. 'If it's them?'

Somer shakes her head. Lucien will have thirteen children with this baby. But only one will be the One. 'I don't know, to be honest. Lucien says that they'll rise up when the time is right and lead us to safety. I don't know if it'll be obvious before that. But we've got to trust his word.'

'Lucien is very wise,' says Romy.

'He *is*,' says Somer, with love and longing. 'He's the wisest.' And she puts her hand where Romy's has lain a few moments ago, and looks strangely melancholic. 'Anyway,' she says, and leads them forward.

'So is it true,' Romy asks, as she helps her mother onto the path that runs along the brook, 'that the Christians ate Jesus?'

'*What?*'

'That was what Kiran said, in the Pigshed. He said they have a ceremony every Sunday where they eat his flesh and drink his blood.'

'*Did* he?'

'Yes.'

58

'Oh, that's—' Somer stops. 'Yes, that's exactly what it is. You're right. Whatever you do, Romy, you want to steer clear of Christians. They're a cannibal cult, and if you're not very careful they'll eat you alive.'

'So nobody lives in Jesus's house?' she asks. She finds it hard to imagine. It seems so ... wasteful. Every inch of Plas Golau has a working function. The inhabitants of the Ark sleep six, sometimes even eight, to a dormitory room, and all the other spaces – the old chapel, the eaves and the attics, the cellars, the spaces beneath things and the spaces above – are overflowing with the necessities of survival. The barns and the godowns, the roof spaces and the rows of hooks along the beams ... everything has a function. Nothing is wasted.

'Oh, no,' Somer replies. 'But it has to be kept perfect for when he moves in. The women go up every day and sweep and clean and polish and make a cold collation so he always has something to eat.'

Romy catches sight of a big healthy shroom over by a rock and trots over to snatch it up. Somer gasps. 'No! Romy! Do you want to kill us all?'

Romy freezes.

'Don't you *look*?' asks Somer. 'Have I taught you nothing at all?'

She looks down. The mushroom, now that she's looking properly, barely resembles the ones they've been picking. It has a sturdy white base, yes, and a generous cap. But it's greenish, and its gills are white.

'It's a *Death Cap*, you twit.'

Romy drops the fungus as though it were scalding. They are taught about the Death Cap, and the Destroying Angel and the Dapperlings, long before they learn to forage. Like yew trees and foxgloves and deadly nightshade, like adders and hemlock and unwashed wounds, they are the stuff of schoolroom legend, drummed into them as soon as they can talk. The land is lovely and will be their salvation, but there are things that grow there that will kill you.

'No, don't throw it away.' Somer gets out the black bag and scoops it up. 'Where did you find it? We need to mark the place, so we can keep coming back and picking them till they're all gone.'

Romy points. Now she's looking she sees half a dozen, near-phosphorescent against the forest floor. 'Don't put your hands near your mouth,' says Somer. 'Literally just one of those can kill a dozen people. You're not to touch *anything* until you've washed your hands, do you hear?' She quickly scoops the remaining fungi up with the bag. 'Come on. We're going to have to go back now. Take them to Vita so she can dispose of them. Oh, honestly, Romy, and it was all going so well.'

'Sorry,' says Romy. Her fingers itch and she longs to wipe them on something. She feels as though the poison is seeping through her pores, will start at any moment to stop her liver. A long, slow death, hallucinating and bleeding from her orifices. She's heard the stories.

'It's okay,' says Somer. 'Just ... be more careful, eh? If this had got in with the others we'd have had to throw the lot away, and then we'd have to confess. It'll be all right. It's good we found them. A good scrub with the scrubbing brush and you'll be fine. And it's getting on. We don't want to be late for drill. What is it tonight, anyway?'

'Toxic gas,' says Romy.

'Ah, yes,' says Somer. 'We've not had that for a while. Good to keep your hand in, eh?'

8 | Romy

September 2001

Everybody is a nobody. Everyone is a someone.

The Blacksmiths beat the letters out in the smithy and fixed them into an arch above the courtyard gate. You pass in, you pass out, you are reminded. They repeat it to each other constantly – as compliment, as negation – for it is a phrase that will work as either. Romy will be well into her teens before she notices the blandness of the words, the shallowness of the sentiment, of so many of the adages by which they live their lives. But their purpose is so high that it won't matter, even then. Daily life depends on a shorthand of proverb and platitude, of automatic response that keeps them on the straight and narrow. And the Ark is working towards a noble goal.

Romy is on her knees in the physic garden behind the old chapel, in prayer position, plucking weeds from the soil around the black cohosh plants. 'A garden,' says Father, 'is like a society. Weeds, unchecked, will choke the useful plants, and steal the nutrients they need to live. We must be vigilant. Bad thoughts, bad ideas, bad people – all of them threaten our survival.'

She's so caught up in her task, reciting the Latin and common English names for the plants around her, that she doesn't at first notice the tall, handsome figure sweeping towards her from the graveyard gate. But then Vita calls her name, and she leaps to her feet. Vita knows all of their names, of course, but it's rare to be addressed by her, so when it happens you feel privileged. And today is special. Her mother went into labour in the dark dormitory in the small hours, and today Romy will become a sister.

Or an orphan, for childbirth is a serious business.

'Hello,' she says. 'Is it over?'

Vita flashes her glorious smile. 'Yes,' she replies. 'You have a sister. Are you ready to come and meet her?'

Romy gulps, and nods. A sister! Imagine! But excitement doesn't stop her from carefully cleaning off her tools in the water bucket by the pump, drying them with a cloth and putting them back on their proper hooks before she follows.

The chapel graveyard, where the Llewellyn family sleep beneath weathered headstones and the honourable dead of Plas Golau lie unmarked and unremembered, is empty of people, but the courtyard is full. Harvest is in full swing and the Cooks have spilled out of the kitchens to use the space, simmering great vats of fruit butters, those little vitamin shots on a teaspoon. But they pause in their work as Romy and Vita sweep through the yard, to offer congratulations. A birth is a rare event, and today Romy has become sister to one of *Lucien's* children. Which practically makes her Lucien's family herself. Of course, Lucien is Father to all of them, but this is different.

Romy has to trot to keep up with Vita's long strides. She waves to people as they pass through, calls out in her soft American accent. *Yes! It's a girl! They're doing great! I should think she'll be back at work in a couple of days. I surely will. No, tomorrow, maybe. We've got her Naming Ceremony later, and I think they'll both need rest after that.*

Everyone smiles when they see Vita. Vita and Lucien. Whenever they appear, everyone smiles. Today, though, the smiles feel different, spontaneous. As though they're pleased, genuinely pleased, for Romy's mother.

As they walk, the second of two airliners is plunging into the shining façade of a tower in Manhattan and the world outside is holding its collective breath. A day when the world really *is* changing. By evening the compound will be abuzz as they race to prepare. *It's happened. It's happened. It's begun.* There is nothing like spectacular mass murder to warm the heart and gird the loins. The 11th of September will gift them their anticipation fix for literally years.

The Infirmary is on the first floor of the Great House, the only sleeping quarters in the building apart from Vita's and Lucien's own. There will be a toast tonight, in the Great Hall, all the adults sinking down a full glass of cider in the baby's honour, becoming silly and garrulous once they've done it. They drink alcohol so rarely that it goes straight to their heads.

On the steps of the Great House stands a man she's never seen. To Romy's eyes he looks old – though not as old as Vita – but still magnificent among the humble bodies she's used to. He's tall and muscular, a strong nose in a suntanned face, his hair unusually short, for the compound style. He holds himself like a god: head up, shoulders back, alert and hawkish. And there's something about his mouth. It's resolute.

'Who's that?' she asks. She's panting a little now, from hurrying.

63

Curious, not worried, because nobody ever comes here without Lucien or Vita's permission.

'Who?' asks Vita, then, seeing the direction of her gaze, 'Oh, him? You don't know who that is? No, I suppose you wouldn't. You weren't even here when he went away. That's Uri.'

Uri ... Romy scans her memory. Then she remembers. 'Father's first son?' she asks. '*That* Uri?' Though obviously there is no other. Although they all share Father's surname, Blake, everyone here has their own unique first name.

'That's right,' says Vita. 'He's been away, and now he's twenty-three and he's come back. He came home yesterday.'

They're getting closer. He turns his blue eyes in their direction, having overheard the exchange, and she sees the lips clamp a little tighter. 'I've been in the army, little girl,' he calls. 'Learning how to keep you safe.'

Vita's smile tightens. 'Yes. Uri is going to train a squad of Guards, to protect us,' she says. 'Father sent him into the army to learn how to fight, and he's been at the Cairngorm property for a while, getting it set up. Now he's here to learn our ways while he teaches *us* how to fight.'

'And it will come down to fighting in the end, Vita,' says Uri, and hits them both with his Father's smile. 'I'm only doing what'll keep us alive. It's not going to be a *nice* world when the End comes.'

'And in the long term we will be more than our fists,' says Vita, and her face twists with something that Romy doesn't understand.

Uri's face is suddenly serious. 'But we can't be anything at all if we don't survive,' he says. 'Surviving is everything, in the end. I wish you'd see that, Vita. We can't have *any* sort of civilisation if we don't survive. That's all I'm here for. To keep us safe.'

Vita is suddenly serious too. 'I understand that, Uri. I do.

Father trusts you, so I must trust you too. Anyway. We're on our way to visit your new sister.'

'*Half*-sister,' replies Uri, as though the correction is automatic. 'Why's *she* going?' He peers at Romy closely, at her dark hair and her olive skin and her green eyes, as though he's never seen such colouring before. Romy wouldn't be surprised if he hadn't. She's never seen anyone who looks like her. Or met anyone who still has the Dead name they were born with. Lucien never gave her a new one, said that Romy was 'good enough'. Romy can never decide if this makes her more special, or less. Different, certainly. Always the odd one out.

'Romy is your half-sister's half-sister,' replies Vita evenly.

'I guess she was born Outside,' he says.

'Among the Dead? Yes. But we don't hold that against people, do we?' she says, pointedly.

Romy knows her history. Uri himself was born before the Ark was established. He must have been. Because that was only twenty years ago.

Romy eyes this man with an assessing eye. He believes he's the One already, she thinks. He believes he's come back to take his rightful place.

Uri shrugs. 'Don't suppose it'll do any harm,' he says. 'Keep a spot of diversity in the gene pool.' And he turns away and walks off down the steps.

In the Infirmary, Ursola, Vita's head nurse, is sterilising the birthing chair while Somer lies among soft white sheets. The only white cloth Romy has ever seen. She sneaks a feel of the sheet as she gets used to this new mother – the weary, smiling woman with a baby in her arms. It's as smooth and as crisp as it looks.

'Come and say hello, Romy,' says Somer.

'Your new sister,' calls Ursola from the corner. 'She came out easy as you like, as though she couldn't wait to be here.'

Romy steps forward and cranes over the swaddling to see the baby's face. A little thing made of beetroot, eyes closed, wrinkles everywhere. Not what she'd been expecting at all. She can't see a single thing about her that's special, any sign that she – not strapping Uri or any of the other eleven – might some day lead them. She seems tiny, too. The way her mother's belly looked yesterday, she'd been half-expecting to get a calf, not a baby. And she feels – nothing. Just a faint envy at the sight of her mother's arms around another child.

'Yuk,' she says.

Somer laughs out loud. 'She'll get better,' she says. 'You looked like a frog!'

Romy laughs too. 'A frog? No, I didn't!'

'You did, you know. All googly eyes and a mouth that took up half your face.'

She's not sure what to ask next. This mother seems like a stranger. Romy knows all about the reproductive process, of course. They all learn, just part of Nature and her routines, the rhythms of life on a farm. The sow goes to the boar and the cow goes to the bull, and the sheep get turned out with the ram when the orders are given, and every solstice Lucien names two women to bring new life to Plas Golau, and chooses a mate for them. They have to keep the numbers down, for survival's sake. Too many infants when the End comes and the burden will destroy them all.

It's been several years since Lucien chose to be the mate himself. His next child up, Heulwen, is almost five. Somer is truly honoured.

'Look, Romy!' she says, and waves her left hand, craning her arm around the baby. On her third finger, a thick gold band.

Romy gazes. This is a much more beautiful thing than the skinned rabbit in the blanket. Adornment is rare among the women of the Ark, but there are two exceptions: the rings that Father gives to all the women who have had his babies, and the medallions, engraved with their name and date of birth, that those babies will wear for the rest of their lives. Her best friend Eilidh wears one, and fingers it whenever she's uncertain. A reminder of who she is; a comfort.

'It's beautiful,' she says. 'Now everyone will know he chose you, always.'

'Yes,' says Somer. 'It's like my medal for valour.'

Romy has no idea what she's on about, and covers it by looking down at the baby again. She's bald. A bit of fuzz on her head, but nothing anywhere else. I hope she'll get eyebrows one day, she thinks. I can't imagine I'll ever want to look at her if she's got no eyebrows.

'What's her name?' she asks.

'We can't be sure,' says Somer. 'Until the ceremony. You know Lucien doesn't actually make the final choice until he's seen you face to face.'

Yes, it needs to be the right name, Romy thinks. The right name, for the One who will guide them in a new world.

And then the old world changes. One moment it's just the three of them, and then there are footsteps and chatter in the corridor and the door bursts open and the room fills with golden people. Lucien's brood, the Family: bigger than her, blonder than anyone, and confident in a way she can never imagine. Uri, Zaria, Rohan, Jaivyn, Fai, Leana, Inara, Lesedi, Roshin, Farial, Eilidh, Heulwen. All twelve of them, now Uri's back – she knows their names the way she knows her catechism – and the baby makes thirteen. They've come to name their sister, and Lucien will be along in a minute. Somer greets them with a complacent smile, a member of their extended family now, and peels the blanket back from the baby's face, so they can see. Romy gives them all a big grin too.

'Okay, you can hop it now,' says Zaria, and jerks a thumb towards the door.

Something drops, inside her.

'No,' she says.

'Yes,' says Rohan, thirteen and stocky.

'Come on, Romy,' says Ursola, on guard respectfully in the corner. 'It's the Family's time now. You can come back and see them later.'

She stares around the faces, those imperious faces. Alights on Eilidh, her best friend down in the Pigshed. The friend she's known since she was eight months old. Eilidh's mouth is open, her little white teeth showing. She looks up at Uri as though she's seen a ghost. And Romy is filled with rage as she realises that despite it all she will never be one of them.

'It's only the *proper* siblings,' says Zaria. Zaria is fifteen and has unexpected red hair. She stands out in the compound like a flaming torch.

'I *am* a proper sibling!' she cries. 'My mum—'

Eilidh stares at her, mouths, *I'm sorry*, and Romy explodes with anger. 'I'm not leaving!' she snarls. 'She's *my* sister too.'

And then Jaivyn, twelve and always horrid, a bully wherever he goes, always arrogant, always taking the best titbits and the most comfortable spots, grabs her by the arm and starts to drag.

Romy fights back. The Teachers have had words and words with her about her temper, about the rage that can swell through her like an ocean wave. 'NO! No! I'm not going!' She kicks out, catches Uri by the ankle. He's wearing mountain boots and glances down as though he's been bitten by a flea. His upper

68

lip curls and his eyes smile. It's all a big bloody joke to you, she thinks, and she spits in Jaivyn's face.

Jaivyn looks startled, then disgusted, and then he turns purple. His big meaty hand flies off her arm and sinks into her hair. Her beautiful, long black hair, all the way down to her waist and a perfect anchor for a big boy's hand. There's nothing she can do. He's twice her age, and twice her size. The pain is vicious and her scalp burns as though it's about to tear right off her skull with every jerk of her body. She's crying now. Hot, angry, acid tears. Her eyes plead with her mother, but she's just sitting there, holding her baby, looking sad. Doing nothing.

She's taken my mother away, she thinks. My mother belongs to *her*, now.

9 | Romy

September 2001

No one comes to her aid. Crying children are always left to cry it out, unless there's actual blood. Manipulative behaviour, Father says, wastes time and undermines. After five minutes, in which the Cooks in the Great Hall carry on laying the tables and sweeping the floor as though she were a piece of sculpture, she wipes her eyes and stands up. Takes herself back to the physic garden and applies herself to the weeds with vengeful ferocity.

She has harvested a full trug and is taking it to the compost heap when Eilidh appears through the arched gate from the graveyard. Romy raises her chin and walks past, leaves her standing by the bitter melon vines. 'Romy,' she says, but Romy walks on. Eilidh follows. Romy knows she'll have to speak to her eventually, but she's not ready yet. It used not to matter, the difference between us, she thinks. But it does now, and it hurts.

'I'm sorry, Romy,' says Eilidh, and Romy feels another stab of anger. Whirls round to glare at her old friend and sees big blue eyes filled with tears.

'Crying is manipulation,' she says. 'Or is it okay for *Father's* children?'

She'll never be the One, Romy thinks, spitefully, as she watches Eilidh try to gulp back her tears. She's too soft. Whoever the One is, they'll need to be ruthless. Not bully-ruthless like Jaivyn, but not soppy like Eilidh, either.

But that's why I like her. I can't be mean to Eilidh. She's never been mean to anyone, until today, and that was only by going along.

'I'm sorry,' her friend says again. 'What was I meant to do? I'm the littlest of all, apart from Heulwen.'

'And my sister,' Romy corrects.

'Yes,' says Eilidh. 'But it's the rules. You know it's the rules. I can't just ignore the rules. None of us can. It doesn't mean we're not friends, Romy. We are. We'll always be friends. We'll survive the End together. But there are *rules*.'

'Even if you're the One?'

'Of course.'

'Even if it's my sister?'

'Don't worry, Romy. We'll be friends always, I promise you.'

'You didn't have to just stand there and let him ...' says Romy, and feels herself welling up as well. Turns away to hide her face. 'He didn't have to do that to me.'

'No,' says Eilidh, 'he didn't. He's horrible. Boys *are* horrible. I think he was showing off to Uri.'

'Well, *that*'s grown-up,' says Romy, and up-ends her trug of weeds onto the compost. Turns back and starts walking towards the bed to pull out another load.

'He's *not* grown-up,' says Eilidh. 'He's just a stupid boy.'

Romy is afraid of what will happen in the End. They all

are – the fear ripples through the compound every time there is news of the Outside – but realising how easily Jaivyn overpowered her has made her realise how great the danger will be. As civilisation collapses and the cities empty, they will be facing thousands of Jaivyns, however well hidden the compound is.

I need to be ready, she thinks. I can't be like Eilidh and just drift along thinking everybody's going to be nice. Uri's right, we do need Guards – but we need to be able to fight back ourselves, as well. Against invaders, but also against the Jaivyns within our walls. I need a weapon. In a couple of years, I apprentice with the Blacksmiths. A knife. That's what I want. A knife so when Jaivyn Blake comes for me I can stab his grasping hands. Everyone gets to make something useful. There's no rule that says it can't be a knife. And I can make the handle when I learn to be a Carpenter, before I make my graduation box. It'll be all made by the time I'm ten.

A long time. But you need to plan, if you're going to survive.

Eilidh follows her and kneels down next to her, starts plucking weeds too, and dropping them in the trug. 'I didn't make the rules, Romy.'

'It's not fair, though,' she says.

'Life isn't fair,' recites Eilidh, automatically. 'The universe is cruel and unjust.'

Romy sits back on her heels and looks at her. 'Do you even *want* to be the One?'

Eilidh shakes her head. 'Of course not. But if I am, if I'm called, I won't have a choice.'

'But do you think you will be?'

'No,' she says. 'And nor will Jaivyn.'

Romy thinks about this. 'I think Uri thinks it's him.'

'Really?'

'He scares me,' she confesses. 'He's so ...'

'Yes,' says Eilidh. 'I know.'

'Are they all like that?' asks Romy. 'The Dead?'

'I don't know,' says Eilidh. 'But I'm glad I don't live out there if they are.'

'Of course, *Eden* could be the One,' says Eilidh, generously, as they wash up their tools. 'It could just as easily be a girl.'

Yes, thinks Romy. And if my sister is the One, they'll have to accept me then. 'Eden,' she says. 'So that's her name?'

Eilidh gives her a beaming smile. She's felt the shift, knows she's forgiven. 'Yes,' she says. 'It's good, isn't it? A good name for a Leader. It's pure, and strong.'

10 | Somer

December 2002

Her bruises are healing, but the fear remains, self-recrimination ringing round and round. Solstice. I *know* about solstice, what happens if you're stupid.

I'm sorry, she tells the universe, I'm sorry. I knew to stay in the light, and still I didn't. Please don't punish me further. Please let it just be a nasty moment, something I can turn my back on and forget. Don't let there be more. Please don't let there be more.

Somer is on duty in the Infirmary with Ursola when they bring Lucien's daughter Farial Blake in from the Pigshed. She's one of their regulars, for she's a strangely clumsy child, always running into walls and falling on her face. She was here two weeks ago for a nasty cut on her foot, so Somer doesn't feel any surprise to see her here again.

And then she sees her face, and her own fears are wiped from her thoughts.

*

They don't let the Littlies near the sharp tools, but no one gave a second thought to letting Farial take apple peelings to the horses until a shriek alerted them to the fact that one of them, in the rush for goodies, had trodden on her canvas-covered foot. A swarm of adults downed tools and ran to help. A badly trimmed iron nail in the horse's shoe had pierced clean through the canvas to the skin, but the ground was mostly mud near the gate where she stood wailing, so to everyone's relief no bones were broken. Vita cleaned and bandaged the wound and instructed everyone to look out for signs of sepsis, and let her limp proudly back to the Pigshed to show her peers. On Friday, her Teacher confessed to carelessness and the Blacksmith admitted sloppy work on the shoe, and they accepted their penalties and all was forgiven. Lucien is a forgiving Leader, and punishments are the same whether the infraction involves the Family or an ordinary person.

Two weeks later, Farial started to grin. Not the normal smiles they all wear to face the day, but something wide and weird and wicked that sent her peers scuttling into corners with howls of fear whenever it happened. She claimed she couldn't help it, but even as she did so she seemed to be having difficulty articulating, and when the Teacher touched her forehead she realised that it was damp and hot.

Somer is faintly irritated that she has to haul herself from the chair where she's rolling bandages and feeling her fear when the Teacher comes in, but then she sees the hobgoblin in her arms and leaps, her lower back twanging, to her feet. 'What's wrong?'

'I don't know,' says the Teacher. 'Maybe it's some sort of prank, but she genuinely can't seem to stop. Even when I tickled her while she was doing it, her face didn't change at all. I thought it would be best to be sure.'

'Of course,' says Somer, and feels the child's forehead, though she can already see that her fringe is slick with sweat. 'Well, she certainly has a fever,' she says. 'How do you feel, Farial?'

'Head hurts.' Her eyes suddenly widen until they are as round as cogwheels. Her lips pull back so far that Somer fears they will split and she grins and grins and grins.

Her teeth, Somer notices, are clamped together.

Ursola strolls over from the only other occupied bed in the ward. One advantage of their magnificent isolation is that outbreaks of disease are rare at Plas Golau. Someone fetched flu in with them, the winter solstice before last, and they worked round the clock for three weeks to keep the fever under control. But the population of Plas Golau is young and fit, by and large, and asthmatics never make it in through the gates, so they emerged triumphant at the other end of the epidemic with not a single death. But most of the Healers' medical duties involve administering to cuts and bruises, the odd burn, the occasional broken bone. And, of course, growing and preserving medicinal plants for the days when nothing will grow at all.

'What's this?' asks Ursola.

Farial grins and grins, and her eyes roll in their sockets. 'Oh,' says Ursola. She turns on her heel and runs to fetch Vita.

There will be no vaccinations in the Apocalypse. So of course there are no vaccinations at Plas Golau. Vaccinations, says Lucien, lead to a weakened bloodline, sluggish immune systems surviving where they would never have done so before. They must learn to live without them, to live more cautious lives. And, although it's not really discussed, requests for vaccines for unregistered children would lead to inconvenient questions down in the valley. The adults, raised in the thoughtless indulgence of the Dead, will of course have been immunised in the normal run of authoritarian government interference. Not so the children. No measles vaccine, no mumps, no rubella. No whooping cough or scarlet fever. No tetanus.

Vita bustles through from the pharmacy, drying her hands on a towel as she walks. Takes one look at the child and orders her to bed.

Farial's straining muscles collapse. Suddenly, she is a skinny ninety-year-old in the body of a seven-year-old. Klimt, thinks Somer. Like a Klimt painting. She is pale and panting, and a little trail of drool slithers out of the corner of her mouth and drips onto the front of her tunic.

There will be no hospitals in the Apocalypse. Besides, in the Apocalypse a hospital is the last place you would want to be. No resident of the Ark has been to a hospital in twenty years. You know that when you come here, when you breed here. Survival is a matter of will, of fighting back and rising above, and, if death overwhelms you or your loved ones, that is part of the contract. Will there be room for the weak, when fire has rained from the sky?

Somer tucks Farial into bed, tries to feed her a glass of water. But her throat is hard as marble and she can barely swallow, the water dripping down and wetting the pillow. Most of Vita's medications come in the forms of liquids. Tinctures, tisanes, drenches, pills and powders. All useless now.

'We'll need to get a feeding tube into her,' says Ursola, 'for the drugs. And another to keep her airway open.'

'A tracheotomy?' Somer is aghast. She's learned the basic technique from books, but no one in the compound has ever needed the real thing.

'Toughen up,' snaps Ursola. Three years as a registered nurse has made her an invaluable member of the community. She may be No. 188 to Somer's 142 in the arrival order, but still she is her superior. 'It's the job. She still has a chance to get through this. People *do* survive it.'

'How many?'

Ursola turns away. Farial may be silent, but she is still conscious.

'Sorry,' mutters Somer, ashamed. Every job has its unpleasant aspects. It's not all willow bark and lavender oil. She strokes Farial's forehead with a damp cloth while Ursola goes away to put water on to boil, to sterilise the scalpels.

Beneath the sheet, Farial's abdomen begins to rise off the bed as though hauled by an invisible winch. Somer can tell that she is trying to scream, but all that emerges from that carved white throat is a hiss of compressed air.

'Someone needs to tell Lucien,' says Ursola, and they stand in a row and stare at her.

'I'll tell him,' says Vita, eventually.

In the morning, Lucien brings Farial's mother, Luz, in to see her. Luz's eyes are red, and no one judges, for, even in this Spartan world, the loss of the only child you will ever have is a heinous loss indeed. And Lucien's eyes, too, are red, for, though he has many children, each life at Plas Golau is precious to him.

She is, at least, breathing now, with the help of the tracheotomy tube. And Vita has broken out some of the small stock of the opium she distils from home-grown poppies. They were concerned at first that the feeding tube would never survive the pressure of that clamping jaw, but one by one her baby teeth have cracked and been spat out, and no longer pose a danger. She lies drowsy and silent against a pillow and twists in and out, in and out of spasm.

78

Luz stands over the bed and gulps air. Somer feels inadequate, unequal to this task. If it were my child, she thinks. If it were Romy or Eden, I would want to die. I would want to die too. Then she thinks, Oh God, please let there just be Romy and Eden. Please let there be no more than the two of them. Please. I'll do anything if you make me not be pregnant. And then she remembers that there *is* no God, and her gorge contracts.

Lucien lays a comforting hand on Luz's shoulder. He is so kind. This loss must be exquisitely painful to him, but always, always, he is there first and foremost for his people.

'Sometimes,' he tells her, 'accidents happen anyway. With all the care we take, with the best will in the world, they happen.'

The patient in the bed at the end of the room lost skin from her hand and thigh when a vat of boiling fruit slipped off its trivet as she walked past it. Jam boils at 105 degrees, and jam is sticky. It clings to the skin like glue. The burn has gone a full half-inch into the thigh, and Vita and Ursola had to spend more of the precious opium to operate and remove the dead flesh before it turned bad. She had her healing visit from Lucien a week ago. You don't expect a second.

'If I'd been there . . . ' says Luz.

'You couldn't have been there,' says Lucien. 'It wasn't your fault.'

Farial spasms again, and her ribs snap like firecrackers. She is screaming inside, thinks Somer, and grits her teeth as the tiny hand grips her fingers so hard she is afraid her knuckles might dislocate. This is awful. It's awful. Are we right to be keeping her here? Should we take her down to some cold, efficient, neon-lit hospital where nobody loves her?

'They fight so hard, the young,' Lucien says. And he looks up and meets Somer's eyes for the first time since he arrived, and she sees no real spark of recognition. I am nothing to him, she thinks. Now I've had his baby, it's as though I never existed. I've been paid off with a ring. And then she forces the thought away.

Vita lays a hand on Luz's other shoulder. Somer watches them, feels their pain. There are tears on Lucien's cheeks. It must help her, she thinks, knowing that they care so much. We're their children, all of us. And she dismisses the flash memory of Lucien's O-face in the firelight in his bedroom and tips a little more opium into the feeding tube.

'You must stay with her,' Vita tells Luz. 'Stay with her all the time. We'll set a chair up for you, make it comfortable.'

'Thank you,' she says, and the words catch in her throat. No hospitals for Farial. We take care of our own, at Plas Golau.

Lucien stays a full hour, sitting quietly by his daughter's bedside, holding her mother's hand. When he leaves, he doesn't return.

Farial takes four days to die, and they bury her in the chapel graveyard. After the burial, they never speak of her again.

Among the Dead

October 2016

11 | Romy

It is very quiet.

Not really. It's just a completely different sort of loud from the rural sounds of Plas Golau. The sound of traffic outside, the rumble of the machines downstairs. I have the windows open, for the heat is stifling on a sunny day in October. Every minute or two, the roar of aeroplane engines as they soar so close to my rooftop that I feel as though, were I standing up there by the chimney of this two-storey building, I could reach out and catch a ride on the great black wheels that hang from their bellies.

Out on the pavements, coming in and out of the Underground, voices, incessant, day and night, far more disturbing than the mechanical rumbles. A jumble of accents, but one particularly harsh and prevalent, which I take to be the local flavour. Many voices speak languages I don't understand. But London is one of those places where the whole world comes seeking the gold on the pavements, and two hundred and fifty languages are spoken here every day. I can't wait to get away. Find my people, and get away.

Eden. It was her birthday last month, which will mean it will have been Ilo's too, though we didn't mark them. She will be fifteen. A ward of the state. My period of rest is up. I must make myself leave this noisy little sanctuary and start to look for them. Ilo's only young. He's strong and brave, but I've got to find Eden and make her safe, and I know he will understand. Now I have you, now you're growing inside me. I need to make her safe, to keep you safe. But not today. The journey here – the speed, the dizzying distance, the million unfamiliar sights – has left me exhausted, and even glancing out of the window at all those passing strangers overwhelms me. Overwhelms me with fear, and overwhelms me with sadness. All those people. All of them, unaware of what the future holds.

Janet's milk is good; the tomatoes are bland and textureless; the bread is woolly. I long for a proper tomato again, warm from the sun through the greenhouse walls, sweeter and more perfumed than a plum. I play with the television for a bit, and eventually find my favourite, a man called Jeremy, who shouts at fat people on channel 27. It was always playing in the rec room at the Halfway. Spencer said that it soothed them, seeing that people like us could get on the TV. It seems as good a place as any to find out about the dystopia I am still learning to inhabit.

I have food for three days, if I eke it out, and then I must go out and brave the world. I never thought of myself as an anxious individual before, but I've found since I came out of the hospital that all sorts of things have become challenges to me. Melanie said that it wasn't surprising, that PTSD is a powerful condition and I must learn not to be hard on myself. All very well for her to say. I have a baby to feed and a sister and brother to find, and that will take courage.

I find myself stringing out the actions of the day, filling the time to soothe myself. Washing up each plate and mug as I

84

use it, making small snacks – a sliced tomato, a hard-boiled egg, a piece of toast made under the grill – one after the other rather than a meal. I unpack Janet's box, arrange the soap-shampoo-conditioner I find in it on the shelf by the bathroom sink, put Melanie's crockery away, string my spare sheet across the bedroom window to stop the people in the flats opposite looking in.

And then I allow myself to open my box. I've been looking at it sideways for a couple of hours, saving it, savouring the prospect. I have a strange feeling that once I lift the lid all the contents will simply vanish into thin air, like the dust of an Egyptian mummy.

I remember everything that's in here. Of course. If your belongings are pared down to everything that can fit in a wooden box twenty inches long by a foot wide by ten inches deep, you don't forget what you own. But oh, to feel them again. These little souvenirs of home. I take them out, one by one, and weigh them in my hands. Small things, vast memories.

A soap that smells of lavender.

Photographs. One of my mother as a teenager, maybe Eden's age, face covered in thick make-up, black lipstick, black lines around her eyes like an Egyptian goddess. One of my mother and her family: an awkward photo, standing on a doorstep, parents behind, children in front. Mum maybe twelve, so I guess her sister Sarah, my aunt, is five.

A tiny strip of three photos of my mother and me. She said they came in a strip of four and she had them done in a photo booth. Cut one off and posted it to my grandparents. She's seventeen or eighteen there. Thin and scared-looking, holding baby-me as though she's afraid I'll break, staring at the lens with wounded eyes. Gone is the make-up, the backcombed hair of the earlier photo. Now she looks like a small albino mouse.

It's one of only two photos I have of myself. Somer gave them to me because she said that she had the memories and I didn't, that I should have something of my infancy. We didn't do photos. Or mirrors, beyond necessary medical or firestarting purposes. Narcissism, Father said.

The other photo: me and my friends Kiran and Eilidh, ready for our first solstice. The one exception to the no-photography rule was that they recorded us as we reached legal adulthood. It was like branding us as Real People, people with a place at last in history, worth recording for the descendants. We kept them as souvenirs of this rite of passage, like our puberty flowers, to be handed down to those who come after. Ursola had a clunky machine that whirred and spat out a piece of white card that gradually, as you waved it in the air, took on colours and shapes and turned into a photograph. She took three, one for each of us. We look so young. Eilidh and me with our crowns of flowers, me still watchful, Eilidh with her big open grin, Kiran standing between us looking straight at the lens, his half-smile that preceded his laugh. Three young people, ready for a party. I miss them. So much it physically hurts.

I look at the pictures for a long while, touch the faces with a fingertip. Want to howl at the sky, for I will never see them again. I don't know what they've done with my mother's body. No one asked if I wanted to claim it – and what would I do with it if I did? – and I don't suppose any of the family that didn't want her when she was alive have done so. I don't know what they do with bodies like that. Just burn them up and never speak of them again, I guess.

I lay the photos aside and go on.

A wreath of flowers, dried and pressed and stored between two sheets of cardboard to keep it from falling apart. A souvenir of the day I reached womanhood, worn over my hair as I walked to have it shorn.

A small wooden horse, whittled painstakingly by Kiran over the course of a long, dark winter when he was twelve. It's clumsy, energetic, mane and tail flying out as it heads into the wind, and he gave it to me because ... because I don't know. I never even questioned it.

And then I *am* crying, for there will be no more Kiran, no more Ursola or Somer or Vita, no more *any* of them. I don't cry. I never cry. But there has been so much loss, so much.

And, when I've finished crying, I put the horse on the little mantelpiece for decoration and I hang my crown on an old picture hook and this dreary flat feels suddenly more like home.

I go back and find something else that makes the tears come. Wrapped in a piece of cloth lies my mother's ring. They threw it away when she got pregnant with Ilo, as though it were tainted, and I sneaked out and retrieved it from our tiny landfill in the medieval quarry from whose stones the house was built – not such a hard task, as we produced barely any rubbish – and slipped it into my box. I'm not sure why. I had a feeling, just a feeling, that it might have a function later. I guess it does, now. I slip it onto my own finger, left hand, third from the right, and look at it. It fits as though it had been made for me. And I stare at it and let the tears fall.

When I'm calmer, I change the channel on the TV and watch a programme about people who are unable to stop collecting things – rubbish, clothes, bits of wood, old newspapers – and whose houses are so cluttered that they have to climb through tunnels of trash. A woman has been collecting cats, out of control, shit everywhere, and the house-clearer has just moved a pile of books to find a batch of tiny kittens, dead and mummified, behind them, and the floorboards rotted by urine.

And I half-watch and wonder about the billions and billions

of us and the millions of the Dead who must be living like this, and I feel around for the marram-grass tab at the bottom of my empty box. My finger grasps it and I lift. The false bottom comes away, and there they are, my last treasures, nestled in their niches and quietly gleaming. The police and the social worker would never have let me have the box if they'd known they were there, but I feel instantly safer when I see that they still are. Wrapped in tissue paper, two items from the modern world: a bank card, and a tiny flat shard of metal and plastic the size of my pinkie nail. A SIM card, to put in a phone and make it one's own.

And, beneath those, my comfort. My protection. My knife.

Before the End

2002–2003

12 | Romy

March 2003

The month before each solstice, the tension grows among the women. They eye each other, assess their own chances, assess those of others. Romy is a long way from understanding this burning urge to reproduce, to fill themselves with baby, but it pours off them like body odour as the nights lengthen and shorten.

A six-month window. It's likely all you'll ever get here. There are more women than men in the Ark, and the chances are that if you fail in your first conception window it will be too late by the time your turn comes round again. Lucien, standing on the Great House steps, watching, playing God. He doesn't like his mothers over thirty, his fathers under. And all the women, even the older ones with their fading wombs, pray, as he passes them by: *me, me, this time let it be me. Let his eye light upon me, let him see me strong and young and healthy. If not for himself, let him choose a mate for me.*

Lucien knows best. Who's fittest, who's ripest, who will make the best babies. Their future depends on his choices, for they can't afford to carry weaklings. The Ark will need strength, intelligence, endurance, to carry them through the Great Disaster, and Lucien can tell, by eye alone.

Sometimes, when the choice has been made, when Lucien has announced the names of the lucky pairings at the choosing ceremony, Romy sees the unchosen women turn and walk away, bury their faces in their hands and weep.

A change has come over her mother, she's noticed it. She's gone quiet, turned inward; flinches if someone touches her unexpectedly, crosses the yard whenever one of Uri's new squad of swaggering, bumptious Guards appears. Walks with her eyes downcast and sometimes, weirdly, wrings her hands. On the morning after solstice, her eyes were red when she came with the other women to let the children out of their overnight confinement in the Pigshed. And later, in the washroom, with the other women turned away, Romy noticed bruises on her shoulders, her thighs. A fall, said Somer. It's nothing. Silly me. I tripped on a stone and went for a burton. That'll teach me, eh? No more cider for mamma. And she was seven and careless, so she laughed at the thought that she should have come from such a clown. Then Farial died, and everyone in the Pigshed was sad, for never speaking of someone is not the same as never thinking, and she just assumed that Somer, who was there when it happened, was sad as well. And then she thought no more of it.

By the spring equinox, one of the current breeders is already confirmed – has adopted the waddle and back-pressing of late pregnancy though she can't be more than a few months gone – and glowing with pride. The other's eyes are ringed with dark circles from her sleepless nights, and her chosen mate walks as though he's carried the good news from Aix to Ghent.

Three days after the equinox, the bell in the chapel tower begins to ring to call a Pooling – the summoning ring, long slow tolls – and the compound drops its tasks and hurries to the courtyard. They know they're not in danger – a double ring, repeated around two-second gaps – and that the End has not begun – fast tolling, constant until everyone is safe – but that something momentous has happened. A betrayal or a triumph, a water leak in one of the food godowns. They eye each other silently. Will someone be disgraced today? Is it you? Is it you?

Busy planting beans below the trellises surrounding the Pigshed wall, Romy jumps to her feet and runs inside to scoop up Eden. She's barely beyond the goo-ga stage – but everyone has to come to a Pooling. She is heavy, though, and wriggles, and Romy's progress is slow. When she realises that they are the last ones left in the orchard, she ignores the squawks of protest and jogs the rest of the way. She weaves a lengthy path around the flowerbeds to get to a place where she will be able to see.

They count off, so everyone knows who's here, and there's a gap after 141, before Romy calls out her own number, and her vague sense of unease, the one everyone shares when these gatherings are called, gets a whole lot worse. She and Somer arrived on the same day, so of course they have consecutive numbers. She calls out Eden's number for her, but she can barely make herself heard, her mouth is so dry.

And then the Great House door opens and the compound sees that the sinner is indeed Somer. A murmur runs through the crowd.

Somer. It's Somer. Eden Blake's mother, for God's sake. How are the mighty fallen.

Downcast eyes with shadows beneath, the skin on her face

red-raw from crying, she emerges from the gloom behind Lucien and Uri, Ursola to her left and Vita to her right, four grim Guards in a row behind as though they expect her to make a break for it. Romy doesn't recognise half the Guards these days. The original corps was made up of people she remembers from the Pigshed, but Uri has brought several in from the Outside, recruited from among his old colleagues in the army of the Dead, some strangers from the Cairngorm compound. Loyalty, he says. The first thing I need from my Guards is loyalty.

Somer's head is bald as an egg. Someone's cut her hair off and shaved her right down to the skin. Vita, probably, because it is usually Vita who carries out this harshest of all penalties.

Minutes pass. Lucien's eyes rake the crowd, search for signs of prurience. His most recent handmaid, a woman so honoured that she bore his child, brought so low that he cannot even look at her. But the Ark see. Oh, yes, they see, now that they're looking. She carries so little flesh – they all do – that it's hard to hide the signs of pregnancy once someone is looking: the swollen breasts, the filling belly. A three-month gestation is impossible to hide. Somer looks as though her uniform has shrunk. Yet she herself is also diminished.

Romy is scandalised. Burns with shame. People nearby have edged away from where she and Eden stand, leaving them in a little pool of space as though her mother's disgrace might be infectious. How could you? she thinks, and her memory floods with images of mating pigs, of the squalls of the semi-feral cats who live around the godowns. How could you? Can you not stop yourself? Do you have no willpower? She's filled once again with the ignominy of her own conception. She's like a rutting animal, she thinks, always on heat, always waiting for her chance to mate. Only a couple of children in the compound have brothers and sisters, but they were all conceived when their parents were still Dead. Nobody has two. Nobody. She will be marked forever, a freak. They all will, all three of them. Even blessed Eden.

Poor Lucien. Her heart burns for Father. What an honour he gave her mother, she thinks, and look how she's repaid him. Eden lets out a squawk, and Romy realises how hard her fingers are digging into the child's tiny arms.

Lucien clears his throat, and speaks. 'What shall we do?' he asks. 'What shall we do?'

He speaks of betrayal. Somer's not the first. The shame is on all of them. They stand where they have landed and listen as the day's light changes, as the fires go out in the smithy and the bread, proving, overflows the pans. Romy wishes she'd brought an overcoat, as the wiser, older hands paused to do before they ran to the courtyard, for once the sun passes behind the house-eaves she starts to shiver. Eden struggles in her arms and, when she realises that she is not going to be let down, begins to wail. Stop, oh stop, Romy begs silently as her neighbours glare at her as though she could, by some magic, shut her up. Her arms are hurting and so are her knees and, for the first time in her life, her back, from the weight of her wriggling burden. And still she holds her, because to do anything else will bring punishment down on her head.

And still he speaks. Vita, Ursola, Uri, the Guards, still like statuary around them, Somer staring at the step on which she stands as the blood crusts on her naked scalp. 'Liars,' he says. 'Lying and thieving and cheating. You swore to us all when you came here that this was an end to that, for you. This woman has stolen from the wombs of her sisters. Every one of you who has done as she has done has stolen their child from somebody else.'

In among the crowd, a woman begins to sob. Because of Somer, one fewer of them will get her own turn, come the next solstice.

'Does anybody else have anything to confess?' he asks. Looks out over their heads in the gathering gloom, as they draw in their breaths and search their souls.

'Not a single one of you? What shall we do?' he asks, as they shiver in the dark, beset by hunger and thirst and cold and the deep, deep wish to sleep. 'What shall we do?'

Ursola steps forward. 'We've all betrayed him,' she says. 'I've looked at my fellows with wicked eyes. I've stolen extra bread. I've rested when I could have been working for all of us. I am no better than many, no worse than many.'

From the bag tied to her waist, she produces the hair clippers. Hands them to Vita, undoes the tie that holds back her mane of hair and drops to her knees before her.

13 | Romy

September–November 2003

He squalls his way into the world when the fruit harvest is at its height and Romy doesn't hear about it, or notice that her mother is missing, for two days. Anyone at Plas Golau who can walk and understand simple instructions is out in the orchards, and his birth has attracted none of the pleasurable anticipation that Eden's did. In fact, Romy only realises that it's happened when Somer, long since demoted to Farmer, returns to the fields looking like a popped balloon. She doesn't go up and ask. She has barely exchanged a full sentence with her mother in six months, even though they sleep in the same dormitory. The shame is almost unbearable, the shaved heads all around her a constant reminder of her connection to the sin.

In the Pigshed, Eden's other siblings have quietly stepped in and taken over her care, and Romy has let them do it, for she knows that this bastard child has effectively cancelled out the status gain of having a sister in the Family. She's no more of a

97

figure to Eden now than any of the older children are. Eilidh is probably as important to her now as Romy is. At least it means she no longer has to fight her indifference. If Eden is the One, it would be useful if she knew who Romy was, but she no longer has to pretend to be devoted to the sister who has never seized her heart.

She doesn't bother to go and visit her new brother. Lucien has called him Ilo, but he just sent the name by messenger to the Infirmary.

He comes into the Pigshed in November, when the frost makes it impractical for him to stay with his mother in a Moses basket in the fields. Ursola arrives, hands him to a Teacher, and the Teacher puts him on the rug in front of the stove and goes back to leading the recital of the Pieties.

Knowing the Pieties off by heart, Romy has the space left over in her brain to allow herself a little curiosity. Standing in the third row, smaller children in front and taller ones behind, she has a good view of the bundle in the hearth.

'A liar is a thief,' she recites. 'Who lies to his brethren steals food from their mouths.' And she sees a little red hand creep out from among the wrapping and wave in the air.

'A promise is an empty vessel,' she says. Eilidh, standing next to her, has lost her front teeth and has particular difficulty enunciating this one. The bundle by the fire wriggles its limbs inside its wrapping. It looks like a maggot, thinks Romy. Like a fat maggot sucking the goodness from the harvest. They'll want me to see him. They'll probably want me to look after him, but I won't. He's not my baby, not my mistake. I won't be punished for it.

Eden, two tiers in front, recites clumsily, but with pious verve. 'Everybody is a nobody, everyone is a someone,' they intone.

'We are the Ark,' they say. 'We are the future. Mankind depends on us,' and then they applaud, as they do at the end of the Pieties every day, and they stand down for morning break.

She's putting on her coat to go out and run off the morning's energy build-up with the others before chores begin, when the Teacher pulls her up. 'Aren't you going to say hello to your little brother?' she asks.

Reluctantly, Romy pauses, arm in sleeve. It's not a question at all, really, but an order. Eilidh stops dressing, too. Always her friend, always loyal, despite her disgrace.

'Ooh, yes,' she says enthusiastically. 'Come on, Romes.'

Romy considers, just briefly, refusing, and then she sighs and lays her coat aside. Eden runs out into the farmyard with Heulwen and Roshin, laughing as though she will never bear a burden. She won't, of course. No one is telling *Eden* to love the bastard. She has a higher purpose.

They go over to the fireplace. She's glad she has Eilidh, because she knows that, without her, doing this alone, with no one but the Teacher watching to see that she shows the correct responses, it would be so much harder.

He is wrapped in linen. No angora from the special herd for Ilo. We have more in common than he will ever know, she thinks. The odd ones out from the very beginning. The outcasts. But that doesn't mean I have to ... oh.

Eilidh has pulled the head-covering back so they can see his face. Romy's first thought is that he is less ugly than her sister was. Her next, piling in on top like a second wave, obliterating everything, is that she can see all of them in his face. Her mother. Eden. And herself. A blond version of me, she thinks. The first time I've ever seen someone else who looks like me. I keep trying to see myself in Somer and Eden, but I can't. But in him, I do. I see me in him. My God, I see me in him.

And his eyes open and they're blue, and they wander for a moment and then they fix upon her face, and he smiles.

He recognises me, she thinks. 'Oh, hello, baby,' she says, and gives him a finger to clutch. 'Hello, Ilo. I'm Romy. I'm your sister.'

Among the Dead

October 2016

14 | Romy

My knife is beautiful. The most beautiful thing I own. It is perfectly balanced, perfectly sharp. I carved the handle from two slim pieces of walnut, made it to fit my palm, to nestle into my grip as though it were an extension of my hand itself, and the Blacksmiths riveted the blade smoothly between the two pieces with a hinge of horseshoe iron, and polished it until it gleamed. The blade's not long, but it's sharp. Just the feel of it in the pocket of my jeans comforts me.

Not enough to make me leave the flat, though. It takes me three full days to do that.

I need food, and cash, and a phone. I have twelve pounds, which must buy me enough for a few days, though honestly I don't really know, but I'm sure it won't buy me a phone. I need to find a library, so I can do the internet. And I need to work out how to get to Finbrough, because really, when it comes to finding my brother and sister, I don't know where else to start.

*

an hour dressing. My choice isn't wide, but still
all that time, for my hands are shaking and I keep
stop to rest, to calm my breathing. Eventually, I take
the beta blockers I was prescribed back in Weston – my
heart simply won't slow – and then I have to wait for half
hour for it to begin to work. I don't want to take them more
than I have to, but my head is spinning and I feel as though my
heart will burst out of my chest. I'm sorry, baby. Your mother
has let herself get soft. I'm not the lioness you will need to
keep you safe.

Once the pill starts to work, I settle on jeans, a T-shirt and a
dark blue hoodie with a big front pocket, because they hide my
knife well and because I want to be anonymous, at least for now.
Once the dressed-for-work crowd has passed, this seems to be
the primary uniform on the streets of Hounslow, and blending in
is good. I pick up my keys and the bank card and put them in my
bra, slip what money I have into my jeans pocket. And then I let
myself out. I don't take my address on a piece of paper. Despite
what Janet thinks, I do, in fact, have a functioning memory.

The door swings to behind me and I'm still alive. No one has
come at me with a machete, nothing has exploded, no boil-
covered plague victim is grabbing at me begging for help. People,
people, swishing past me on the pavement, and no one so much
as looks in my direction. A plane passes overhead, so much
louder without walls and tiles between us, and I cringe, cling to
the wall behind me. And then it's gone, and I'm on my way to
find the Magic Piano.

The bank card was a brainwave of Vita's. We all had one,
leading to an emergency fund, in case one of us was separated,
or kidnapped, or trapped in some way, and needed the means to
bring ourselves home. Home no longer exists, of course, but the

money is most likely still there and she would agree, I'm sure, that I'm going to be using it in the spirit, at least, for which it was intended.

I find a Magic Piano (this is what Spencer told me it was called) recessed into the plate-glass window of a supermarket. A man sits on the pavement beside it, with dirty hair and a dirtier coat, and a friendly brown and white dog, a polystyrene cup with a couple of 10p pieces in it resting on a piece of cardboard that reads HOMELESS AND HUNGRY, PLEASE HELP.

I wish he weren't there. Maybe that's what everyone thinks, which is why he's homeless and hungry. I can't give him anything until I've been to the Magic Piano, and I really don't want to go to the Piano while he's there. I slow down as I approach and try to look as though I'm dawdling while I make a decision.

'It's okay, luv,' he says, and his voice sounds as if it's coming from a storm drain: all cracked and grimy and full of flotsam. 'I'm not going to *rob* you.'

A challenge. 'Is that what you thought I was thinking?' I say.

He jingles his dog's chain. 'People always think that, when they see a Homeless,' he says.

'With good reason?' I ask, and he looks aghast. Then he laughs.

'Wow,' he says. 'Haven't met a Millennial with a sense of humour in a while.'

'No one's told me I *had* a sense of humour in a while,' I tell him. The ice is broken and I'm not worried by him any more. I dig in my pocket and find the cash card from my box. Put it in the slot and punch in the number. 0712: Father's birthday.

It thinks for a moment, then a figure flashes up on the screen that makes me blink. 73,887.00.

I stare at it. I'm not sure I knew there was that much money in the *world*. Maybe there's a mistake with the decimal point?

I have just over £400 in my benefits account. We didn't spend much, at the Halfway House.

73,887.00

My hand is actually shaking, slightly. YES, I press. Then CASH WITH RECEIPT. I suppose I should get a receipt, so I can show it to someone, if they ask. If there's anybody *to* ask. They could all be scattered to the winds, the Ark lost forever, for all I know.

I choose £200. I have no idea how much a phone costs. Hopefully it will be enough. I wait, nervously, for alarms to ring, but after a couple of seconds it spits out the card, whirrs deep inside and then follows up with the cash.

'Spare a quid for a cup of tea?' asks my companion, immediately.

I give him ten pounds, which should be enough for him to buy some bread and cheese, or gin or heroin or whatever. I've learned a lot in the Halfway House.

'Wow, thanks, luv,' he says, and tucks it into a filthy pocket.

'I don't suppose you could tell me where the library is?' I ask.

He shakes his head. 'I think there's one up by Hounslow Central.'

'I mean, to walk?'

'Have you tried looking it up?'

I grind my teeth slightly. 'I don't have a way of looking it up. That's why I want the library.'

Another funny look. 'Well, hang on,' he says, and the hand goes back into the pocket. Comes out with one of those little screens I see people staring at as they blunder into each other on the pavements. Prod, prod, prod, he goes, and then 'There you go,' he says, and shows it to me. There's a map. A map! It's too small for me to see properly, so I hunker down on the pavement beside him.

'Wow,' I say. 'You have the internet in your pocket?'

'Where've you been?' he asks. 'Mars?'

'Wales,' I say, and he accepts this as an adequate explanation. I look at the map, try to memorise it, but it's too small to read the road names. He does some swipey thing with his finger and thumb, and suddenly it's expanded. 'Wow,' I say. 'What's this machine called?'

He laughs. 'Mobile phone,' he says. Like, mo-bile-phoooone. When they trained us how to put the SIM in and work one, the mobile phone was a little thing with push-button numbers on the front and a little tiny screen that showed you what you'd typed.

'Where can I get something like this?' I ask. If I have one of these, I won't need the library after all. It seems extraordinary that a tramp should be walking about with such a miracle of technology in his pocket.

'Doh,' he says. 'Shop.'

'What sort of shop?'

'If you want a new one, phone shop,' he says. 'But I got this one from Crack Converters. The pawn shop. It was only about £20.'

I can't hide my astonishment. All the information in the world, in your hand, for £20? I could buy ten of these with the cash I have right now. Well, nine and a half, now he's got my ten pounds. But still. 'Where's this Crack Converters?'

He points up the street. 'Get to the main road and turn left.'

'Wow, thanks,' I say. 'That was worth ten pounds.'

'Oh, don't,' he says. 'You're a funny sort of Millennial. You're not meant to believe in swapping cash for services. You're meant to give me money and then tell your friends how virtuous you've been.'

'I don't have any friends.'

'Well, you'll be able to tell the whole of the internet now,' he says, comfortingly. 'That's almost the same.'

I get home £60.05 poorer – £40 for the phone, £10 for the charger, and £10 for a two-minute tutorial from the man in Crack Converters on how to switch it on, plus 5p for a bag to carry my purchases in. Extraordinary. It will take me years to understand the relative values of things. Six eggs are £1.79 in the Bath Road Minimart, and this bag will last literally forever.

Back in the flat, I find the contacts folder and press it to open. I only have one contact, stored for years on the SIM for emergency use. I touch it for a moment, wait, and it starts ringing.

He picks up on the eighth ring, just as I'm starting to think that he's not going to answer. That it really is all over. That maybe he will never answer and I really am alone.

'Bloody hell,' he says. 'I thought you were dead. What are you doing in Hounslow, 143?'

How does he know? A sudden flurry of paranoia. I glance around the room, half-expecting to see one of my former comrades standing in the corner, watching me.

'I saw someone had been using a card in Hounslow,' he says. 'Seriously didn't expect it to be you. Where've you been, 143? Having a little holiday in the fleshpots?'

'I'm sorry,' I say. 'They took my box for evidence. They've only just given it back.'

'Yeah, enough of the petty details,' he says. 'What do you want?'

'I want to come back,' I say. 'I want to come home.'

15 | Romy

'Home?' Uri splutters. 'You think there's a home for you here?'

I'd half-expected a response like this. I need to play it carefully. 'Yes,' I say. 'I belong with you. I always have. I would be with you now, if I could be. Lucien always said that we should stay together, no matter what happened. You know he did. He always wanted us to gather around the One.'

Flattery. Not a lie, as such, because lying comes hard to me. But if Uri thinks I mean *him* when I speak about the One, there's no harm in that, is there, baby?

A silence. It goes on for so long that I take the phone away from my face to see if we're still connected. Eventually: 'And what makes you think I'd take you back?'

'I—'

'You didn't make the bus,' he says.

A little chill runs up my spine. 'Uri!' I protest. 'You left me behind!'

A sardonic chuckle. 'To be fair, 143, I was pretty sure you weren't going to make it.'

I'm lost for words. I thought I could handle this. Handle him.

Then he laughs. 'You've shown you're a survivor, I'll give you that.'

I try to avoid the memories. Most days I am successful, but pleading with Uri brings them crashing back. I hope, baby, that you never know anything like the pain of lying pinned to a bed while over a hundred people die outside your window. Shouts. Then screams. Then howls of pain. You can hear all those things through glass, and wood, and even stone. But no one can hear you calling back. People scrabbling to get up the stairs to where I was, not to find me but to save themselves. They never made it. My mother. I heard her, calling my siblings, her familiar voice ringing out clear above the hubbub. And I heard her stop.

Then silence. Days of silence before anyone found me. The wings of carrion birds as they found the banquet on the court-yard gravel.

'Please,' I say. 'Tell me where you are. Let me come home.' In my mind's eye I see him in the courtyard at Plas Golau, though it must be the last place one would find him now. But he must be some place similar. A central core, easily locked and easily defended, and easily locked to keep the people in, with open country all around to afford a view of approaching attack. Mountain country. But I've looked at the Cairngorms and they are huge. And, even if I did find them, I won't make it inside without an invitation.

'Yes, you have my respect, I'll give you that,' he says. 'But that's a long way from having my trust. There's been a lot of water under the bridge here, 143, and you've been out of contact for months.'

'You know what happens when you stop a course of anti-biotics halfway through?' I ask. 'It's not good.'

'And yet, here you are,' he says.

'It's not an excuse, it's a fact. And they took my box for evidence. You know when I got it back? Yesterday.'

Plus or minus three days. He doesn't need to know everything. Especially the bits that might suggest that I'm weak.

'Excuses.'

I backtrack. 'Okay, ask me,' I say. 'Tell me. What do you need from me?'

'Have you found your siblings?'

'I'm looking. They're minors. Apparently I can't just be told where they are. I need permission from whoever's in charge of them. I'm not exactly on the list of approved guardians. What with the mental health facility and the mass suicide and everything.'

'Jesus, 143,' he says. 'What have you been doing all this time?'

'Waiting to get released.'

'You need to find them,' he says.

'I *know*.'

'We should have taken that boy with us,' he says. 'He was good. Talented. Showed real promise.'

'They come as a pair,' I tell him.

'Well, I suggest you make her safe, then.'

I stay silent. Don't trust my voice. I haven't even found her yet. Haven't looked her in the eyes and remembered that she was once my sister.

'There are three left,' he says. 'Not just her.'

'Really?' I'd thought there was one more. Not two. Who's the second?

'I need you to find them,' he says. 'There's no certainty for any of us unless we know for a fact that they're safe.'

I lay a hand on my abdomen and stroke the place where I imagine your head to be with my thumb. It's okay, baby. Once they're all safe, you're safe too. See? We're already one step closer. I wait, three beats, to make it sound like I'm deciding. 'Who else?' I ask.

'78,' he says.

We would count off every night before dinner, to make sure no one was lost or sick or AWOL, and I remember, after twenty years of constant repetition, almost everyone's. I was 143, my mother 142. Eden is 201, Ilo 226. Uri loves to call us all by number. Only his Guards had names. They spoke of us *en masse* as 'the Drones'.

78 is Jaivyn Blake. I'd assumed it would be him, as he was already on the Outside when he made his break for it. I didn't like Jaivyn. He didn't like any of us, either. Not even his peers, as far as I could see. I still remember the way he manhandled me, the day Eden was born. It will be a pleasure to find him.

'And 139,' he says, and my heart skips a beat. Eilidh.

'Oh,' I say. 'I thought she was . . .' I begin, and then I stop myself.

I didn't *see* her die. Not like Zaria or Farial. Didn't see a body, just assumed that her vanishing meant what I thought it meant. It was me who cleared her box out from the dormitory and gave it to Vita. Surely you wouldn't leave, and leave your box behind? Just . . . one day she was there and the next she wasn't, and we never spoke of her again.

'Where is she?' I ask.

'Working on that,' he says. 'And now you can, too.'

'I'd thought we—' I begin.

'There is no *we*, 143,' he snaps. 'Find them and show me evidence that they're safe, and we'll talk.'

'I don't know what to do,' I say. 'Where to start.'

'Start with your own,' he says. 'And keep this phone on. We'll be in touch when we know anything. And find me that boy too. If he's still alive.'

16 | Sarah

As she's leaving, the case worker takes Sarah out for a 'chat' on the brick parking space that her neighbours all refer to as their 'drive'. Hands her a bulging folder of paper. 'Sorry,' she says, 'it's a bit chaotic. Had to shove it all together. You'll need to sort it out before you hand it over to the new case worker.'

'Um,' says Sarah, 'thanks.'

'No, I mean, there's other stuff in there that you'll want to keep here, not hand over. Their birth certificates, for a start. You'll need those. It took a while but we got that done for them – it was pretty much impossible to do anything else without them. You can't really have someone in the government systems if they don't officially exist, can you?'

'I suppose not.'

'Anyway. You need the papers. As their legal guardian. You'll need them for the school, for a start, especially if they're going in after half-term. And their vaccination certificates. The schools are getting tougher about letting kids in unvaccinated. Herd immunity and that. There's a few second-doses you'll need to get sorted once you've got them registered with a doctor. I'm afraid we had to take a guess at their actual birth dates. Well, Eden was reasonably easy; she swears she was born on 9/11. Ilo, though ... he seems to have a good idea when he was conceived, so we've extrapolated forward from that.'

'That's odd.'

'Winter solstice, apparently,' she says, and shrugs. 'They seem to have had a bit of a thing for solstices. Though I don't think his conception was anything official, as such. Just a party slip-up by the mo— your sister.'

Not the first one, Sarah thinks, and is shocked at her own spitefulness.

'Anyway, we made it the 14th of September, as that probably isn't too far off.'

'Two birthdays in a week,' she says. 'Heavens.'

The bright Case Worker Smile flashes at her.

'I wish I'd known at the time. We could have done something to celebrate,' Sarah says, and gives the Smile right back to her in return. 'Thanks for getting this sorted,' she says. 'I wouldn't even have known where to start.'

'Pah,' says the social worker, 'we're not actually in the business of incubating whooping cough outbreaks in our children's homes.'

'Thank you,' says Sarah.

They're standing out on the drive, by the woman's car, and she's fiddling with her car keys and her briefcase full of sandwiches and folders, clearly keen to get back on the road. It's a long drive back to Dolgellau. Sarah's glad that she at least won't have to make *that* again.

'They're nice kids,' the case worker says, optimistically. 'Polite.'

'Yes,' says Sarah. 'They seem it.'

'Anyway,' says the case worker, eyeing Sarah's generous dwelling and obviously drawing conclusions about her income, 'I must get on the road. Long trip back. Oh, and—' She delves in her pocket, produces a piece of folded A4. 'I meant to give you this.'

Sarah unfolds it. It's an address, somewhere in the TW post-codes. 136b Bath Road. Where is that? Twickenham? Hampton? Somewhere around Heathrow?

'It's the half-sister. I thought you should have it. There are reasons why we can't give yours to her, as the kids are minors and she's an adult and we don't really know all that much about her. And she's been in rehab until very recently. You'd need to bear that in mind. Maybe assess her a bit before you plunge in. But maybe you could sound them out? See if they're wanting to be in touch? If they want to be, it would be no bad thing, I'd have thought.'

'Thank you,' says Sarah. 'I don't suppose there's a phone number, is there?'

'Not as far as I know.'

'Okay.' Sarah folds up the paper. She'll put it in her wallet while she thinks, so she doesn't lose it.

Ilo is staring at portraits of his ancestors. They've taken themselves as far as the dining room, at least. Some signs of curiosity.

'Who are these?' he asks.

'Your forebears,' she says, 'on your mother's side. They all lived here before us. This one—' she points to her great-grandfather '—built this house.'

'They don't look very happy.'

'Oh, I think they were happy enough. There's a type of person who finds being miserable more satisfying than just about anything.'

115

Ilo turns and looks at her. Studies her face for a moment, then nods. 'I understand,' he says, and smiles.

At the table, Eden has settled into the chair at the head, the one Sarah thinks of as her father's chair. Sarah feels oddly uncomfortable about it. She's never sat there herself, even though she has been head of the household for some time. It just doesn't feel right.

Eden has taken two wooden boxes from the bags and lain them on the surface in front of her. She sits quietly and watches her brother, as though she's waiting for him to join her before she opens them.

'What are those?' asks Sarah.

'Our boxes,' says Eden, as though the answer were self-evident. They're beautiful boxes. Very plain and simple, but sanded to silken smoothness, the grain of the wood – walnut for one, what looks like cherry for the other – fed and polished until they shine.

'They're beautiful,' says Sarah. 'Did someone make them for you?'

Eden looks surprised. 'No. *We* made them.'

'Yourselves?' she comes closer and runs her fingers over the polished wood of the cherrywood box, the one into whose lid the name ILO has been painstakingly etched with a childish hand. Brass hinges, a tiny hook and eye holding it closed. Beautiful. Who would have thought a child could make something with such skill and attention to detail?

'We all have one,' says Ilo, coming up beside her and taking his box in his hands. He hugs it upright against his chest, as though the very feel of it comforts him. 'Had,' he corrects.

She wonders what's in them, decides it's probably wrong to ask. Let them have some secrecy, some private places. If they want me to know, they will tell me in time.

116

'Cup of tea,' she says. The solution to all awkwardness.

'Thank you,' says Eden. 'We haven't really drunk tea before.'

'In the Home, we did,' Ilo reminds her. 'We had it at breakfast.'

'Oh, yes,' she says. 'Would it be possible to have a glass of water instead?'

'Of course,' says Sarah, suppressing a smile. 'I'll show you where everything lives.' This is it, she thinks. This is my life now. And it's theirs, too. She clears her throat. 'I want you to feel at home here,' she tells them. 'This is your home.'

'Thank you,' they say, in unison, like little robots.

'I hope you'll be happy here,' she says. 'I don't expect it to happen overnight, but I hope you'll be happy with me.'

Eden smiles. 'We were happy at Plas Golau.'

'Oh, yes,' says Ilo. 'We were happy there.'

She doesn't know what to say to that. Plas Golau, from what she's read of it, seems to her like very hell on earth. But it's where they've come from. I mustn't sweat it, she thinks. It's inevitable that they'll have brought a bit of it with them, the way they've brought those boxes.

'Well, I'll do my best to make it okay for you here. If there's anything you need,' she says, 'just say. We'll have to go shopping over the next couple of days. Get you kitted out for school.'

She catches them glancing at each other. 'Thank you,' they say again.

'No, seriously, don't be shy. It's a lot to take in all at once, I know. A big change. You've had a hell of a lot to adjust to. At least I guess you've got a bit of time to settle in before you go to school. I'm sorry we couldn't get things organised so you could join at the beginning of the year. You need to be ready to be a bit conspicuous, I'm afraid. But if there's anything you need, if you think of anything ...'

'It looks like you've already got everything in the world,' says Ilo.

117

Sarah looks around her home and feels sad. All those blond-wood, sleek Scandinavian dreams she shared with Liam reduced to a few sticks of Ikea furniture stored in the garage because they looked so out of place in here. She'd intended to have it all cleared out by now.

'I'm sorry,' she says. 'It's grim, I know. It's hard, deciding what to keep when you've inherited it. I promise I'll get to it. We'll pick the stuff we want to keep and get other stuff that suits us better.'

They side-eye each other again. 'No, no,' says Ilo. 'That's not what I meant. We're just ... not used to so much *stuff*.'

'It wasn't our way, at home,' says Eden.

'Well,' she says, hopefully, 'I guess communal living is different. You must have been pressed for space.'

Eden shrugs. 'Yes. And possessions won't mean much, after the Great Disaster.'

'They get in the way,' says Ilo. 'They weigh you down.'

'That's all,' says Eden. 'We're not, you know ... *judging* you. But presumably you have a plan.'

'A plan?'

'For what you'd take if you had to run? And where you'd go?'

'I ...'

Not even lunchtime, and already she's flummoxed.

'Not really,' she says, 'but ... maybe we can work on one together.' Good lord, they still believe all that stuff. Just as my parents believed that Jesus really was a bloke who wanted a nice suburban house to live in, or Momentum members believe in Magic Grandpa. You never totally get it, do you, till it slaps you in the face?

'Bedrooms,' she says. 'Let me show you your bedrooms.'

Their eyes meet. 'Bed*rooms*? One each?' asks Ilo.

'Yes. Of course.'

'Oh.'

'We've got plenty.'

'I suppose so,' says Ilo, and she's flummoxed again. Even identical twins long for their own space when they're teenagers, surely? 'I just ... it seems so ...'

It's going to be so tricky, finding ways of showing them how the normal world lives without seeming to criticise the one they've come from. But the overcrowding at Plas Golau must have been practically slumlike. No wonder they never had any belongings.

'Thing is, I don't think Social Services like the idea of siblings of different genders sharing rooms,' she says. 'So we're going to have to do what they expect, at least until they're not watching us any more.' *By which time, hopefully, you'll have got used to it.* 'Come on,' she says, and leads them upstairs.

From the landing, four bedrooms. First, her parents', with her father's reading glasses and tumbler – water long since evaporated – still in place on his bedside table. Two smaller rooms in the middle, which were once her own and Alison's, Alison's stripped and turned into a sewing room within a week of her leaving. And the Bishop's Room: what in any normal house would be called the spare room. Smaller than her parents', but twice the size of the little ones. She's almost embarrassed to admit it, but she herself moved straight back into her childhood bedroom. Doesn't want to take over her parents' room and can't face clearing it out. All those clothes. The shoes unworn for two years, the strange lizardy feel of anything they've touched. It wasn't meant to be forever. But time slips away when you're lonely. Loneliness saps your energy. You can stare at the same cobweb for years on end, watching it blacken, and still not think to find a duster to remove it.

She opens the door to the spare room. 'I thought you could be in here,' she says to Ilo. 'It's bigger, but I'm afraid the window

119

just looks out on next door. And this one's your mother's old room.' She throws open the door to Eden's.

Eden stays in the hallway, says nothing, but her eyes blaze.

'What's wrong?' asks Sarah.

'Nothing,' says Eden.

'It has its own basin, look.' She points to the pearlised pink pedestal sink on the far wall. 'It was your mother's room, when she was your age,' she repeats, hopefully.

'It's okay, Eden,' says Ilo. 'I'll take it. It's fine.'

'I thought,' Sarah says, finds herself stammering, 'it would be nicer. You've got a lovely outlook, and a decent wardrobe.'

Eden's eyes flash at her.

'She should have the bigger room,' says Ilo, and walks into Alison's. Lays his box down on the desk, sits on the bed. Eden says nothing, but walks into the other and closes the door.

It will get better, Sarah. It's day one. It will get better.

17 | Sarah

They're fascinated by the footbridge. But then, they're fascinated by everything, with very little distinction, like a toddler spotting a pigeon in a zoo. A puzzled look crosses one or other of their faces five times an hour, because they literally know nothing. It's lucky, really, that the school couldn't take them till half-term, as their goggling astonishment at everything they saw – piercings, cats' eyes in the road, post boxes, trains, washing machines, blue hair, Marmite, the sea, pugs – would have marked them out for bullying in an instant. She took a couple of weeks' unpaid leave before the half-term holiday to get to know them, and in the hope that she could introduce them to enough of the world that they don't attract too much attention when they have to navigate it without her.

It's only partly worked. Merely crossing a bridge is something special to them. Though the bridge is, in its way, a special experience. Looking down onto the windy chasm of the motorway is a strange sort of time-travel experience. It makes you feel, as juggernauts blast past beneath your feet, like a Stone Age hunter

121

finding yourself in the land of dragons. Ilo stops and leans on the railing for so long that she almost tells him to hurry up. But then his curiosity sparks a curiosity in her. I've never actually done that, she thinks, and climbs onto the ledge that supports the railings beside him.

It's a unique sensation, she discovers: the puffs of air that hit the face when even a small car whizzes beneath them, the fact that that sort of speed is so unnatural, so beyond anything one would experience in nature, that when you watch you can actually feel your brain adjusting to fit the phenomenon in with the surrounding reality. Eden climbs up on the other side of her and she has to fight a strong urge to put out an arm to stop her tipping over, as though she were a toddler.

'How fast are they going?' Ilo asks.

'Oh, I'd think somewhere between seventy and eighty.'

'Miles an hour?'

'Yes.'

He doesn't seem particularly impressed. 'An asteroid enters the earth's atmosphere at 45,000 miles an hour,' he says.

'Apophis,' says Eden.

'You what?'

'It'll pass inside the orbit of our communication satellites in 2029,' she says.

'Yes,' says Ilo. 'And that might alter its orbit enough that it hits us the next time round.'

'Goodness!' she says. 'And when will that be?'

'2036,' they both say complacently.

'But obviously most of humanity will be long gone by then,' says Eden.

'Yes, but it'll be a long winter,' says Ilo.

'Come on,' Sarah says. She's getting used to this habit they have of spotting the links between things they see and world-crushing phenomena. It doesn't mean anything, really. It's just a reflex, like crossing yourself when you see a magpie. 'We don't want to be late on your first day.' And he climbs down obediently, though he casts a look of regret over his shoulder.

She looks at them. Funny creatures. Is there more going on beneath the surface, or are they really this calm? Helen says to be patient. 'It's early days,' she says. 'They need to trust you first.' Maybe the daily counselling they've got arranged with her will help; teach them, at least, to open up. She finds it hard to know what to do when most of the time they treat her like a pleasant stranger, not the friend she'd imagined she would be. She would have a better idea of how to be around them if they treated her the way all the kids at the school do – like the enemy.

And talk of the devil: they turn the corner and run smack into Marie Spence, and Lindsay, her morning bodyguard. It's not that surprising. She lives on the Canaan Estate, in one of the houses the Congregation sold off in the Noughties, her parents' matching red Jags in the driveway and a swimming pool where the rhododendrons used to be, so she'll inevitably take the same route to school if she's walking. But Sarah wishes that today had been one of the days her father decided to give her a lift; that the children's first experience of their schoolmates didn't have to be her.

She's Abi Knowles all over again, thinks Sarah, remembering her own nemesis, her own adolescent misery. They're part of every ecosystem, and God, I wish they weren't.

'Morning, *miss*,' Marie says pertly. She is wearing rattling silver bangles – lots of them, layered – and big hoop earrings that dance against her cheeks. Her feet, for the journey from house to school, are clad in spike heels so high that to Sarah her arch looks vertical. More drag queen than teenager. But still she's confident that Marie won't look back at teenage photos

123

and feel as bad as Sarah does when she looks at the pudding-basin haircut and the apron-pinafore combinations that feature in her own.

'Who's this, *miss*?' asks Marie. She has no fear of adults, and no respect, either. She probably doesn't even know Sarah's name. It's not as though lowly office drones figure much in her world.

'This is Eden Blake, Marie,' she says. It's bound to get out that the children are related to the staff eventually, but no point in cursing them with that by actually announcing their relationship on their first day. 'She's starting in your class today. And this is her brother, Ilo. Eden, Ilo, this is Marie, and Lindsay. Eden's going to be in your year. I'm sure you'll be making her welcome, won't you?' she adds, and the bright tone she attempts sounds a lot like pleading.

Marie's eyes scan up and down Eden, then Ilo, then Eden's clean-scrubbed face and knee-length uniform skirt again, and her upper lip curls. Whatever the disappointments of her adult life, Sarah is grateful every day that she never has to be a teenager again.

'Yeah,' says Marie to Eden's unbranded trainers. A hand comes up and flicks the shiny red extensions.

'Who was that?' asks Eden, as they turn the next corner. She sounds neither impressed nor apprehensive.

'Oh, don't worry about them,' says Sarah, more confidently than she feels. 'There's a Marie in every school.'

'How does she walk in those shoes?' she asks.

'God knows,' says Sarah. 'She'll have to change out of them when she gets to the gates.'

'Ah,' says Ilo, 'that's why she has such a big bag.'

Well, it sure as hell doesn't have any books in it. 'I know. You wouldn't have thought it was worth the effort, would you?'

'She has very long eyelashes,' says Eden.

'They're not real,' says Sarah. 'She gets them glued on once a month. By the end of the month they're shedding down her cheeks like spider's legs.'

Helen is waiting on the steps as they arrive, dressed in her full soft-jersey-waterfall-cardigan professional counsellor gear, lots of pockets for Kleenex and large round breasts for weeping on. 'Hi, guys,' she says. 'Ready for the fray?'

They go inside and Sarah is glad that she's spent so much effort and money on acclimatising them to crowded places in the past few weeks, for without it they would probably be frozen to the spot right now. The pre-registration cacophony is enough to make a healthy adult quail. The air is rich with that particular heady smell that comes off a body old enough to be using deodorant but not old enough to have discovered independent washing, and the air reverberates with shouts and screams. They hover just inside the doorway to let themselves adjust, and she feels Eden's speedy breathing.

'It'll be okay.' She attempts to sound reassuring. 'You'll get used to it, I promise.'

They set off through the surging bodies to the corridor that leads to the principal's office.

Before the End

2008–2010

18 | Romy

2009

Boys become men at thirteen. For girls, it's more of a moveable feast. Romy gets almost a year longer in the Pigshed than Eilidh does. Their low-protein, low-fat diet tends to delay puberty for the girls of the Ark in comparison with their contemporaries among the Dead. But she's fourteen, and she has finally become a woman. She secretly finds it a bit icky that so many people should be so interested in her bodily functions, but everyone seems so excited, so pleased for her, that she keeps the thought to herself. Besides, she's been bored, locked up in the Pigshed, waiting, and she's wild to find out what she will become.

Her first thought, when she sees the stain, is why did it have to happen in winter? She even considers, briefly, hiding it until the spring, but the prospect of another long winter in the Pigshed, waiting to start her life, reading Shakespeare and Dickens and Tennyson to while the hours away while Teachers who are now no more educated than she is concentrate on the little ones – and the danger, of course, of being caught in a lie – are worse than the prospect of the sudden exposure to cold and life in a woollen beanie hat that adulthood represents. So she goes to Ursola and tells her and gets swept immediately into the overwhelming current of adulthood.

Preparations for her ceremony are hurried, for Lucien likes it done while the girl is still bleeding. And the embarrassment is so profound that she swears, deep inside, that no one will ever know such detail about her again. She shows on Monday, and her ceremony is scheduled for after evening meal on Thursday. The Cooks rustle up a batch of honey cake and the Farmers slaughter a dozen of the chickens that have passed laying so that everyone will have a taste of meat, and three flagons of cider come up from the vaults, for everyone to toast the new adult. The Healers scout the hedgerows and the herb garden for flowers and foliage for her coronet: not such an easy task in November. In the end they find penstemons and campion and pennyroyals, and wind them all up with stems of fragrant evergreen bay. Not the prettiest crown, but she is pleased, for it will dry well, and there's something pleasingly witchy about bay.

The women come for her at the Pigshed at four o'clock. At the door, they place the coronet on her head and lead her across the farmyard to the Bath House. Inside is a whole bathful of hot water, dried rose petals floating on the surface. A hot bath all of her own, no recycled water, no one waiting to follow her and cursing her if she lingers and lets the water cool. A roaring fire in the hearth, a bar of special lavender soap that's usually reserved for sale to the Dead, now her own to keep. A towel warming on a clothes horse in front of the fire and a dress laid out on a chair. She feels like a queen.

Even more so as she walks through the dining hall with Vita, once Counting Off is done, in her new linen dress. She sees her mother, one hand on her collarbone, gaze at her as though she wants to hold the image in her mind forever. Her little brother lets out a whoop at the children's table and is hushed by the adult sitting with them; but she manages to throw a shaky smile in his direction and sees him catch it. He's the thing she'll miss the most about the Pigshed: the way he still bounds around her like a puppy, the way they often understand each other without the tedium of having to speak.

Then she looks up at her destination and has to remember to breathe.

Lucien, seated at the High Table among his children, watches her as she makes her way towards the steps. Leans to his side and says something into his daughter Zaria's ear. Even from halfway across the hall, Romy sees the colour rise in Zaria's face. She stands, stalks up the table and throws herself into a chair next to Jaivyn. Then Lucien is standing and waiting for her, smiling, smiling all the time as she walks. She feels his ice-blue eyes run over her, taking in her woman's body, and blushes to the roots of her hair.

'Sit, my dear,' says Lucien, and points to the chair beside him. She sits, and Vita places herself on her other side. She wishes she felt more honoured, less conspicuous. Her seat is more throne than chair. It has a padded base, arms, and a back. You can lean back and let the wood take the weight from your spine. After fourteen years of benches, it's certainly a novelty.

'Welcome, my child,' he says. 'And welcome to womanhood.'

He helps himself to a piece of bread and tears it between his fingers. Romy is too nervous to eat. She picks up her water glass and takes a drink, and her hand is shaking. Vita, sitting on Romy's other side, puts a hand on her shoulder and smiles into her face. 'Don't be nervous,' she says. 'It's a breeze.'

131

Romy gives her a wobbly smile.

'I'm very practised,' says Vita.

'I know. It's all the people,' Romy confides.

'That you see every day.'

'They're not all watching me every day.'

Vita raises an eyebrow. 'So you don't like being the centre of attention, then?'

'Do you?'

Vita blinks. 'Sometimes one has to accept things one doesn't enjoy for the greater good,' she says. 'We all do.'

'Yes,' says Romy.

'You will be surprised by what you can do, when it's necessary.'

'I hope so,' says Romy.

The food arrives on platters, as it does in the main hall. They seem that little bit fuller up here, though. Not by much: an extra inch of potato here, half a dozen pieces of chicken there. Nothing that would be obvious from the tables below. When the platter arrives in front of her, she hesitantly takes a thigh with the fork and spoon laid on top, puts it on her plate and puts her hands into her lap while she waits for everyone else to be served.

'Come on, child,' says Lucien. 'Have another.'

She gapes. Never, ever in her life has there been a second piece of chicken. For the Farmers and the Builders maybe, at times when the work is especially intense, but not for the likes of her.

'Special food for a special occasion,' he says. Smiles down at her and jerks his chin encouragingly. Lucien has recently grown a close-cropped beard, and there's a peppering of silver in among the golden hairs. She wonders briefly if this is some sort of test, but then she looks down the table and sees that there are two pieces on most of the plates. And Father doesn't lie, she tells herself. He hates lying, so why would he do it to me? She takes a drumstick and adds it to her plate. Saliva floods onto her tongue.

'So tell me, Romy, how old are you?'

'Fourteen,' she says.

'A late bloomer!' he says. 'Never mind. Well worth the wait.'

Romy goes scarlet, stares down at her plate in confusion.

'Lucien ...' says Vita, and she sounds as though she's warning him.

'Are you ready for your responsibilities?'

'I hope so,' she replies again.

'And what will you be, do you think?'

I want to be a Healer, she thinks. Please let me be a Healer. But she knows the right response, and she uses it. 'I shall be whatever Vita and Uri say I should be,' she says. She'll find out soon enough. Vita and Uri will tell her her assignment in the Council Chamber when the feast is done.

'Good girl,' he says, 'good girl,' and he picks up his cutlery and begins to eat. 'I should think,' he says, 'you can't wait to grow up.'

'Which is still in four years, Lucien,' says Vita.

'Oh, yes,' he says. 'Plenty of time to look forward in.'

There is butter on the winter cabbage. She never knew how delicious cabbage could be.

The Guards have taken increasingly to taking their own evening meal together, in the new house they've had restored for their use by the reservoir despite Vita's indignant protests, but Uri has come across to sit with the Family tonight, specifically because of Romy's feast; there's a three-line whip for the birth family, where feasts are concerned. He doesn't look as though he's relishing the experience. He sits between Eden and Heulwen, the two youngest, and eats without speaking. I wonder, she thinks, what they did that has made him not like them?

The two girls look a bit cowed, sit with their elbows on the table and their hands supporting their heads as they stab at their food. Eden is toying with her food more than eating it. If she were down in the hall, she would be earning a stiff reproach from the Cooks.

She looks across the table at Romy, and calls out, 'So you've got your period, then? What's it like?'

Romy's face flames.

All the way down at the foot of the table, Eilidh shines her sweet smile on her and waggles her fingers in greeting; rolls her eyes to show she knows how she feels. And Romy feels better, because if there's Eilidh she will always have support. Eilidh and Ilo will always be on her side, however embarrassed she is.

And then the apples are eaten and Lucien pushes his chair back and rises to his feet. Romy's stomach lurches. Childhood is over.

'Today is a day to rejoice,' says Lucien, and the room erupts. Banging on tables. Spoons on glasses. The Cooks bustle up the aisles dispensing cider and squares of honey cake. Everyone apart from the children gets a glass of cider and everyone will drink. Romy sits with downcast eyes, for even on this special day there will be people watching her for signs of vanity. Especially her, with the mother she has. But she can't stop a little smile from playing on her lips as she blushes. *Me. They're cheering for me.*

'Tonight,' continues Lucien, 'we welcome one of our young to the challenges and responsibilities of adulthood. Tonight, she is no longer a child, but stands shoulder to shoulder with us all. Welcome, Romy Blake. Welcome to the future.'

She stands. The room erupts again. Thunder in her ears, part pulse, part deafening noise. Lucien, all smiles, presses his palms to her cheeks again, then enfolds her in a paternal, masterly hug.

134

He smells of soap and wood smoke. And some rich woody fragrance that she doesn't think originates among the flora of north Wales. When he lets go, he manoeuvres her round to face the crowd. She sees her friends from the Pigshed, applauding. Her mother's hands clasped in front of her face, in prayer position.

Lucien raises a hand. His people sit. It's funny, thinks Romy, that I don't have to say anything myself. But I suppose it makes sense. I may feel special, but all I'm really doing is becoming a part of the great totality. I've a long way to go before I'm important enough to speak. And part of her feels glad, for she's not sure that her voice would work. She looks up at Lucien and feels a glow of love. She feels energised, electrified, changed. Ready.

A chair is placed at the front of the stage by two of the Cooks, in front of the Family. Beside it, a little table. On its surface, the large shears they use for cutting sinew in the kitchen, the clippers, a small blue bag. She steps away from Lucien and takes her new seat, hearing the thud thud thud in her head. And then Vita is there, bending down to her, smiling into her face and planting a light, rose-scented kiss on each of her cheeks. They smell so good, the Leaders. 'Congratulations, Romy,' she murmurs. 'Welcome to the world.'

Romy sits. Bows her head while Vita removes her coronet and lays it gently on the table. Then Vita takes the shears, brushes Romy's mane of thick, shiny, waist-length hair off her face, coils it around and around her hand until it is taut, and turns her into an adult.

She has never felt so naked. She longs to put a hand up and feel the shape of her skull, run her fingers over her moleskin scalp. So this is how my mother felt, she thinks, but without the shame. Her warm blanket of hair, protection against the cold, has been tied with a ribbon and dropped into the blue velvet bag. She will never see it again. Vita replaces the coronet. It itches and prickles, the newly exposed skin tender as a baby's. She will wear it, nonetheless, until it begins to wilt, and then the Cooks will take it away, hang it on a chimney wall to dry, wrap it in tissue paper and give it to her for her box, a souvenir of her great day.

She doesn't know it, but her eyes look huge. Bambi eyes.

19 | Romy

2009

At the end of her Assignment Ceremony in the Council Chamber, Vita stays behind when Uri leaves, with some pretext of Women's Talk that sends him hurrying for the door. Then she closes it behind him and turns to Romy with the sweet smile they see too rarely these days.

'Are you happy?'

Would it matter if I weren't? thinks Romy. But she smiles back and pronounces herself delighted. In a way, she is. She's not to be a Farmer or a Launderer or a Cook. But nor is she a Healer or an Engineer. She is to live outside the Hierarchies. Attached to the Healers but not of them. Special, and yet not. Medical Horticulturalist: the only one in the compound. Always just on the outside, looking in.

'It's not the end,' says Vita. 'Understand that. We can't just *make* you a Healer, not straight away. We made your mother one, after all, and she let us down.'

'I'm not my mother,' says Romy.

'No,' says Vita. 'And you can earn your place.'

'Thank you,' she says. 'How?'

'By proving that the trust we've put in you is justified, Romy,' says Vita. 'There's hardly anyone in the compound, especially not one your age, who gets so much trust.'

'Thank you,' she says, meaning it a little more as she thinks about the estate, the farm, the moorland, the woods. It will all be hers. As long as her work is done, as long as they can see that her work is done, she will be able to go wherever she chooses. Maybe one day she will even get to go out among the Dead and see their world, for she is to apprentice with the Beemaster as well, taking care of the hives that remain when he takes the others out into the world to pollinate orchards and market gardens and great fields of flowers and bring back the foreign honey. Honey is life itself. The Cooks use it in the kitchen and the Healers keep it sealed up in sterile jars, as an antiseptic for dressing wounds.

My knife will be useful, she thinks. I'm glad I made it. I shall need a sturdy blade, to harvest tough stems. A blade and a spade and an eye for ripeness. I've learned the plants already; that's why they've chosen me. All that time I've spent in the physic garden, the lessons I learned from Somer, the books I carried with me everywhere: I may not be a Healer yet, but I shall at least be a Someone.

She is to take charge of the physic garden. But more. Romy is to be both forager and protector. She is to cover the whole of Plas Golau with her observant eye, ripping up Destroying Angels as they sprout, plucking out the hemlock, the ragwort, the henbane, the bryony, the water dropwort, the nightshades: everything poisonous to livestock as well as humans. She is to carry bags for the good, the bad and the in-between, and bring the latter two to Vita for disposal. Vita disposes of all the poisons herself, since the accident when two people collapsed after inhaling the fumes from burning rhododendron.

She can earn her way into the Infirmary, they have assured her. Do her job well, be diligent, be tireless, bring home the analgesics and the antipyretics, the unbroken cobwebs for clotting wounds, the docks to soothe the rashes, the mints to settle stomachs. The poisons, as well. Many poisons are also medicines, of course. The plants that both cure and kill must come back to the Infirmary with her in a basket, as undamaged as she can manage. *And bring them back well enough and one day, one day, Romy, we will trust you to do more.*

'I need you to do something for me, Romy,' says Vita. 'We're old friends.'

Romy glows.

'Lucien is very tired,' says Vita. 'Caring for us all, making decisions for us all, worrying for our future – it takes it out of him. Do you see?'

Romy nods. 'He is so good to us.'

'I do what I can to ease his burden.' Vita sighs. 'He can't be everywhere, but nor can I. And people – some people – they're not as loyal as they should be. We need to work together. You know that. We're only as strong as our weakest link.'

Romy falls quiet. Sometimes, in the dormitories, in the kitchens and the corridors, she has heard rumbles of discontent. Complaints, contempt, bad words about their peers. It's the fact that she was still a child, of course. People forget that children have ears.

'I need you to be my eyes, Romy,' says Vita. 'You can be anywhere. That's the great privilege of this position. I need you to be my ears. People see me coming and they change. You, they won't even notice.'

Romy gulps, nods. Vita wants her to be a spy. The price of her freedom will be spying on her comrades.

'I don't want you to denounce,' says Vita. 'Not that. I'm not asking you to have people punished. It's just for me. So I know. So I know when there's a problem beginning. So I can do something to help. Do you understand? Just pause, when you're near, and listen. To the Farmers, the Blacksmiths, the Teachers. To the Guards, down in that house away from all the rest. I can't be everywhere. Just listen, when you can.'

The Guards. She'd known that they were going to come up. The unease between Vita and Uri is ever more noticeable: The flow of words that stops when the other comes within earshot, the tiny jerks of the head that indicate offence. She wants me to watch the Guards, she thinks. And she's not surprised.

The first hill frost has settled while she's been indoors. She gasps as she pulls open the door to the Great Hall, begins instantly to shiver in her silly thin dress, her naked scalp exposed to the blasting cold. The dormitory she shares with seven other women – she stopped sleeping in the same quarters as her mother when she was seven years old – is two hundred yards away. It's an old wooden chalet beyond the courtyard wall that used to be the home of a single counsellor back in the days when Plas Golau was a prison for troubled teens, and she's privileged to be there rather than in the old potting sheds where Farmers like her mother live. But she is barefoot, and it never occurred to anyone to bring a coat for her from the Bath House, and the air is cold, and once she's beyond the courtyard wall she will be all alone in the dark.

She holds on to the banister as she descends the Great House steps, for the stone can be icy on a cold night. And when she hits the gravel she starts to run, eager for the warmth awaiting her.

A figure steps into the gateway and bars her way. It's Uri.

Romy skids to a halt ten feet away, eyes him suspiciously, unsure whether to go back or forward.

'Hello, 143,' he says. 'A word, if you don't mind.'

Among the Dead

November 2016

20 | Sarah

There's a toilet at the back of the staff room, and although there's a general one much closer to her office she tends to use this one, because a toilet used by adults is always going to be more fragrant than one accessed by several hundred children. She likes to use it in the middle of the second period in the morning and the first after lunch, when most of the staff are in classrooms or meetings and the coast is likely to be as clear as it ever will be. A strange inhibition left over from her upbringing: that the sound of other people sharing the space makes her bladder freeze. The relief when she's out in public and finds a disabled toilet is always intense. As a child she would run home in lunch break simply to pee, and then – oh, the fear that she might be too late one day – to change the bulky towels with which her mother preserved her putative virginity. You don't shed inhibitions like that overnight.

Ten a.m. and she's sitting on the toilet when the sound of the outer door opening makes her muscles clench. She checks her watch. Another twenty minutes until the next changeover. She has time to sit it out.

'. . . who it was?' asks a voice as it passes through the door. A woman, with another. Not all the staff are teaching all the time, of course.

'I should think someone on staff with kids in the school, don't you?'

'Careless talk costs lives.'

'Little pitchers have big ears.'

'True. Anyway, whatever. It took three weeks but the cat's well and truly out of the bag now. Tricia says the phone's been ringing all day.'

Tricia. The principal's PA. Something wrong, clearly.

'It's ridiculous. It's not like either of them was implicated. They're hardly, you know, going to be poisoning the water supply.'

Oh, hell. This can only be about one thing.

'Try telling that to the parents.'

'I know, I know. It would help if they weren't so weird, though, wouldn't it? Have you got them in any of your classes?'

'The girl.'

'I've got both. Do they ever take their eyes off you for one second?'

A shiver-laugh. 'No! It's freaky! It makes me feel like I must have my skirt tucked into my knickers!'

'Oh, I think Ben McArdle would let you know if that were the case!'

'Or Marie Spence.'

'God, I wish someone would poison *her.*'

'Tell me about it.'

The doors either side of her cubicle close and lock. I could make a run for it now, she thinks, but toilet gossip – so unguarded – is the best chance for information that she'll get.

'Poor sods,' says the voice to her left, 'they don't stand a chance, really. Even without everyone finding out. I mean, she's a bit weird herself, isn't she? Who's going to show them how to be normal?'

'Oh, I know. Scurrying around like a squirrel, apologising all the time.'

Sarah's cheeks burn. It is never a privilege, hearing how other people see one. *You don't have the first idea!* she screams inside her head. *How brave I have to be every single day just to leave the house.*

'Isn't she part of that Congregation lot on the High Street?'

'Is she? Well, the apple doesn't fall far.'

'Imagine,' says the voice to her right, 'you get freed from one cult and they put you straight back into another.'

'It does seem tough.'

'What does Helen say?'

'Oh, you know Helen. All "I daresay"s and "maybe"s. You'll never get a judgement out of a therapist.'

'And in the meantime we get to deal with the fallout.'

'I don't know, maybe we need another bullying assembly or something?'

'Oh, please God, no. It was bad enough after the last one when half of Year Nine decided they were non-binary.'

'Yes, but I do feel sorry for them. That Marie's a stirring little minx.'

'What's she done?'

'Says they smell, says the girl has a thing for her, keeps asking people if anything's gone missing from their locker while staring at them. The usual.'

'They don't help themselves, though, do they? All that walking around together like he's her bodyguard or something.'

'And the clothes! What was she thinking?'

'I know! The shoes!'

'And those smiles! They're like . . . puppets or something.'

A flush on one side, a flush the other. The doors unlock.

'Well, we shall see what we shall see.'

'Yes, well, they'll either carry on being freaks or they'll learn to fit in.'

Footsteps cross the floor and the door slams shut behind them. Sarah finally urinates, and burns with rage. They talk about my children like that, she thinks, and they don't even wash their hands when they've been to the loo, the dirty bitches.

21 | Romy

Two years after my brother Ilo was born, four young men with
backpacks full of explosives entered the London Transport
system. They never left, and nor did fifty-two commuters who
shared their bus and railway carriages. In Tokyo in 1995,
members of the Aum Shinrikyo cult released sarin gas on the
subway, and twelve people choked to death on their own bodily
secretions. In 1987, a mix of hair, skin flakes and grease, built
up on the underside of an escalator, burst into flames and the
rising tunnel funnelled the blazing heat straight into the faces
of thirty-one people in the ticket hall of King's Cross station. It
took seventeen years to identify one of the bodies.

Millions ride it every day, but just the thought of entering
those tunnels sends a shiver down my spine. Father got hold of
photographs from inside those train carriages and showed them
to us on the dining hall projector screen. Blood and intestines,
jagged metal, body parts, a handbag abandoned on a slatted
wooden floor. Safe in Plas Golau, I never dreamed of putting
myself at that kind of risk.

There are buses to Finbrough. They go from a town called Reading. But the buses to Reading go from Heathrow, and Heathrow is two stops on the Piccadilly line from Hounslow West and the police will pick you up if you try to walk along the airport roads. It might as well be in Croatia. No amount of beta blockers and mindfulness and breathing techniques will get me through those tunnels. I went into the station concourse, and the rush of hot wind coming up the escalator felt like the very breath of hell, and sent me back into the flat for two more days. I'm not the person I was, baby. I've seen death, and it's left me weak.

So I try hitch-hiking. Somer used to do it all the time, she told me, with me tucked into a papoose across her breasts. We spent the summer after I was born on what she called the 'festival circuit', her running Chai Tea stalls and bacon sandwich stalls and delivering something called 'e' to tents while I crawled about in the mud under the *laissez-faire* eyes of people with dreadlocks and tattoos and feathers in their hair. It was on that circuit that she met Vita, who gave her work in the Ark's mobile café in August and took her to the Glastonbury house when the season ended in September. So, in the end, hitch-hiking is what made me. Made us. Brought us to Plas Golau.

It's surprisingly easy. I don't have to stand for more than ten minutes on the A4 with a sign I've made from cardboard before a woman in a vehicle so grand I have to step *up* to get into it stops and throws open her door.

'You really shouldn't be hitching,' she says. 'I only stopped because frankly you look as if you don't know what you're doing. It's not safe, you know. There's all sorts on the roads.'

'I know,' I reply. I'm getting better and better at making up stories. 'But the car broke down and I promised I'd take my grandmother to church.'

'Well, that's good of you.' The seat is made of leather and I swear there's a heat source somewhere inside. I settle back and feel my aching hips go *aaaahhhh*. 'But I bet she wouldn't want her granddaughter standing on the side of the A4 looking for lifts. I'm sure she'd be okay to miss church just this once.'

'She's in a wheelchair,' I say. And this seems to satisfy her.

She goes out of her way to drop me in Finbrough – she's going all the way to Newbury to look at a horse, she says. I'm surprised there are no horses closer to London to look at, but perhaps it's a special horse. She gives me a thing called an energy bar to eat as we join the M4 motorway, and asks when I'm due.

'February,' I tell her, which I think is about right. But I'm a bit appalled that she's spotted it so easily. I'd thought the extra weight I'd put on was a good enough disguise, but six months is six months, I suppose.

'Well, promise me you won't be such a fool again,' she says, and presses the accelerator to take us into the fast lane.

It's not much of a place. To come from. Or to go to. In Plas Golau, I imagined it to look a bit like Dolgellau, the only town I'd ever visited. You construct your imaginary landscapes from the things you know, so the birthplace I'd imagined was all narrow winding roads, tall narrow buildings, small windows, granite walls, hills. Everywhere on the Outside looked like Dolgellau in my head, except the Taj Mahal and Angkor Wat, because there were pictures of them, I've never known why, on the Pigshed walls.

I wave goodbye to Caroline, my chauffeur, and look up and down the London Road. Finbrough is bungalows. Paved forecourts, squat black-and-white signs naming the roads. Roundabouts. Endless little roundabouts, and pedestrian sanctuaries every two hundred yards. I look up my map on my telephone, and then I walk back a couple of hundred yards and turn up Cardigan Street, for buried behind these shabby little houses is a much older town.

The motorway is less a sound here than a feeling. If I stand stock-still and hold my breath I can hear the traffic rush by out there, the building and waning drone, and though I'm not aware of it at a conscious level while I'm walking I guess some bit of me must be, beneath the surface. I feel restive, unsettled. But maybe that's because I have a mission, and I have no idea how it will turn out.

Then the sound of people. Voices – calling out, talking, laughing – clanking, footsteps, the occasional grumble of a car engine, music; something that goes thook-thook-thook and, competing with it, a woman singing – wailing – about sex or dancing or something. And then I turn the corner into the High Street and I'm in the middle of Finbrough market. Rows and rows of little stalls, vans with open back doors and watchful men taking cash and ready to run. Colour everywhere, men shouting, women shouting, children shouting. Lucien would literally have his eyes screwed shut right now and his hands clamped over his ears. He hated people shouting. *Avocados free for a pahnd, getcha cleaning products*. A dozen food smells tumbling over each other: spice and oil and caramel, the scent of grilling meat. I recoil at all this brightness in this grey little place, and then I plunge in.

I am dodging through a world of strangers, and any one of them could be armed, could be waiting for their opportunity to be the catalyst that sparks the revolution. Any one of them could be incubating the final pandemic. Any one of them could do something that starts a stampede.

Then a scent so overpoweringly delicious that it snatches my breath away snaps into my nostrils, turns my head. It's so strong, so hypnotic, I swear I can feel you shift in my belly to turn towards it too, though I know that's just fantasy. Or a growling stomach. I've never smelled anything like it. Heat and citrus and salt and crimson-brown in my head. I look, track it down to a stall where a black man with a great bunch of snake-like tendrils tied against the back of his neck is turning chicken pieces over and over on an open grill. I go over. He's old. He must be forty at least. But he smiles at me as if we're contemporaries.

'What *is* that?' I ask.

'Jerk chicken, my love,' he says.

'What's that?'

'Old Jamaican recipe. You bite it and your head *jerk*,' he says, and jerks his head in illustration.

'What's in it?'

'Secret recipe,' he says. 'I don' share my trade secrets wi' no one. Want to have a try?'

'How much?'

He picks up a knife and a fork and nicks a thumbnail of flesh from the blackened outside of a drumstick. Offers it to me on the point. I take it gingerly between my fingers, sniff it and pop it into my mouth, and the whole universe explodes. I think my head actually *does* jerk, because the man's smile practically splits his head in two as he bellows with laughter. It's hot – so, so hot I think my tongue will ulcerate – and ... I don't know how to describe it. Complete. It feels completely whole, as though all the flavours in the world have come full circle. I didn't know. My God, I didn't know. I didn't know that food could be like this.

'Oh, my God,' I say.

He smiles a slow, crafty grin. 'Best jerk in the West Country,' he says. 'All the way from Bristol, with love.'

I need this. I want to buy everything on his stall. I want to throw my arms round him, round his food, round the whole world. 'How much?' I ask again.

153

'Six pieces for a fiver,' he says. I have no idea if that's cheap or expensive or what. According to the internet it's the bus fare back to Reading. I dig in my pocket and find five pounds, press it into his hand, then I snatch the chicken from him and practically run to find somewhere to sit.

A few yards along, I find a low wall in front of a building set back from the road. It has railings, but there's enough wall in front to give purchase to my buttocks, and my need is so urgent that I'm happy to make do. I perch and open my box, breathe that heavenly aroma once again. And then I pretty much inhale a thigh and a wing. I actually close my eyes to concentrate on the complexity, the challenge, the greasy caress of the flavour, actually hear myself letting out little grunts and 'oh's of pleasure. Never, I think. Never, never, never has food felt like this, in my whole life. How can people who make food like this be bent on self-destruction?

I suck the last of the meat from the bone and drop it back into the box. Just one more. If I just have the other wing, there will still be enough for later. People walk past me, unaware. People in jeans and dresses, in sweeping coats and sharply cut jackets, people in boots and leggings, people with scarves wrapped round their shoulders, slung round necks, tied round heads like turbans. They're fascinating. Every one striving, in some way, to stand out, to project some part of their personality for the rest of the world to see. There's a scarf in among my donated wardrobe: lightweight green wool with black silhouetted songbirds printed on the weave, faded but still charming. I must try these other ways of wearing it; it had simply never occurred to me that they had a function beyond keeping the neck warm.

Oh, stop, Romy, stop. They warned me over and over of this danger, of the seductive veneer of the world of the Dead. You can become addicted, they said. Enslaved. You will only truly be free if you keep yourself separate. Four and a half months in and I'm already looking for fashion tips. And then I bite through the crisp skin of the chicken wing and am once again filled with this weird nostalgia for a life that never was.

I stand up and go over to a rubbish bin to dispose of my bones. An old lady in a pink tweed coat gives me a big wrinkly smile. 'Heaven, that, isn't it?' she says. I nod, for I'm still so caught up in the flavour that I can barely speak. 'I don't know,' she says. 'You hear all that grumbling about immigrants, but I'm old enough to remember how *boring* this country was before them. People used to think olive oil was something you bought in a dropper bottle, to put in your ears, you know.'

She obviously wants to engage, so I take the opportunity to look at her. I've not been up close to many old people and it would be good not to show shock when I meet my grandparents. We didn't do old people at Plas Golau. They just seemed to melt away when they reached their fifties, and, as it was our custom to never speak of a deserter again, one just didn't ask. Father was the oldest there by some years, and he was only sixty-six when he died. I guess I just didn't think about it much. I suppose it made sense, that we were mostly young. You don't make old bones in the Apocalypse, and the main use for someone who can no longer work would be as a back-up food supply.

But I'm surrounded by them now. Shuffling along with their sticks and their bags-on-wheels. They don't scare me any more.

'Do you know,' I ask, 'where I can find a place called the Lord's House?'

'The Lord's House?' she asks. 'No. Is that a café?'

'No,' I say, 'it's a church.'

'Oh,' she says. 'What sort of church?'

I'm a bit stumped. Then I think of something.

'Not church,' I say. 'Congregation.'

'Congregation,' she says. Then, 'Oh! That lot! You're standing right outside it!'

She points at the railings where I've just eaten my spectacular meal. And there it is, baby, and I was so distracted by my food that I simply didn't notice. The place my mother came from. The railings enclose a flagstoned front yard, and behind it is a large and elegant house, all oblong windows and handsome cornices. I don't know how I didn't notice it before, but a large black notice-board stands above the railings, on which the words 'Finbrough Congregation' are picked out in fading cream.

But it's empty. There's nothing pinned to it, nothing written there apart from someone's initials done with a tin of spray paint. The gate is closed and secured with a chain and padlock. And the yard is full of drying leaves, though I can't see any trees from which they might have come.

'I don't know if they're still going any more,' says the old lady. 'Used to see them bothering people with leaflets all the time on market days, but I've not, for a while, come to think of it.'

'How long for?'

'Gosh, no idea. There was something happened, but I can't remember what. I think someone died. Best part of a couple of years, I'd say. Something like that.'

'Oh,' I say.

'Sorry,' she says.

'It's not your fault,' I tell her, which when you think about it is pretty obvious.

So Eden clearly won't be here. I'm not sure what to do next. Uri certainly won't think much of my seeking skills. There's probably something about what happened on the internet, but all I did was look up the address.

Then I look harder. There's nobody here any longer, but it doesn't look derelict. Maybe there's something inside that can

156

lead me to where I'm trying to go. Their address, perhaps. Then I can go to their house and see.

I go for a walk through the streets until I fetch up at the back of the building. There's not much to see. A terrace of red-brick houses and, halfway up, an alleyway topped off with a high wooden gate. I walk down and test it. Locked. Hardly surprising. But it looks like a simple enough lock. I guess I'll have to wait till it's dark, though. Till there's no one around to see me picking it.

22 | Sarah

She comes home to a dark house, and she feels surprisingly disappointed. After three years of turning on the lights herself, it's been nice to find someone else there when she opens the door.

She switches on the hall light and hangs up her coat. Takes a breath to call out, but something stops her. This quietness is like the quietness when they first arrived. When she would come home to the house uneasy and still and they would emerge from one bedroom or the other, always together, and greet her with that spooky smile. There has been less of that lately. She's started to look forward to their presence. Sometimes they will even have made a start on dinner. Ilo, it turns out, is a good cook, and she's eaten better since he volunteered that information than she has since Liam left.

But now the house is cold and quiet.

And then she hears a sob.

Sarah freezes in the hallway, the very hairs on her body listening. As her ear tunes in, she hears voices.

Who's crying? It sounds like Eden. And then she hears hissing, angry tones of accusation, and Ilo's light, breaking tenor, propitiating.

Sarah hangs on the bottom step. Of course she has known that this would come eventually. But they didn't do tears in the Maxwell household, especially once the tempestuous moods of the rebel daughter had been dispatched. Liam said that there was something wrong with her. Women cry, he told her. It's what they do. His little girlfriend cried all the time, she's sure of it. Cried to display her womanhood, cried to persuade him that his wife had no emotions. But, if your early training teaches you that tears bring penalties, you learn not to show them unless you're alone.

What do you do with tears? She's not trained. No one has ever cried in front of her in her life – well, not anyone who mattered, about anything that mattered, and it sounds as though this matters. She has no idea what to do with it.

Despite her covenant with herself that she would not be dishonest with them, that she would not be the sort of person who spied on children without their knowledge, she creeps to the top of the stairs and listens.

The sob was an angry one. Definitely. 'You're meant to look *after* me, Ilo,' she says. 'Where were you?'

'I'm sorry,' he says. 'I was in the entrance hall. Waiting for you.'

'Well, that's no bloody good, is it? You're meant to look *after* me.'

'It was crowded,' he says. 'There wasn't anywhere to stand.'

Eden makes a sound of frustration. Of contempt. 'You're fucking *useless*,' she says.

'I'm sorry,' he says again. 'I'll do better.'

A wail. Despair. 'It's too late now! Oh, my God, what am I going to *do*? I will *die* without it, Ilo! I will *die*! Don't you understand?'

Sarah tenses. The hyperbole of adolescence, or should she be worrying? Eden sounds ... deranged. What's made her this way?

'I'll get it back,' he says.

'How? Go on – *how*?'

'I'll ask.'

'*Ask?* They'll laugh in your face. You won't even get close. Ilo, I'm going to *die* without it. Don't you understand? You don't seem to have the first idea how dangerous it is out here, for someone like me. I'm *nothing* without it. I might as well ... just do myself in now ...'

'Eden, I – no – maybe if we ask someone ...'

'Who are we going to ask?'

'I don't know. Aunt Sarah?'

'And what's *she* going to do?'

'Eden, she's meant to be on our side.'

'Oh, come on,' snaps Eden. 'Nobody's on our side. We're on our own, Ilo. It's just you and me, so really it's just me, isn't it?'

'Eden—' he begins, but she cuts him off.

'You're nothing,' she says. 'If I die and the world ends, it's your fault.'

Sarah feels a sting of hurt. All that effort and Eden, at least, clearly trusts her no more now than she did at the beginning. And then she has a pang of conscience about what she's doing. You should have learned your lesson about eavesdropping in the toilet on Monday, she thinks. Serves you right. And if they don't trust you, you need to put more effort in to *make* them trust you.

She retreats to the foot of the stairs and calls out. 'Hello? Anybody home?'

A ringing silence. The way cicadas go quiet in the night at the sound of a predator. Then the door opens, and there they are, smiling. Smiling, smiling. No sign of ill temper on Eden's face, no apology on Ilo's. They're totally playing me, she thinks, then no, come on. They just don't know you yet. You're the grown-up. It's up to you to gain their trust, not the other way round.

'Hello, Aunt Sarah,' says Eden. 'You're early.'

'Friday,' she tells her. 'Poet's Day.'

Little frowns of incomprehension cross their faces.

'Piss off Early, Tomorrow's Saturday,' she says, coming back up the stairs, but not even the mild cuss word seems to amuse them. 'I was getting a bit worried for a moment. You were so quiet I thought you'd run off and left me.'

'No,' says Ilo. 'We were just . . . up here.'

'How was your day?'

Come on. Trust me. Tell me. How are we going to move forward if you don't trust me?

'Okay,' says Ilo, and Eden says nothing.

'Are you all right, Eden?' she ventures.

Eden's hand paws at her breastbone, where that ugly little pendant usually lives.

'Have you lost your necklace?' she asks.

Eden turns round and slams her bedroom door closed. Ilo stands awkwardly on the landing.

'Is she okay?' asks Sarah.

He looks forty years old. 'She will be,' he says. 'She's stronger than she thinks. It's okay, Aunt Sarah.'

'Would it help if I—'

He shakes his head. 'Not right now, I think.'

Don't push it. It's the difference between cats and dogs, she thinks. You go to dogs, if you want them to love you. Cats, you have to allow to come to you.

'Have you eaten?' she asks.

He shakes his head.

161

'D'you want to come and give me a hand? We can take some up to her if she doesn't want to come down.'

Ilo even seems to *like* cooking.

'Perhaps you'll be a chef,' she says. 'You're so skilled already.'

He brightens with the praise, dispatches an onion at the speed of light, his blade flashing as he chops. 'Thank you,' he says.

'Did you cook much, at Plas Golau? You've got amazing knife skills. You're practically professional!'

Seems a bland enough sort of question to bring up the subject with.

'Yes,' he says. 'In the Guard House. I wasn't much use for anything else, as I'd only just joined. But it's good practice.'

'I can see!' she says. 'So I have to ask, Ilo. Has something happened at school? I can't pretend I haven't spotted that Eden's upset.'

The knife pauses, carries on. 'It's nothing,' he says. 'Just stupid stuff. She gets upset. It's difficult for her. Harder for her, being normal, because of who she is. It's easier for me. I was never particularly special.'

'Who she is . . . ?'

The knife pauses again. 'Sorry. I thought you knew she was Lucien's?' he asks, as though that were explanation enough.

'Oh.'

How many questions is too many? At what point does it stop being interested and start being intrusive? I must remember that this stuff is still real to them.

'Of course,' she says. 'Has something happened, though? She seems like . . . '

'She's lost her medallion,' he says.

'Her what?'

'The medallion she wears round her neck. It's important to her.'

162

'How important?'

'It's a ... symbol, really. All of Father's children wore them.'

'A sort of amulet – a good luck charm?'

He considers. 'Sort of. It's hard to explain. They're part of them, those medallions, from the day they're born.'

'So she feels naked without it?'

Ilo nods. 'Yes. Like that. Exposed.'

'Oh, God. When did she lose it?'

'In the playground, today. As we were coming out to go home.'

'Did you find it?'

Ilo gives her a look that reflects how stupid the question is.

'Sorry. I mean, did you look?'

Again the look. *Back off, old person. If you're going to ask questions, ask intelligent ones, at least.*

'I'm sorry. Is it valuable?'

'I don't suppose anyone on the Outside would think it was. But she does.'

'Okay. I'll put an alert on when we go in in the morning. Put a notice up on the noticeboard ...'

Ilo pulls a face. 'Someone's got it, I think,' he says.

'Well, that's stealing,' she says, firmly. 'There are punishments for that.'

He pulls another face, scrapes his onions into the casserole dish to fry.

Eden comes down to dinner, and she's cleaned her face and plastered that smile on again, but she refuses to look at her brother, ignores him when he puts a plate in front of her at the table, like an Edwardian lady in a restaurant. I'm not going to get anything out of her tonight, thinks Sarah, and tries anyway. 'Eden,' she says, 'if there's something going on that's upsetting you, you would tell me, wouldn't you? It's what I'm here for. To help.'

163

Her voice rises and takes on a tone of command. 'It's Ilo's fault, Aunt Sarah. It's up to him to sort it out.'

'But,' she protests, 'you don't have to do this stuff on your own, Eden. It's what I'm here for. There are rules, you know. If you're being bullied, if someone's picking on you, they're breaking them.'

Those clear blue eyes, gazing straight at her. 'Oh, in the end, I don't mind that,' she says. 'I want my medallion, but I feel sorry for *them*. For all of them.'

'Why's that?' asks Sarah.

'Because they're stupid,' says Eden, 'and they will all die screaming.'

Once they've retired to bed, she goes out into the garden for her evening cigarette. She allows herself two a day, as much in defiance of rules as for the actual pleasure they bring.

She sits on one of her parents' green-painted cast-iron chairs at their cast-iron table and smokes as slowly as she can, tapping her ashes into her mother's green-and-beige St Ives School cachepot. I'm no good at this, she thinks. Who do I even ask? Everyone I've talked to sees the whole Ark thing the way I do, as some sort of crazy world organised around theories we don't really understand that don't make sense, but God knows the world's full of catastrophists waiting for the sky to fall. They're hardly the only ones. I need help here, and it's not finding someone I can talk to, it's finding someone *they* can talk to. Someone who won't constantly be biting their lip or saying the wrong thing because they don't understand what they believe. There's always going to be a degree of mistrust if I can't show them in some concrete way that I'm on their side.

She gets out her wallet and looks through the notes section. Finds her niece Romy's address. Stares at it as her cigarette burns down to the filter, then makes her decision as she stubs it out.

23 | Romy

As I thought, the lock on the gate is simple. I get it open in under a minute with the help of the two metal skewers I bought at the kitchenware stall for £1.35. I check behind me in the alleyway, pull the gate open slowly, in case it creaks, and slip inside.

I'm in another little courtyard, more flagstones, a line of wheeled bins lying on their sides to stop them filling with water. A dreary outlook for the Lord, though: the backs of other people's houses, too close for privacy and barely room for a table and chairs in the fresh air. Perhaps he'll use the front court, so people can watch His Glorious Majesty drink his morning coffee.

A porch overhangs the back door. A nice bit of privacy for me.

The door has a mortice and a Chubb. The first will be easy, the second more complicated, but nothing I've not cracked before. We did lessons, in the Pigshed. You never know when you might need shelter when you're in flight. It takes three minutes to hear the satisfying clunk of the mortice and five more before I persuade the inner barrel of the Chubb to turn.

Inside is pitch black and smells of spiders. I'm tempted to

flick the light switch, but control myself. For God's sake, Romy. You're trained to face the end of the world. You're not blowing it because you're scared of arachnids.

I close the door behind me and switch on my new torch. I'm in a plain little room that looks more store cupboard than anything else. A couple of broken chairs, a line of empty coat hooks, a pile of missals on a battered console table. On one of the chairs, a cardboard box. *Please respect the Lord's House*, reads a sign taped to the front. I look inside. A collection of white cotton bonnets, tapes hanging from their undersides to tie beneath one's chin. They're spotted with mould. It must be damper in here than it smells. They're the same bonnets as Hester Lacey wears in the portrait on Wikipedia. Imagine. Wanting to dress up like that warty old monster. What a strange way to show your faith. My mother must have worn one of these, every Sunday till she was seventeen. A door leads out the other side, a heavy bolt holding it shut. It slides back easily, with a satisfying clunk. I try the handle and it turns.

A huge space, for its shrivelled occupants. I play the torch about, drinking in the detail. I recognise it all from her stories. My mother did her homework here, in the back pews, as her father talked of hellfire from that ebony lectern to my left. White walls. Black wood. I walk inwards, head for the high arched door at the far end. Turn and look where I've come from. A plain table on which sit two brass candlesticks, a pewter chalice and a pewter plate on a square of linen. Above it on the wall, painted on the stone surround of an arched window, the words *The Lord Thy God Is a Jealous God*; above the door I'm aiming for, *The Wages of Sin Is Death*. Cheerful people, my forebears. But so caught up in their imaginary afterworld that they didn't give a thought to the calamity howling towards them in the real one.

No decoration, no embellishment. We didn't use the Plas Golau chapel for religious purposes, obviously – it had long since become food storage, with its nice cool even temperatures – but it still retained impressions of a jollier era: death's heads carved into memorials, a brass eagle designed to hold an opened bible, fluted pillars holding up the roof, winged babies weeping at the feet of a crabby old couple, fixed forever in marble on a carved marble bed. They suggested a playfulness, a level of morbid enjoyment, buried in there somewhere among the serious business of worship and death. Here, it is clear that God allows no fun at all. It's years since I believed the stories about the Christians eating Jesus, but it's clear that my grandfather's church was no barrel of laughs.

Father saw rage in me, he said. Even as I proved, over and over, how obedient I was. And even as he said it, I felt fizzing bubbles of rage between my shoulder blades, and my scalp contracted in preparation for the fight. And then I saw that maybe he was right. Rage *does* drive me, in many ways. It consumes me now. Rage with the world, rage with my grandparents, rage with Eden and Ilo because they've disappeared and left me on my own, rage with Uri because of what he is asking me to do. But everything, everything, comes back to these people, the people who used to worship here. Cold and judgemental and destructive in their pursuit of their morality. Wallowing in their own superiority. I'm going to find them, and I'm going to make sure they understand the true meaning of wickedness.

You killed my mother, I will say. *You couldn't have killed her better if you'd used a knife.*

Revenge, Father said, is a self-destructive urge. Father knew freaking *nothing*. Vita knew more about the world than he did. Far more. And Uri. That's why Uri's still alive and they are dead. Father clearly never had someone to hate, and with such good reason, as I do, and that means that for all his fine words he knew *nothing*.

I look around this place where my mother's misery began and realise with a shock that maybe the rage comes all the way from them. No one gets pleasure from the thought of eternal hellfire if they've not got a load of rage stored up inside them. No one enjoys the thought of eternal damnation unless they hate the world.

My mother was so lucky, getting away from them. Well. Maybe not, in the end. But she saved me, and I can only ever be grateful for that.

I never knew it until this moment, but I am their grandchild.

It smells of dust and, faintly, of wood polish. I run a finger over the back of the nearest pew and the pad comes up grey. There's been no one here in a long while. I head for the door and go and look for the basement. I remember my mother saying that that was where they kept their offices. If the information I need is anywhere, it will be there. So damp. It hits me the moment I step onto the stairs. It's been shut up, unheated, for as long as the rest of the building. Which gives me hope. Because if it's been shut up, that means nobody's been in to take away the paperwork. They've literally just locked it up and walked away. I wonder where they are now. Was the man who died my grandfather? A bit of me hopes so, because the sooner he discovers his own hellfire the better.

At the bottom, I assume it's safe to turn on the light. A ceiling bulb bathes everything in an unearthly glow that makes me think of vampires. A dreary room. Two long tables and two chairs on wheels, white-painted brick. Plastic trays filled with pieces of paper that have begun to crumble. A line of filing cabinets.

I go to open them, and the door opens at the top of the stairs and a voice says, 'Clarion Security. Can you come out, please?'

There are two of them, and they're wearing uniforms to make them look like policemen. I know they're not, though, because they would have said that they were. The hall blazes with light, and the chapel, too.

'How did you know I was here?' I ask, because I'm genuinely intrigued.

'Alarm, love,' he says.

Ah. How come it didn't ring? Are there silent alarms? Have I been tripping them as I've walked about the world?

'Can you tell me what you're doing here?' he asks.

I put on my best waif face. Let my jacket drop open so he can see my swollen abdomen. 'I was looking for somewhere to sleep,' I say.

'In the basement?'

I shrug. 'I'm not proud.'

'Bedrooms usually live upstairs.'

I shrug again.

'You know you're breaking and entering, right?'

'I didn't break anything. The back door was open. I just wanted somewhere to sleep,' I repeat. 'It's cold.'

I size them up. I think the older one's my best bet for a calm exit. He looks old enough to have a daughter my age. 'I'm pregnant,' I tell them.

'So I see,' he says, 'but you're still breaking and entering. Or trespassing, anyway. Stand there,' he says, and points to a corner, turns away to speak into his phone as though doing so will somehow prevent me hearing what he says. 'Terence. Yep, we've got a burglar at Finbrough High Street. Call the constab, there's a love.'

'Don't,' I say, 'please don't,' and I look at him, pleading, vulnerable. It doesn't work. He just stares at me under his peaked cap and I know I'm not going to talk my way out of this. So I take my only other option, and run.

They're slow-moving, as I'd hoped: even slower than I am with my limp and baby. The older one has slower legs and the younger a slower brain, and I have muscle memory, and once I start to run my body remembers how to do it, though I've not even tried in months. They're still cursing and bouncing off each other in the hallway by the time I'm halfway up the aisle, and I've got the door to the little back room bolted by the time they slam into it and curse some more. I run out through the back door, tear up the alleyway and make for the main road.

You somersault inside me as I jounce along. Get used to it, baby. Life isn't easy.

I jog away from the High Street, since it seems fairly obvious that that will be the way the police will approach the building, then I run up two roads and turn left. And there I slow down, make myself walk slowly, loosely, as if I'm just out for a stroll. Nobody comes looking for me. Perhaps they didn't even call. I stick my hand out into the London Road, and hope someone will stop soon for the poor pregnant girl.

Anger makes you careless. I'm not really thinking about who might be in these cars that swish along the darkening road. It takes less than a minute for one to stop, and I get in without even looking through the windscreen. I just throw my backpack into the footwell and don't even look into the face of the driver before he has stepped on the accelerator. Rage has made me forget another thing that Father always said: that decisions made in anger are seldom wise ones.

Before the End

2010–2011

24 | Romy

2010

She's almost on top of the body before she sees it. A woman. Fallen, by the looks of it, from the high boulders below the dam, and lying face-down in the pool where the big trout dream.

The woods are silent. Just the quiet singing of the water at her feet. Romy looks away, searches for the comfort of tiny pale patches of night sky between the tree branches. Looks back again. The body is still there.

Romy feels herself sway in the night air. Something flaps away in the canopy and she jumps.

That's her brain, she thinks. I can see her brain.

She's broken on the way down. A sharp end of bone sticks through a rip in her sleeve and her head is on crooked. Not the first corpse she's seen, but the worst, by a long chalk.

Should I be this calm? she wonders. Am I not meant to be trembling?

But her training is stronger than her shock. She's been raised from infancy to face death with equanimity. I'm meant to be harvesting mistletoe, she thinks. What do I do? If I don't come in with mistletoe at dawn, Ursola will report me to Vita and I'll be even further from the Infirmary.

She looks again, for the corpse is sort of fascinating. That white brain, how easily a skull cracks, like walnut.

Maybe I should see who it is, she thinks, though the coppery shade of the stubbly scalp, even in moonlight, gives a clear indication. She tugs the unbroken sleeve, but it's waterlogged, heavy. Eventually she has to heave the body like a sack of wet cement onto the bank, onto its back, to verify that it's Zaria Blake. Eyes wide, lips parted, the gash in her skull black and white in the moonlight.

She sits on a mossy rock, takes a drink from her water bottle and considers what she should do. I should walk away, she thinks. Pretend I've seen nothing. Who would I tell? Or, rather, who would I tell first? They both expect to be top of the list, they've each made that clear to me. I've kept them both at arm's length with a steady drip-feed of inconsequential detail, but how could I do that with this?

Then she hears footsteps, high up in the pasture path that leads from the Guard House to the dam wall. And she's on her hands and knees in a moment, scrambling for the cover of the bracken behind a tall horse chestnut. She always has the estate to herself at night, apart from the odd patrolling Guard. If someone's coming here so directly, so boldly, they must know what they're going to find.

They don't like spies, the Guards. They don't like spies and traitors, unless they're *their* spies and traitors, and they don't like people who question them or answer back. Perhaps it would have been better to show herself straight away and plead her innocence. In the dark, cut off from the moonlight, she feels grateful for her dark colouring, for it helps her disappear into the shadows. If I vanished tonight, she thinks, I would simply vanish, the way people do, and no one would question it. Not out loud, anyway.

Her vision adjusts to the gloom and she watches them come. It's Uri, and his Number Two, Jacko, and Dom, one of the soldiers they brought with them from the Dead, and Willow, one of the few girls plucked from the Pigshed to join their ranks.

Romy concentrates on slowing her breathing, on staying still. A dead body in the night might not make her afraid, but Uri's soldiers do.

They pass her, gather around the body. The three men look down at Zaria with absolute indifference. Willow seems to struggle for words.

'What happened?' she asks.

Uri shrugs. He's not bothered. A silence falls that fills the night.

Romy watches Willow strain to keep her expression blank, to match her comrades'. She mustn't say the wrong thing, thinks Romy. And she knows that. She's just found out one of the secrets of the Guard House, and so have I, and if either of us drops our defences we'll end up just like Zaria.

Lucien's children have a high attrition rate. She's noticed it and other people must have, too. Last year, eleven-year-old Roshin Blake ate yew berries and died in convulsions on the floor of the Pigshed. The year before, Leana Blake, seventeen, caught her sleeve in the hay bailer and bled out from her arm socket while a Healer tried hopelessly to staunch the blood that would not stop coming. They both had honourable burials in the chapel graveyard, of course, but then, as always, nobody spoke of them again. And then Jaivyn slipped off during an outreach expedition to a rock festival in the early summer – took his box and his shoes and the weekend's takings and disappeared with the crowd – and there was hell to pay. Vita herself was in disgrace for a month.

She worries about her sister.

Zaria stares at the moon and Willow, after some thought, clears her throat. 'Those shoes are slippery when they're wet,' she says. 'And the moss on these rocks is horribly loose. Stupid to be climbing there.'

It's clearly the right response.

'Whatever,' says Uri. 'She's safe now.'

The men grunt in approval and Dom switches on a torch. Jacko drops his backpack to the ground and feeds a long expanse of fabric from its top. It's a canvas duffel bag, big enough to hold a body.

She assumes they'll head back up the bank to the Great House, but to her surprise they turn, once they've manoeuvred the corpse into its carrier, and head deeper into the woods along the path that runs the length of the river.

'Where are we going?' asks Willow.

'What?' says Jacko. 'You think bodies bury themselves?'

'She probably thinks the magic pixies do it,' says Dom. 'You still believe in magic pixies, 193?'

Zaria flipflops about inside her wrapper, throwing the Guards off balance in the dark. Romy takes the chance that they are making enough noise, their speeding pulses rendering them deaf to furtive sounds in the woodland, and creeps along in their wake.

Willow teeters on a patch of slippery mud on the riverbank, barely saves herself. The men, holding fast on to their corners of the bag, roar with laughter as they watch. So strange, the sound of laughter.

Dead girl. It's a dead girl, and they're handling her like meat in a slaughterhouse.

*

176

Halfway down the hill, a set of stepping stones leads across the water to the other side and the men wheel round to cross. 'We're going off the estate?' asks Willow. Her voice is shaking. She's scared, thinks Romy. More scared even than I am. She knows the stakes here as well as I do. One look, one word out of place, and she'll be gone along with Zaria, some story concocted of Sapphic assignations or a taste for frippery, and everyone will shrug contemptuously and forget about them. But once she's gone through with this, once she's obeyed her orders and over-come her revulsion, Romy knows she will be even more theirs than she was before.

'Set-aside,' says Uri. 'Area of outstanding natural beauty. The EU pays us to keep it like this.'

'And a nice bit of armour against the hordes,' says Dom. 'By the time they get through those brambles they'll be too tired to attack. We can pick 'em off one by one as they wade across the stream.'

And a good place to hide things.

They drop the bag onto the soggy ground and Jacko starts across the stepping stones to the wild land. The woods on Romy's side are kept under control naturally, by the daily pas-sage of foragers and guards. Firewood is collected almost before it falls and dead bracken brought up to the light to dry for kin-dling. Over there, the brambles entwine thick around the feet of the trees and the ferns grow to head height. Romy can't see how they will get through it, for it grows as thick as treacle.

Then Jacko simply picks up the landscape and lifts it aside.

Camouflage. It's a camouflage of deadfall. She can see, now he's moved it, that it's backed with cloth, the fallen sticks and foliage nailed to a frame. Behind it, a path. Clear steps up the bank and an arch of brambles into which to vanish.

She holds her breath.

'How ... many ... ?' pants Willow. 'Where ... ?'

From up ahead, Jacko's mocking laugh. 'That'll be the secret, 193. And now you know where you'll end up if you talk about it.'

Willow shivers, for she knows that this is not an idle threat. 'I didn't mean ...'

'Stop making a fuss,' says Jacko. 'We'll be using them for protein come the Great Disaster.'

25 | Romy

2010

The Guards are drilling, and Romy, in the hemlock grove, watches with her knife in her hand, a sack of flower heads open at her feet. It's such a tough weed, hemlock, that all she can do until the winter is make sure it doesn't seed, and then dig up the roots when it's dormant. And besides, dead-heading gives her a reason to hang about the Guard House without attracting attention.

They have become magnificent. She sees that. Beneath the khaki jackets they wear in public spaces, their muscles ripple and their limbs are strong and straight. Like Lucien's children, they are gods among the peasants. Twelve of them on morning drill, while twelve sleep off the night and twelve do the day patrol. She watches, notes, imagines the muscle movements. Kick, step, punch, kick, step, punch.

Romy is good with her knife already. After months of solitary practice, she can flip it from pocket to hand, closed to open, in a second, the hinge oiled assiduously and worked and worked through the nights until it moves as smooth and loose as a falcon's wing.

But they're strong. So strong. Stronger than Romy, stronger than all of them. Watching them punch the air, watching grain dust burst through the canvas of their improvised punch bags, leaves her awestruck. And certain that, were she to take even one on – even Willow – she would go down with the first blow.

Only thirty-six of them – thirty-seven including Uri – but they would be strong enough to destroy us all, she thinks. None of us is trained for fighting, despite Uri's long-unfulfilled promise to teach us. Am I the only one who sees it? Vita must, I'm sure of it. But he's Lucien's son and he might yet be the One, and in the end that will surely count against her.

She has read enough history to know that a usurper is only a usurper if they fail. And that the vanquished end up in unmarked graves.

The beehives are kept in their own little section of the orchard, fenced off with high evergreen hedges to keep the children out and largely avoided by people afraid of stings. When the Beemaster is on the road, he leaves her to manage the day-to-day maintenance, and she often has the whole place to herself and a reason to be there. She has never known such luxurious privacy. And it gives her a place, every morning and every evening, to drill. If she can't find a way to prepare her fellow Drones for the onslaught, she can at least prepare herself. She does what she's seen the Guards do. The jumps, the kicks, the lunges. Punches the air with her fists and slices it with the sides of her hands. She bends and lifts and crawls on knees and elbows, pirouettes on the spot until the earth stops spinning, hangs from branches and slowly learns to pull herself up.

If you want to survive, you need to be prepared. Every moment of her education has taught her that.

When the feasts approach, she watches through the slaughter-house window to see how the butchers handle their knives. Looks to understand the casual way with which they find a jugular, cut a tendon. Volunteers to help dress the carcasses, so she can accustom herself to the feel of death.

Zaria's glassy eyes stare up at the moon in her dreams.

She runs between assignments. Willow can run from the bottom of the drive to the top of the moor, a rise of three hundred and sixty feet, in fifteen minutes, so Romy must at least be faster than Willow.

She's running one day from the physic garden to the moor, where she's set a hive to gather nectar from the blooming bell heather, when little Ilo drops the bucket of water he's been bumping against his shins on his way to the chickens' trough, and falls into step beside her. He's seven years old now – the age at which they're old enough to work in the afternoons and take the blame for their mishaps – and growing handsome, his eyes blue and his hair blond like a proper child of the Ark. Romy glances at him as he keeps pace with her, surprised by how fast he seems able to run.

'Shouldn't you be doing chores?' she asks. She's only been running for six weeks, and is delighted to find that she is already able to conduct a rudimentary conversation while doing it, even when going uphill.

'I can help *you*,' he replies, and there's barely a pant as he says it. Romy feels a bit resentful. It doesn't seem entirely fair that she's been training all this time to do things this child with legs two-thirds the length of her own can do with ease. He's a natural athlete, a born survivor.

'I'm not sure I need help,' she says.

She likes Ilo. Always has. But she's been out of the Pigshed and working for a year now, and he's matured so much in that time that he already seems like a semi-stranger.

'Everybody needs help, though, don't they?' he asks. 'I thought that was the whole point? That we can't do it all alone?'

'I suppose you have a point,' she tells him. 'Better keep up, though. I don't have time to dawdle just to support weaklings.'

'That's okay,' he says cheerfully, and pulls ahead of her on the path.

The boy can run like a greyhound. Romy is hard pressed to even maintain her dignity beside the little squit. They pound up the moorland track, eyes fixed to the ground for treacherous flints. Romy can no longer talk. It is all she can do to push through the burn in her lungs and the sweet-sharp rush of lactic acid in her legs. She can't allow herself to be beaten by a seven-year-old. She finds another ounce of will and forges ahead. Ilo laughs out loud and passes her as though on wings.

At the top of the moor, by the tumbledown slate wall that marks the border between their land and the National Trust's, they collapse into the heather by the beehive. Prickling, scratching stems above and yielding peat beneath. No longer cooled by the breeze of speed, Romy feels sweat burst from her skin and her face turn purple. She is blown: spent. Rolls onto her back and feels the ache of exhaustion sweep through her limbs.

'Where the hell did you learn to run like that?'

Ilo does a shrug that consumes his whole body. 'I don't know,' he replies. 'I just . . . can. And I want to be a Guard when I grow up, so . . .'

She rolls back onto her front, props herself up on her elbows. 'A *Guard*?'

Ilo nods.

'Really? I had you pegged for an Engineer.'

'It's the obvious thing to be, if I'm going to keep you all safe.'

Safe. The word makes the hairs on her arms rise. I saw the brain through the hole in her skull, she thinks, and pushes the thought away. 'We'll all keep each other safe,' she tells him.

He wrinkles his nose. There are freckles across the bridge, like on their mother's, brought out by the summer sun. 'Yes, but somebody's got to do it properly,' he says. 'Eden may be the One, but she's a long way off being able to look after herself. I know they won't want me, but I want them. What they can teach me. So I've got to be the best I can be. Be better than everyone in the Pigshed. So they can't say no.'

The heather hums with seeking bees and a lark sings, some-where up there in the blue. She looks at her little brother and she thinks about how best to make sure the One survives.

'Well, then, you'll need to learn to fight,' she says, and pushes him down the slope.

Among the Dead

November 2016

26 | Romy

The driver smells – musty. As though he's been kept in a damp cellar between trips in his car. A headful of unruly black curls, pubic sideburns all the way down to his jaw. One of those simian faces with eyes that narrow to slits when he smiles.

'Looks like someone's having a good day,' he says, and laughs like a barking dog.

I pull myself out of my blur of rage and size up my situation. I'm sitting on a seat that feels, from the way the frame digs into my thighs and buttocks, as though the stuffing has fallen out of it. In the gloom of the interior, I see that this car is old. Older than I am, probably. The winding handle for the window to my left has fallen off, just a cog in the door where it should be. On the dashboard, a plastic model of a piebald bull terrier nods and nods and nods, and a length of silver sticky tape holds the glove compartment closed. Around my feet, a sea of paper and old soft-drink containers.

I look at him. He's grinning at the road ahead through the windscreen, his teeth improbably white.

'What you been up to, my duck?' he asks. The heater blows scalding air onto my feet, yet my shoulders are surrounded with chilly autumn draught. I pull my hoodie up to cover the back of my neck. Stupid, stupid me, letting the red mist override my ability to look before I leapt.

'Been to visit my grandparents,' I tell him.

'Grandparents, eh?'

'Yes,' I say. Not sure how to play this. Friendly, so he thinks he sees a come-on, or standoffish, which would be likely to enrage? Or tough, so he knows not to fuck with me?

'And what do they think to a great-grandbabby?' he asks.

Babby. There's something primeval about the misuse of the word. I'm in a lot of trouble, here. 'They're old-fashioned,' I say.

That laugh again. 'Babby got no daddy, eh?'

I'm going for standoffish. Let him think I'm a dumb chick who thinks that grand manners are enough to keep her safe. 'What an intrusive question,' I say.

The grin flashes off. 'Oh, no offence, maid,' he says, and turns onto the motorway slip road. We've not slowed down enough at any point for me to try the door. Not without risking harm to you, baby. 'Although on second thoughts it's a bit late to be calling you *maid*, eh?'

He puts his foot down as we hit the motorway and the car roars and lurches into the centre lane. I'm probably safe at eighty miles per hour. It's when we return to the side roads that I need to be prepared.

Maybe if I engage him. At least I can get the measure of him then. He might just be very, very stupid; not realise how he comes across. Or I might be paranoid. It's not beyond the realms of possibility; I was raised paranoid. And he's not done anything yet. Much.

'So where are you off to?' I ask.

'That depends,' he says, and gives me a flash of his big white teeth. Falsies, I think. No way they'd be that white in a face so begrimed. He puts his hand on his gearstick and caresses it with his thumb.

We pass Reading, then Slough, in silence. He weaves in and out of the fast lane while I stare ahead through the windscreen. Then he hits his indicator and turns off, goes through a tunnel under the motorway, and takes us along a road leading south. Winter trees, scrubby undergrowth, no people.

'Where are we going?' I ask.

'Short cut,' he says.

Every bone, every hair, on my body, is alert now. 'Short cut to where?'

'I told you,' he says. 'That depends.'

I look out through my side window. We're entering an area of scruffy old storage units. The sort of dead zone that lurks on the edge of every town I've ever been through. Streetlights illuminate shuttered doors and blank, windowless corrugated walls. Weeds grow up through potholed concrete; skips are filled with wooden pallets and broken chairs. The Outside is full of places like this: places where buildings have lost their purpose and everyone who used to come there has moved on and left them behind.

'Costs me a lot in petrol, this,' he says, and that thumb strokes, strokes, strokes.

Oh, Romy, you are in so much trouble. Don't say anything. Don't speak. Anything you say will sound like you're afraid.

'How you going to pay me back, maid?'

In a broad stretch of emptiness, a crossing signal turns red and he pulls to a halt. Nowhere to run to, but I grab my chance, pull on the door handle. It flips loosely in my hand, and nothing happens. That face turns towards me and he

189

grins: a death's head that smells of tobacco smoke and sebaceous secretions.

He pulls away. Swings the wheel and pulls into a cul-de-sac. Metal walls and a high brick border, no light. Elder and buddleia shedding fading leaves, their roots embedded in the gaps between the walls, their feet buried, like mine, in litter. That wall in the headlights is too high for scaling, even if I were fit.

'Back in a minute, maid,' he says.

'Where are you going?'

'Need a slash,' he says. 'Don't you be going anywhere, eh?'

I test him. Make a move to put him at his ease, give him reason to think he's the one with the power. 'Please don't hurt me,' I say.

The grin again. 'Why, maid, whatever makes you think I'm going to do that?'

Options. I cycle through them as he stands with his back to me in the headlights, raising himself up and down on the balls of his feet as though the better to pump urine from his bladder. Wriggle myself behind the steering wheel to his door and trust that I can do it fast enough to get out before he's back on top of me? Run? Not an option. I could outpace him with ease, even as I am, but I can only outpace a moving car if I have somewhere to run *to*. Steal the car? He took the keys with him when he went. Talk my way out? He doesn't seem like a talker.

I slide my knife from its holster and slip it into my hoodie pocket.

I see him zip his jeans up, and then his head drops and he becomes immobile. I wait. It's gone silent inside right now. Where there should be a person, a personality, is a howling void. All that empty blackness, waiting to be filled. I put my hand in my pocket, caress the handle of my knife, rest my thumb on the button that will make it spring open. It feels solid. It comforts me.

When he comes, he comes fast. His head snaps upright, and then he's running towards me, and in the headlights his face is the face of the devil.

Three steps is all it takes to cross the yard and get his hand on the door handle. And then his fingers are buried to the palm in my hair and he's pulling me out onto the concrete.

Despite myself, I am taken by surprise. I'd forgotten, so long is it since I last had it, how vulnerable hair makes you. And I remember Jaivyn doing this to me when I was five, and I am filled with rage. My scalp shrieks with pain. He's strong. Manual-labour strong. No dexterity to what he does, just brute force and indifference to my humanity. I buck and try to grab at the hand. He hauls me into the open, drags me backwards into the shadow of the building. I try to dig in my heels, but it's useless against the backward impetus. And then he punches me sharply in the side of my head, and the world goes white.

Play dead. I have two things to my advantage: that he thinks I'm unconscious and that he believes me harmless. I let my body go limp as I wait for my brain to recover, hear him grunt with the effort of dragging my dead weight. Not yet, Romy. Not yet. Not while he's behind you.

He drops me. Throws me onto a bed of gravel and broken things. Stands over me in his big old boots. They are covered in drips of paint and plaster. I wait. Release a noise between a groan and a whimper.

He laughs into the darkness. He believes me. He thinks he's won. That's good. My right arm is half-pinned beneath my body, the hand still safely in my pocket. No power to swing it like this. Wait, Romy, wait. One chance is all you get.

With the tip of a boot, he rolls me onto my back. I open myself up, lie with my eyes half-closed, and watch through my eyelashes. And, when he raises a leg to step over and straddle me, I strike.

It's not accurate, but it doesn't need to be. The femoral artery runs close to the surface at the groin, and my blade is wide and sharp. Flat-out on the ground isn't the best angle to hit from, so I hit with all my might, while he's off balance. Feel my glorious blade glide through denim and flesh as though they were made of butter, feel the tip hit the bone, slide sideways. Artery, testicles: either one will stop a man stone dead.

He screams. The sound bounces off the metal walls. I pull the knife out, quickly, before he crumples. Scoot backwards with my heels as he falls to his knees. He's no longer looking at me. He's gone inside, where the pain is. His eyes are shut and his hands are clamped over the deep black stain that spreads over the tops of his thighs.

'You cunt!' he screams.

Not down yet. Not entirely out. One chance to make sure. No need to torture him, but you need to be sure. Go for the side of the throat. Don't waste energy on the gristle of the oesophagus. Go for the artery. If you're going for a swift kill, arteries are your friends. I flip the handle of the knife across my palm and slash.

He dies quietly. I wonder, as I elbow my way backwards, if he feels proud that his last words in this world were 'you cunt'. Maybe he has other things on his mind. Or nothing at all. Blood loss affects the brain quickly, especially if the leak is near the head.

He spurts. Warm, salty liquid smacks my face.

He moans. No more of that barking laughter now.

Another spurt. It spatters my hoodie, the front of my dress, my skin. There's disease in blood. I don't have time to worry about that. The front of his jeans is soaked, all the way to his

192

knees. Blood drools from the cloth, creeps across the concrete. So much blood. There's over a gallon in the human body. I scoot back once more, and his final pump spatters harmlessly to the left of my legs.

He crumples. To knees, to face. His hands have not left his groin.

I blink. My eyes sting as his cooling blood slides off my brow. One last groan, and nothing more.

You kick, deep inside me. The man spasms a couple of times and lies still. I pull my sleeve down over the heel of my hand and wipe my face. Roll over onto my hands and knees. There was a time when I could get to my feet from the ground without the help of my arms. Not now.

I wait five minutes, but he doesn't move again and the blood slowly stops spreading. Out on the road, the swish of car tyres, a brief change in the pattern on the shadows in our yard. No one comes to investigate the noise. In the bleaching light from the headlamps, the man looks silver-grey, the viscous pool that surrounds him a deep, reflective black. In the morning, when daylight comes, it will be dirty, flaking red-brown.

I pick my knife up. Take it over to a skip that squats further back between the buildings. Fish around until my hand finds a dirty rag and wipe it off. Blood is bad for metal joints, and hard to remove; gluey, once it's dry. I cleaned mine every night at Plas Golau, regardless of whether it had seen use. Love your weapons and they won't let you down.

I fold the rag up and put it in my pocket. It's twelve miles to Hounslow from Slough. I can dispose of it on my walk, along the top of the motorway embankment, where nobody ever goes. It's a long walk, but I should make it before morning.

Before the End

2012

27 | Romy

2011

The latrines are built into the south wall of the courtyard, where on the outside the land slopes sharply off into the woods and a path runs down to what was once a piece of useless bog by the main road. It's far away from the house and far enough below the reservoir that it's ideal for their discreet little bio-gas plant and slurry pit.

Eight latrines serve the main compound: little stinky sheds that no one would dream of using to snatch a moment's privacy. Rough wood planks suspended over blue plastic barrels in the hole beneath and tubs of water and ladles for washing off once your business is done. The barrels can be accessed via wooden doors off the path, and doing so is one of the Dung Squad's duties.

Collecting the barrels and taking them down the hill was once a communal duty done on rotation. It was Uri who came up with the idea of Sanitation Engineers. The fact that Squad membership can double as fatigues goes almost unremarked. The Sanitation Engineers clean out these, and the Guard House latrines, and the little septic tank behind the Great House, muck out the pigs and the cattle and the horses and the poultry in the winter, pick up after them in the meadows in the summer and, in February, dig out the digested manure and give it back to the land.

They may be called the Sanitation Engineers in official language, But Uri quickly coined the epithet 'Dung Squad' and allowed it to spread through the compound like muck on a field. And now they have their own separate table at the back of the dining hall and a dedicated dormitory, for, try as they might, the stink never really washes off.

The narrative of equality rumbles on. Everybody talks the talk, but when it comes to walking the walk it's different. Though no one would ever call it demotion out loud, everyone knows that wrongdoers are invariably sent to duties agricultural. And, when they're already wallowing in mud, the Dung Squad is the only way down. There is no level below Dung Squad, beyond leaving, quietly, in the night.

Somer is their Leader. It was her choice. Stay a Farmer, or become a Leader. Go down, to go up. Leaders get to attend the Council. She may smell of shit, but she's back, in a way, in the inner circle.

Uri's getting stronger. They all see it. Lucien came off his horse a couple of summers ago and spent the night unconscious on the moor before they found him, and there are people among them who wonder occasionally if he has truly recovered. He walks with a cane now, and spends more time in his quarters, and when he appears he seems mellowed, somehow: distant. Though smiling. Always smiling. And then they dismiss it straight from their heads because he's Lucien, Leader of Leaders, and everything they are and everything they will be comes from him.

Romy and Ilo train every day, slipping off together when the Pigshed lets out. Down in the woods, up on the moors, in the hive compound, in the godowns. Step and *kick* and step and *kick*. She can stand one-legged like a stork for fifteen minutes and still kick out to head height when she stops. Can pull herself up all the way to her breasts on the barn crossbar a hundred times. Shin up a tree trunk all the way to the branches on thigh power alone. Lift a cider barrel above her head. She works her knife as she harvests: the slash and the slice; the upward cut and the twisting stab. All theory, so far, but muscle memory is a wonderful thing. If I have to fight, she thinks, I will be able. My arms and legs and hands and torso will know what to do, even while my brain is catching up.

She has been volunteering to help the Farmers butcher the livestock when they're brought in for feasts and preserving for a year, now. She's watched, quietly, through the window. Seen Fitz and Jacko and Willow dispatch animals with single, skilful, unhesitant lunges – a guard duty and privilege, to accustom them to the shock of death. She has yet to bring about the act of slaughter, but Romy knows how it feels to slice from groin to sternum, to have still-warm innards tumble out onto her slicing hand. She knows how it feels to bury her arms to the shoulder in a stag that had been strutting proud on a mountainside an hour before, to hack through the trachea to pull out the lungs. She can strip the pelt from a rabbit with two cuts and a single wrench of the wrist.

Ilo has a natural talent, although he's only eight. Old enough to learn. An hour each day, the two of them, dancing their dance of secret violence, hitting with all their might and rarely making contact. She'd like to train Eden too, but Eden's not interested. She's ten and knows her status. She's done her carpentry apprenticeship, but no one has asked her to hammer a ploughshare or stoop down in the fields. Eden will go straight into Leadership training when she's grown. But she's never seen the poison in their garden, as Romy has. Never seen the secret graveyard. Doesn't know how unlikely it looks that she will ever be grown at all, unless her siblings form her bodyguard.

They practise stalking, in the woods. Take turns to be pursuer and prey, practising camouflage and silent movement. Sometimes they follow a Guard on patrol, track them all the way from the gate to the dam, or wait with frozen limbs to catch a squirrel, tickle a fat brown trout out of the water and watch it gape for water on the bank.

They're returning to the compound over the wall by the privies when Ilo touches her arm and presses his finger to his lips. She stops, listens. Someone is down there, talking, and their mother's voice, low and submissive, replies. Romy signals her brother to work his way along the bank and climb the old Scots pine twenty feet along so they can see.

It's Willow. Stern and stiff-backed as she's become over the two years since she left the Pigshed. She watches as Somer empties cupboard No. 5. The barrel is brimming and Somer is hurried and self-conscious as a girl nearly half her age supervises her. As she thumps the metal lid into place, its liquid interior splashes out around the seal, coats the cupboard wall, sends a fine spray of droplets onto her right cheek. She doesn't flinch.

Willow stands there with her crossbow and pulls a face of pure disgust. 'You're going to have to clean that up,' she says.

'I know that, yes,' says Somer patiently.

'No need to be insolent,' she says.

'No,' says Somer.

'You shouldn't let them get that full,' says Willow.

'I know,' says Somer. 'But you can't predict how people are going to use them. A couple of the others were almost empty.'

Willow tucks her thumbs into her toolbelt. Uri does that, Romy's noticed. They're all starting to mirror his gestures. 'Are you trying to blame other people?' she asks.

'No, Willow,' says Somer, 'I'm just stating facts . . .'

'Well, don't, 142,' she snaps. Somer starts, and gazes at Willow with big, hurt eyes. Then her shoulders slump and she turns away. She may be a Leader, but she knows who's boss. She edges the barrel out of its cupboard and leaves it on the path, fills a bucket from the pump and crawls inside with her scrubbing brush.

Romy swells with shame and rage in equal measure. How can Somer be so humble? How can Willow have turned into such a monster?

Willow opens cupboard No. 1. All clean inside, the blue tub in place, scrubbed and only slightly soiled. She checks the three others, looking for fault, finds none. When she emerges from cupboard No. 4, Somer is standing on the path, picking at her rubber glove. She gets it off and dips the hand into the bucket, splashes the water onto her face.

'Not much point in doing that,' says Willow.

A flash of defiance. 'I don't need your permission to wash my face,' she replies.

Willow raises a hand, and slaps her. Not a lady slap: the full whack, hand cupped to catch the ear. Somer goes down without a sound. Crumples to the soiled earth and clamps a hand over the ear, her face white where the blood has rushed away.

'Don't ever, *ever* speak back to me like that, 142,' snaps Willow. 'Once more and it's Purgatory.'

Somer doesn't move.

'Do you understand?'

Still no movement on the ground.

'*Do you understand?*'

Somer nods. From their perch in the tree it looks as though even nodding hurts.

A rustle of leaves. Ilo has tensed. Romy keeps her eyes on the scene below, puts a hand out to hold his arm. *No. They don't know we're here. Better that way.* His small, hard bicep flexes, relaxes.

Somer sits on, staring at the trodden earth, as Willow walks away. She lays the flat of a hand to her cheek, but her eyes are dry. Romy and Ilo slip down from their hiding place and go to her. She looks up as they approach, and mortification fills her face.

'I wish you hadn't seen that,' she says.

'Are you okay?' asks Ilo.

'Yes.' She drops her hand from her face and they see the imprint of Willow's hand. Nothing half-hearted about that slap. They're getting bolder, thinks Romy. Not even waiting for Lucien and the elders to judge infractions. Summary punishments, and no one's discussing it.

The Dung Squad is not Uri's only innovation. He's turned the crypt beneath the chapel – too damp for food storage, too airless for even one of their cramped dormitories – into a sort of jail. They call it Purgatory, and no one who's spent a night or two there wishes to return. Punishments have got harder, and are handed out more frequently as well: short rations and extra work, night shifts added in until rule-breakers are stumbling with exhaustion, obedient zombies. There's not a day passes when someone isn't in Coventry, shunned and eating alone on the Great House steps.

Ruaridh, Leader of the Blacksmiths, fifty-five, former owner of nightclubs across Glasgow and Stirling and recruited from a rehab where Vita was working as a locum, lost his temper when

Uri announced in the Council Chamber one evening that there would be spot inspections. Leapt to his feet and roared in Uri's face: *Nobody's made you Leader yet, bhoy! You're not the boss o' me!* Five days later he disappeared, taking his box and his leather boots, and they never spoke of him again.

Romy knows where he went, though. Oh, she knows.

Romy holds out her hand and helps her mother to her feet. A smear of privy mud runs up her body from knee to elbow. Yesterday was laundry day. She will have to wear her uniform like that until Saturday now, or rinse it out and wear it damp in the autumn chill. Ilo picks up her knitted hat, brushes it down and holds it out.

Somer pulls it over her vulnerable skull and looks at them with injured eyes. 'Don't ...' she says.

I will, thinks Romy. Just a bit. Just enough to make her sick. She's on my list now.

But she says nothing.

Somer turns away and levers her tub of effluent onto her trolley. Plods down the path towards the slurry pit without another word.

They stand and watch her go. She looks smaller, thinks Romy. But I suppose that's because I'm bigger. A bit of wolfsbane in Willow's boots, that's what I'll do. They all leave their footwear on a rack outside the Guard House door at night. I'll slip some in and it will work through her socks and into her skin. Just enough to lay her low. Not enough to stop her heart.

'She won't survive without us,' she says to her brother, and he knows who she means.

'No,' he says.

'So do you still want to be a Guard?' she asks.

'Oh, yes,' says Ilo, and glances in the direction Willow has taken. 'Absolutely.'

203

Among the Dead

November 2016

28 | Romy

So that's how it feels to kill a human being. I didn't know. In many ways, it was more upsetting to kill a pig.

I follow the road back to the motorway roundabout. It's not as far as I'd thought. Time and distance expand in times of stress. It felt as though we were driving for ten minutes after he turned off the motorway, but it turns out that it's only maybe a quarter-mile.

It's nearly midnight. At this time of year I have the cover of darkness for another seven hours, before I will need to be in the sanctuary of my flat, no one looking at my rainbow face and wondering. Though maybe, if they do, they'll just think I'm a Hallowe'en stop-out dressed as a vagrant or a deranged serial killer. My nose feels strange, as though it's been popped out of alignment, one of my eyes is already beginning to close, and I can feel my split lip swelling. Only a mile and three-quarters to cover every hour. It should be easy.

I killed a man tonight. Not exactly in cold blood. I should feel something, but I don't. Perhaps what Uri's asking of me won't be so hard after all. Especially if I start with Jaivyn. Jaivyn will be more like practice, the way the man was practice.

The others? I don't know.

What I will do to keep you safe, baby. You must be the size of a kitten now. I wonder if you felt it all, buried as you are in the cushioning of my internal organs? You must at least have felt the adrenaline, must have jarred and bounced as he dragged me, dropped me.

You must trust me to keep you safe. I will do anything to keep you safe.

A road, another roundabout, another bridge. Two a.m. and I doubt I've gone more than two miles. I slide down the bank, jog across the tarmac with my head bent down, scramble up the other side, and in the adjustment from streetlight to moonlight through shadow I put my foot on something that rolls, wrench my ankle and hit my bad leg on something hard as I go down, and a supernova explodes inside my head. Something hard and sharp has stabbed straight into my scar, and the pain is so intense I can do nothing more than whimper. God, don't let it have broken open. I roll onto my side and curl up in the foetal position.

I will not survive if I am this weak. We will *die* if I am this weak.

I breathe. In through the nose, out through the mouth, the way Vita taught us. And eventually I can open my eyes, and see that I've hit my leg on an old water tank, dumped among the stinging nettles. Hard edges, but not sharp, thank God. I lift my hands from where they're clutching my thigh. The blue of my leggings is still uniform. A streak of mud on the grey marl of my hoodie sleeve. But no blood. No more blood, I mean.

I sit up. I hurt so much. Grazes and bruises, and now this. I think I'm still on the eastern outskirts of Slough. I will never make it to Hounslow before day. If I'm not careful, I won't make it at all.

My walk lasts well into daylight. As we get closer to London the traffic builds and the motorway splits and splits again and I'm forced off it for fear of getting mown down, forced to use footbridges hundreds of hobbling yards up the subsidiary roads. My ankle throbs and my thigh throbs, and every piece of me is pain, and a blister in my other boot sings out a sharp note in my brain.

Fields give way to the remains of villages, built up, filled in, unloved and shuttered, their street plans a blow to my fantasy of walking straight home. Judging from the map on my new phone, staying to the left of the airport is pretty much all I can hope for. A plane passes over while it's still dark, cruising in to land. Then another, then another, and then the villages join up into one long sprawl of roads and mean concrete houses and frustrating cul-de-sacs, and the lights start to come on, upstairs at first and then on the ground, at kitchen level. People start to emerge onto their weedy concrete parking spaces and notice me. Their eyes look up and see my face, and look hurriedly away.

They think I'm a Homeless, like the man outside Iceland.

I tighten the cord on my hoodie to cover as much of my face as I can, and concentrate on putting one foot in front of the other. My blister is bleeding now, and that's something of a relief, for at least it lends a slickness to the lining of the boot. But with each step I'm getting weaker – my thigh jars with every step and my ankle is screaming and I have to grind my teeth to hold in my keening.

I get to Bath Road at half-past nine, and I start to weep with relief as I pass the little café and smell the bacon, the coffee. We can lie down soon, baby. Lie down and take the pain away.

And then I see my mother sitting on my doorstep, and for a moment my heart leaps. And then I realise that it's my aunt, and my hopes implode.

29 | Sarah

Pregnant. That's something she hadn't been expecting. But the pregnant young woman limping towards her in a stained hoodie is definitely her niece. She can tell from the way her pace breaks when she sees her sitting on the doorstep, and then from the way her hair falls over her face as she resumes her approach like a charging billy-goat. Alison used to do that. You'd see her coming down the street head-down and eyes glaring out beneath her fringe, and you knew not to get into a disagreement with her. It's only now Sarah sees her that she remembers, and realises how much of it was just teenage bluster. She doesn't see much other physical resemblance, but she recognises her as Alison's daughter from that alone. She gets to her feet and waits.

She's little. Four or five inches shorter than Eden, and light-boned, with a swirl of thick, shiny black hair. She's chopped it off at chin level and hacked a rough fringe into the front, and it looks spectacular. As she gets closer, Sarah sees that she has the most beautiful almond-shaped jade eyes. And that her face is covered in livid bruises.

Sarah wants to turn tail and run. This isn't what she'd envisaged at all. But the girl knows who she is – she clearly knows who she is – and it's too late now. I shall be British about it, she resolves, and pretend I haven't noticed a thing.

Romy stops six feet away and stares at her challengingly. Her skin has an unnerving yellow tinge. Jaundiced yellow, or at least, she judges from the sheen on her forehead, the bleaching of illness. The bruising must be more extensive than just on her face, if it's causing her to turn yellow.

'You know who I am?' asks Sarah.

Romy nods curtly. 'You're my aunt. You look like my mother.'

She's surprised. She has never thought of herself as looking like Alison before. But twenty years will change anybody. 'Yes. Sarah. Sarah Byrne.'

She offers her a hand. The girl looks down at it with something like surprise, as though the gesture is unfamiliar. Then she slots her palm against Sarah's and gives it a sharp shake. The hand is a bit damp, and there are brownish stains further up her wrist where her sleeve has slid up. Sarah wipes her own surreptitiously on the back of her coat when she lets go. She has a little bottle of anti-viral gel in her handbag; she'll rub some on when her niece turns her back.

'Romy,' she replies. 'Romy Blake.' She fishes some keys from her pocket and eyes Sarah uncertainly. 'Do you want to come in?'

'If that's okay.'

Romy shrugs, as though she doesn't care much either way. Then she opens the door on to a dingy staircase covered in green lino and limps ahead without looking back.

The flat is grim. Low ceiling, windows covered in condensation, sad old broken-down furniture. It's a little-old-lady flat. Probably died *in situ* or got carted off to a twilight home. Sarah

212

bets there are hand rails in the bathroom. A little row of kitchen cupboards in olive-green formica. Miserable blue and yellow curtains that end a good inch from the windowsill, half-closed. Romy goes over and throws them open.

'I need to pee,' she says, and leaves the room abruptly. Sarah stays where she is, unsure whether her invitation extends to sitting down. A scratched little coffee table, one of those oval ones from the 1950s with the three spindly legs. Flowered wallpaper gone grey with age, a patch of damp high in one corner, a blackened Axminster carpet. It's hot, from the launderette downstairs, and yet feels strangely, unwelcomingly cold.

How awful, she thinks, to be having a baby here. And then she thinks of Alison, caring for this very girl as a baby in a caravan in the middle of winter, and feels unspeakably guilty again.

She's gone a long time, for someone who's having a pee. Sarah hears the sound of water running in the bathroom, a door opening and closing in the corridor. She feels awkward, doesn't want to touch anything in case doing so violates her welcome. Eventually she wanders over to the window and looks out at the street. Run-down, respectable west London, two tube stations conveniently close by. She could have fetched up in worse places.

Then a plane thunders past so close to the roof that she ducks and covers her head. Maybe not. It must be torture, living here.

The door closes in the passage again, and her niece comes back, with clean hands, and in clean clothes – leggings and a black jersey mini-dress with one of those flippy hems. Thoughtlessly stylish. But her face is a sight and she's still limping on her bare feet.

'Would you like to sit down?' she asks.

'Yes,' says Sarah, 'thank you,' and lowers herself gingerly onto the sofa. It's not dirty, at least. The girl clearly knows how to clean, like her siblings. But it's a joyless place. She's tried to

213

cheer it up with a scattering of bric-a-brac on the mantel over the old gas fire, but otherwise there's very little evidence that she lives here at all.

Romy, still standing, considers some more. 'Tea,' she says. 'I have tea. Would you like some? I have milk too.'

'That would be lovely,' says Sarah. She watches as Romy fills the kettle and puts it on to boil, then gets a single plain white mug down from a cupboard, opens a box of PG tips and takes out a bag. 'Aren't you having any?'

'No,' says Romy. 'I don't drink it.'

'Oh, I'm sorry. I didn't mean to be a bother.'

The girl's eyes narrow. She's trying to work something out. 'Oh, right,' she says. 'You're not just meant to give it to people, you're meant to have some yourself?'

'Yes, that's sort of normal,' says Sarah, and now she sees the children in her. Half-feral and trying to work out the mystery rules – only Romy is having to do it all alone, with no one to help. 'It's like a custom. To share a drink, or some food.'

'Oh, the breaking of bread,' says Romy, and turns back to the cupboard. When she reaches for a second mug, Sarah notices that her hand is trembling.

'Are you okay, Romy?' she asks.

'Yes,' says Romy. 'Bad night, that's all.'

'Can I ask what happened?'

'I got – what's the word? Mugged. I went into London a couple of days ago and I got mugged.'

'My God. Jesus, are you okay?'

The girl shrugs. 'I will be.'

'Where did it happen?'

She gulps, as though she hadn't been prepared to be questioned so closely. 'I'm not sure. I went to King's Cross, just to see. It was somewhere near there.'

'I'd thought it had got better up there, with the regeneration! What did they get?'

'Not much. Some money. They seemed to be angry because I didn't have anything else.'

'Not your phone?'

She shakes her head.

'Did you call the police?'

A what's-the-point face. Just like Ilo's when she offered to get the amulet back. God, Sarah, she's living in a different England from you. The England you see on the news, not the one most of us live in. It's weird, in a place like Finbrough, how easy it is to forget that for other people robbery and stabbing and damp walls is just another day at the coalface. Actually real, not drama designed to make the comfortable feel happy with their lot.

That face looks *nasty*, as though someone has punched her full in it.

'I know you probably get a lot of opinions,' she says, hesitantly, 'what with the baby and all. I know everyone has unsolicited advice to offer when you're pregnant ...'

'How do you know that?' She doesn't turn, just stares at the empty mugs. 'Have you been pregnant?'

Crikey. Defensive or what? 'I – no, I haven't,' she says.

Liam has two children now. Probably thinks that the little girlfriend's fecundity is just more proof of her own emotional coldness.

'Best keep yours to yourself, then,' Romy says, and Sarah shrinks into the couch.

The kettle boils. Romy pours water into the mugs and stirs vigorously. 'Do you have sugar in it?' she asks. 'I know some people drink tea with sugar.'

'Sure,' says Sarah. 'One, if that's okay?'

Romy opens a drawer and produces a sachet of sugar from a

215

café. Rips it open and dumps the full contents into one of the mugs, then adds the best part of a quarter-pint of milk to each. Brings them over. 'Do you need something to eat? I have apples.'

Sarah suppresses a smile. 'No.' She sips gingerly from her lukewarm milky drink and fights to hold back a grimace. 'This is lovely, thanks.'

'Okay,' says Romy, and lowers herself slowly down beside her. Something's hurting, thinks Sarah. She's off balance because of the baby, but it's more than that. She's moving like an eighty-year-old.

She sees Sarah notice, shakes her head. 'It's not as bad as it looks,' she says, and winces as she leans forward to pick up her tea. Turns to face her. 'So why are you here?'

'I'm sorry,' says Sarah. 'I would have given you some warning if I could. But I only had your address and I didn't know how else to contact you.'

Romy nods. 'Do you know where my brother and sister are?'

'Yes. They're with me. That's why I wanted to find you.'

She blinks.

'Oh, no, I'm sorry.' The words rush out. 'I mean, that's not the only reason I'm here. But I didn't know. About what happened. Not till a couple of months ago. I didn't know you were there.'

Romy looks away. 'Never mind,' she says, and sips her tea. Pulls a face and puts it back down on the table.

'Well, I'm sorry anyway,' says Sarah. 'You've had a lot to deal with all alone and I should have thought of that. And, for what it's worth, I'm sorry I never tried to find you before. You and your mum. I know I was a kid when you were born, but I've been an adult a long time now.'

Another blink. Her big eyes are such a vivid green and the lashes so thick and dark that she looks for a moment like one of those animatronic dolls that sad men buy for pleasure.

216

'Yes, well. I had a family.'

Had.

'I'm so sorry,' says Sarah. 'About your mum. About your ... friends.'

'Family,' she corrects, with an edge of defiance. That eye looks really painful. It's swollen half-closed. If that's two days old, she must have been close to death. She's really ill, thinks Sarah. They're made of tough stuff, my sister's children, but I don't think I've come at a good time. Or maybe I have. I should think she could do with some support, however prickly she is.

Romy coughs. 'So tell me about Eden and Ilo,' she says.

'They're fine. Well, as fine as you could expect – I don't know. I have no idea what you would be expecting. I'm sorry. I'm making a hash of this.'

'Yes, well.' She coughs again. She really doesn't look well. 'I don't suppose this is a commonplace experience for either of us.'

Sarah smiles. 'No,' she says. 'I'm glad you understand.'

A superstorm of suppressed emotions passes across her niece's face. Then she pulls herself together and goes blank again. 'I'm not sure how much there is to understand. It is what it is. Thank you for taking them in. Where do you live?'

'Finbrough,' she tells her. 'It's a little town a bit of the way up the—'

'I know where Finbrough is,' she snaps. 'Are you telling me you've been there all along?'

'I – well, I left for a bit, when I was married. I lived in Reading, but – oh, you mean with the children. Yes. Well, not all along. But once Social Services released them to me, yes. Have you been looking?'

She looks miserable, as though she's being crushed by an unseen hand from above. 'Yes.'

'Presumably you tried the church?'

217

'Yes,' she says. 'But I couldn't get through. There's a website, and I called the number there, but nobody answered.'

'I'm sorry. It's been closed for a couple of years, since your grandfather died.'

'So I gathered. About the church. I didn't know he was dead though.'

'And you didn't know where the house was? Your mother didn't tell you?'

'Well she told me *about* it,' says Romy. 'But she didn't exactly give me an address and directions, no.'

'No. I suppose she wouldn't.' She thinks of those letters and feels a surge of rage. 'I don't suppose Alison wanted you to have anything to do with them.'

'Somer,' Romy corrects.

She checks herself. 'Yes, I'm sorry. I've just been thinking of her as Alison all these years, and it's hard for me to shift. Bear with me.'

Another of those thunderous looks.

'Anyway,' she continues, trying to act as though she hasn't noticed, 'they're well. But they miss you.'

The look goes from thunderous to thunderstruck. 'They said that?'

'In so many words. They talk about you.'

A flicker of the eyebrow. God, these people are so hard to read. Blank walls with hairline cracks in the plaster. 'And I think,' she continues, 'that I might need your help.'

'My help?'

'Yes. If you … I know I have no right to ask you for anything …'

'No, you're right. But I'm listening.' She puts her hand on the sofa arm and bends backwards, as though she's trying to clunk something out in her spine.

'I … look, I'm glad to meet you, and honestly, if there's

218

anything I can do ... but I need your help. You're the only person who ... well, you know. Knows. Knows them. Knows what they've been through. Knows about the way they grew up ...'

'And me,' says Romy. 'It was the way I grew up, too.'

'Yes. I get that. That's why I thought maybe you ... I just ... they're having trouble fitting in. I can see it. And I wondered if maybe you ...'

'You think I know?'

She's brought up short. 'I ... gosh. I don't know. I'm sorry if that was offensive.'

She shakes her head. 'Not offensive. Just a bit stupid.'

'You're older,' she says. 'When they're not at school they're at home all the time, with no friends. I mean, I only moved back to Finbrough quite recently—' she's embarrassed to admit that it's been three years and she's still a virtual recluse '—so I've not really got much of a circle myself, and anyway, people my age, you know, they're mostly just starting out having babies. It's rare for someone my age to have a fifteen-year-old ... and I don't see how they're ever going to learn to fit in like that. And they *need* to fit in. They're out in the real world now and they need to learn how to negotiate it.'

Another flicker of the eyebrow. Probably didn't like that 'real world' thing, but at least she's not clammed up the way *they* did.

'I thought we were getting on okay,' she says, 'but I don't ... I've realised that I don't know how to talk to them. And I think they might be having trouble with some of the kids at school, but they won't confide in me ... I don't know how to ask the right questions. Help them open up.'

'No, I can see that,' says Romy. 'So you want me to?'

'It's ... or advise me. I don't know. I'm so surprised, some-times, by the things that matter to them. And the things they don't trust me about.'

'Such as?'

'I don't know. Like, Eden lost her necklace the other day, and ...'

Romy jolts. Literally jolts. Looks at her with dark, suspicious eyes. 'Necklace? Metal thing, like a medallion?'

'Yes. Ilo says it's important to her, but they seem to be dead set against me putting out an alert for it in the school, and I don't know ... I don't know who else to ask.'

'And you want me to ... what? Get it back?' she asks.

'I ... no, it's not that. It's that – you know – their lives have been so different from mine. From anybody's, really. And there's this disconnect because there's stuff they take for granted that I just don't even know about, and probably quite a lot of vice versa, too. I thought maybe if they could see someone who's ... who knows all the stuff I don't ... someone who's had the same experiences but is a bit older ...'

'I see.' Romy's nose wrinkles. 'I'm not sure I'd be that much help. If you want me to explain how the world works. I can't even make tea properly.'

Sarah can't stop herself smiling. 'I'll teach you that, if you like.'

'I'll think about it.'

She risks pushing further. 'It's not so much *here* I need explaining to *them*, Romy. It's *there* I need explaining to *me*. I've tried to ask them, but ... I realise I don't really have the first idea what you believed – believe – sorry ... I know I'm getting this all wrong. But that's it. That's the problem. I just feel I'm constantly putting my foot in it, making wrong assumptions, but it's as though we speak a different language or something. I feel as though I need someone to translate.'

Romy looks surprised. 'Oh,' she says. 'You're the first person who's not assumed it was something lacking in *us*. Okay, then. When do you want me to come and talk to them? Now?'

Sarah panics. No. No, no, no, I should have thought this through better. I can't just have her tip up covered in bruises with a baby hanging off her. 'I . . .' She hunts her brain for a way to backtrack without being rude. 'They're at school now,' she says, 'and I haven't talked to them about you. I would think it would be a bit of a shock if you were just *there* when they came home.'

'Oh,' says Romy.

'Have you got a phone? Can I take your number, maybe? If we could maybe talk a bit more, when you're feeling better, and I can get to know you a bit . . . ?'

'Yes,' she says, 'but I don't know what it is.'

'Okay. If I tell you my number, you can send me a text. Then we can both store each other's. Then we can talk more.'

'Oh, okay,' says Romy, 'yes.' She pulls herself up from the sofa. Takes two steps towards her bag on the countertop, and her knees buckle under her. She drops to the ground like a chainsawed ash.

30 | Romy

They come and sit nearby, sometimes together, sometimes alone, but I pretend not to see them. I've got myself here now, and, now that I'm in this comfortable bed in this quiet road with curtains that block out all the light, I realise that I am, in fact, dog-tired and hurting, and a couple of days' sleep and recuperation is just the ticket. She brought a doctor with grey hair and spectacles, who took my temperature and listened to my chest with a stethoscope and decided that I wasn't in imminent danger of death, and prescribed delicious painkillers and large amounts of water 'whether she wants to or not – flush those contusions through her kidneys and liver'. And I certainly look the part. I crept into the bathroom and had a look in the mirror when they were all asleep. I look like chopped aubergine.

No wonder she believed I'd collapsed for real.

My aunt feeds me neon-orange soup from a plain white bowl – oh, the sheer deliciousness of little strips of buttered toast; she makes me drink a glass of water every hour I'm awake, puts a funny little bell by my bedside, chases the children out when they've been there silently staring at me as I pretend to sleep, for too long. And I spend more time than I would have thought possible unconscious in the clammy dark, as though a few bruises might actually have made me sick.

My dreams are chaos. A swirling vortex of chaos, punctuated by screams of rage. Have been all my life. It's mostly just darkness and movement and a sense of being followed.

But in a dream in this bed I go back to Plas Golau, and the man is lying at my feet halfway up the hill road in the woods. He's grinning that open-mouthed grin and his hands are claws. But he's dead. I've made sure of that. There's a pool of blood beneath him. I roll him with my toes until he hits the slope and disappears into the undergrowth. He won't be bothering me again. I'm done with him now. And I walk on, up the hill, back to my home.

I cross the orchard. Laundry flutters like carnival banners in the breeze. I remember what it was really like – the drooping grey, the drizzle that filled the air – but this is another day, a day before the people came. No one is here but me.

A lark sings, somewhere in the blue, and the approach, through this beautiful countryside I know so well, makes me feel so full I could explode. We made a place of beauty, up here in the hills, Cader Idris soaring above us, its colours changing with every passing moment. It's the thing the Dead will never understand. That life was hard at Plas Golau, but what we made was beautiful.

And then I turn through the gates and see that the Great Disaster has arrived.

A sharp pain in my ribs snatches my breath away, throws me from sleep. A cramp. I must have been panting, and set it off. I don't know which way to go to stretch it out. Either way the agony will be worse before it gets better. Eventually, I stretch. Hiss as the muscles ripple red-hot between my ribs and the spasm goes all the way to my spine.

'Oh,' I say, 'oh,' and then I look up and see that Eden and Ilo are sitting at the end of the bed, looking alarmed. 'Aaaaah, sorry,' I say, pushing myself into a sitting position against the pillows. 'Cramp.'

Ilo gets up and walks to my end of the bed. 'Where?' he asks. I point. Bottom of the ribcage, left-hand side. He bends his elbow and digs it into the ball of molten metal under my skin and it shrieks, fights back, relaxes.

I exhale with relief. 'Thanks.'

'That's okay,' he says, and walks back to sit by my sister.

'Where have you been?' Eden asks.

'Weston-super-Mare,' I say, 'and Hounslow.'

'Where's Hounslow?'

'East of here. Near London.'

'You're meant to look after me,' she says.

'I'm sorry,' I say. 'I was looking. But I was ill. For a long time. And you had Ilo.'

'What if I'd died?' she asks. 'Where would we be then?'

And I look at her and look at her, and I remember how she was when she was a little kid, and I'm glad you'll never grow up like Lucien's children, baby. Knowing you're special is a long way different from *being* special.

'How are you feeling?' asks Ilo.

'I don't know,' I say. 'Like I've been run over.'

'Aunt Sarah said you'd been robbed.'

'Yes.'

He frowns. 'That doesn't sound like you.'

'They caught me off-guard. And I'm not ... as fit as I was. What day is it?'

224

'Sunday.'

'What time?'

'Half-past ten,' says Eden. 'You look a lot better. When are you going to get up?'

'I probably stink,' I say.

'There are three bathrooms here,' says Ilo. 'There's actually one through that door over there, look, for this room alone. You've been peeing in it, but you probably don't remember. You've been delirious.'

'On sweet,' I say, looking at the door. They look blank. 'That's what it's called,' I say. 'An On Sweet.'

They both look doubtful.

'She said to call her when you woke up,' says Eden, 'so she can make you some breakfast.'

'She?'

'Aunt Sarah.'

'Oh, yes. Of course.'

Eden nods. 'Apparently you collapsed.' She doesn't sound very impressed. 'This is our grandparents' room,' she adds.

I pretend to look around, though I've had plenty of time to familiarise myself with the taupe walls and the beige carpet and the two hard-backed armchairs, all of it looking like no one ever stopped living here. 'Is it?' I ask. 'In Finbrough?'

'You've been looking for us, then?' asks Eden.

'I told you. Where were you?'

'A place called Barmouth. Quite close to home. Then she brought us here. We go to school now.'

'How's that?'

'Weird. Boring. They're all interested in stupid things and don't know about anything useful. I like you with hair, by the way. It suits you.'

'You too,' I reply. I look at them both. Grown some, and she's pretty with her mop of curls. He's looking thinner, softer than he was when I left him. Life on the Outside weakens you. Well, it has me.

'I should go and get her,' Eden says. 'We're going to go up to the supermarket when it opens. Did you know? They buy a whole week's food in one go, most of them. Can you imagine?'

'Have you tried jerk chicken?' I ask. I know. Shallow talk. But food was a lot of what we talked about. We thought about it, all of us, all the time. There never, despite all our work, seemed to ever be quite enough.

'No,' she says. 'Have you tried Indian food?'

'No.'

'There's a restaurant on the High Street. Near our grandparents' church.'

'You can buy jerk chicken from a man literally *opposite* there,' I say, then think, shit, that's probably more information than I wanted to give. I know I said I'd been looking, but I don't necessarily want Aunt Sarah knowing how close I came. But they don't seem to notice.

'She gives us ten pounds a week, *each*, you know,' says Ilo.

'Wow,' I say. That's a lot of jerk chicken.

'Aunt Sarah smokes,' he confides. 'I smell it sometimes after we've gone to bed. She goes out into the garden.'

'Mm. I suppose you don't worry too much about that sort of thing when you're already Dead,' I say.

'I guess,' says Eden. 'It's a shame, though. I like her, even if she is. We're going to save her, if we can.'

'Don't hold out too much hope, E,' I tell her.

A tap on the door, and the person outside waits until we invite them in. What a world. It's my aunt, in a long flowered skirt that makes her look a bit like a dinner table. Now that I'm not taken by surprise, now I'm feeling better, I can tell that Eden is right.

There's something about her that's just *nice*. A strange, warm contrast to this sad and featureless room. She has a nice smile – real and immediate, not like ours. It's the smile that reminds me most of Somer, I think, though the way she was frowning on my doorstep yesterday, all uncertainty, was what made me know her instantly. I must practise. It would help us fit in.

'How are you feeling?' she asks. 'I thought I'd leave it to these two to wake you up.'

'I'm . . .' I think about it. 'Thank you,' I say. 'I think I'm better.'

Actually, I am. I don't think I was as not-ill as I thought, even if I did ham it up to get here. That was some beating that man gave me. Still. I gave him more.

'Those are some nasty bruises,' she says. 'I had a fair amount of trouble persuading the doctor to leave you here.'

'For a few bruises?'

'You can get a sort of jaundice when the blood reabsorbs,' she says. Then blushes, rather sweetly, as though she thinks she's showing off. 'Or something like that.'

'We don't do stuff like jaundice,' I tell her, and see that mystified look Melanie wore a lot. 'It's fine. I'm fine.'

'Anyway,' she says, 'you stay in bed. Don't get up. You need to rest. There'll always be someone about if you need us. We're all going to have to go in to work tomorrow, but you're welcome to stay and rest up, and I'll just be at the other end of the phone.'

I look at Eden, startled. 'You work? I didn't think you were allowed.'

Sarah laughs, nervously. 'No, no, sorry. I work at the school where Eden and Ilo go. I work in the office.'

'Oh, right.'

'How do you feel? Up to some breakfast?'

'I would sell Ilo for some breakfast,' I say. Charm. I am all charm. I learned a lot from Lucien.

She laughs. 'I'm not sure how much he'd fetch. But you can make her something, can't you, Ilo? There's eggs, and bread for toast, and some orange juice,' and at the thought of all that I am practically weeping.

'Thank you,' I say, and I mean it.

'Eden and I are going to the supermarket. Is that okay? You'll be okay with Ilo?'

My little brother. Five months lost. 'Of course,' I say.

31 | Romy

When they close the door, he hurls himself on me like a sheepdog looking for bacon.

'Ow!' I croak, and hug him so hard I think I'll squeeze his innards out. 'Fuck's sake, Ilo, that hurts.'

I've missed him, I've missed him so much. He smells of chemical flowers and his skin is six shades paler than it should be. But he's still Ilo. I can feel those wiry muscles under the layer of softness he's put on. I can have him back.

'I thought you were dead,' he says. 'I did. When we went to the Infirmary. When I saw you. I thought you were dead.'

'Well, I'm not. I'm like the cockroaches. When the world ends, I'll still be here and you can eat me.' And we both laugh, because Uri once tried to start a rule that we all had to eat insects once a week, and cockroaches featured high on his list, termites being in short supply in north Wales. Even the force of Uri's will wasn't enough to make people co-operate with that one.

'What the fuck happened to Eden's medallion?' I ask.

He colours. 'I'm sorry. It's this stupid girl at school. She snatched it off her neck on Friday, and she's got these friends, and when I tried to take it back they were all, like, throwing it over my head, and then one of the teachers came along and chased us off and her father turned up in his big car, and ...'

'We need it, Ilo. She's worth absolutely nothing without that medallion.'

'Yes, she is! She's still Eden! Come on!'

No, you're right, Ilo. She's worth nothing to *me* without it. Or I'm worth nothing to Uri. Without it, she could be just anyone.

'Who is this girl?' I ask.

'She's a ... she's stupid. She's called Marie. Her hair's made of plastic and so are her fingernails, and she swanks around the place like *she's* the One, and they're all so ignorant, they follow her around like sheepdogs. And she hates Eden because she won't bow down to her. It's horrible. I don't like school. Romy, can we go? Can you take us away?'

'It's not as easy as that. I can't just kidnap you.'

'But you're our sister.'

'And now Aunt Sarah's your legal guardian. I can't just take you away.'

'I thought that was only because they couldn't find you,' he says. 'You're back now!'

'No. They knew where I was. But I don't count as a responsible adult, apparently. There are laws.'

'We're not subject to their laws,' he says, confidently.

'We are now. They'd come after us.'

'Oh.'

'And anyway, she seems kind.'

'I think she is. But she hasn't got the first idea. She's made no preparations. Literally none. We've tried telling her and it's like talking to a brick wall. How are we going to survive?'

'I'm working on it.'

'And you're pregnant. Like a football.'

'Good observational skills. I taught you those.'

'What would Somer have thought?'

'She knew. I told her.'

'Oh.'

'She wasn't thrilled.'

'Oh,' he says again, then, 'bit hypocritical.'

I shrug.

'I won't hold it against you, though.'

Too right, you *literal* little bastard. You're the last person in the world who should. 'Thank you,' I say.

'Whose is it?'

I shake my head. 'It doesn't matter. He's dead.'

'Aren't you scared, R? I mean, it doesn't matter *how* nice Aunt Sarah is, does it? I'm literally scared all the time. Do you watch the news? She puts on the television at six o'clock every night, and it's nothing but people screaming at each other and people getting blown up and volcanoes and burning buildings. And she doesn't seem to see it at all. She watches it like it's some sort of entertainment. They're all going to be turning on each other soon. How can she not see it? Imagine when they all come pouring out of London ...'

I put a hand on his shoulder. He's such a kid. I'd forgotten. 'I know,' I say. 'I do.'

'But what do we do?'

'Keep your pack packed. Be ready, always. If we can't get her to understand before it's too late, we'll have to leave her behind.'

'And go where?'

'Cairngorm. They're there. Uri and the rest. That's where they went.'

He drinks this in. I guess they didn't tell him everything,

in the Guard House. He'd only been there a little while. He's only young.

'And how are we going to do that?' he asks.

I tell him. Well, not all of it. Not yet. Give him a chance to get used to the easy bits first. He's not stupid. He'll work it out.

Before the End

2012–2014

32 | Romy

June 2012

On the other side of the hill pass, a silvery-black lake reflects the sky, nestled in the heather. Every year, the morning after the summer solstice, when the party is over and the children have been released from their confinement in the Pigshed, the women carry the remainder of the solstice feast up into the hills to eat on the heather and enjoy the bitter mountain waters. Their moment of liberty, if just for the morning. Lucien doesn't like mixed bathing. For the moment, for the rest of the morning, they can do what they want, but they must be back in their clothes, modesty recovered, by the time the men come up after clearing the courtyard to share the meal.

Eilidh throws herself down in the heather and Romy drops down beside her. All around them, women are stripping off their dresses, exposing pale bodies to the air. The Plas Golau suntan: brown faces, scalps, forearms and upper feet, and sharp lines of demarcation with the white beneath. Romy, with her olive

235

complexion, feels conspicuous in the women's Bath House, when she finds herself surrounded by all this ivory skin. She never really wonders who her father was, for his part of her story most likely ended with ejaculation, but she does wish, sometimes, that he'd been a normal blond like everyone else in the world. Eilidh is so white she feels concerned for her, for the dangers from the mountain sun.

'This is the life, eh?' says Eilidh.

Romy strips off her top and rolls onto her back, arches her spine. Is there any bed more comfortable than a blanket laid over the natural bounce of living heather? She can't help scanning the bodies of the three female Guards. In this gathering of rib and hipbone and breasts that have lost their stuffing till they dangle from chests as though they don't quite belong there, Fitz and Ash and Willow are lionesses. Muscles that ripple in their arms, thighs and bellies hard as granite. Their skin is smooth and lustrous, for Uri insists that they bathe daily and oil themselves afterwards, to protect against infection and the elements. Romy rolls onto her belly. I might get dressed in a bit, she thinks. For, although she's rougher round the edges, she feels slightly nervous that someone might notice that she looks more Guard than Drone.

Down the slope, Vita, magnificent in an emerald-green swimsuit, her silver hair tumbling down to her waist, leads the charge into the water. Her mother, freed from the Dung Squad for the day, joins in for all the world as though she belongs there, whooping with shock as she runs into the mountain-cold water in her underwear, looking younger than Romy has seen her look in years. She's hand in hand with Eden, laughing. Eden's still fond of her, despite it all. She may be part of the Family, but she never forgets who her mother is.

'You not going in?' Romy asks.

Eilidh shivers. 'Maybe once I've got myself nice and hot.' She fingers her medallion as she watches the other women. 'It's pretty cold in there.'

'I guess it'll clear their hangovers,' says Romy.

Eilidh laughs. 'Is *that* why they do it?'

'I heard,' says Romy, 'that you can drink as much as you want.'

Eilidh's eyes grow wide. So many things you want, at sixteen. 'Really? D'you think Kiran ... ?' Their old friend Kiran passed into full adulthood last night, and they're burning to hear his account of his first solstice party. It sounds so wild, through the Pigshed walls. The drumbeat so arousing, the cries of the women sounding, if they didn't know better, for all the world as if they're in pain.

'I should think so. Wouldn't you? Anyway, I guess we'll see soon enough. And there's food and food and food. No portions. They killed two pigs and three sheep last week, you know.'

'Waah,' says Eilidh.

When Lucien comes, astride his big black horse and leading his men, they've long since left the water. It's a beautiful thing about him, thinks Romy, that he still loves that horse despite the fact that it nearly killed him. Our Father is so kind. He forgives everything. Then she sees Kiran, skin grey and shadows under his eyes, and she waves and nudges Eilidh.

'There he is,' she says.

Eilidh looks, wrinkles her nose. 'Is there really any fun so good it's worth feeling like that for the picnic?' she asks.

Fitz and Ash, altered and eerie in feminine garb, come over to join them on their blanket, chat amiably as though they were equals. They respond to the girls' attempts to pump them about the night by smiling and laughing and turning away. You'll see soon enough, they say. And yeah, we had a good time. You think

237

this picnic is good, but there's so much food you don't know where to start.

'Some people don't know where to stop, either,' says Ash, and Fitz laughs. Out of her green fatigues, Fitz is pretty. Smooth golden skin and a smattering of freckles, eyes as blue as robins' eggs. Perhaps it's the change in her expression. Around the Guard House she mostly wears a slightly feral frown, as though she feels that to be a Guard she needs to be *on* her guard all the time. Out here with the women, her face is relaxed, the brow no longer knitted, the corners of her lips turned upwards.

'Yeah,' she says. 'Too right.'

'Did anyone get drunk?' asks Romy. Some of the women are quiet today. Slow-moving. And they're drinking deeply from the elderflower cordial in the flagons, diluted with water from the lake.

'Not us,' says Ash.

'No,' says Fitz. 'We've got more sense.'

The men reach the water and start to strip. Romy wonders passingly why it is that the men can show their skin in front of the women without kicking off a frenzy of lust. It's just always been that way. But she looks anyway, for she's not seen Kiran without his top since last year. He's grown up fine, his body slim and muscular from his work in the smithy. She's surprised to realise that she's enjoying the view.

She turns away. 'Is there dancing?' she asks.

'Oh, yes,' says Fitz. 'There's dancing.'

Lucien joins them at four o'clock. They've moved into a circle, the older teens, the younger twenties. People who've grown up together, old comrades from the Pigshed, flirting and fooling, for all the world as though they have no duties.

He's been attracted by the laughter, she realises, as he gets up and walks towards them. He's been glancing over every time they've guffawed. He's so familiar, and yet so not. A presence who moves among them every day, guiding, but aloof, retiring early to his quarters, for Vita says his burden is heavy and he has to think late into the night. He is never like this – one of them – apart from today. It's part of the magic of the longest hours. It must be hard for him, she thinks. To have to be *the* Leader. He must be very alone.

He looks Romy straight in the eye and asks if he can sit, just like a normal person, just like a human being. And Romy gets goosebumps, but she plays the game and moves casually aside to make room for him just like he's one of them. He drops from standing straight into the lotus position, and smiles at them all in turn.

Lucien is sixty-two. His hair has gone white and his neatly trimmed beard to match. His body is still lean, though a little old-man paunch is just faintly visible beneath his tunic. His teeth, she sees, are snaggled, and eyes that she remembers from her ceremony as bright blue have faded to a blueish grey. A face surprisingly unlined, but for the creases around his eyes when he smiles. If it weren't Lucien, if she didn't *know* how deep and great his deliberations, she might well have assumed that the smoothness indicated a mind untroubled by thinking. But he is, and he's here among them, and they're all trying to hide their excitement, to pretend that this is an event that happens every day.

'What are you all up to?' he asks.

Someone has to speak. Come on, someone. Romy looks at her companions beneath her eyelashes. The longer the pause, the more awkward we make it, the higher the barrier we put between him and us. She glances at Eilidh. *He's your father*, she projects at her. *You at least should be able to talk.*

And then she's speaking, because she's realised that everyone else is more tongue-tied than she is, and he's smiling at her and nodding, as though every word she has to say is interesting.

'It's just a silly game.'

The blue-grey eyes continue to rest on her, and she's drowning. They may have faded, but still they are clear and piercing. From a distance, you feel as though they can see right into your soul.

And then she's cold all over, because she's realised that, when you see them close up, there is nothing behind them.

'We . . .' she stammers ' . . . just Simon Says.'

'Oh, that old game,' he replies, and helps himself to a handful of berries from the bowl they've hived away for themselves. Trickles them between his lips and holds her eyes with his.

There's nothing there. Nothing. He's as empty as a prayer bowl. The heat has gone out of the sun.

'So did you all have a good time last night?' he asks.

'Yeah,' says Fitz, 'it was good.'

'It was great,' says Kiran. 'Not that I've anything to compare it with.'

Lucien ignores him. Looks again at Romy. 'And you?' he asks. 'It must have been your first time?'

She finds her voice, though it's small with shock. How can this be? How can we follow him, when there's nothing there?

'No,' she says. 'Next year. And not till winter.'

A little tic of a frown. 'Next year? How old are you? I thought you came of age this year?'

'Next November,' she tells him.

'Ah, still,' he says. 'Not long till you're ready.'

33 | Romy

December 2013

She's preparing to leave the Bath House when Somer grabs her by the wrist. 'Listen,' she says. 'Stay in the light.'

Romy stops. 'What?' she asks. She feels uncomfortably unconstructed in her long, loose dress. It's the first time she's worn it since her maturity rite four years ago, and it's no more comfortable now than it was then. It has had to be let out at the shoulders, for she's taller and broader by several inches.

Her mother seems to have shrunk again, her daily humbling showing literally in her stooping shoulders. If that's what thirty-five looks like, thinks Romy with all the certainty of godlike eighteen, I would rather die in battle. And then she feels a wash of guilt, for this is the woman who bore her, nursed her, brought her here to safety, and drops back.

'Tonight,' says Somer. 'You've not been before.'

'I know that.' She's trying to look cool as a vixen, but inside she prickles with nervous excitement. Eighteen, and never been

241

to a party. Tonight is the night. All the abandon she's heard through the Pigshed walls all these years – this time she'll be part of it.

'Listen to me, Romy,' says Somer. 'This is important.'

By the fireplace, Eilidh laughs loudly in the middle of a group of older women, and a knot of envy forms in her sternum. It's Romy's first solstice too, but no one is gathered around *her* draping her with garlands, tying friendship bracelets around her wrist, smoothing unguents into her skin. Sometimes she feels as though she and Eilidh live on different planets.

'Stay in the light,' says Somer, again.

Her head snaps back into the here and now. 'What?'

'You don't know,' says Somer. 'It's not like you think. Lucien, Vita, Uri – they're not there tonight.'

She wants to let out a loud 'doh'. 'I *know*.'

'*Listen* to me, Romy.'

She listens, resentfully.

'Drink slowly,' says Somer. 'You're not used to it. None of us is, and it can get away from you before you know it. People ... aren't the same tonight. You'll see.'

Eilidh brushes past. 'Are you coming?'

'Yes,' says Romy. 'Hang on. Don't go without me.' She turns back to her mother. 'I can take care of myself,' she says confidently.

'I know. I know.' Somer lets her arm go, looks suddenly tired. 'Just ... stay in the light.'

In the courtyard, Kiran presses tankards of cider into their hands. She drinks, and nearly spits, for her first taste of alcohol is not, as she had expected, like a particularly nice form of apple juice, but sour and bitter at the same time. Kiran laughs at the expression on her face. 'You'll get to like it,' he assures her, and she takes another sip. Without the element of surprise it's closer to palatable, but she can't imagine she will ever grow to like it. But hey – you can pretend to like *anything*.

Ursola approaches, smiling, her strange boxy camera in her hand. 'You two,' she says. 'Solstice photos.'

The girls straighten up, feel strangely self-conscious. Photographs aren't part of their lives. Kiran makes to step back, but Eilidh holds his arm. 'Can we have Kiran too?' she asks.

'Really?' asks Ursola. 'You don't want your very own?'

Eilidh shakes her head. Smiles her sweet smile. 'I don't,' she says. 'I want it to be the three of us. It'll always be the three of us.'

'Well, if you're sure ...' says Ursola. 'Is that all right with you, Romy?'

'Yes,' says Romy, and crowds in the other side of Kiran. Feels warm and loved, and part of something.

'Smile,' says Ursola. 'Say cheese.'

This is a splendid party. Trestle tables piled high with dried fruit, the pork and mutton they reaped in honour of the occasion earlier in the week, great heaps of flatbreads. No holding back tonight. The Leaders have locked themselves away and the people are free to cut loose. A tradition. Freedom, for one night and one day, two nights a year. The courtyard is strung with paper lanterns, candles burning in Mason jars, two great bonfires blasting out heat. By the makeshift dance floor the drums are starting up, a steady, heady rhythm that makes her want to sway her hips, throw her hands in the air. Women, in dresses, heads wrapped in garlands and cloth turbans in place of hair, are already straying into the open space, still in groups, starting to dance, throwing back their heads and laughing. She feels at once shy and arrogant: uncertain of how one approaches these people in this mood. An electric anticipation hangs in the air that she's never felt before.

'This is going to be a good one,' says Kiran, with all the knowledge of three solstices under his belt.

It's four o'clock and dusk is drawing in.

The Guards are there. Not in uniform, but still clumped together, keeping apart from the rest of the Drones. Another tribe within their tribe. They lounge on straw bales like watchful cats, the three women as uneasy in their dresses as she is in her own. They don't talk, she thinks. The men and the women. Not with us, but also not much amongst themselves. Several of the men are smoking, a habit she's heard of but never seen.

Off the leash like the rest of us, she thinks, and takes another drink. Her cheeks are oddly flushed and the drumbeats, which sounded so outlandish when she was a child, are making her want to dance. And then Dom turns his head and stares at her. His eyes narrow and his lips move. He's saying something about her. Just a couple of words, but it is enough to make all of them turn to follow his gaze. The men, the women: still as statues and staring, as one being.

She blushes and turns hurriedly away to look at her friends. The way they look, she thinks. I don't like it. It was as though they were sizing me up.

Midnight, and Romy is drunk. Smeared with pork juice and sugar, ripe with sweat. The Guards still stand by the barrels, watching, eyes narrowed, exchanging comments from the corners of their mouths, and Romy is on the dance floor, shaking her body. This is something different. Something primal. There is no music. Just drumming, drumming, drumming: the men queuing up to take over as others tire, the firelight licking the

244

walls and making their shadows huge across the ground. I understand the dress now, she thinks. The freedom of her unclothed body beneath feels louche, delicious.

She throws her hands in the air and jerks her hips, side, side, forward, back, and then, from the crowd, Kiran is there with her, dancing in her rhythm, his feet moving to match hers as though they are one person. There's a sheen of sweat on his face and in the firelight his cheekbones are so pronounced they throw shadows. And her hips fall into line with his hips and they raise their arms together in the air, no touching, no speaking, just looking, and she is filled, suddenly, with a rush of lust that terrifies her.

And then Eilidh has her by the hand and she's sliding off through the gyrating bodies, and she's laughing with relief. My God, look at us. We're adults at last! Us, from the Pigshed, dancing as though the world will not end!

'This is amazing!' cries Eilidh.

'Isn't it?' cries Romy, and pushes away the disturbing thoughts. Throws her arms round Eilidh because she needs something physical, a touch from someone, *anyone* but him. I must not think of it, she thinks. It's forbidden, and besides, it's *Kiran*.

She can smell alcohol on Eilidh's breath, realises that she's far drunker than Romy is herself. She wobbles on unsteady legs as Romy holds her and nearly takes them both over. Staggers back and pushes her slipping garland back onto her head. Laughs like a child and turns to Rohan, starts once again to dance.

On, and on. The drums thunder into the darkness and bodies move closer and closer. How do they keep it up? she wonders. Now she's stopped, she doesn't want to go back. She wanders over to the food, slaps a chunk of pork into a flatbread and eats. The meat is cold and greasy and the bread is turning stale, but she is ravenously hungry. It's two in the morning. A few more hours until dawn begins to creep over the horizon and the solstice is over.

On the dance floor, a hand reaches out and touches a buttock, is slapped away. A woman sways, sandwiched between two men, and suddenly Romy feels uncomfortable. She looks around and sees the adults, smeared and bleary, and senses that the atmosphere has turned. Men are grouping together, standing on the edge of the dance floor, watching. Licking their lips.

She turns to the nearest person, who turns out to be one of the Guards. 'I could do with a nap,' she announces.

'Fucksake,' says Dom. 'No stamina.'

'She's stocious,' says Phil.

'Not as stocious as that one,' says Ace, and points at the dance floor. In her own little space, as though the crowd has parted to make room for her, Eilidh sways in her sweat-stained dress, small breasts proud under the flimsy cloth, her crown long since gone. She gazes up at the cold sky, though the stars are obliterated by the glow of the firelight.

'Come for a walk,' says Dom. 'You're overheated. It's cooler in the orchard.'

'No,' says Romy. 'I want to go to bed.'

'I'll bet you do,' he says.

Suddenly, the three girl Guards, Ash and Fitz and Willow, are standing beside her. 'Come on,' says Fitz to Willow. 'I'm done. Let's get 143 home before she keels over.'

'Hold on,' says Dom. 'I'm coming with.'

'Not a fucking chance,' says Ash.

'I don't want to go yet,' Romy protests. The drums are still thundering and she feels she shouldn't leave until they stop, though she longs for sleep. She staggers slightly, bumps into the table, sends a clatter of empty tankards crashing to the ground.

Fitz's strong arms, hauling her upright. 'Oop,' she says. 'That's enough for tonight. You young 'uns.'

'You're only twenty-two,' says Romy.

'A world of difference,' says Fitz.

On the dance floor, Eilidh suddenly clamps a hand over her mouth. Too late. People jump backwards as cider and fruit and not much bread burst out over her feet, over the gravel around her. Romy laughs, goes to point it out to Dom, but finds that he is no longer there beside her. 'Hunh,' she says, and staggers again. Ash slams her drink down on the table and grabs her other arm. 'Right,' she says, 'we're out of here.'

Romy lets herself be led away. She is very tired, and longs for her bed. And then her mother, and Cara, the Cook who shares her dormitory, loom out of the gloom and reach for her arms. 'We'll take it from here,' says Somer to Willow, and Romy is surprised to find that she is glaring.

'We were just—' says Willow.

'I know,' says Somer, 'thank you,' and they take the weight from her legs of jelly and walk her home.

She glances back as they reach the field gate and catches sight of Eilidh, running unsteadily towards the alleyway that leads to the chapel, her hands clamped over her mouth again.

A few seconds later, several Guards slip quietly into the dark behind her, for all the world like a pack of wolves on the scent of prey.

34 | Somer

February 2014

And then there is no more Eilidh.

She vanishes one day, just like that. Vita goes to Glastonbury that morning to sort out a crisis that has arisen there, and Lucien is locked in his quarters, meditating, so only Uri is in charge. Ursola, coming down to check on her when she fails to show in the Infirmary for her shift, finds her bed made, her box beneath it and all her clothes still hanging at the end of her bunk, only her medallion gone, and after a few hours of calling and searching they give up and stop speaking of her, take over her tasks as though she had never been. And Somer finds Romy crying silently behind the godowns for her lost friend, but you never talk of the ones who've gone, so she just gives her a consoling pat and moves on with her duties.

They don't see Vita for another week. On the seventh day, as Somer and Ursola are sharing a jar of peppermint tea in

248

the corner of the orchard – how well she is beginning to be reaccepted, since she became a Leader – Somer hears the Guards' radio network crackle, and moments later Uri strides across the orchard towards the road gate with thunder on his face. He stands in the middle of the drive, folds his arms and waits.

Vita crests the hill in the car, sees him in her way and pulls up. Gets out, and the shouting begins.

They don't need to eavesdrop. They're near enough, and invisible enough, and, even if Uri and Vita have noticed that they're there, it seems that their emotions are running so high that they don't care. Ursola sits rigid beside her, slows her breath. Perhaps they *want* this to play out in front of witnesses. For the rumour of discord to sweep the compound. It must be in someone's interest, though whose is anybody's guess.

'Where is she?' he asks.

'Gone,' Vita replies.

'Gone where?'

'Gone. I took her out of here. I'm not having it.'

'Not having what?' he sneers.

'You know. Jesus, Uri. You think I'm blind? Even your father ...'

A laugh from Uri. Not a nice one. 'Well, aren't *you* the clever one?'

'That poor girl. Jesus. Can't you keep them under control?'

He laughs again. 'Who says I want to?'

'They're not ... toys. They're not bloody treats for your robots. And Jesus, Uri, she's your *sister*.'

'Half-sister.'

She shakes her head as if in disbelief. 'I don't believe you. What the hell has happened to you?'

He folds his arms again. Doesn't answer. Then: 'He's furious, you know.'

'I doubt he's even noticed.'

'I don't suppose he would have,' he says, 'if I hadn't told him.'

Now she folds her arms, too. 'Oh, you are the funny one. I suppose you think that's going to undermine me.'

'Well, I'll enjoy watching you explain.'

'It won't take much explaining, Uri. If their Father can't keep them safe, their Mother will have to. Simple as that. And you know what? He'll accept that, because I've been running this place for years.'

'Bullshit,' he says.

'Oh, come on,' she says. 'Who do you think's been keeping this place going? Your father?'

Somer realises that Ursola is looking at her. Turns and sees that her face is tense. She's as uncomfortable as I am, she thinks. I've never seen Vita this passionate before. She's the calm at the centre of our world. The eye of the storm. What's *happening*?

'Well, if you think *you're* in charge, you're even more deluded than I thought,' he says. 'It's *me*, Vita. He's just been waiting for me to get old enough and strong enough. You're nothing. You're a ... a ... placeholder. If you were in charge they'd all be dead on day three.'

'Wow,' she says, 'you really think that highly of yourself?'

'Just ask him,' he says. 'You just ask him.'

'Oh, kiddo,' she says. 'How old are you? Thirty-five? And you still haven't worked out that your father will say anything as long as it makes people like him? Are you ever going to grow the hell up and figure out how things really work around here?'

She starts back towards the car.

'Things are going to change,' she tells him. 'Your little personality cult has got way out of hand. This is the final straw, Uri, I'm telling you. It was bad enough when it was just you exerting your *droit de seigneur*. You can't have a whole pack of them created in your image.'

To Somer's surprise, Uri responds with a laugh. 'Just extending the privilege,' he says.

Vita stops, a hand on the door handle, and looks up. 'What's that meant to mean?'

'Like you haven't been his personal procurer for years. Why, Vita? You need to ask yourself that. Are you really so scared of him leaving you that you have to pimp for him?'

'Don't be ridiculous.'

He folds his arms again, waggles his shoulders.

'There were plenty of women,' she says, 'who were ready to mother the One.'

Somer feels sick. I don't want to hear this, she thinks. I don't. I don't want to hear it.

An explosion of mocking laughter rings out across the orchard. 'Yeah,' he says. 'That really was a stroke of genius, my love. It's been such a sacrifice for him, making all those babies.'

Vita slams the car door. Marches back across the sward. 'You know what, Uri? You're way too confident. Way. This place wasn't founded on tyranny and it won't survive on it. You can rule people with fear for a while, but you can't rule that way forever.'

'Oh, you stupid old woman,' he says. 'You stupid old woman. You're a fucking relic.'

'Well at least I'm not a fucking *rapist*,' she snaps. Gets back into the car and slams the door.

Somer doesn't speak until Uri has marched away towards the Guard House. 'So Eilidh's gone, then,' she says.

Ursola nods. 'Yes.'

'Another victim of solstice?'

Another nod. Somer feels a stab of anger. No one smuggled *me* out, she thinks. No one showed me anything but scorn.

'Somer?'

She turns to look at Vita's deputy. 'Yes?'

'I think something's coming,' says Ursola. 'I think this place is changing and it's going to get worse.'

Somer considers what to say. Words like this from someone so deeply embedded in the higher ranks of the Ark are two things at once. Flattering, to be taken into confidence after all these years. And frightening. For all she knows, this could be a test.

'We're all here by Father's grace,' she replies eventually. 'Uri as well.'

And one day Father will no longer be here, she thinks as she drinks her tea. And someone else will lead. And he said it himself, over and over again. There can only be One. Not two.

Among the Dead

November 2016

35 | Sarah

The Year Tens are holding an anti-bigotry demo on the lawn outside the science labs. They have wrapped their faces in scarves and pulled slogan T-shirts over their uniform jumpers, and are punching power fists into the air beneath banners on sticks that read JC4PM, FUCK THE TORYS, PUNCH A TERF TODAY and TRUMP OUT. In front, a gaggle of Year Sixes play some complicated skipping game without ever glancing in their direction. The rest of the school is looking at its mobile phone.

'Ah,' says Helen, 'schoolyard politics. Always one execution away from utopia. They'll tire of Magic Grandad eventually.'

'I do wish they'd learn to spell "Tories", though,' says Sarah.

'Or go and look "bigotry" up in the dictionary,' says Helen. 'And since when has "feminist" been an insult?'

'Well, it always was in some quarters,' says Sarah. 'Just not among progressives.'

'Ack, "progressives",' says Helen. 'Another word that knots my knitting.'

'D'you think we should break it up?'

'On what grounds?'

'Swearing? Inciting violence?'

'Mm,' says Helen. 'I suspect the fact that no one's paying the slightest attention might undermine our argument. How's home?' she asks. 'The kids tell me the half-sister has come to stay?'

Sarah grins. 'Yes. I went to talk to her and ended up bringing her home. Did they tell you she's pregnant?'

'No!' Helen leans in, fascinated. I suppose *she* can pump *me* for info, thinks Sarah. Just a shame I'm not allowed to do it the other way round, now my children are her clients.

'Yes. And she wasn't . . .' Some instinct makes her pull back from mentioning the injuries. 'She wasn't coping all that well. I thought I should. She was ill. I couldn't not, really.'

'Just mind you don't turn into one of those people who collects rescue dogs.'

'Oh, no,' she says, 'it's not like that. She had . . . flu. She was totally in a state of collapse. She's much better now. She's been in bed all weekend but she's completely *compos mentis*.'

'Good. And how long's she staying?'

'A few more days, I guess. It's good having her. She's only been properly with us since yesterday lunchtime, but she's really brought Ilo out of himself already.'

'And Eden?'

'Not so much. But I think I'm starting to understand the dynamic now. Romy's already told me a lot I didn't know. Those two have spent much more time together. Eden is a . . . I suppose what you'd call an aristocrat. You know: Brahmin class, because of her father. I hadn't really taken that on board. It does explain quite a lot. I think she'll need more time, is all. It must be hard if you've been special, getting used to being ordinary.'

'Yes,' says Helen. 'Well, it'll be a while before either of them attains ordinary, I should think.'

Sarah spots Eden, on a bench with her back to the netball courts, reading a book. Reading a book: a surefire way to put a target on your chest in the world of school playgrounds. Ilo must not have emerged from the lunch hall yet, or he would be sitting with her.

'They shouldn't be covering their faces, though, should they?' Sarah asks.

Helen looks at the protestors. 'Pfft, better here than in Trafalgar Square. Besides, I can tell who they are at a glance, can't you?'

A littlie trips on the skipping rope and falls to the ground. They both stand and watch, sip their coffee, wait to see if there will be wailing. There isn't. She scrambles up, brushes down her hands and knees and goes to take her turn at turning. 'Phew,' says Helen. 'Wouldn't want to have to *do* anything on lunch duty, would we?'

Over by the art block, next to Year Eight's chickenwire cart-horse, Marie is sitting on a bench examining her fingernails. She does that a lot, though uniform rules prevent her from having more than a French manicure. Mika and Lindsay and Ben McArdle (there are some people whose surname just naturally falls from your mouth whenever you mention them) form an indie band around her, lounging and sprawling and emanating disdain for the whole world.

They're looking at Eden. Mika nudges Ben and says something, and they both laugh. Sarah suppresses an 'ugh'. 'I wish that lot would just can it, though,' she says, tipping her chin in their direction.

'Oh, they're just kids,' says Helen. 'They're not exactly gangsters, are they?'

257

Sarah shrugs. No, she's right. None of Marie's crew is going to be bringing a gun into school or flogging crack or raping their classmates. They're just ordinary overindulged brats of the provincial suburbs, sneering at their peers for lack of anything else to do. She shouldn't mind them so much. Marie Spence dissing your trainers is hardly going to count in Eden's world when you think about all the other things she's seen.

Ilo comes out of the main doors, looks around. Looking for Eden, she thinks. But no. He sees his sister, nods, and sets out across the tarmac towards Marie.

Sarah feels herself tense. Ben gets up from his perch on the back of the bench and the three girls straighten up, watch him approach with their ankles pressed primly together.

He looks so small, she thinks. I will not go over there. It's not my business.

Ilo stops in front of Marie. His stance is relaxed; his hands hang by his sides. He says something, points at what looks from this angle uncomfortably like her bosom. Marie sits back and fingers her necklace. Smirks and shakes her head.

He speaks again. Ben takes a step forward. Ilo looks at him calmly, then his hand strikes, like a cobra, on Marie's collarbone, and he's wrenching and she's struggling and the two girls are shouting, and then whatever it is he's pulling at snaps suddenly loose, and his hand flies sharply into the air and instantly Marie is screaming and blood is spouting from her nose.

Shouts ring out as Helen and Sarah start to run – 'You hit me! You hit me! Oh, my God, you've broken my nose!' – and Ilo is stepping back with the necklace clutched in his fist and Ben is jumping onto his back. And then Ben is flying through the air like a marionette and everyone within twenty feet has started screaming.

258

Ilo looks as calm now as he did a minute ago. He turns and walks across the playground to where Eden sits, and holds out his fist. Drops the necklace into her outstretched palm.

She smiles at him and puts it in her pocket.

'This is *outrageous*!'

Sarah's voice is high-pitched and wobbling. Not the powerful voice it needs to be: it's the voice of the professional victim. Shit, she thinks. I never *did* learn to assert myself, did I? 'It was *her* who started it. It was *her fault*. She's been bullying my kids, she and her . . .' she looks around them all, hates them all '. . . little *friends*. Why aren't you disciplining *them*?'

The principal's office is crowded. Marie and Ben sit in two chairs in front of the desk, Eden and Ilo in two more, separated by three feet as though to put them closer would be to invite another outbreak of violence. Lindsay and Mika stand over by the window, all aggrieved expressions and tearful sniffs, though nothing has happened to them at all. Helen has been called in with her counsellor hat on and the three heads of year have been fetched from their classrooms. And Ray Spence and Sarah make thirteen.

Ray Spence has been shouting since he arrived eight minutes ago. '*Look* at her!' He points to his daughter. She is, it's true, a sorry sight. Her nose is swollen, one eye is black, and a chip has come off a front tooth where her face hit the bench when Ilo judo-flipped Ben. They're veneers anyway, thinks Sarah spitefully. It's not like it'll have *hurt*.

'I asked,' replies Ilo. He seems to be treating the whole thing as though it were an intellectual exercise. Does he even realise how much trouble he's in? 'But she refused to give it back. It's Eden's medallion. It's important.'

'Of course I was going to give it back,' sniffs Marie. 'You just didn't give me a chance.'

259

'How many times should I have asked, Marie?' he asks, and Sarah cringes. Stop being so *calm*, she thinks. You're coming across like a psychopath, Ilo, and I know you're not one.

'Bullshit!' shouts Ray Spence, and, although several adults cringe slightly at the word, no one reprimands him. Spence advances on Ilo, and the form teachers rush to get between them. 'Never. Ever. Hit. A. Woman!' he bellows over their shoulders, jabbing his finger repeatedly through the air in time with his words.

'I didn't hit anyone,' replies Ilo, still calm. 'My hand slipped when the medallion came loose, and I employed some basic self-defence techniques when Ben came at me. Anybody would have done it. If Marie had just given it back to me when I asked, none of—'

'Well, you're paying for the reconstructive surgery,' bellows Spence, and his face turns a shade of puce that perfectly matches the shirt beneath his shiny grey suit. Oh, great, Sarah thinks. Marie gets the nose job she's probably been agitating for since she was twelve, and we get to foot the bill. That man is everything I hate about the world of now: people who think that never backing down is a virtue.

'Well, I think it's unlikely to come to that,' says the principal. The school nurse has pronounced her bruised but whole, no need for A&E, except that she's definitely in need of a dentist.

Sarah clears her throat and speaks up, concentrates on dropping her voice, sounding authoritative. 'None of this would have happened if your daughter hadn't stolen my niece's necklace,' she says. 'And it's hardly the first thing she's done. She's a bloody menace. She got what was coming to her, frankly.'

Oh, God, that came out wrong. She needs to remember that this is her workplace.

'I don't think that's very helpful, Mrs Byrne,' says the

principal. No Sarahs now, not while the other parents are in the room.

'Well, he hit *me*,' Ben McArdle pipes up.

'I pushed you, Ben,' says Ilo. 'You were running at me and I stepped aside and just gave you a helping hand.'

'Are you hurt?' asks the principal.

Ben holds up his right hand, on which a large piece of gauze has been affixed to what looks like a small graze. 'I think it's sprained,' he says.

Oh, bugger off, thinks Sarah. Boo hoo. There's no one like a bully for claiming victimhood. She feels a powerful urge to scream. FUCKSAKE, she howls inside her head. But sense steps in and reminds her to be the better person.

'Mrs Byrne,' says the principal, 'the fact is that there was a violent incident between your wards and their schoolmates, and we can all see who has come to harm. We need to decide what action to take.'

'Me?' Eden comes out of her meditative trance and sits up. 'What did *I* do?'

'Come on, Eden. Your brother's younger than you. No doubt he thought he was doing the noble thing and protecting you, but you need to own responsibility too.'

'Own responsibility?' Sarah is outraged once again. 'I was watching the whole thing! She was reading a *book*! Literally on the other side of the playground! And what about *Marie*? None of this would have happened if she hadn't stolen her necklace!'

Ray Spence points at Eden. 'What, *that*? What would she want to nick that for? My daughter shops at Zara, not the Pound Shop.'

They crane to look. It does seem a tawdry thing: a strip of leather and a round of hammered iron. Hardly Marie's Swarovski style. 'It's not the value,' says Sarah. 'It's the principle.'

The principal, as if responding to her title, purses her lips. 'Right,' she says. 'I think I should probably talk to Mrs Byrne alone now. Mr Spence, are you okay to get Marie home, or do you want us to call you a taxi?'

Ray Spence whirls a key fob around his index finger. 'I've got the Jag,' he says.

Of course you do.

He turns to Sarah. 'Don't think you've heard the last of this,' he says.

'I don't doubt it,' she snaps.

36 | Sarah

A whole month. They're excluding him for a whole month. Right up till Christmas. What's she going to do? How will she watch him and work at the same time?

And some friend Helen is, sharing her reports on the kids with the principal, giving her the ammunition she needed to claim they weren't fitting in.

'But what were you thinking, Ilo?' she says. 'What were you *thinking*?'

'I'm sorry,' he says. 'I wasn't. Force of habit.'

I don't think he gets how serious this is. I don't think either of them does. They wouldn't be so calm otherwise. Look at me. Am I calm? Why won't they take a cue from me? 'Force of *habit*? Are you serious?' What on earth did they get up to at Plas Golau? Were they really that violent?

'I'm sorry, Sarah,' he says.

'But he got me my medallion back,' says Eden, as though this were the most important issue. Maybe it is, to her. She'd seemed so diminished without it. 'I'm safe now,' she says.

'Safe?'

'Nothing can touch me if I've got it on,' she says, and beams disconcertingly.

They all sit side by side on the sofa, Romy like a Buddha with her bump resting on her crossed calves, Ilo with back straight as though sitting to attention, palms flat on his thighs, Eden with one knee crossed over the other. Sarah is too agitated to sit. She stalks up and down on the other side of the coffee table, straightens the contents of the mantelpiece, plucks imaginary fluff from the curtains. 'You're just lucky,' she says, 'that the school managed to talk the father down. You could be getting a criminal record if they hadn't.'

Romy drops her feet to the floor. For someone with two black eyes, she looks remarkably surprised. 'Really? Violence is illegal?'

'No *shit*, Sherlock!' she snaps. 'Jesus.' She squeezes her eyes closed. 'So what other basic rules of a functioning society do you not know?' she says between gritted teeth, and immediately feels bad, because, well, it's hardly their fault. And then she opens her eyes and sees that Ilo's are filled with tears, and she wonders, just for a moment before she dismisses the thought, if she's being played.

She takes a deep breath.

'Sorry. That was unfair. Yes, it's illegal. I had no idea you didn't know. I thought it would just be so obvious.'

'But then how are we supposed to protect ourselves?' asks Eden.

'That's the point. In a civilised society we don't *need* to protect ourselves.'

They look sceptical.

I should've helped them, should never have let them get to this stage. I should've gone over their heads and reported it and followed the proper protocols. Why didn't I? Because I kept hoping

264

it would blow over and Marie would move on. Because nobody did a blind thing when Abi Knowles was doing the same things to me, poking me in the back with her compass from the desk behind, tripping me up in the corridors, pouring milk into my bag so it smelled of vomit for the whole of the rest of my time here, so more than a bit of me assumed that no one would do anything for them, either.

'And when the Great Disaster happens?' Eden asks. 'What then? We have no idea when it's going to start. It's not *scheduled*. We can't just not be prepared.'

Something in her snaps. 'Oh, for Christ's sake! Stop it. Just *stop* it. There's not going to *be* a Great Disaster. It's nuts. It's just stupid talk. Stop it!'

Their expressions change and she knows at once that she's made a grave mistake. Their mouths snap shut and their chins jerk up, and she sees without question the bloodline that runs from them to her parents. Damn it, she thinks, oh, God *damn* it, I of all people should know better than to get into one with people about their dearly held convictions. It never changes anything, direct confrontation. If anything, it makes them worse, when they feel they're under attack. Always that same look, doesn't matter what the belief. Scientologists, communists, fascists, Jehovahs, Buddhists, Islamists, Justin Bieber fans. Always the same: that moment when their eyes go blank and they hang like a computer. In two seconds they'll reboot and start firing out learned-by-rote challenges and unanswerable questions, gaslighting me till I'm too tired to argue any more. You can't convert a true believer. All you do by trying is entrench their position for them. It's Cult 101: cognitive dissonance strengthens loyalty, it doesn't weaken it. I've just sabotaged weeks and weeks of being patient, of letting them work it out for themselves.

'Why do you think that, Aunt Sarah?' asks Eden.

'It's not as though the world hasn't ended before,' says Ilo. 'It's a living system in a living universe.'

'We're a long way from being the first dominant species,' says Eden. 'What makes you think we'd be the last?'

'The world's nearly ended a dozen times in the past century alone,' says Romy. 'Why would you think that's over?'

Sarah is well practised in the arts of deflection and distraction. You don't live through adolescence in an evangelical household without saying or doing something wrong at least once a day, even if you *aren't* a rebel or a fighter. This recitation could go on all night if she doesn't divert their attention, and she, with her lack of dedicated zeal, will get tired long before they do.

'Okay,' she says, 'well, I'll tell you what, I'm not going to discuss it with you any more tonight. You can go to bed, both of you. And understand that you're in disgrace, okay?'

Their jaws snap shut. 'Okay,' says Eden.

'Sorry, Aunt Sarah,' says Ilo.

A disastrous day. She'd thought she was getting a handle on this new life, but all she's been doing is fooling herself.

She makes herself, despite her upset, give them a kiss and a hug goodnight. Tells them that it will all be okay, that they'll find a solution, though she very much doubts that what she's saying is true. Then she makes herself a gin and tonic, takes the blanket from the lounge sofa and goes out to sit at the garden table in the cold to smoke her evening cigarette. It might have to be two, tonight.

Now she's calmed down a bit, she's grateful to the principal for keeping it under wraps. But still, here Ilo is, out of the educational system for the time being, and no doubt there are bureaucrats about to open the case files and start asking how she plans to look after her disgraced minor ward while she's at work.

266

They really believe it. How could I have been so stupid as to not understand that, just because the people in charge of their cult turned out to be spectacularly psychotic? You see it all the time: people moving the goalposts so their principles can remain intact. *Well, the Border Wall was only ever metaphorical. Yes, I know Stalin killed twenty million people, but see, that wasn't proper socialism. I'm not antisemitic: the Zionists have it in for Jeremy. Yes, Lucien Blake's cult killed all its members, but that doesn't mean he was wrong about the Apocalypse.* She feels more alone, more at sea, than she has since the months after Liam left. She doesn't even know where to start. Searches her memory for clues to how she broke her attachment to the Congregation. She knows it wasn't a sudden thing. Vividly remembers thinking until she was at least Eden's age that Alison had deserved her exile. She was at university before it occurred to her that the idea that Jesus would elect to live in Finbrough was frankly bonkers.

She hears the French doors open and looks over her shoulder. It's Romy, still dressed, and wrapped in a shawl against the early winter cold.

'Hello,' she says. 'Can I join you?'

'Of course.' She makes a lacklustre gesture towards one of the cold metal bistro chairs. 'I'm sorry. Did I disturb you?'

She sits down. 'No, of course not. And besides, it's your house.'

Doesn't feel like it, she thinks. Never has.

'I just smelled a cigarette and thought I'd come down.'

Sarah looks at her fag. 'Really? You smelled it?'

'I've been keeping my bedroom window open. It's so nice to be able to. Can I try one? I've never smoked before.'

'Are you sure?'

'Why? Is it instantly addictive?'

'No—' Sarah nods at her stomach. 'I was thinking about the baby, more.'

'Oh. Is it bad for her?'

'Yes, it is. So it's a her, is it?'

'No idea,' she says. 'Figure of speech.'

'Anyway, yes. I'm surprised nobody's told you. Which reminds me. If you need, you know – if you need to go to a check-up or anything, you'll let me know, won't you? Unless you're ready to go home, of course. Sorry. Assumptions.'

A tiny little pause. Then: 'No, it's okay. I'm not due anything. Aunt Sarah, can I ask you how you're feeling? I don't think anybody's done that.'

A lump forms in Sarah's throat. 'No. Thank you. I'm okay. Well, I'm upset, if I'm going to be honest. And worried.'

'We should always be honest,' says Romy.

'Yes. Yes, you're right, of course. Okay, yes, I'm upset. I don't understand how Ilo could have been so reckless. I'm afraid I don't know how to communicate with them. I'm scared I've made a dreadful mistake.'

Romy's expression is inscrutable. Sarah starts to lose confidence. 'I mean – I don't mean for a minute that I'm thinking . . . you know. But what on earth am I going to do now? I can't leave a thirteen-year-old home by himself all day. I don't suppose it's even *legal* for me to leave him home all day. It's less than three weeks till the Christmas holidays, and I already used unpaid leave getting them settled in . . .'

The words come at such a pace that she runs out of breath. Romy just sits quietly and listens, her eyes meeting Sarah's all the while she's speaking.

'Would you like me to stay? At least till you find a better solution?'

Relief floods through her. The thought hadn't even occurred to her.

'Would you?'

Romy nods. 'Of course.'

Sarah puts her face in her hands. She finds herself filled with love for her niece. 'God, that would be amazing,' she says.

Romy shrugs. 'Don't be silly. You've been so kind, helping me. I don't know how well I'd have done, by myself in that flat.'

'No,' she says. 'It worries me, you being all alone in your ... state.'

'I'm only pregnant. Not dying.'

'I know, but still.'

'If you want me,' says Romy, and looks unutterably sad for a moment, 'that would be wonderful.'

It's a solution for all of us, Sarah thinks. At least for now. And next year? Maybe I need to learn to worry less, to take one day at a time a bit more. Maybe it'll be better in the long run if he and Eden aren't spending every waking moment together.

'Honestly, stay as long as you want,' she tells her. What's one more on top of all the new souls Gethsemane Villa has taken on this year? All of them, chasing out the ghosts. Some kind of strange family.

'I'll try to be helpful,' Romy says. 'All I want is to make sure everyone's safe. And that you're okay, Aunt Sarah. I want you to be okay too.'

Sarah stubs her cigarette out on the leg of her parents' green metal table. 'Thank you, Romy,' she says. 'I can't tell you how grateful I am.'

37 | Romy

'Are we going to drill?' he asks, once Eden and Sarah leave for the day.

'We can,' I say, 'but it's not going to be the same. I don't think I'll be high-kicking again for a good six months.'

'That's okay,' he says. 'You can still do squats and stuff.'

'I can't run.'

'Not at all?'

'I did, a couple of weeks ago. I thought my stomach was literally going to bounce off.'

'You've got soft.'

I poke his midriff and it gives under my fingers. 'You don't have an excuse, like me,' I tell him.

'Romy?'

'Yes?'

'Is she still angry?'

'I don't think she ever was, honestly.'

'I sometimes get the feeling she *is* angry.'

'Not about you, Ilo.'

270

'What about?'

'Her life. Our grandparents. Her husband. Marie Spence.'

'Her husband? I didn't even know she had one.'

'Ilo, you need to start asking questions.'

'I thought it was rude, to ask questions.'

'Who told you that?'

'In the home.'

'Oh. That's different.'

'Different how?'

'If you want Cairngorm, Ilo, you need to make friends with Sarah. I told you.'

'Friends?'

'Yes.'

He thinks for a long time. 'How do you make friends?'

'You ask questions, and you listen to the answers.'

'Oh. How do you know that?'

'I had a friend called Spencer in Weston,' I tell him. 'He told me.'

'Spencer? What happened to him?'

'He fell off the wagon.'

'Ouch. Badly? Was he hurt?'

'He died,' I say, and I feel a bit sad. I kick Ilo's feet out from under him.

On the grass of our grandparents' lawn, he lands with an 'oof', raises himself up on his elbows and looks at me with his piercing eyes. 'But Aunt Sarah … she's never going to just hand me over.'

I give him a hand up and all the stretched muscles in my abdomen pull so hard I have to stay bent and clap my hands to my sides until the cramps pass. 'That's up to you,' I say. 'She can come too, but that's up to you.'

'And how can we take Eden to Cairngorm?' he asks. 'We can't just leave her here all by herself. She'd never survive.'

271

'Don't worry,' I say, and I massage my intercostals. 'She'll be safe. But we have things to do first.'

'It's in here,' Ilo says, and lifts the garage door.

'Oh, my,' I say.

It's a boxy car, all corners and straight lines. Dark blue, tweed seats. Not a scrap of damage or rust, though it must have been sitting here unused for two years and it's clearly a lot older than Aunt Sarah's silver runabout with the scratch on the wing mirror and the dent in the door. Much older. But it's a car, and a car is what I need, if Uri wants me to go around the country at his behest.

'Don't you think she'll notice?'

'I've not seen her come in here since we arrived. Not once.'

'But she'll notice when we come in and out.'

'Not if we do it when she's at work. We can park it round the corner if we don't know if she's there or not.'

Sounds reasonable.

I take the key. The lock is slightly stiff and the door creaks as it opens. I settle into the driver's seat. My grandfather was clearly taller than I am. I have to stretch to reach the pedals. I put my key in the ignition and turn it. Nothing happens.

'It's dead.'

'What sort of dead?'

'You heard it. Dead dead.' I knew my luck wouldn't last. It would just be too damn simple.

'Mmmm.' He ducks in around my knees again and pulls a lever that pops the bonnet. I might have known he'd know how to do these things. He was always engine-mad, hanging around the Farmers in the hope of getting a drive of the tractor, hanging around the Engineers doing things with fulcrums. 'Hold on.'

While he's out of sight I check my reflection in the mirror. My nose has shrunk back down to its normal size, which is good. I'll be attracting less attention in the suburbs, anyway. I've still got the black eyes, but there's less blood in them now. I'm getting old. I used to heal from a bruise in no time.

'Try again,' he calls.

I turn the key and the engine springs to life. He slams the bonnet and gets in beside me, grinning with self-congratulation. 'Someone unplugged the battery,' he says. 'They do that sometimes, if a car's going to be sitting a while.'

'Told you I needed you,' I tell him.

He grins. 'Some of us paid attention when we did the Engineer apprenticeship.'

'Whatever,' I say. He wouldn't know wolfsbane from hogwort if you shoved them under his nose.

We are in the car turning the engine over to build up the battery when Uri calls. 'Where are you now?' he asks.

'Finbrough,' I say.

'Oh, right,' he says. 'Closer, then. Jaivyn is in Bristol, you'll be glad to hear.'

Bristol. I remember that. That jumble of houses, warehouses, blocks of flats that went for miles below the motorway with the glittering sea beyond.

'How do you know?'

'Same way I knew you were in Hounslow,' he replies. 'He's started using his card. I guess he must be running low on other sources. Or maybe he thinks that now Vita's dead it's just free money sitting around. He's taken £300 out every day this week. So he's either eating off gold plates and bathing in asses' milk or he's saving up to make a run for it. You'd better get down there sooner rather than later.'

I look at my little brother, and nod at him. His mouth drops open, just a little bit.

'Bristol's a bit of a vague destination,' I say. 'I went past it once. It's huge.'

'The Old Red Lion, Strickland Road, St Paul's,' he says.

'What, now?'

'It's a pub. He's been withdrawing cash in a pub. Been using ATMs all over the place, but he gets a couple of hundred out there a couple of times a week, too. Either that or he's drinking enough to do your job for you.'

'Okay,' I say. 'What do you want me to do? Hang around the pub till he turns up?'

'Yes,' he says.

Yes, that'll work. A pregnant woman with a faceful of cuts and bruises will never attract attention in a pub. My lower lip is still so swollen it sticks a full half-inch out from my face.

'I'll see what I can do,' I say.

'Don't see about it,' he says, 'do it.'

38 | Romy

I've never forgiven Jaivyn for the day Eden was born. You don't see that level of contempt on someone's face and forget it easily. I guess he must have been twelve, almost Ilo's age now, when that happened. The beginning of adolescent arrogance, the last throes of infant narcissism, exacerbated by the ego boost of knowing you're special. But still.

He'll still be bigger and stronger than me now. He was one of the tallest of us, over six foot by the time he hit his majority.

But I guess I'll have the element of surprise.

After he ran, things got worse for us. Lucien was furious. They were all furious, and we all kept our heads low and hoped that we would not be the next to be punished. That was the end of outreach. The gates were closed and nobody left, apart from Vita or Uri, unless they were accompanied. A dozen people got demoted to farm work and half a dozen more were shunned for months. He didn't believe that none of them had known what Jaivyn was planning. I wondered why someone would have helped him plan his bunk and not gone too, but Lucien said traitors were everywhere. 'I can no longer trust you,' he said that Friday. 'From now on, none of you are to be trusted.'

And, when the punishments were done, we never spoke of him again.

Jaivyn could never be the One. He could never be a Leader. If anybody had been going to run, it was him. Always the first to the food, always the wildest at solstice, always looking at the girls as though they were his houris, always arguing back when someone gave him an order. If he were the One, we'd all die off in a couple of years. Discipline. You need discipline, if you're going to survive.

So funny: by the time Eilidh went, Lucien barely even seemed to notice. I guess he'd got used to losing children by then. By the time Lucien died, he only had six children left. Now there are only four.

Strickland Road is a grim little road where blankets hang in windows and rusted cars line the gutters. A few trees try bravely to lift the mood, but even they are grey with dust, stunted in their little paving-slab beds. I looked St Paul's up on the internet and it said that the area was gentrifying, but there's little sign that the gentrification has reached as far as here. The Old Red Lion is small, and the old brass plating on its windowsills looks sticky, even from a distance. Three men, different colours, different ages, same tracksuits, stand around a huge cylindrical ashtray. Each has one hand in a trouser pocket, fondling his balls, and the other cupped around a cigarette as though trying to hide the glow of the cinder from a sniper. One of them speaks to the air; the others just stare vacantly at the wall beside them.

I park. It's already four o'clock and dusk is beginning to make itself known. Sarah thinks we've gone to Hounslow to collect the rest of my gear and that we're staying for a couple of days. She trusts me already.

'You can do your maths while you wait,' I tell Ilo. 'Okay?'

He rolls his eyes.

'No, seriously, Ilo. You need to keep up your school work.'

'It's miles behind where I've got to,' he says. 'It's like they think I'm stupid or something.'

'You're in disgrace. I think they generally don't expect high academic standards in kids who fight in schoolyards.'

'Thanks,' he says. 'I only did it 'cause you told me to.'

'I know. I didn't actually tell you to punch anyone, though.'

'To be fair, you wouldn't have me now if I hadn't.'

'Just make sure that workbook's completed, okay?'

He nods and gets out his phone, sinks down in his seat and I go into the pub.

Will it be okay, leaving him out in a car by himself in this place? Of course it will. He's Ilo.

I've never been into a pub before. It was against the rules at the Halfway – drink, and that. But I've seen them on TV. The Old Red Lion is really barely recognisable as the same sort of establishment as the Queen Vic and the Rovers Return. For a start, both of those are clean.

I open the door to one of those rooms where the lamps sticking out of the walls actually seem to absorb the light. A long room that runs all the way to the back of the building, with a cramped bar on one side and a series of wood-walled booths on the other. A pool table, the lights hanging over it unlit, in a gloomy space by the stairs. So this is what pubs are like. You don't really pick up the sour-beer-and-damp thing from the television.

It's not very full. A handful of men stare at me silently from the bar. Two women sit in a booth. One has a black eye and one has no teeth. I should fit right in.

I walk to the bar and manage a smile for the man behind it. He's five and a half feet tall and not much less wide. Eyes me with little enthusiasm, but I get the feeling that that's just his normal greeting.

'Yes, love,' he says, and picks up a tea towel. Spreads the sticky patches across the surface of the bar with it.

'A G&T, please,' I say in my confident voice. People order those all the time in the Queen Vic.

He eyes my belly. 'Single or double?'

I think I'll see if I like it first. 'Single.'

'Ice and slice?'

Someone sniggers.

Must be a trick question. 'No, thanks,' I say.

He takes a glass and goes over to one of the bottles hanging upside down against a mirror. Pours a measure into the glass. Bugger, it's gin. That must be what the G stands for. 'Can I have a glass of water as well, please?' I ask.

He sighs as though I've insulted him in some subtle way, but pulls out a little hose from under the counter and squirts water into a second glass. Presses a button on the top, and whatever the T is – it's fizzy, I know that – goes in with the gin. He plonks them down on a towelling mat. 'Anything else?'

'Have you got any food?'

Another snigger. 'It's a pub, not a restaurant,' he says. 'I've got cheese and onion, salt and vinegar and dry roast.'

'Dry roast,' I say, because that sounds the most substantial. He reaches behind him and pulls a small pack of peanuts from a display. 'Not sure you're meant to eat those when you're pregnant,' he says. A bit of an afterthought in a man who's just sold me gin.

Oh. What a lot of rules. At Plas Golau the only rule of

278

pregnancy was 'don't make a fuss'. 'Well, maybe cheese and onion, then,' I say. He reaches beneath the counter and produces a bag of crisps.

For a moment I want to cry, because I know absolutely nothing and this exchange has just reminded me of that. Instead, I give him Uri's money and take my drinks over to an empty table.

They're all drunks. Dedicated, isolated drunks. Not completely at the bottom of the heap, because I don't suppose people at the bottom of the heap can pay for drinks in pubs. But you don't spend your days silently soaking up the booze in a place like this if you have many choices in life. The women don't speak; just sit together drinking the coloured liquids the men occasionally carry over to them, staring at their phones, staring at their chipped nail polish.

'You meeting someone, love?' calls the landlord across the room.

'No,' I tell him, because it's true. I'm not meeting Jaivyn, in any orthodox sense. 'Just got to wait somewhere for a bit.'

'Fair enough,' he says, and goes back to wiping the bar top.

I think they think I'm waiting to ambush the father of my child.

I text my brother. *U OK?*

Yes, he texts back. *S called. I said you were on the bog.*

I have trained him well.

Once night falls, which at this time of year is not far off four o'clock, the place starts to fill. The accomplished drinkers don't change, as though they're simply keeping going with their maintenance dose rather than looking to change their world. The people who start to trickle in drink faster, talk louder, eye the

279

table I'm taking up with greedy eyes. There's a circle of space around me, and, though they throw glances in my direction, they stand with their backs turned firmly to me.

And I'm about to give it up as a bad job for the night, go out and find the boy, when Jaivyn walks in, large as life and a lot uglier.

39 | Romy

Whatever he's been spending Uri's money on, it's not his appearance.

He doesn't see me. Well, he does see me, for he glances in my direction, but he looks straight through. In the six years since I've seen him, his blond scalp-stubble has grown out mousy brown and hangs down to his shoulders to mingle with a raggedy beard. An alky Jesus. Grey jeans wrinkle around his crotch and an oversized plaid shirt feebly struggles to disguise his bulk.

His eyes skim over me and he goes back to his dealings. He's bought a pint of yellow beer, and gulps from it between sentences with the open-gulleted greed of someone for whom it is more than simply a pleasure. He wipes his beard on the back of his hand, and droplets seep onto his shirt.

I drop my head and leave, before something about me can remind him who I am.

It's half-past eight and the street is dark and empty and ominous. The pub looks like an oasis of warmth and hospitality in comparison, the dim light spilling through its frosted windows showing up how few lights are on in buildings elsewhere. It's cold. Cold enough to make my breath cloud as I exhale. The air this close to the sea is damp and clings to the skin. I get into the car.

'He's there,' I say. 'He just came in.'

'I wondered if that was him,' he says. 'I was just about to text.'

'How did you recognise him?'

'I don't know,' he says. 'I just ... did.'

'Right, well, we're going to have to wait. Have you done your maths?'

'In about five minutes. And I've done my English and French, too, for the week. They don't expect much from you, do they?'

'I've no idea. Why are you learning French?'

He jumbles out a garble of meaningless consonants, and smirks as I stare at him. 'You should learn it too. Then we could talk to each other without anyone understanding.'

'I think quite a lot of people speak French, Ilo. I mean, how many were there in your class?'

'Oh.' He looks disappointed. Brightens up again. 'How about Arabic, then? That way we could even write each other notes.'

'Good thinking,' I say.

All the things that will be lost. The languages, the art, the music, the food. It didn't affect me so much when they were an abstract concept, but now I've seen more of the world the thought fills me with melancholy. We must follow Lucien and Vita's example, baby, and make sure as much as we can save is preserved. I don't suppose Uri is thinking about that side of things at all. A world led by Uri would be a bleak old world of drilling and killing.

I could totally go some jerk chicken right now. I'm starving. I do hope I'll taste that taste again before the world ends.

As if he hears my thoughts, Ilo announces that he's hungry. I tell him we have to wait. Sometimes the job comes first.

And we have an important job to do tonight.

They come, and go, and come and go. Mostly by themselves, sometimes in pairs. The Old Red Lion isn't somewhere you go *with* people, the way they show on the television. It's where people with no one go to be alone in company.

The same three men are still smoking around the ashtray. I'm not sure I've seen any of them go inside. The clock on the dashboard ticks on. 'What did Aunt Sarah say,' I ask, 'when you called?'

'She said we shouldn't be worrying too much about cleaning a place like that and what were we going to do about food?'

'And you said?'

'I said it would be fine, we'd go to the shops.'

'Good,' I say.

'She's a worrier.'

'Yes, but she has a lot of worries, I guess. And she's not used to them. She's not even used to living with people.'

'Okay,' he says.

'She needs to learn to trust you.'

'I'm not sure that's ever going to happen now. I think I might have blown my chances,' he says, mournfully.

'Well, you need to make it happen, Ilo. You'll never get anywhere if you don't.'

He sighs. 'Okay. How do I do that, then? I don't get the impression she even *likes* us much. She's very nice and everything, but it's all so ... polite.'

'What have you done to make her like you?'

'*Make* her?'

'Oh, Ilo.'

He's only thirteen, Romy. Keep remembering that. Think how you were at thirteen.

He looks up. 'Oh. Is that him, coming out?'

I look where he's looking. 'Christ. Yes.'

He walks, loose-limbed and smoking a cigarette, not looking around him at all, certain of his own wellbeing. God, of *course* he was never one of us. Not by talent nor habit. Lucien's or not, he was just careless, relying on everyone else to keep him safe, never really aware of the dangers we protected him from, a bit like Eden. I'll make sure you never let your guard down that way, baby. You're going to need every wit you have.

I turn on my engine, but don't turn on my lights. No point trying to follow on foot. He's a hundred yards ahead already and we'd have to run to catch him up, and even someone as drunk and complacent as Jaivyn would probably be alerted by the running footsteps of a pregnant peg-leg. I turn the car round and watch till I see which way he turns at the corner before switching on the lights. Then I follow and pass him, and he sends not a glance in our direction.

A couple of corners on, I pull into a space up ahead of him. Drop Ilo off and he melts into a doorway. Bleak façades of red brick, pools of dreary sulphurous light from wide-spaced street lamps. Every city has one, I guess. These places where the world has moved on and left nothing but rot in its wake. Where you can be surrounded by 615,000 people and still be completely alone.

One day the whole world will look like this.

Jaivyn walks past and turns the next corner. When I turn, I see that this street is empty, desolate, perfect. A dead end with only a narrow alleyway leading out at the other end. I drive up to the end, park. Get out of the car and hear his footsteps hesitate for a moment, then speed up again as I turn side-on to show him that all that's ahead is a slight and pregnant woman fiddling with a door lock. I walk towards him with my head bowed and my hood still up, and my hands buried deep in my pockets. My right hand clasps the handle of the filleting knife I took from Aunt Sarah's kitchen drawer, and my thumb caresses the back of the blade.

Men are meant to cross the road when they see a lone woman in the dark. Simple etiquette, really.

Sometimes, though, they should cross the road because not all lone women are potential victims.

Jaivyn just keeps coming. Too drunk, perhaps, to think of other people. Or maybe that domineering streak he showed at Plas Golau, the brushing past, the slamming of doors, the pulling by the hair, has turned, in the Outside, into a genuine pleasure in frightening women.

I stop ten feet from him and lower my hood.

He stops, too. Peers at me through the gloom. 'Do I know you?'

I raise my chin and look into his face. It takes him a moment, then 'Oh, it's you,' he says. Then, 'Why aren't you dead?'

And then he says 'Oh, you're pregnant,' and Ilo comes up silently behind him and his lovely blacksmith knife slides into Jaivyn's back as though it were made of cream cheese.

'Oh,' says Jaivyn.

There's a brief period, when someone is taken by surprise, when you are completely in control. It takes them anything up to five seconds to fight back. That's what my training was for. To cut out the what-do-I-dos and make use of every second. He's teetering and gawping, and I step forward and bury my own knife in his abdomen, slice down towards his groin, to make room for my fist to enter his body. Like gutting a pig. And then I bury my hand to the wrist in his pulsating viscera and turn the blade up to meet his heart. Not the best knife I've ever used, but it does the job.

'Oh,' he says again, a coil of gut slipping out through the hole in his trunk, and then he falls to the ground and my hand and knife slip, with a smooth sucking sound, back out into the air.

Ilo looks at me and his eyes have gone dark.

Jaivyn is dead already. I've opened up too much of him to ever put it back. A waterfall of blood cascades into the gutter and I step back, watch as he twitches, and wipe my blade on my left sleeve, for my right is already too bloodied to salvage this top.

Ilo takes the photos. His first kill. He deserves the honour. And besides, he already knows how to work his camera. Uri won't trust me enough to believe I've got the job done based on the medallion alone. I feel around inside Jaivyn's collar and my hand closes on a leather string. Even after all these years, even when he must long since have given up on being the One, he's still wearing it. I cut the string with my blade and slip it into my pocket. One down.

In the outskirts of Bristol, before we hit the motorway to Hounslow, Ilo spots the golden arches and bleaching halogen of a fast food restaurant and I pull in, because our hunger is as bad as it's ever been. They seem to be everywhere, these places. I park and go in in my clean clothes and buy four things called Big Macs, which we eat in the car park, leaning against the car, washed down with a bottle of water. They're bland yet highly flavoured, a strange mix of slimy, dry and crunchy, and I eat mine in three bites each.

'So how do I make her like me?' he asks.

I learned a lot from Lucien, shut up in that room with him, listening to him ramble.

'It's easy to make someone like you,' I tell him. 'You ask them about themselves. Like I told you before. Have you even asked her a single thing about herself yet?'

'Oh,' he says. 'I see. She's always asking us questions. I didn't realise that was what it was about.'

'Yes. And then the other thing you do, you listen carefully to the answer, and you ask more questions based on that, to show you're listening.'

'Okay,' he says.

'And you praise her,' I say. 'Tell her how great she is. Tell her when she says something smart or wise, let her feel appreciated.'

'Wow,' he says.

'I know,' I say. 'They love that shit.'

Before the End

2014

40 | Romy

She's nearly nineteen when Vita comes to her in the physic garden, where the foxgloves are going over and she's harvesting the seeds by tying paper bags over the flower heads.

'You lucky girl,' she says.

Romy nearly wipes her forehead with her glove, remembers in time and strips it off. She was cutting hemlock yesterday and the outer layer will still be soaked in sap. 'What?' she asks.

'He wants to see you.' Vita's a bit grim about the mouth, not her usual self.

'Who?' she starts to ask, and then she realises what she's saying and she's speechless. 'Me?'

'Yes. I thought he was done with all that, but it seems you've caught his eye.'

'Oh,' says Romy. She feels slightly sick. Lucien is her Father. It has never occurred to her to expect anything else.

'It's a great honour,' says Vita, but her expression doesn't match her words.

'Yes,' says Romy. 'Of course. I am honoured. I just ... I wasn't expecting ...'

'I can imagine,' says Vita. 'Well, there you are. Looks like you've drawn the long straw. But don't be boasting or telling people.'

'No,' says Romy.

There's a spiteful edge to her next words. 'And don't think this makes you special.'

Romy's face flushes. 'No,' she lies. 'Of course not.'

'Your mother thought it made her special,' says Vita, 'and look what that did for her.'

'I understand.'

'You're a vessel,' says Vita. 'That's all.'

'Yes,' says Romy.

'Right. Tomorrow, after lunch.'

She nods, her mouth dry. Not me, she thinks. I don't deserve this. I don't want it. But how do you refuse?

But there's an itch of excitement beneath her skin. Maybe I can save our family. Maybe if he's pleased with me, my mother will be forgiven. Maybe I will mother the One, and that is why I'm here. Why I've always been here.

'I'll be waiting by the door once the Cooks have finished clearing,' says Vita. 'Come clean, and bring your solstice dress.'

'Yes,' she says, and returns to her toxic harvest.

292

41 | Romy

Romy's life is less monitored than that of the average Drone. But still, she spends the next twenty-four hours feeling as though she has a flashing beacon attached to her back and everyone is staring. But the day goes on and nobody looks and nobody comments, and she goes through the motions without anyone spotting that something is different in her world. And, inside, little grains of fear and anticipation. Because, whatever Vita says, having Lucien's eye light upon you will change your life forever.

She takes her time in the Bath House in the middle of the morning, when there's not much competition. Washes twice with the lavender soap from her box, rinses and rinses her naked scalp, trims her fingernails and toenails, and goes to find her solstice dress. It lies, ironed and neatly folded by the Launderers, beneath her spare uniform. It's not hard to slip it into her backpack that's usually full of tools and take it with her without anyone noticing.

*

In the Great House, Vita waits for her where the sweeping staircase meets the first-floor landing, and leads her briskly, in silence, past the series of knocked-through bedrooms that constitute the Infirmary and its pharmacy, to the door that leads to the private quarters. The number of people who have gone past this door can be counted on one's fingers and toes, and they never speak of what they've seen.

I'm one of those, now, thinks Romy. Me, who has always been an outsider here.

Vita fetches a key from her pocket. Turns and looks Romy up and down. Then she shakes her head slightly, as though the sight of her leaves her mystified, and opens up.

They step onto a staircase. Soft moss wool carpet, white walls. The carpet is so thick that their footsteps are muffled as they walk. Vita stops at the first door in the corridor at the top, pushes it open. 'You can get changed in here,' she says. 'I'll wait outside. There's an en suite. You might want to wash, I suppose.'

She goes in. It's a bedroom, the sort she's read about in books. High ceilings, high windows, a four-poster, a chaise longue, a full-length cheval glass in one corner, a linen press, a dressing table. She's surprised to realise that she knows all the words, although she has never seen such furniture in the flesh before. That extra year in the Pigshed, reading, when she was fourteen. The room is spotless. Not a mote of dust in the shaft of sunlight that falls through the curtains, the bedclothes folded neatly on top of the bed, awaiting an occupant.

She puts her rucksack on the chaise.

Who cleans this? she wonders. It's not just sitting here. Someone comes in and cleans. A Launderer, I suppose, sworn to secrecy.

She goes through the door to the right, and gasps. There's a bath. A whole bath, for one bedroom. And a basin that sits atop a cupboard and what she can only assume is a flush toilet. That can't work, surely? All this way up in the top of the house? How does the water get here?

She turns a tap on the sink and hot water gushes out. They have plumbing downstairs, of course, but the water comes in a trickle, to preserve resources. She puts her hand on the handle that sticks out of the porcelain cistern above the toilet, pushes it down and laughs in astonishment as water thunders into the pan. She's heard of these, but never seen one. It's like magic.

She washes her face perfunctorily, sniffs her armpits, but despite her nervousness she can still smell a faint whiff of lavender. On the sink lies a whole bar of the same soap, still wrapped in its greasproof paper. She makes a note to bring her old bar and swap it for that one, if she's invited back. And allow time for a bath all to herself. *If* she's invited back.

Of course I will be, she thinks. He won't find me wanting.

She changes into her dress and studies herself in the mirror. Long and thin and strong and tanned, eyes big and green and frightened. I look vulnerable, she thinks. He'll like that. I can kill a sheep with my bare hands – *have* killed a sheep with my bare hands – but I know what he'll want today is an innocent to teach. I can give him that. I shall give him anything he wants, because the world depends on it.

She lets herself out.

'Rules,' says Vita.

'Yes,' says Romy.

'You never speak to anyone about anything here.'

'No.'

'And you do what he asks and you never question him.'

'Of course,' says Romy. 'I always have.'

'And you leave when he tells you to.'

'Yes.'

'And you must please him, or you won't be asked back.'

'I want to please him,' she says. 'I want nothing more. But I'm afraid I won't know how.'

Vita looks suddenly softer. 'Don't be afraid, Romy. Everyone's a bit afraid, their first time. Just be grateful that it's Lucien. You'll get used to it. Just remember that he wants the best for all of us.'

'I know,' she says. 'Oh, I know.'

'Right,' says Vita, and knocks on the door to Lucien's quarters.

There's a strange smell. Oily, chemical and yet not. As if he's been burning something. Lucien stands in the doorway, blocks her view of the rest of the room, and leans a forearm on the jamb. He's wearing loose cotton drawstring trousers and a billowy shirt in some feather-light, soft material that she's not encountered before. Silk? Cotton? She's not sure. Its buttons are undone halfway to the bottom, and she sees a medallion on a leather cord like the one his children wear, and a sea of curly white chest hair.

'Romy,' he says, 'come in, my dear.'

As she crosses the threshold she glances back and sees Vita standing at the door to her own quarters. The look on her face is odd. Despairing. Lost. She loves him, she thinks. Then: no, she loved him once and now she doesn't know what to do with that. And then she steps into his room and he closes the door behind her, and she becomes the next in line.

She's in a large room, a salon, doors to the left, door to the right, panels of blond wood on the walls and two huge sofas in dark green velvet. Lucien goes over to one and throws himself upon it, stretches out and leans on one elbow to drink her in. 'I've been looking forward to knowing you,' he says.

'Thank you,' she replies, proud and uncertain. Music – some music she doesn't recognise, no voices, soaring – coming from black boxes sited on either side of a working fireplace. A table at the back of the nearest sofa, on which a silver tray laden with a dozen, two dozen bottles resides. A huge screen hanging on the wall. She realises that it's a television. Of course. He has to record the news from somewhere. He watches it on this, plays edited highlights on the projector in the dining hall. She takes a couple of steps forward.

'Don't be shy,' says Lucien. She walks over and looks out of the tall windows. He must watch them all from above, like God studying ants, as they scurry about their business. And then the view beyond the woods. Spectacular. The most spectacular thing she's ever seen. The chequerboard of green that stretches to the distant blue hills, the small white houses crouched by clumps of trees, the two shades of silver where a river meets the sea.

She turns back to him. 'It's beautiful,' she says.

He throws himself to his feet with remarkable energy. 'Come,' he says. 'Come and sit with me. But first, a drink. What would you like?'

'I don't—' She looks at him standing by his drinks tray, sees the tendons straining in his throat as he gives her a broad, wolfish, empty smile. Drugged, she thinks. He's drugged. Is that what that smell is? 'I don't know what anything . . .'

'No, of course you don't,' he says. Picks up a series of bottles and studies their labels. 'Cherry brandy,' he says, 'you'll like that,' and he slops a large measure of something deep red and sticky into a glass. Carries it over to his big green sofa. There's a sheepskin on the floor in front of the fire. Long hair, combed and silky. She's never seen such wool.

'Merino?' She gestures to it.

297

'Leicester longwool,' he replies. 'From before you were born. Come. Sit.'

She obeys. Perches on the edge of the sofa, like a débutante at a ball. Lucien presses her drink into her hand. Picks up a glass half full of some golden liquid and takes a gulp. His pupils are tiny pinpricks in those faded blue irises. There's a dish on the coffee table, and lying in it is a long white roll of paper, like a cigarette only longer and fatter, half charred. It's this that the smell's coming from, she thinks. He's been breathing in the smoke. She sips from her glass. Strong and acrid, and yet noxiously sweet. This will make me drunk really fast, she thinks, and then she thinks, maybe that would be a good thing, and takes a larger sip. Lucien watches her through narrowed eyes, little ripples of self-satisfaction playing over his lips.

'I'm not your Father any more, Romy,' he says. 'In here, by ourselves, I'm not your Father at all.'

Among the Dead
November 2016

42 | Romy

The flat smells the way Plas Golau did that day. The smell is so strong it hits us as we walk through the street door. 'Wow,' says Ilo.

'It doesn't usually smell like this,' I say, as though my house-keeping skills mattered all of a sudden.

It's the man's blood, of course. I stuffed my bloody clothes into a carrier bag, still damp, and shoved the bag into the cupboard under the bathroom basin when I changed in a hurry for Aunt Sarah, and now they've rotted and the blood has turned. And a fly has got in from somewhere, though all the windows are closed, and its eggs have hatched. You wouldn't have thought that a polycotton blend would provide much nutrition, but the maggots are cheesy-fat and squirming.

Ilo stares at the bag. 'What's in there?' he asks.

'Oh,' I say, 'I got some blood on my clothes and I had to change them in a hurry.'

He looks at me, lowers his head as though he's peering over a pair of reading glasses. 'Is that how you got—'

'You should see the other guy,' I say. 'Well, you wouldn't want to now.'

He doesn't say anything, just picks up the bag and ties the handles around the top, his mouth working. He never used to be squeamish, my brother. Didn't seem to turn a hair as Jaivyn bled out in front of him. Maybe his thing isn't blood, it's rot. Or maybe what happened at Plas Golau has changed him. I hope not. I need him as he was.

'I think maybe we need another bag,' he says, 'to put this one in.'

'Yes,' I say, and go and look in the kitchen cupboard.

'Actually,' he says, 'maybe we should split them up. Drop them off in different places.'

'Have you been watching movies?' I ask.

'Yes. I rather like television.'

'So do I.'

'Have you seen *Judge Judy*?'

'Yes.'

'She should be the One, really. She doesn't take any nonsense.'

'Bit old, I suppose,' I say.

'But tough,' he says. 'Like beef jerky.'

All I could do with my knife while Sarah was there was rinse it off while I was in the shower and wipe it down with toilet paper. I almost weep when I see it in the cupboard under the bathroom sink, its beautiful blade devoid of shine, rusty brown already showing around the hinge. 'I'm sorry,' I tell it, 'I'm so sorry,' and I take it through to the living room to save it.

Ilo looks horrified when he sees it. 'What did you do?' he asks.

'Aunt Sarah was here, in the living room. She surprised me. I did all I could do with someone I'd never met in the flat.'

He takes it from me and strokes it like an orphaned kitten, his face filled with longing. He always loved my knife.

'D'you want to clean it?' I offer.

He turns his face up, and it's shining. 'Oh, yes.'

As I'm sorting through my sad little collection of clothes and starting to pack my box, my phone starts to vibrate in my pocket. I get it out and look – now two people have my number – and see that Uri has called while we were on the road and again just now. I call back.

'What are you doing not answering, 143?' he says. 'You should keep your phone with you.'

'I was taking a shit, sir,' I say, silently thanking Ilo for the idea. Uri is squeamish about gut functions. That's why the Dung Squad was the worst punishment he could think of, before torture and death.

'Oh, right,' he says. 'As you were, then. What news?'

'It's done,' I tell him.

'And did he still have his medallion?'

'Yes, and the boy took photos.'

'Good,' he says. Not much of an obituary. 'Hey – did you say you have your box?'

'Yes.'

'Good. You solsticed with Eilidh, didn't you?'

'Yes.'

'Still got the photo?'

'Yes.' It's in the living room, on the mantelpiece.

'Send me a copy,' he says.

'What's the address?'

Uri laughs. 'Haha – very clever. With your phone, stupid.'

'With my phone?'

He sighs. 'Take a photo with your phone and send the photo to me as a text message.'

303

'What for?'

'I want to braid my hair and take a stroll down Memory Lane,' he says. 'No, I have an idea.'

'What idea?'

'Shut up, 143. Just do it.'

'Okay,' I say, and he hangs up.

Ilo's cleaning my knife on the sofa and watching a film about cars that turn into robots that looks so excruciatingly boring only a thirteen-year-old boy could like it. He looks up as I come in, with a blanket over my arm. I hand it to him. 'You might as well turn in when you've done that,' I tell him 'You must be tired.'

'Not really,' he says.

'Well, we've got to get this place cleaned up in the morning, so you should get some sleep. Sofa okay?'

'Sure,' he says, and his eyes swivel back to the television.

I collect the photos and Kiran's little horse from the mantelpiece, my crown from the picture hook. Might as well put them all away now.

Sitting on the bed with the phone, I look at the photo. We look even younger, now, than we did a month ago. Dead Kiran and doomed Eilidh and me. Things are going to get harder now. I must be kind to Eden.

I wake with a start as my bedroom door opens in the darkness. 'Romy?'

I'm almost asleep. Lift up the covers to let him get in. Little brother, here you are. I've missed you.

'Romy?'

'Yes?'

'Your baby. It's His, isn't it?'

I consider lying for a moment. But what's the point? He will have to know some time. 'Yes.'

He doesn't say anything.

'How did you know?' I say.

'I just ... I just realised. Just now. I thought it might be Kiran's, before. I know you liked him. But then I realised.'

'Well, yes,' I say.

A silence. A long silence so complete I can hear him blink. He's thinking. Mulling over what this means. For all of us. He's not stupid.

'Romy?'

'Yes?'

'Does she have to die?'

'Yes,' I say, and as I say it my throat fills with tears. 'You know it's not her, Ilo. You know she will never be the One.'

'But why does she have to *die*?'

I'm stumped. I've never even questioned it. Not as I watched them all die off one by one, not even now. Until now. It just was, like Lucien was, or the coming Apocalypse. Because the strongest will be the One? Because surviving in itself is a show of strength? Because the One will keep us all safe. Because I have to get us to Cairngorm, baby, and there's only one way he'll let us in. Because sacrifices have to be made. Because the Great Disaster is just around the corner and we're out in the open with no defences. Because Uri says so.

'We have to sacrifice to survive, Ilo,' I say. 'You know that. If the loss of the few means the many survive ...'

'I love her,' he says.

'I love her too,' I say, though maybe I didn't know it until now.

He falls quiet again. I lie in the darkness and listen to him breathe. It's not fair, this, baby. I know nothing about the end of the world is fair, but Eilidh and Eden ...

'Romy?'

'Yes?'

'Promise me one thing.'

'Tell me.'

'Make it quick,' he says. 'Don't let her see it coming.'

43 | Sarah

She stops into the garage on the way home from work and notices that it has Christmas trees. It's not even December until tomorrow, but the lights have been up in the High Street a fortnight already. She buys one, and five strings of LED lights with battery packs and a big box of assorted baubles. Of all the crap in Gethsemane Villa, the one thing she knows for certain there isn't is Christmas decorations. Christmas in the Congregation was a long and dreary day of sermons topped off by a cold collation of every family's most colourless dish.

Of course we didn't do Christmas, she thinks. Why would we do anything that suggested that life could be fun? Well, these young people are going to get some fun this year, if it kills me. I don't suppose Christmas was a barrel of laughs at Plas Golau, either. That's something we have in common.

She comes in to a savoury scent and all the lights blazing. In the hallway, by the ebony umbrella stand, a small pile of luggage: a battered suitcase, a duffel bag, another of those beautiful polished boxes like the ones Eden and Ilo brought with them. Carrying all that on public transport would have been a nightmare by herself even if she weren't up the duff. Sarah's glad she let Ilo go and help.

She calls out. They're all in the kitchen, the room warm, something delicious in the oven, radio playing, volume on full. Gloria Gaynor singing loudly on the radio and the three of them singing along, dancing, smiles on their faces, Eden waving a wooden spoon in the air like a conductor's baton. They have beautiful voices and they harmonise with professional confidence. Who knew? She pauses in the doorway to watch, feels a smile spread across her face.

'*Your bones will turn to stone,*' they chorus, '*you'll be petrified.*

'*And then your flesh will melt away, you'll lose your appetite.*

'*And then you'll spend so many sighs because your future will be bleak,*

'*And you'll grow weak,*

'*And your last breath will be a shriek,*

'*And with a flash, from outer space,*

'*The light will sear the skin and eyebrows from your boiling burning face ...*'

Ilo catches sight of her, nudges his sisters. They break off, see her and their smiles widen. Eden turns the radio down. 'Hi, Aunt Sarah.'

'Hi,' she says, and puts her bag down on the table. 'Good to see you all having fun.'

'We love that song,' says Eden. 'We used to sing it at home. I didn't know you had it on the Outside too.'

'So I guessed,' she says. Restrains herself from pointing out that the original lyrics are a tad gentler. I'm learning, she thinks. I'm getting better at accepting who they are. 'Hey, listen, come and give me a hand. I've got some stuff needs bringing in from the car.'

I like them, she thinks. I actually like them. Amazing what a difference Romy's already made to the children's spirits. I didn't think she'd be much help when I first met her, but I was judging someone who was clearly not well. Look at them now. Ilo's like a whole new person, and even Eden's laughing and joining in.

They've put the tree by the fireplace in the drawing room and spread the baubles out on the coffee table, and she's opened a bottle of Riesling and given them each a glass. Hester Lacey looks down and judges. 'I don't think she approves,' says Ilo, and nods up at her.

Sarah looks around. All those old dead people, disapproving. All my life, she thinks. All my bloody life. And she stands up. 'Yeah, you know what? If she doesn't like it, she can go and sit in the study.'

She unhooks Hester and a cloud of dust bunnies falls to the floor from behind. 'Bollocks,' she says. 'Mind that when you get the others,' and carries Hester ceremoniously through to lean against the study wainscot. As she goes back to fetch the hoover, she crosses paths with the three of them, a little queue of removals people carrying a portrait each.

'Who are these ghouls, anyway?' asks Romy.

'Your sainted ancestors,' she replies. 'They didn't rate Christmas.'

'How was your stay in Hounslow?' she asks as they hook baubles onto the branches. It's a good, sturdy little tree, lots of foliage. 'Did you get any sleep?'

They glance at each other the way Ilo and Eden used to do. Maybe it's just a Plas Golau thing: that everyone checks with everyone else before they speak. It would make sense, really, if you've lived in a world so ordered, so constricted. She should read less into things. Be less paranoid.

'Yeah, it was fine,' says Romy.

'What did you eat, in the end?' she asks.

'Big Macs,' says Ilo. 'And how was your day, today?'

Another first. My God, she thinks, this woman's a miracle. Here for a few days and he's totally noticed that there are other people in the equation.

'Not bad,' she replies. 'Straightforward, at least. A bunch of form-filling and a load of filing.'

'Mmm,' he says. 'I know I should know, but what do you do?'

'I'm the school administrator,' she says. 'Well, one of them. Mrs Field is the other. Have you met her?'

'Oh, yes,' he says. 'The lady with the gammy eye.'

'We don't say "gammy", Ilo,' she says. God, she sounds like Helen. 'Sorry. I mean, just that it's generally frowned on to point out people's disabilities as a way of describing them.'

'Mm, okay,' he says. 'It must take a lot longer to describe people if you don't mention the most obvious thing about them, though.'

'It's just good manners.'

'Okay,' he says. 'So can I say something like "the pregnant lady" about Romy, then? Does it apply to temporary stuff that stands out about them today, too, or only, you know, permanent things?'

'You never told us who the father was, by the way, Romy,' says Eden.

'It doesn't matter,' says Romy, and she doesn't look at her. 'He's dead.'

A little drop in volume, a little chill in the room. Romy gives them a smile. 'That shepherd's pie must be ready by now,' she declares.

They remove the ancestors from the dining room as well, and the place looks immediately brighter, as though they've actually changed the light bulbs. The shepherd's pie is delicious. Hot and savoury, with nutmeg in the mash.

'What's your favourite food, Aunt Sarah?' Ilo asks.

'Ooh, I don't know. French, maybe? Or maybe – no, Chinese. Chinese is my favourite.'

'Ooh!' echoes Ilo. 'What's Chinese food like?'

'It's good. Lots of textures. Lots of flavours. I'll take you up to Man Ho on the High Street before Christmas. You'll like it.'

'I'd love to try it,' he says. 'I want to try a lot of stuff before—' and she feels him consciously check himself. 'Have you been to China, then?' he asks instead.

'No. I'd like to go, one day.'

'Really?'

'Ilo, I'd like to go *everywhere* one day.' Might as well be honest. What's the point of pretending that all she ever wanted for her life was Finbrough?

'Really?'

'Yes. Wouldn't you?'

'I don't know,' he says. 'It's a long way from home and there are a lot of people, aren't there?'

'Over a billion,' she tells him, and he suddenly looks faintly green. Eden is fading out, looking suddenly bored. I won't worry about it, she thinks. It's so nice to have a conversation that just flows. She'll learn, one day. 'I guess that sounds a bit daunting if you've spent a lot of your life in the same place,' she says.

'Yes, it does. So where *have* you been?' he asks. 'Tell me what they were like. What was your favourite place?'

So curious, all of a sudden. But it's so nice that he is. He's really very charming, when you get to know him.

'Not many places.' Liam was big on all-inclusive. Thought holidays were for resting and didn't much care about leaving the pool, so there wasn't much point in taking long flights when the experience would basically be the same. 'Mallorca, Cyprus, Malta, Tenerife,' she says.

'Where's Tenerife?'

'It's a volcano off the coast of Morocco,' she says, ashamed to hear herself trying to make it sound more glamorous, more adventurous, than the package tour it really was. 'And I've been to a few cities in Europe. Paris. Florence. Madrid. And the Algarve. I went to the Algarve. That's in Portugal.' She'd been planning to make her first ever foray out of Europe this spring, to Thailand.

She only realises she's heaved a sigh when Romy puts a hand on hers and knits her eyebrows.

'Sorry,' she says. 'Silly.'

'No, I'm sorry,' says Romy. 'We didn't mean to interrupt your life this way.'

She feels comforted, guilty at the same time. What emotions these people are bringing out in her. 'No, Romy, it's not like that,' she says. 'Life's not like that. Doing the right thing is a reward in itself really. Even if it does mean having to put stuff off for a bit.'

'That's what Father used to say,' says Ilo.

'Well, he was right,' she says, and she's glad to be able to find something to acknowledge about Lucien, to be able to agree that he was right about something.

'So if you were to go, to travel, where would you most like to go?' he asks.

She thinks. So many places. So many oceans. 'Australia,' she says, 'and New Zealand. The other side of the world. As far away from Finbrough as I can get. And you?'

'Tahiti,' says Ilo, decisively, as though it's a subject he's already given hours of thought to. 'Palau. And Tierra del Fuego. They're all a long way from anywhere else.'

Romy's phone buzzes as they're finishing off the tree. She pulls it from her pocket, looks at the screen. 'Oh, sorry,' she says, 'I should take this,' and goes out through the front door to the driveway.

They go back into the drawing room and Eden picks up a pair of glorious golden baubles. Holds them like earrings on either side of her head and makes them laugh.

'Very glamorous,' says Sarah.

'I like earrings,' says Eden.

'Do you? Would you like some for Christmas?'

'Oh!' she says. 'Really?'

'Of course. You could get your ears pierced as part of your present, if you like.'

'*Part* of my present?'

'Yes!' she says. Seeing them so animated, she suddenly has plans. I'll show them, she thinks, and I'll show myself. We'll make a proper family yet. 'It might be a bit late, but I could probably get you something made that would go with your medallion, if you'd like.'

Eden looks stunned. 'You could do that?'

'I don't see why not. And Romy too, if you think she'd like that. Do you think she'd like to stay for Christmas? Ilo?'

She turns to look at him and is taken aback to catch the oddest look on his face. He's looking at his sister and he looks . . . melancholy. Then he snaps his eyes shut and looks at Sarah. 'Sorry – what?'

'Do you think Romy would like to stay for Christmas?'

'I don't know,' he says. 'Maybe. She might.'

313

The front door closes and Romy comes back in. She looks a little pale, a little serious.

'Has something happened?' asks Sarah.

Romy shakes her head. 'Stupid. Apparently I have to pay some rent, or something. I thought I'd paid it, but the landlord's complaining, and Social Services say they have to inspect me in the flat.'

'They called you at this time of night to tell you this?'

'Is that odd?'

'Yes. They must be hacked off.'

'Yes,' says Romy.

'I'm sorry,' she says. 'What a pain. You've only just come back. I'd run you up there tomorrow, but ...'

'No, it's okay,' says Romy. 'I know how to do it now. It's easy. I'll go after breakfast.'

Ilo is watching her. 'Do you want me to come?' he asks.

Romy gives him a smile that seems suddenly full of tears. 'No, it's okay, kiddo,' she says. 'I'm going to have to do this one by myself.'

Before the End

2015–2016

44 | Somer

2015

Now that Ursola has broken the silence, she sees it everywhere. Wonders how she could have been so blind for so long. But then, so is everyone around her. Changes happen so slowly you don't really see how different it has become until you stop to look. You're like a lobster, boiling up slowly in a pot. There have been no new arrivals since Jaivyn Blake left; no new eyes through which to see the limitations of their world.

The Guards are everywhere. She remembers, like waking from a dream, how Plas Golau used to be before he arrived. We were equals then, she thinks. The world was going to end, but we were going to build a better one. There were rules, of course, lots of them, but you could see the intent behind them. They were about discipline, yes, but discipline based on trust. On mutual trust. Lucien trusted us and we trusted him. And if there was discipline, it was about survival, not . . . subjection.

She sees it everywhere, now. The silent war between Vita and Uri, and Lucien barely to be seen any more.

On Eden's birthday, three big trucks appear on the drive, breaking branches with their roofs as they go, carrying away a whole section of the drystone wall as they turn into the orchard. And Uri calls the Farmers in from the fields to the godowns and orders them to load them up with their carefully husbanded supplies. Somer stands and watches as sack after sack of wheat and chickpeas and potato flour, whole pallets of bottled, preserved, dried, tinned produce, their insurance against the end of the world, make their way from the shelves to the hoists as the brigade of Guards stands by and urges the labour to hurry.

The Cooks come from the kitchens, the Blacksmiths and the Engineers from the workshops, the Carpenters, the Launderers, the Dung Squad, the Teachers. And they gather to watch, aghast. This is too much, they whisper. We can't afford to give so much. There will barely be enough to see us through the winter. What will we do, if the Great Disaster comes before we replenish?

But nobody says a word out loud. The Guards have batons and everyone knows how easy they find it to use them.

Then Vita's there, hurrying out of the courtyard gate. 'What are you doing?' she shouts.

'Needed at Cairngorm,' he says.

'On whose authority?'

'On mine.'

'Not on mine.'

'Ah, well,' he says, 'if you want to ask Father ...'

'I will,' she says. 'You can't just—'

'I can, you know,' he says. 'We're bigger now, and we need to feed the people there.'

'Just wait,' she says. 'Don't you dare leave with all that. I shall go and ask him now.'

'Help yourself,' says Uri.

Vita hurries away, and he stands, arms folded, and smiles as they watch her go.

She doesn't return.

An emergency Pooling in the evening, all the leaders in the Council Chamber, protesting. Too late, of course. The trucks have long since headed north. But they gather anyway, and shout. *What have you done? What have you done to us? How will we live? How will we survive?*

Uri stands in front of them, arms across his chest, and waits. He doesn't seem afraid, or even ashamed. He just waits. And when they finish shouting he says, 'Are you done?' and they shuffle and glare, but nobody speaks. 'Good,' he says. 'You need to learn some discipline.'

Discipline. Discipline.

'But how are we to feed ourselves?' asks the Leader of the Cooks. 'What good is *discipline* if we starve?'

'Stop gorging,' says Uri, 'and remember that you're not the only ones on Earth.'

'But that's *our* food!' cries the Leader of the Farmers. His face is leathery after years of hillside labour, and he's missing two fingers from his right hand.

'And you'll grow more,' says Uri.

'But what about the Great Disaster?' asks the Leader of the Engineers.

Uri shakes his head. 'We all have to make sacrifices,' he says. 'You'll just have to hope it doesn't come till you're done. Why should Cairngorm die and you survive?'

'We've always been here,' says the Cook. 'Always. If Cairngorm can't be self-supporting, then what's the use of it?'

'It will be. But it takes time to establish a place like this. You

319

know that. We've too many eggs in a single basket,' says Uri. 'Two locations is safer than one. A greater chance for humanity.'

'But Lucien!' cries the Engineer. 'This wasn't what Lucien—'

'It's what he wants now,' Uri snaps.

An intake of breath, an outbreak of muttering.

Somer finally finds her voice. 'But how can there be two places?' she asks. 'What about the One?'

The smile he gives her sucks the heat from her bones. 'I guess you'll have to hope you're the lucky ones. I'm not going anywhere. For now.'

Vita sits silent at the back of the room, and waits.

When he's gone, they turn to her. Start to babble out their fears. *What's happened?* they cry. *What has Father done to us? He is too strong. How did he get so strong? Where is Father? Where is he? Why has he betrayed us?*

She stands. Clasps her hands together, low on her body.

'I'm sorry,' she says. 'I've let you down. An adder has entered our garden and we must tread carefully.'

'It's all over,' says the Cook. 'If he's in charge, we will never survive.'

Vita smiles. 'Oh, children,' she says, 'you must trust me more than that.'

320

45 | Romy

2016

She keeps the key in her box and Vita no longer bothers to meet her on the stairs. It's a practical solution, for Vita occasionally leaves the compound for days at a time and Romy must still respond to his command. Three times a week. Three times a week for eighteen months, although, as it turns out, the idea of a young, willing body is often more potent than the reality. He likes the ritual, she thinks, more than the mating itself, though if he takes one of his tablets and his old-man cock is on parade he will go on and on, pounding into her, often from behind, her face pressed into the pillow, or the sheepskin, or the sofa, until she longs to beg him to stop.

She never does.

I must be here, she tells herself as his scaly hips pump back and forth, back and forth and his hands dig deep into the back of her neck, for the sake of the future. I must stay until I get with child – God help us if it never happens – or until he tires of me. One or the other. The one is my duty to humanity and the other ... well, you're a fool if you reject the master when you have nowhere else to go. As Khrushchev said, 'When Stalin says dance, the wise man dances'.

Sometimes she makes it bearable by imagining that the body behind her is Kiran's. Young, strong Kiran who she sees in the smithy every day, who smiles at her as though he understands. But then she is forced to open her eyes, and her dreams dissolve.

Most of the time, though, she's more nursemaid than houri. She discovers his secrets quickly, for in the privacy of his quarters he is garrulous in a way he never is outside. Uri knows it, clearly, and so does Vita, but the rest of Plas Golau continues to overlook the telltale signs. But if they were to break through the door one day they would discover that the man who leads them, inspires them, judges and chastises them, is a shell. That he spends his day in a haze of drink and drugs, that he relies on Vita or Uri to administer the shots that will turn him into Leader for his brief performance at the evening meal. They've been running the rest, between them, however fractiously, since he came off that horse, and no one has noticed because, in the end, no one *wants* to notice.

I must not forget, she thinks. I must always remember that what he is now is not what he *was*. I never knew him young, not even when I was a child, but I remember so clearly the glory of him. A light seemed to shine from him, when I was young. And, though his time is nearly over, we must always love him, for he led us to safety. Literally saved our lives.

His quarters are a padded cell. Every surface is soothing. She comes in often to find him lying upon the couch like a pasha, smoking one of his cannabis cigarettes and drinking brandy in the afternoon. Those are the best days, for then all she has to do is listen. Pose attentively, naked on the sheepskin, or at his knee or, on his orders, open-legged on the carved wooden throne by the fireplace. On those days their congress is brief and unspectacular. Lucien likes to look. It helps him feel his power, she thinks, though the sight of him clutching foggily at his crotch as he recites past glories is something far removed from power.

But he's the Progenitor, not the One. It doesn't really matter what he's like, because his function is to father the one who will save them. He has often said so himself.

And then there are the days when he is felled by pain. When the most he manages is to make it from bed to sofa, if even that. On those days, his appetite for Vicodin is inexhaustible. On those days, there is nothing she is expected to do but sit by his side and comfort him.

And because he is the Progenitor, she will suck at his flaccid member all afternoon, if it brings the One nearer to being.

I cannot love him, she thinks as she mounts the stairs. He isn't our messiah. But my baby will save mankind, and that is everything.

Vicodin is an opiate. A very strong opiate. Vita takes her into her confidence, because once you've seen him close up, seen the empty joviality and heard the slurring, it's hard to ignore. You must keep an eye on him, she says. You have no idea, the pain, and he has to carry on for all of us. Do you see? If the people see that their Leader is weak, their confidence falters. They fall to squabbling over who will be next and unity collapses. We need him to carry on. But keep an eye on him. He likes it too much and it's easy to overdose. On the bad days he'll gobble them up like wild strawberries, pop them into his mouth without a thought. You need to keep an eye on him on the bad days, Romy. Remind him how much he's taken and don't let him drink.

*

323

She misses her period in late May, but she doesn't speak of it. And then her breasts become tender and her body temperature rises, and she starts to feel somehow Other, as though the life she suspects is growing inside her is infinitely more precious than the life without. A strange, distant, altered feeling. But she waits two weeks, always looking for signs of failure, before she accepts that they have succeeded and Lucien's child is dug deep into her sheltering womb.

Between breakfast at six and the beginnings of the lunch preparations at eleven, the Great Hall is usually empty. She enters through the back door from the chapel graveyard, and no one sees her as she mounts the stairs and lets herself into the sanctum. She doesn't bother with making herself nice in the ante-room; just goes down the hall to tap on his door.

The voice that answers is feeble, nasal, and she knows that today is a Bad Day. A perfect day for her. She cracks the door, peers round it and sees him on the sofa, on his back, hand to his forehead like Branwell Brontë. His eyes are sunk deep in pools of charcoal grey, his lips are dry and cracked.

'Not today, Romy,' he says. 'Not today.'

'Oh, Father,' she says, and comes in despite his words. 'I'm sorry. You're in pain.'

She kneels at his side and takes his hand. The table in front of the sofa, where he's spreadeagled her a hundred times, is scattered with the litter of sickness. Blister packs and cardboard boxes, used tissues, a smeary water glass, a joint half-smoked in a brass ashtray. Tears pour from his eyes and for a moment she feels intense pity. To be so old, with only this to look forward to. The good days will become fewer and the bad days closer together until one day it will be only this. Only this until death.

She picks up a blister pack. There are three more of them on the table, shaken in haste from their box. One strip of seven is empty, and four in the strip she holds have gone. She pops another out, puts it in his hand, helps him drink from the glass. There are drinking straws on the sideboard especially for days like these. She'll get one in a minute. She lights the joint, the oily smoke acrid and disgusting in her mouth as she sucks to get it going, then hands it to him.

'Has no one been in to see you?' she asks.

'No,' he says, and the pain makes him petulant, childish. 'I've been by myself all day.'

'I'm so sorry,' she says. 'If I'd known, I'd have come before. Is Vita away?'

She knows that Vita is down in Dolgellau. It's why she's here now.

'I don't know,' he snaps.

'I'll get you a drink,' she says. Goes to the drinks tray and pours him a brandy. Rémy Martin, his favourite. She doesn't know how these things get into the compound unnoticed. In Vita's luggage, she supposes, along with all these other things – the little luxuries, the pharmaceuticals – that she finds in his room. She pours one inch, two inches, adds a little more, then tops it up with soda. Brings it back with a straw sticking out of the top and presses it into his hand. Gives him a Vicodin, and he takes it, absently, as though he's already forgotten the one she gave him before.

She rolls him another joint. She hated to be around it when she first came here, but he's gentler, less rough, when he's smoked one, and for that she has come to like it. It's a skill at which she has become quite adept, for he likes to watch her. On good days, he likes to watch her roll them naked. Today, he hasn't even noticed that she's still in her uniform.

She gives it to him, holds a flame to it as he inhales. After a

325

while, he sinks into his cushions and gives her a weak smile. 'You're a good girl,' he says.

'For you,' she replies. 'Father.'

She pops another Vicodin from its foil and hands it over. A whole foil gone, now. He's had fourteen. Maybe another foil's worth, to be sure. Lucien mumbles it into his mouth, then sucks and sucks through his straw until his brandy glass is empty. She takes it from his hand.

'I have some news, Father,' she says as she refills. There is still plenty more in the bottle; it was almost full when she got here. I'll bring it over to the table, she thinks. Leave it there, to save the trips.

He's drifting, quite happy now – his pain, if not forgotten, irrelevant. Vicodin makes him genial. He's taken enough now that he's putty in her hands. She pops another, hands it to him as she resumes her seat on the rug.

'What news?'

'I'm pregnant,' she says. 'I have your baby growing inside me.'

She gives him his drink. Lucien sucks on the straw and smiles at her with his empty blue eyes. 'It will be the One,' he says.

'I know,' she says. 'What a blessing you've given me.'

'*He* won't like it, of course,' he says, though he doesn't seem particularly bothered.

'I know,' she says, and puts another Vicodin into his hand.

326

Among the Dead

December 2016

46 | Romy

It's a hundred and ninety miles from Finbrough to Southwold, and it takes three hours to get there. As the crow flies, it's shorter, but of course there is the whole of London between the two. Six hundred and eleven square miles of it, eight million people crammed in like ants in a formicarium. That's thirteen thousand people to the square mile. One of the problems at Plas Golau, according to what I've read, was overcrowding, and there were a hundred and sixty of us to a farm of roughly a square mile. If overcrowding caused our meltdown, then London must be an open powder keg waiting for a spark.

One day, before I leave, I shall go into London and look. But not now, not now. Now, I have to go and kill my oldest living friend.

Ellie Dracoulis. It sounds like a vampire, sounds dark and brooding and Transylvanian. Nothing blonde in that name. Where does it come from, I wonder? Has she married? Or was that her mother's birth name, as Maxwell was mine? You can find

329

anything on the internet. Even, it seems, a face from years ago, matured and living incognito.

I must try to think of her as a stranger. As someone I didn't break bread with every day of my childhood, share beds with, share laughter. It will make it easier. I hope she understands.

The road gets gradually narrower, slower, bleaker, great beds of reeds springing up from pools of ominous green water. Single lonely trees against the sky, an eerie sense that the sea is right behind each hedge.

I don't see the sea until I am nearly upon it. And then houses rear up from the flatlands and suddenly, there it is. The North Sea, my first sight of it. Different from the sea I know. This sea is stern and black and slow-moving. When I open my window to hear and breathe it, instead of the whoosh of the sea at Weston I hear the gelid suck that drowned a thousand longships.

It's a beautiful town, a glorious town. A good place to hide, to recover. After the usual approach through a hinterland of battered nonentity, I reach a place where the roads narrow and wind, and flat-fronted cottages open straight onto pavements. A lovely fishing village, protected by its isolation. On the front, genteel villas gaze out at stormy water, little beach huts painted in primary colours huddle below a bank of green, a pier strides boldly out across the waves. Wide golden sand that makes me long to strip my boots off. I park up on North Parade and watch the ocean as I drink my coffee and plan my next move. Christmas lights everywhere, cheerful in the winter gloom. I don't suppose I shall ever see the festival itself.

Once you have someone's name, you have almost everything. She's got careless, has Eilidh. Now Uri has found her, I see Ellie Dracoulis everywhere. Bubble-headed Ellie, smiling her big smile from the Southwold Arts staff page, smiling her big smile

330

from Facebook and countless photos by her tag-happy friends on there, on Instagram, on Twitter. Ellie at a barbecue, Ellie dressed as a squaw, Ellie hugging a big sandy dog, Ellie laughing, approaching the camera on a water slide with a screaming toddler in her lap. The toddler turns up in lots of pictures. She looks about two. Oh, God, Eilidh, I didn't know you had a daughter. It all makes sense now. And I know, just from looking, that I would still like you.

Southwold Arts is based in a small office that used to be a shop, in one of those cute little cottage streets. The plate-glass window has the organisation's name spelled out in childish cardboard cut-out letters glued to its inside. On the sill, on a stand, a huge oil landscape of a ruined boat and a water tower. Three desks, modern, curvaceous, facing each other, and Eilidh sitting at one, side-on to the window, on the telephone, blissfully unaware of me. I only pause for a moment, to look, to be sure it's really her, and then I walk on down to East Street and back to the front.

My knife is in my jacket pocket. My hoodie's so snug these days it stands out unmistakeably in the front pocket.

I find a chintzy little café almost directly across the road and buy a scone and a cup of tea, though God knows I don't want them. And I sit in the window – the place almost empty, two old ladies discussing some man's prostate troubles and the woman behind the counter already beginning to wrap up the cakes in clingfilm – and watch.

The office looks warm, welcoming. I hope that she's had a good time here. That life among the Dead has been good to her. Her remaining colleague, late thirties, horsey, is facing me, and they're having an animated conversation, heads bobbing, hands waving and the occasional pause while she stops to laugh. Ellie

Dracoulis. Popular. A much-loved colleague. Beloved mother of Suki, daughter of the late Marnie. You won't die forgotten, at least. Three hundred and seven friends on your Facebook page, and, from the way you all talk, I bet you know a good quarter of those in real life.

I don't remember her being particularly artistic. She was all thumbs. But maybe you don't need to be artistic to be a junior co-ordinator. I have no idea what that is.

I crumble my scone between finger and thumb, take a taste. It's floury and solid, and I'm glad I'm not going to be eating much.

The colleague leaves as Eilidh gets to her feet and starts packing up her desk. She collects a handful of mugs, carries them through a door at the back of the room. She's gone for a few minutes, long enough that I begin to wonder if there's a back way out, and then she emerges, wearing a sweet black velvet frock coat that comes all the way to her knees and pulling a woollen shawl over her shoulders. She reaches back through the door and turns the light off behind her, then she comes to the front door and turns the lights off in the office. I haul myself to my feet – and doing that takes some time nowadays – wave a five-pound note at the woman behind the counter to show her I'm leaving it, and come out to follow her.

She doesn't look around. Why would you? It's four o'clock on a drizzly evening in Southwold. It's not a place where stag parties roam, like Weston, or where someone could throw you down and snatch your bag, like London. It's just ... coming home from work in a small North Sea town, thinking of the central heating and picking up the kid. She turns down towards the sea, pulls her shawl up against the wind and I do the same with mine. It's bitter, out here in the sea wind. There's no one to be seen, no lights on the pier, curtains drawn across windows.

I call her name. Her name from home, the one I know her by.

It will be the last time I ever speak it, I guess. I have to call it twice, for the wind carries it away the first time.

Eilidh turns with her big wide smile to see who wants her. And she sees me and the smile drops away. 'Oh, Romy,' she says.

I look at her and bury my hands in my pockets.

'I knew one of you would find me, one day,' she says. 'I just wish it wasn't you.' And she starts to cry.

47 | Romy

She didn't fight. Didn't argue. In the end, we are what we are, and Eilidh, despite the clothes and the make-up and the new life, was still a child of the Ark. The obedience was hard-wired within her, whatever the veneer. As it is in me. As it is in all of us.

A car swishes past in the lane where I've pulled up to rest and weep, and its headlights bring me back, set off a fit of coughing, for my throat is dry as sand. There's no sign of the sky lightening, but I know from the feel of the air that dawn is near. You know these things, if you've lived in nature, as I have. I need to get on the road. He'll be walking her to school at half-past eight, and I know that if I hesitate, if I don't go through with it now, these memories of Eilidh will stay my arm and all will be lost.

My knife still has her blood on it.

By the time I get to Finbrough, my brain is fuzzed with weariness. I caught the rush hour halfway round the M25 and spent an hour crawling, stopping, crawling, stopping. Fell asleep during one of the longer waits and flew awake with a start to the blast of a queue of car horns behind me. You're quiet inside me. Sleeping, I hope. If you've died while I've been travelling, it will all have been for nothing.

I find a space two roads over from the bridge, by a hedge of overgrown box. It's eight o'clock and my heart is racing. I consider taking a beta blocker, but decide against, in the end. If I'm going to do this, I must face it with every cell in my body, or in time all this will become a dream, the sacrifice diluted, the value of the lives lost diminished. I must never forget the sacrifices that have been made for you, baby. For the world.

Oh, Eilidh, oh, Eden, I never knew I would be your avenging angel.

Before the End

June 2016

48 | Somer

She's on privy duty when she sees Vita come home from one of her trips to the outside world. Somer wonders, sometimes, if she will ever see that world again. She's been here so long that its speed and garish colours, its noises and its endless stimulation, seem more dream to her than real-life experience. When she came here, Vita's hair was still blonde. Uri was a sulky young man who came on access visits from the army. And Lucien was the most beautiful thing she'd ever seen; a sun-god of strength and vitality, an inspirer, a true Leader. She'd longed to be chosen by him. Had been beside herself with joy when she'd found she was carrying his child.

He's a shadow of himself now, she thinks. How funny. We're really only keeping his legend going through the force of our will.

Somer sees Romy, all by herself, walking briskly towards the orchard wall. She stops when she gets there, scans all around to see if she is being watched. Doesn't even notice her mother in the shadow of the privy door. Somer is used to that now. She's been invisible here for so long. Romy hops over the wall and vanishes across the road, into the woods. That girl's up to something, thinks Somer. I wonder what. Then she looks away to fix the lid onto her barrel of shit and thinks no more about it.

She's loading up her cart – Vita got them a cart recently so that they can carry three barrels at a time rather than labouring to get them one by one down the hill – when a flurry of movement catches her eye. Ursola running out of the courtyard gate. It piques her interest. Life is slower here. You rarely see anyone over the age of ten running. Their days are too long and their work too hard to waste energy that way.

Somer straightens up and watches her go. She's heading for the Guard House. Very odd. Running may be an unusual occurrence, but she has never, ever seen someone run *towards* the Guard House.

A couple of minutes later, Ursola returns with Uri, both of them jogging as he buckles up his belt. Ursola looks almost panicked and Uri looks suddenly about twelve again, his natural disdain wiped away by a look of – *something*. She's unsure what. Not fear, as such, but certainly some form of dread, of uncertainty. Then Vita comes through the gate to greet them and Somer sees that she is crying. Her hands fly up to cover her face when she sees Uri, and she comes to a halt on the drive in a pose of abandoned grief.

Oh, God, thinks Somer, something's happened. Something terrible. Are we to see the End after all?

Even now, in his moment of crisis, there is no physical contact between them. Their relationship has always been cold. Uri was six when Lucien left his mother for Vita, or so the story goes, and he's never really got over his resentment. They stand facing each other for a moment, then go back into the courtyard side by side, and disappear.

Somer finishes loading the handcart and starts to haul it carefully down the hill. It's an improvement on how things were done before, but it's a job that must be done with caution, for the path has never been paved and its earthen surface is riddled with tree roots.

She's halfway down when she hears a walkie-talkie crackle into life. There must be a Guard on the other side of the wall, lurking the way they do, waiting to catch the unwary in dereliction of duty. 'Dom to all Guards,' it goes. 'Whisky Tango Foxtrot repeat Whisky Tango Foxtrot, over?'

Somer gets chills. The Guards have a series of call signs on their radios. They probably think they're secret, but they use them so carelessly, talk so thoughtlessly among themselves, that most of the compound knows what they are. Alpha 1-2 means that the End has started. Victor Bravo is a medical emergency. And Whisky Tango Foxtrot means 'major emergency, all Guards to Guard House'.

She leaves her burden and hurries back up to the privies, where she can take a better look. All across the compound, khaki-clad figures hurry towards their goal.

Up at the house, the great bell in the tower on the roof begins to toll.

49 | Somer

Silence. Then silent tears. They stand with their heads bent and weep for their loss. And in among them, Vita. Still there, still with them, still mother to them all.

She moves between them like the spirit of their world. Vita who is, who always has been, their continuity and their kindness. Pale with grief, but still finding it within herself to smile. A face touched here, a palm pressed to the back of a hand, a pair of arms to wrap yourself in. She sees Somer, even Somer, and envelops her in her golden web of fellow feeling. Presses her forehead against Somer's, holds it there, holds her hand. Moves on.

He loved you. He loved you all. Each one of you was special to him. He has left, but he is not gone. He will live on with all of us, in everything we do.

Somer is dazed. The beautiful day, the blue sky above, the people with whom she has shared her life for all these years, seem unreal to her, like ghosts or distant wood smoke. He never forgave me. I waited and waited, but forgiveness never came, and now he's gone and I will live my life like this.

The Guards are gathered with them, Ilo among them, his face blank as though someone has erased the soul within. Eden weeps with her remaining siblings and never casts her a glance. Over by the gate she sees Romy, standing alone, dry-eyed like her brother.

The surprising sound of an engine beyond the wall. They turn to look, wonder who is disturbing their sorrow. Then they see that it is the compound car, Jacko at the wheel. He drives through them like a cop through a demo: slowly, slowly as they part, carefully, so as not to inflame. Vita glances, then glances away. Keeps her back turned as two Guards emerge from the kitchen door and begin to load it up. Three canvas bags on the back seat, a box in the front.

They know what it means. Now Lucien is no longer here, Vita's days at Plas Golau are done.

They wait.

The bolts draw back on the Great House door and the people of the Ark look up as one. Faces animate, and she is surprised to read hope on many. They hope he's going to come out now, she realises, and tell us it was a mistake. They hope he isn't dead.

And then Uri comes from the shadows within and their shoulders slump and they exhale.

His Guards straighten up. Stand to attention, separate their legs and stand at ease. Like soldiers. Like proper soldiers. Uri sweeps them with his eyes and what they see on his face is ... triumph.

Silence. They hold their collective breath. Vita turns round slowly to face him and her shoulders straighten. She holds her head high, like a queen.

'You can go now,' he tells her.

343

When she speaks, her voice is clear. 'These aren't your people, Uri,' she says, 'and this place isn't for you to take.'

He is white with fury. And still no grief.

'It's mine! He wanted *me* to have it,' he shouts. 'He told me. It was always going to be me!'

Vita, now the moment is here, is as calm as he is enraged. 'But Uri, he left it to me. I'm his wife. You have Cairngorm. That was what he wanted you to have. It's all in the will, if you want to look.'

Lucien, keeping everybody happy, playing them all.

He is robbed of words. His jaw works, but no sound comes out. For a moment she thinks he's going to call his Guards to action, that battle will break out here and now. Then he blinks. Grinds his teeth.

'You are not his heir,' he says. 'You're not the One. And you're nothing without him.'

Vita tosses her beautiful silver hair. 'Whatever,' she replies.

The strain of self-control must be monumental, thinks Somer, as he marches down the steps, head held high, back rigid. He walks to the car and removes Vita's bags from the back seat and hands than to the people nearby. Takes her box from the passenger seat and lays it gently on the steps, feigns respect for her hated possessions.

'We'll stay for the funeral,' he says.

'Of course,' says Vita. 'Anyone who wants to stay afterwards is welcome, as well. There will always be a home here for the members of the Ark.'

His eyes bulge for a second. Then he throws himself into the driver's seat and starts the engine. Turns the wheel with a crunch of gravel and drives away. Sees Romy standing by the gate, drops down a gear and accelerates as he approaches. Swipes her with his wing as he passes.

Somer's daughter flies through the air like a ragdoll, all dangling limbs, and hits the finialled gatepost with a crunch that echoes through her very viscera. As though she can feel her own bones breaking.

50 | Romy

The first thing she knows, when she knows anything at all, is pain. Swimming around in the dim grey of unconsciousness, she feels something grab hold of her leg and sink its teeth in. And she tries to pull away, but it comes with her, won't let her go. And then she's awake and lying in a bed in the Infirmary and crimson agony shoots through her body and eats her alive.

Romy freezes where she lies. If moving makes the pain worse, then maybe lying still will make it stop. The fierce, mauling pain recedes, but still, down in the upper reaches of her right leg, a ball of molten metal throbs with every beat of her heart. She waits, forces herself to focus, and listens to the rest of her body to see if there is pain elsewhere.

There is. Another throbbing pain, in her head. I remember hitting that, she thinks. On a car. I was standing in the court-yard, and . . .

Her head thumps.

What was I doing there? There were people. I remember, there were people.

Nothing.

There's a crumpled, chalky pain in her middle fingers. She gingerly raises the hand to see in the dim light from the pharmacy door. The fingers are wrapped together and held with a splint. Where else? A graze, down her upper arm, covered in gauze and held on with more sticky tape. I was wearing a jacket, she thinks, and is thankful that she was.

She lifts her other hand and feels her face. Tender places, but the skin feels intact. A lucky break, she thinks, then chuckles internally at her pun. Then she falls asleep again, as quickly as if someone had thrown a switch on her consciousness.

Daylight. The pain is worse. Now her whole leg is made of molten lead. I must have been drugged last night, she thinks. Lies still and concentrates on breathing the pain away.

The pillows are deep. And yet at the same time light. They must be filled with feathers.

She wakes, and it's evening, and this time the pain is so strong that she lets out a groan. In the ante-room someone moves, and Ursola pops her head out to look. 'Oh, thank God,' she says, 'you're awake. We were starting to get worried.'

The pain soaks her in sweat. She grits her teeth, tries to pull herself upright, but the drag of her heel across the mattress wrings a gasp from her lips.

'Don't move,' says Ursola. 'You want to keep that leg as still as you can. I've got it splinted, but you've got to stay still. It was a nasty break, that. I'll rig up a sling tomorrow. Get it into the air out of harm's way.'

'What happened?'

'You've had an accident.'

347

'I can tell,' she says, but the rudeness just makes Ursola smile. 'What have I done?'

'Broken your leg. Clean snap through the tibia, as far as I can see, and it looks as if you've torn the ligament that attaches your fibula to your knee. Your foot turned clean round, you know.'

Hearing the detail does little to reduce the pain.

'And you've bashed your head. And a couple of fingers. You've been out for the count for—' she looks at her watch '—nearly thirty hours. What do you remember?'

'I was in the courtyard,' she says. But she doesn't remember why.

'Oh, well, that's good. At least you remember *something*. How's the pain?'

Be stoical. Be a Spartan. Come on. You're a survivor.

'Awful,' she replies, in a tiny voice.

'I'll get Vita,' says Ursola.

Vita swishes in, and she's aged two decades. Lines have embedded themselves in her skin like cracks in a riverbed and her eyes are rimmed with violet. She takes her pulse and feels her forehead, and Romy winces, for she's bruised where Vita's hand touches.

'How do you feel?'

'Not great.'

'I'm not surprised. You took quite a bash. How's your head?'

She thinks. Better than when she first woke, but there's a blank space where there should be memories. 'I don't remember anything. But my leg's worse.'

'Yeah,' says Vita. 'Well, a broken tibia's a big thing. You won't be getting up for a while.'

'How long?'

'We're not talking days,' says Vita. 'I'll get you some morphine.'

'I – Vita, I'm pregnant.'

A million emotions. Then Vita's eyes fill with tears. 'So you did it,' she says. 'Oh, my darling,' and Romy doesn't know if she's referring to her, or to Lucien. Then she shakes her head. 'It's okay,' she says. 'Acute pain will be worse for both of you than a bit of morphine. You should have an antibiotic as well. Broad-spectrum. You've quite a few cuts.'

'We have an . . . ?' she starts to ask, but shuts her mouth and thinks better of it.

Vita leans in close, grips her by the wrist and looks her hard in the eye. 'Romy, listen. There will be changes, now. Big changes, I have no doubt, and I can't be sure of the way they'll go. But you've got to promise me two things. That you'll stay with the Ark, whatever you do, whoever's in charge. And that you'll never tell that man who your baby's father is. Ever. Do you hear me? I realise now. It doesn't matter whether or not people *know* that the One is the One. That's not how it needs to be. I wish he'd never started that now. Making them special. Making them stand out. The One will rise whether they're known or not, do you see? But you must never, ever tell Uri, because Uri can never be trusted.'

51 | Romy

She is woken by the sound of the door opening, but there is no light. They have electric light in the Great House, on the upper floors at least. The only reason someone wouldn't reach for the switch on the wall is because they don't want to be seen. Then the beam of a torch comes on and she knows it. She's the only patient in the Infirmary. The Healers have gone to the dormitories till dawn.

Muffled movement. A group of people. A small number, maybe two or three. Moving so quietly that they can only be Guards. Romy closes her eyes and pretends to be asleep. Footsteps pad past her bed, pause for a fraction at the end, and the dark behind her eyelids briefly lightens. They carry on to the pharmacy door.

She lies in the dark, and listens.

A clink of bottles and jars, low voices murmuring. She risks lifting her head off the pillow and strains to see, but all she catches is a hint of khaki, a marching boot.

They're looking for something on the shelves. She hears his

voice. *Where does she keep them? Where the hell does she keep them? It has to be here.*

She is trapped in the bed. Even lifting the covers off her leg will give her more pain than she can bear. She will never get far enough to call for help. Only Vita is nearby at all, sleeping her widow's sleep in the eaves above their heads, and if she came down now it would be the end of her.

Something smashes and Uri swears. He switches on the light. 'Well, as the patient will obviously be awake now,' he says, 'we might as well see what we're doing.'

Romy clamps her eyelids and begs for unconsciousness.

It doesn't come. Instead, a rough hand shakes her shoulder and pain makes her eyes fly open. She cries out. Then blinks and attempts to look surprised when she sees Uri and Dom standing over her.

'Don't pretend you didn't know we were here, 143,' says Uri.

She doesn't have to pretend too hard to be confused, fuddled with drugs. Vita gave her a shot of lovely morphine before she retired for the night and it's still coursing around her system. 'Whu ...' she says. 'What are you doing here?'

'Need your help in the pharmacy.'

'I ...' she says. 'I'm not really a Healer.'

'I'm sure you know enough,' he says. 'You're the one who's harvesting all the good stuff, after all. Where does she keep it?'

'Keep what?'

'The stuff you bring her. Hemlock. Belladonna. Yew. Destroying Angels. Death Caps. Aconite. You think I didn't know? We know *everything*, 143.'

'Those are disposed of,' she says.

'Right,' he says. 'Not.'

'I don't know, then,' she says, tired, nothing making sense any more. 'I don't know where she would store them.'

In the highest cupboard on the far wall, above the filter cones, are some jars, neat labels turned in to face the wall. But she's not telling him that.

'Oh, I think you do,' he says, and grips on to her knee. Gives it a good shake.

Romy shrieks and the world goes grey.

When they're done, by the time they have their booty, her sheets are wet and her teeth are chattering. In the end, the threat to haul her from the bed and drag her into the other room was too much to bear. Whatever they do, whatever blood they spill, is on her hands now. She has become a Judas. Though nobody made Judas make his choices with torture.

They decant the berries, the seeds, the fungi into a bag, tie the top of the bag, steal filter cones for good measure. I must remember this, she thinks. I must remember, when they come in in the morning, and warn them, she thinks. Something – someone will be poisoned by tomorrow. I must warn them. When I wake up, before it's too late.

Willow approaches and stands over her bed. 'Sorry, Romy,' she says. 'No hard feelings, eh?'

'That's okay,' she says. 'I'll kill you one day.'

'Very good,' she says, and laughs. Produces a hypodermic, holds it up to the light falling through the pharmacy door. 'Anyway. Sorry about the pain. This'll sort it out.'

'What is it?'

'Just a nice shot of morphine.'

'No,' she says. 'I had some earlier.'

Willow smiles. 'So you'll know what it's like, then.'

Among the Dead

December 2016

52 | Romy

I have to stop on Bridge Approach Road to catch my breath, for it is coming short and fast and my legs have no strength. I prop myself on a wall and breathe. In through the nose, out through the mouth. You *can* do this, Romy. There is no alternative. Fast. I'll make it fast and unexpected, as he asked, but I must get there first.

The sound of shoes and laughter. Running footsteps slowing, and three girls come towards me through the kissing gate. The tall one has scarlet hair and her eyelashes are improbably long, as though two spiders have been smashed onto her face with a sponge. I have a good idea who this is.

And she's carrying my sister's medallion.

It dangles from her fist on its broken string and they're laughing. They stop near me as though they don't even see me and laugh until they hug their stomachs.

'You're awful, Marie,' says one of the girls.

'I *know*! Isn't it great?' she replies.

Micro-glances in my direction, showing off. It's not that they've not noticed me. See us, the girl gang, they say. Envy our youth and power, pregnant woman. I remember being fifteen. There's no scorn like the scorn of a teenager.

I heave myself to my feet, walk over and snap the necklace out of Marie Spence's hand.

'Oi!' she shouts.

I give her the Look. She's four inches taller than me, but she has the wisdom to back away.

I walk on to the footbridge.

My siblings have got into a routine. Every day at half-past eight they leave the house and Ilo walks Eden to school. Routine. Something Uri is fond of. Something Lucien and Vita adored. Routine is convenient, but it also makes you vulnerable.

Oh, baby, can you feel my heart? Because it's heavy with sorrow. Will I tell you, one day, of the things I have done for you? I don't know. You will need to understand that sacrifices must be made, but will it make you think less of your mother, as a person?

I walk up to the bridge, the necklace pressed deep into my palm, and even as I reach the kissing gate I hear the sobs. It rises above the blast of the traffic: the wail of a banshee, the howl of a wolf. And I'm lumbering at speed up the incline to get to them, my bloodied knife in my pocket.

I crest the top, and see Eden, back against the safety barrier, body convulsed, the contents of her book bag spilled at her feet, pages flapping in the wind from lorries passing below. She is purple in the face, and Ilo, beside her, attempts to put his hand on her shoulder. She bats it away. Her curls toss in the wind and tears stain her cheeks.

I can't do it. In this moment, I realise that I *really* can't do it. I'm so sorry, baby. We'll have to take our chances. I am not made of such stuff. I'm not strong enough, after all.

I call out her name above the traffic boom, but she doesn't hear me. She's shouting at Ilo, now, flailing her hands at him. 'You're meant to take care of me, Ilo! You're meant to protect me!' Her head jerks as she scans the ground, as though she hopes Marie will have thrown the necklace down.

I call out. 'Eden!'

He hears, glances over, sees me and his face goes pale. He thinks the time has come. Thinks he knows why I'm here. I give him a little shake of the head, just a tiny jerk, but he sees me. I know he sees me. I can talk to him later, tell him why. For now, though, I just need to get her necklace back onto her neck, get her calmed down, work out what to do next.

I advance, hold the medallion out at arm's length, call her name again. 'Eden! It's okay! I have it! Look! It's okay!'

She doesn't hear. She's gone so deep inside that everything beyond her mind is just background noise. I stop. Stand beside her, open my hand with the medallion and its broken cord on the palm.

She slaps the palm away.

The world stops.

'*Eden!*' I shout in horror, and she freezes, looks up. The necklace glints in the morning sunlight as it slices the air. I dive after it, too late. Snatch at nothing as it falls onto the motorway.

'What?' she says. 'What was that?'

She doesn't even ask what I'm doing here. I think she's forgotten I ever went away.

Despair overwhelms me. 'I got it back,' I say. 'I got it back! Oh, *Eden*!' and I climb onto the parapet to gaze down at the road below. Some stupid instinct to see the thing that is forever lost, one last time.

Ilo stares at me. Oh, don't, little boy. Don't judge me. I'm not a monster. Even after all this, I'm not a monster. Then he drops to his knees and starts gathering up the spilled contents of her book bag, crawling forward and sweeping pencils, paper, phone, maths primer, into his arms.

Eden stops still. Climbs up onto the parapet beside me and cranes out into the wind. 'Where is it?' she asks. 'Can you see it? Where is it?'

She leans out further, strains to see the road beneath our feet.

Down below her, Ilo grasps both of her ankles with his hands, and yanks them towards him.

She goes without a noise. Just a gasp and a windmill of arms, and she's gone. And then a mighty juggernaut roars out from beneath the bridge, and there's a dull liquid boom, like something exploding in the distance, and brakes shriek and tyres squeal and metal starts to crumple like paper on the crash barriers, and the world below disappears in a mist of scarlet.

We stand back and face each other. He looks more thirteen at this moment than at any time since I found him. There's camomile growing between the cracks of the paving, and his face is white.

'I knew you couldn't do it,' he says. And he starts to weep.

53 | Sarah

After Ilo leaves to walk Eden to school each morning she has roughly fifteen minutes of quiet time before she gets into the car herself. After years of getting up in solitude, she is quickly adjusting to enjoying these brief hiatuses in the day's business. A final cup of tea, a morning cigarette: this has become her ritual.

She's out at the garden table when she hears the noise. A sound she's never heard before: a horrifying mix of impact and metal and stone.

She jumps to her feet. '. . . the fuck?' she says, to no one.

Then she notices that the motorway has gone silent.

She stabs out her cigarette and goes inside. Starts to put on her shoes, for she is still wearing slippers. Through the stained glass panel by the front door she sees people run along the street at the end of the driveway. Towards the footbridge.

She goes out. Sue from two doors down is standing on the pavement, mulberry towelling dressing-gown pulled around her pyjamas, staring down the road. 'What was that?' she calls. 'Did you hear it?'

359

The silence feels unnatural. These houses haven't been without a background hum for fifty years. Even at three in the morning, the quiet is still broken by the sound of passing engines.

Someone runs round the corner from the Canaan Estate. Ray Spence, England rugby colours pulled over formal shirt and trousers, hair still damp from washing.

'What's going on?' calls Sue. 'Do you know?'

'Something's happened on the road,' he calls back, all animosity forgotten. 'Sounds like a pile-up. Did you see Marie this morning?'

'No,' she says. 'I've been indoors.'

He runs on. Sarah starts to walk towards the silence.

All the neighbours are out. As she approaches the bridge, new sounds replace the growl of traffic. The slamming of doors, the groan of settling metal, and, slowly rising, a clamour of voices. Screams, shouts, appeals for help. Oh, God, she thinks, it's really bad. In the far distance, to the west, a growing cacophony of car horns. And, approaching, the rising wail of a dozen sirens.

She hesitates. The air is fresh, damp, with a hint of overnight frost. Should I go? she wonders. Should I join the mob? Can I help? Or would I just be another sensation-seeker looking for an anecdote?

The thought of the children pushes her forward. What if they were on the bridge? What if they hadn't got safely into Finbrough before they saw it?

You can see the road before you hit the bridge, from the path. Down below, fifty yards to the London side, a Stobart truck straddles the lane divider, miraculously upright. Three cars wedged beneath its wheels and a dozen more higgledy-piggledy across the road, pointing anywhere but east. And, all along the fifty yards, a red-black smear of something dragged along the tarmac, something that's broken up as it went. Something that was once alive.

She walks on. Weaves her way through silent, gawping neighbours. Below, a flashing blue light challenges the morning gloom and a squad car crawls out from beneath the bridge along the hard shoulder. Someone throws up, bent double, into a patch of nettles. A woman sobs. A man puts his arm around the shoulders of a boy in Wellesley Academy uniform and tries to turn him away. They were going to be late, she thinks, nonsensically. They've got an excuse now. And still she walks on, cranes to see the little knot of people who have made it to the middle of the footbridge.

They're bending over something. Too far away for her to see clearly. Heart sinking, she keeps walking forward. The westbound lanes are chock-a-block, moving forward at a crawl, indicators flashing where the cars in the fast lane are forced to move across to steer around the stricken cab of the lorry.

Twenty feet away, and one of the knot of people moves aside, stands up, bends to pick up what looks like a book that threatens to blow through the bars onto the carriageway. Around their leg, she gets a view at last of the focus of their attention.

It's Ilo. All alone, sitting with his back against the railings. Knees drawn up to his chest, and rocking.

54 | Sarah

He can't stop crying. She's not sure she has ever seen so many tears. He's only a little boy, she thinks again, though the little boy's voice has broken and the sobs that come out of him come in a round, rich tenor. Romy sits beside him, encircles him with her arms, and tears pour down her own face as she does so. Seven hours, it took her to come down from Hounslow on the bus after Sarah's call to her mobile, the motorway closed from Slough to Newbury and the traffic on the alternative routes moving at a crawl. There's not been a pile-up this bad since the 1980s, says the radio news, and because of the requirement for forensic investigation and accident enquiry it's unlikely to get better for forty-eight hours.

Eden killed six people in her fall, and another three hang by a thread in the Reading ICU. How do you miss the fact that someone's so close to the edge that they don't even care whose life they destroy when they die? I will never forgive myself, Sarah thinks. Never.

This is a part of parenting that nobody warned her about.

362

How could they? She wants to weep alongside him. Wants to howl at the night sky, rub ashes into her hair, scrape her skin red-raw, close the door and pull the curtains and crawl beneath the covers to wait for this to go away, but she is the adult now.

'It's my fault,' he sobs. 'I killed her,' and it feels as though it's the millionth time she's heard the words. So much so that she no longer bothers to protest. If he needs to say it, he needs to say it, she tells herself. It's part of the process, for him, clearly. Perhaps if he says it often enough, if no one denies it or tells him to shut up, he will eventually accept that the responsibility is Eden's alone. And Marie Spence's. Not his.

Perhaps I will, too.

The images conjured by his words will haunt her forever. All she can see when she closes her eyes is that poor child, struggling and struggling to hold her back from the blustery edge.

'I killed her,' he says again, and rocks in his sister's arms.

'You didn't,' she says. 'Oh, Ilo, you're the bravest of all of us.'

'Yes,' says Romy. 'What you did ... you were braver than I ever could have been. You are a warrior. You are a hero. I know, if you could, you would save the world entire.'

People keep coming up the driveway. Each time she looks out, the bank of cellophane-wrapped flowers leaning against the front of her house has grown. At least the garage will be experiencing a profit bump, she thinks, resentfully. Why do people do that? *Why?* What makes them think that a family in mourning will mourn better amid the smell of rotting foliage? That our lives will be improved by having to find a way to dispose of it all?

It's just getting in on the act, really, she thinks. And then she hates herself for the sort of person she is.

The Christmas tree is still up. She wants to tear it down, hurl it into the street. There is no place in this house for such vulgar splendour. Never was. Never will be. How did I not know that her good spirits when we hung those baubles were all a lie? That those sunny smiles hid someone so easily tipped over?

At five, full dark, she hears movement outside the window, the sound of murmuring voices, a strangled sob. Cracks the living room curtains to see the intruders and feels a rush of rage.

'Oh, this is too much!' she says, and heads for the front door.

Romy looks up. Ilo has curled up on his side beside her and finally fallen into an exhausted sleep. 'What is it?'

'Helen Brown.' Her voice comes out high with strangled fury. 'Helen bloody Brown. And she's brought that girl with her. That bloody, bloody girl.'

'Girl?'

'Marie Spence.'

Romy looks startled. Sits bolt upright in her seat as though she plans to leap to her feet and run.

Sarah storms through the hall and throws the door open. 'Get away from here!' she shouts. 'Just get away!'

Marie and Helen both start. Marie is wearing no make-up: the first time she's seen her without, ever. She seems to have shrunk. With her red-rimmed eyes and her colourless lips, she looks diminished. The urge to march out there and start laying her fists about is almost too strong to overcome. 'Get away!' she shouts again. 'What are you *doing* here? What are you even ...?'

'Sarah ...' says Helen.

'Oh, don't you even start,' she snarls. 'Don't think I don't blame you too.'

Helen looks gobsmacked. Well, so you should, she thinks with a jolt of satisfaction. It's as much your fault as anybody's, pretending to be their counsellor and betraying their confidence.

364

'And you!' She turns on Marie, all contempt. 'I don't even know how you have the gall to come here. How do you feel now, *killer*?'

Marie shrinks even more. Finds her words, pushes them out in a little-girl voice. 'I was going to give it back,' she stutters. 'It was only a joke.'

'A *joke*!'

'And the woman came along. We were waiting where you come off the bridge and I was going to give it back, and she took it. She just grabbed it, and—'

'Oh, fuck off,' she says, and takes a step out of the doorway. Sees them recoil, sees fear on their faces. I must look like a banshee, she thinks, and then she thinks: good. I want them to be afraid. I want them to know what they've done. 'Get away from here!' She sweeps a hand through the air. 'Just get away!'

Their eyes drop and they turn to go. She slams the door. There will be no forgiveness. The world is spoiled.

Romy must have gone to her room while she was in the hall, and Ilo, alone in the drawing room, has woken up. 'What was that?'

'Never mind,' she says. Goes and sits beside him. 'How do you feel?'

'I killed her,' he says, his voice strained and empty, and she wraps him in her arms.

Romy stays in her room for half an hour. When she reappears, she has her phone in her hand. Stands over them on the sofa and says 'Ilo, I've been talking to Uri.'

He straightens up. Sarah feels something change in him. 'You found him?'

Romy blinks. Stares long and hard into his eyes. Then: 'Yes,' she says. There's a hesitancy to her voice. 'No, he found me.'

Ilo stares back. She clears her throat, and when she speaks

365

again the assurance has returned. 'It's been on the news, appar-ently. With her name. He called when he heard.'

'Oh,' he says, and his eyes fill once more with tears.

'Do you want to speak to him?'

Ilo nods, swallows.

'Who's Uri?' Sarah asks.

Romy's eyes move over to her face. 'Eden's brother.'

'Half-brother,' says Ilo, automatically.

'He ... there were other survivors?'

'They left before it happened,' says Romy. 'They got out before it was too late.'

'Oh. "They"?'

'Other people. They left. Before it happened. But they stayed together.'

Sarah drinks this in. 'I'm not sure ...' she says. She's never heard this name before. Feels herself slip out of her depth again.

'Please, Aunt Sarah,' says Ilo. 'He knew her. He knew her then. He knew me.'

The world seems to be slipping through her fingers, but she thinks she understands.

He picks up at the first ring. 'It's me,' says Romy. 'Yes, he's here. Of course.'

She holds the phone out. Ilo, small, defenceless, takes it.

'Hello?' he says. Listens and seems to shrink into himself. His eyes fill once again with tears. 'Thank you,' he says. Then, 'But I don't understand why she had to die.'

His voice breaks. He presses the handset to his face and begins to rock. 'Yes,' he says. 'Yes, thank you. I understand.'

He listens some more. Is he getting comfort from this? she wonders. Have I done the right thing? But then she sees his facial muscles begin to relax, and she knows that she has. People who

366

knew them then. Of course that's what he needs. Romy too, probably. I may have learned to love them, but I didn't know them *then*.

'Yes,' says Ilo. 'Yes, she was. I know. I just don't know ... Why does it have to *hurt* so much?'

Should I go and make a cup of tea? She wonders. Give them some privacy? And suddenly the gloom descends. I am alone again, she thinks. Once again, I am on the outside.

Ilo looks up at Sarah. 'He wants to speak to you,' he says. 'He wants to know if that would be okay?'

When she thinks of it later, the voice comes back to her as the most beautiful she's ever heard. Deep, masculine, strong. But full of kindness, full of understanding. The sort of voice that makes you feel that it has wisdom to impart.

'I wanted to say,' he says, 'that I'm so very sorry for your loss.'

And suddenly she is the one who is crying. 'And for yours,' she says.

He thanks her. 'She was a beautiful creature.'

Grief will colour everything beautiful. 'She was. Oh, she *was*. I loved her,' she tells him. 'I want you to know that she was loved here.'

'She always was,' he says. 'She was easy to love. I know you've been good to her. I know she was lucky to find you.'

'Thank you,' she says. 'It's going to be ... I don't want to be here any more. This town. This house. Christmas ... '

'I understand,' he replies. 'I hear your pain.'

Before the End

June 2016

55 | Somer

There are not enough tears. There will never be enough tears. She has loved him for twenty years, and that love has been everything to her. The hope that she would one day return to his good graces has kept her here for thirteen years, and now he's gone and the world is hollow. Without him, the prospect of surviving seems futile.

She wakes before dawn on the day of the funeral, slips from her bed and watches her daughter. So beautiful in the half-light, golden lashes brushing golden cheeks. Eden still sleeps the way she did as a toddler, body wide open to the world, fist clenched upon the pillow. My beautiful girl, she thinks. You are the best of me, and of your father.

She goes out into the cool morning. The courtyard all prepared, the pyre awaiting Lucien's body, the trestles and the flowers. Every inch of it familiar; a whole world that has been the whole of her world. Everyone has put their love into this task; even the Guards, though they're packing up their belongings

371

in preparation for leaving, have been amazingly helpful. Have thrown themselves into the preparations, bringing up a barrel of cider from the godown, cutting great branches of rhododendron to include in the pyre because, they say, the green leaves will make the smoke smell sweet.

In the orchard she picks an apple and crunches it slowly, watching the sky behind the eastern hills turn slowly blue, watching high wispy clouds catch fire. So beautiful, this place. Even with him gone, even with a funeral to get through and those Guards still here, still giving us the evil eye. There won't be anywhere more beautiful, out there. Am I the only one here who's wondering if they've given up their adulthood for nothing?

And she remembers Lucien the first time she saw him, coming out of the Great House doors to greet them as Vita opened up the minivan, and the tears come again. He was old even then, to her eyes, but he was so beautiful. So radiantly beautiful, and all those people working diligently in the vegetable beds, smiling, smiling, and standing up to greet him as he emerged. This great, beautiful, golden being she'd been longing to meet for months. And he looked at her and then he looked up at Vita, and he smiled and said, 'You've done well'. And she'd glowed inside. He was everything. All the things she'd been missing among the Dead: all the warmth and the beauty and the purpose.

He had come down the steps and stood over them, and taken Romy by the hand and shaken it, solemnly, and then he'd bent down to look her in the face and said, 'Welcome. You're the future now,' and she knew she had come home, to him.

I can't leave our home, she thinks. It's all I have left of him. And she sinks to her knees in the lush summer grass, and she cries and cries and cries.

*

She goes to see Romy. She's barely awake, drowsy and complaisant with morphine. Vita will have dosed her up when she came in this morning, but still she seems more drowsy than she should, not far off comatose. Shock, she thinks. We must keep an eye on her for shock. And concussion. Maybe the concussion hasn't gone yet.

'How are you?' she asks.

'I'm ...' says Romy, and seems to forget what she was going to say. Her leg has been raised by a hoist from the roof and hangs in the air in a sling. Her foot is black where the bruising from the break has spread, and her face is an ugly mess of swollen lumps. Vita says that she's better, that the head injury wasn't catastrophic, that she will recover. But Vita said that about Lucien after his accident, and Somer doesn't trust anything Vita says any more.

'How are you?' Romy asks instead.

'My heart is broken,' she says.

'Mine too,' replies Romy.

'We're cremating Father today,' she says. 'I wanted to come and tell you.'

'I won't be able to come,' says Romy.

'No,' she says. 'He would understand.'

Romy nods. Drifts. Looks back at her. 'There was something,' she says. 'Something I needed to tell you. But I don't remember ...'

'It's okay, darling. I'm sure it can wait.'

'No, it ...' She pauses, frowns as though she's searching her memory. 'I don't remember.'

'Don't worry.'

'It's important. I know it's important. I ...'

'Would you like something? For the pain? I don't suppose you can have more morphine, but we might have other things in the—'

373

Romy shakes her head, wildly back and forth like a drunk. 'I'm pregnant, Somer. I'm going to have a baby.'

'Oh, my God!' It takes a moment to sink in. 'Does Vita know?'

'Yes.'

'And she's not angry?'

'No, she's glad.'

'I . . .' She thinks. It seems so unlikely. And then she thinks some more and then she says, 'Oh,' and her heart collapses.

And then she says, 'Oh, God.'

And she says, 'Oh, God, is it His?'

My daughter's going to be this baby's sister, and its aunt. That's disgusting. It's disgusting. He didn't, did he? He's known her since she was eight months old.

Her gorge rises.

She claps a hand over her mouth until it passes. Stares at her daughter and sees that she is smiling. She doesn't see anything wrong, she thinks. She doesn't see that there's anything wrong in this. But Somer sees everything that is wrong. Everything.

'Oh, my God,' she says. 'What have I done? What have I done to you?'

Romy raises her head from her pillow and smiles. 'Done?' she says. 'You gave me the chance to carry the One.'

She can't look at her. Just turns on her heel and walks from the room, down the corridor, down the stairs. She feels as though she has gone blind. Finds her way to the outdoors by feel, struggles to breathe. He wasn't a god. He wasn't a saviour. He was a . . . dirty old man. That's what he was. A dirty old man. He was fifty when he pinned me down and made Eden, and I was so blind I thought it was an honour. But it wasn't. He would stand on these steps and eye us all, and every now and then he'd pick one out. He didn't care about the children. He wasn't doing it to make the One. It was all just one big ugly story so he could have his pick of the passing flesh. A dirty old man, and Vita pimping for him.

Out in the courtyard, the cider is set up on the trestle and the people are gathering. A last chance to speak of Lucien before he is scattered to the winds. So many tears.

She burns inside. With humiliation and with shame. I did this. I made those choices. They said I'd go to hell, the Congregation, and guess what? I'm there already. I did this. In the end, it's me to blame.

I cannot be angry with her, she thinks. This is my doing.

But the ugly bit inside knows that she will hate Romy forever.

The Guards arrive together, marching in step from the Guard House, Uri at their head. They line up, together, always together, along the back wall by the gate, and stand in silence with their hands behind their backs, Ilo gazing longingly at them from where he stands by his sister. We shall have trouble with them later, she thinks. They don't think they're Of Us any longer, any more than I do. I don't think there'll be one staying behind, except for Ilo, and I'm not sure if he'd be staying, honestly, if he weren't still legally a child. He likes being with them. I can't pretend otherwise. Maybe he'll go to them, when he's old enough.

Vita comes onto the steps and she is wearing black. They stand up straight and watch as she comes slowly down, a picture of dignity. I never really knew her, thinks Somer, and doubt I ever will. She's a mystery, more of a mystery than even he was, really. Manipulating us all. Even him.

We'll leave tomorrow. That's what we'll do. There will be no Guards on the gates and no one with the strength to stop us. I'll take the children and run, and we'll find a way to survive, somehow, among the Dead. There will be other places, other ways.

Tomorrow I'll take them and I'll find a story to tell, and Romy can go to hell. She can go to the hell of her own choosing, with her bastard baby and her lying smile. If I'd never had her, none of this would have happened. If I'd never had her, I would be free.

The Cooks distribute glasses, fill them, and they cradle them, waiting for the signal to drink. From the corner of her eye she notices that the Guards, as one, are holding up hands and refusing to partake. Wonders if they're staying sober because they have something in mind, then dismisses it. It's just their way. Placing themselves apart, as though we care.

She sees Ilo reach for a drink, hurries over and takes the glass away.

'Awww,' he says, and she almost laughs. Hysteria so close to the surface she has to fight to keep it in.

'You know the rules,' she says. 'Not til you're eighteen.'

'They let me drink in the Guard House.'

'Well, you're not *in* the Guard House,' she says firmly. She hands the glass to Ursola, brings him back to the middle of the crowd with her, to keep an eye. Always one kid, she thinks, who sneaks away and steals a drink. It's a rite of passage. From the corner of her eye she sees Horus and Sana snatch glasses of their own and run away behind the greenhouses. I'm not their mother, she thinks. And I'm not part of this community any more.

And then Vita has a burning torch in her hand, and she's standing by the pyre. She raises her glass and faces her people. 'Lucien!' she cries.

'Lucien!' they cry back.

'Burn in hell,' Somer mutters, and downs her cider. It's disgusting. Cloyingly sweet, and it tastes of foliage.

Among the Dead

December 2016

56 | Sarah

It rises up above the trees like a rocket ship, and for a little while she thinks that it's just another of the junkyard scraps and bits of crane you see strewn along the sides of motorways. And then its wings unfurl in front of her and she realises that it's a sculpture.

'What's that?' asks Romy. 'Over there?'

'That's the Angel of the North,' she says. 'Wonderful, isn't it?'

Her breath is taken away. I should have seen so much more of my own country, she thinks. There's so much here, so many extraordinary illustrations of human magnificence. I've wasted so much time sitting in my small town, dreaming of distant lands, when there was so much on my doorstep.

It should be ugly, this square-armed thing of corroding steel. A blot on the landscape, a ruination of the green hill below it. But it is one of the most beautiful things she has ever seen. Against a steely winter sky, a couple of tiny figures wandering at its feet, it soars. And she feels for a moment as though she is soaring with it.

'So we're in the north now?' asks Romy.

'Of England, yes. It won't be so long til we're in Scotland.'

She rolls down her window and lets the sharp northern air blast around her. Far away from Finbrough, and getting further with each passing second. The house abandoned, the Christmas tree dropping needles on the carpet, the portraits still propped against the wainscot.

If I never see that house again, she thinks, I don't care. I'll put it on the market when we get back, and be done with it.

And now that they're in the north, now that they've left behind the synthetic sense of safety created by the green fields of the south, the world takes on a raw beauty she isn't used to, that makes her feel small in a way she appreciates. They rise and rise, and the skies get huge and the land spreads away and away, and they can feel that the air is different from the air where they've been. Stronger, more potent. Newcastle upon Tyne, Morpeth, Alnwick, Berwick-upon-Tweed, and then they're in Scotland.

They stop for petrol in a small town whose pink granite terraces are strung with white lights, but the streets are empty and the shops shuttered, even though it's barely four o'clock. It's different here. It's probably not much smaller than Finbrough, but the commercial urgency of approaching Christmas doesn't seem to have infected it much. Finbrough High Street is host to a council-sponsored Christmas market every day now, complete with licensed *Glühwein* stall and a criminal-record-checked Santa. The memory of Eden is already lost in the rush for luxury foodstuffs, the memorial flowers on the bridge removed in case they blow off and cause another pile-up.

The pub around the corner from the petrol station is enticing – warm light spilling through windows and a pleasing smell of roasting meat wafting through the door. But the Travelodge they've booked into is ten miles the other side of the Forth, and Romy is dozing, so she decides to press on.

380

She's slept so little since it happened, she thinks. And, although she never complains, that baby must be sucking out her strength with every passing day. She's in the front seat beside her, for the belt in the back refused to stretch across her abdomen. It's going to be a biggie, that child. Despite everything. This will probably be our only trip before it's born. They say we're welcome for as long as we like, but she's not going to manage a car journey like this again if we stay too long.

Romy's doze deepens and she curls up against the passenger door, Sarah's big wool shawl wrapped close around her though the car is toasty from the heater. Sarah glances in the rear-view and sees that Ilo, silent since Berwick, is wide awake nonetheless, gazing out at the dark. Or at his own reflection in the window. One or the other.

'Is that pillow in the back with you?' she asks.

She had a job persuading them to bring anything other than their boxes, but the boot is filled with suitcases of clothes against the northern cold and her own sits, held in by the belt, on the empty seat beside him. He looks down, scans the footwell.

'Yes.'

'Can you maybe lift your sister's head up and put it under?' she asks.

'Oh.' He sounds surprised by the suggestion, his inner Spartan still working despite his time out in the world. 'Okay.'

He manipulates her surprisingly gently, his face a frown of focus, and she doesn't wake. Just snuggles in deeper as her face finds the softness. Romy lets out a snore that rattles the windows, and their smiling eyes meet in the mirror.

'She's tired,' he says.

'I should think we all are,' says Sarah.

'But we've just been sitting all day.'

'It's not just that, though, is it, Ilo? It's all of it. Sadness makes you tired. It's totally normal.'

And not just sadness, she realises with a prickle of surprise. Loneliness, too. I've been so much more energetic since they came to live with me, and I hadn't even noticed. In the week since Eden died, the weariness has come crashing back over me like a wave, but it's a different type of weariness. It's grief. It's exhausting, but sharp and intense. *Real*, somehow. Not the same as the leaden burden of an abandoned heart.

'How do you feel?' she asks. And there he is again, the young boy bereaved, his face working in the mirror. He's had so much loss to live through, she thinks. Far more than anyone so young should have to bear. It's good that we're taking him to a place where there are people he knows. I know it's not the same as his home, but some taste of the familiar – having people around him who share his memories – must do him some good.

'I miss her,' he says.

'I know you do. So do I. That's okay. It's how you *should* feel. But she's still here, in a way. She'll always be with us, when we think of her.'

He pauses.

'I'd like to never think of her at all,' he replies, and she feels herself well up in sympathy. I hope he starts to feel better when we get there, she thinks. I hope he gets some comfort. Perhaps Uri can reach him. He certainly sounded willing to try.

I could do with some hope, she thinks. Some indication that there's something better. That life won't just be a slew of sadness in a crumbling world.

There are container ships out on the Firth of Forth. Floating tower blocks, lights twinkling through the misty dark, filled with sailors thousands of miles from home as Christmas begins.

The deep orange glow of Edinburgh behind them, little pools of light in the dark on the far shore. Ilo gazes out, then studies the map on her phone, like a normal teenager. Reels off clumsy pronunciations that the locals wouldn't recognise. Dalgety Bay. Aberdour. Burntisland.

'It's beautiful,' he says.

'I'm glad you think so.'

'A lot of the world is beautiful,' he says, and looks wistful in the glow from the dashboard. 'There's a lot to be lost.'

'I know,' she says. 'I know.'

Epilogue | Romy

In the night, we cross a bridge over a river that looks like the sea, and I remember how frightened I was on a similar bridge only a few months ago, and how bold I have become. We eat lasagne and ice cream in an empty service station dining room where a sleepy Slovak waits to shut up shop, and then I get into a bed so comfortable that I want to cry for what will be lost, and then I am aware of nothing until someone starts running a vacuum cleaner up and down the corridor outside my door and it's morning.

It's almost seven in the morning and pitch black outside. It was never dark in Hounslow, not even when it should have been. All there is to see in the light falling from my window is sleeping cars on a sea of tarmac. I shan't miss this. Even getting up in the dark at Plas Golau wasn't so bad, as the sky flushed gold over our labouring heads and the mountains turned from black to red to silver. I imagine that Taigh na Solas will afford us similar beauties.

I take five minutes to luxuriate in my clean soft bedclothes, then I get up and have a long hot shower. Let the water stroke my aches away as I stare down at my drum-tight belly, the gigantic breasts that seem to have sprung from nowhere. I liked my breasts as they were before: small and neat, not impairing my freedom of movement or pulling on my upper back til it aches. I hope they go back once their function's done with.

It's funny to think that you will probably never have this experience, which seems so simple when you're out here among the Dead. This is probably the last time I shall sleep or bathe alone for a very long time.

I will miss things the Dead take for granted. Television. Soft beds. The ease of the internet. Jerk chicken. Long baths. Solitude. But what price your survival, baby? What price the world entire?

Mid-morning, we reach the mountains. Mountains on mountains on mountains. And castles and a great iron-grey glittering sea, and wild, wild moorland that stretches further than I can see, and snow on the peaks and little houses with their backs turned to the wind and roads that pass through valleys so deep that the sun doesn't reach them until it's well past noon, and I start to feel safe again for the first time since they took me away from Plas Golau.

Plas Golau is empty now. The winter rain will have washed the compound clean.

There's a Guard on the gate with a walkie-talkie, and he just waves us through as though we are royalty. Sarah's surprised to see him, but I point out how annoying it would be to get all the way up the hill and then find out you were in the wrong place, and she seems satisfied enough with that. 'I suppose that's what lodge gates are for,' she says. 'I'd never thought of it that way.'

The road that leads up to Taigh na Solas from the river Don

is three miles long. And when we get there my heart leaps, for Cairngorm is different and yet the same: a big house with a walled garden and a U-shape of barns that form a cobbled court. High walls in the process of construction, to join them all together and enclose the land within.

Uri is standing in the courtyard when we arrive. I pull up in the middle and get out, swing my duffel over my shoulder and walk towards him. Sarah sits on in the car, and Ilo sits behind her, speaking quietly.

'You took your time, 143,' he says. 'And I see you're as pregnant as a dairy cow.'

'Sir,' I say.

'Aren't you the sly one?' He sounds faintly admiring. 'I'd thought we'd kept an eye on you two.'

'An eye?'

'You didn't think we hadn't noticed, did you? Good grief, girl, you were the talk of the compound.'

I feel myself go hot with fear. He knew? He knew all this time? Was all of this just so he could get me up here and make you safe?

Relief floods through me with his next words. 'You were practically fucking on the dance floor on your first solstice. I mean, I know you weren't used to drink, but they said it was like watching a pair of feral cats.'

He's talking about Kiran. He thinks Kiran is your father, baby. He hasn't even guessed where you came from.

'Right,' he says, and holds out a hand. I dig in my coat pocket and drop the two medallions into it.

'Only the two?'

'The third was lost on the motorway, sir,' I say.

'Fair enough,' he replies. 'I saw enough proof on the news. When are you going to drop that squalling infant? We don't have much by way of facilities here yet.'

'February, sir,' I say.

'Shame you couldn't have brought its father,' he says. 'We need bodies.'

'Shouldn't have poisoned him,' I say, and he raises an eyebrow.

'Sorry. Shouldn't have poisoned him, *sir.*'

'Who's in the car with you?' he asks.

'The boy. And the aunt.'

'Good work,' he says.

'Good work of your own, sir,' I tell him. 'We'd never have persuaded her without you.'

Uri nods, speaks into his walkie-talkie, 'New arrivals,' and then he turns back to face the car and his face is filled with melancholy kindness. He is his father's son as though he were reborn.

We walk back to the car and the others get out.

'Welcome back, son,' he says to Ilo, offering him a hand, then a brusque, fatherly squeeze around the shoulders. 'You've been missed.'

'Thank you,' says Ilo.

Then he turns to Sarah and bathes her in his charisma. 'Welcome to Cairngorm,' he says. 'I'm so sorry for your loss. We'll look after you here. We'll keep you safe.'

I see her melt beneath his clear blue gaze.

And here we are, baby, safe from the Dead again. There are only fifty-two of us here so far. I'm already in charge of the Infirmary, for Uri forgot, in his rush to take his revenge, that there's more to survival than merely fighting, as Vita said so many times. He didn't think the skills component through at all, really. Ilo is already the entire Corps of Engineers, all by himself.

I'm sharing a room with Willow. I'll never forgive her, but for the time being she seems glad of female company, and I am content enough to watch and wait, and have you in peace.

387

But I am watching, and waiting. I made her a promise that night in the Infirmary. She may not know it, but I always keep my promises.

I've noticed already that she's particularly fond of mushrooms.

The food is good and the company is rough, and the mud comes in with you wherever you go, but we're far enough from a town that no one will bother us, and the hills are full of sheep and deer and rabbits. Sarah is helping out the Cooks – baking bread, plucking chickens, collecting eggs – and already there's more colour in her cheeks and a light in her eye. We still sing at night, still plan for the End, the way we did at Plas Golau, and she's already learned the words. We don't talk much. New arrivals have always been separated from the ones they arrived with, until they can be trusted. She sleeps in a dormitory with three of the older women, and she seems content. I wave at her when we pass in the compound, and the smiles she returns to me are full of hope.

And as I wander the land looking for medicines, planning what we shall need to plant, my knife in my hand ready for the harvest, I also follow Uri around and watch him, so that I can learn his habits. He likes to take a walk each day, out onto the wild moorland. And one day, once you're born and I can move again with stealth, I know he will go out alone. And then he will meet me coming the other way at the edge of the woods, where no one can see.

Maybe not this winter, though winter lasts a long, long time in these mountains. I can wait. I can always wait. One day, I shall follow. There are many places here where you can be alone, and in the winter the snow lies very deep.

And, once he's gone, we will never speak of him again.

Acknowledgements

All books have their challenges, their deaths and disasters, and each one involves a learning of some sort. This one has taught me that one should trust the right people – and gosh, I've been blessed with the right people – to help when one's in trouble, and that one should never trust a dermatologist. With beautiful irony, given the title of the book in question, one poisoned me so thoroughly as I was setting out to write it that I lost my ability to hold a thought or a memory for well over a year, an experience both terrifying and exhausting.

The patience, forbearance and support I've received from the people in my professional and personal lives (and the crossover) have been an absolute revelation to my untrusting soul. And the calm with which everyone greeted my mess of a first draft, the clarity and skill with which between them they nursed, prodded and guided me through hacking it back and finding the sense within still leave me breathless with respect and admiration. From the bottom of my heart, I thank everyone involved.

Laetitia Rutherford, my amazing agent, who like a swan gliding through the water never betrayed the frantic paddling beneath the surface as she negotiated the logistical ramifications while making me feel protected and supported. Having an agent with such a sharp editorial eye is also an extra, extraordinary gift.

Cath Burke at Sphere, who has always handled my eccentricities with calm and kindness, and to whom I owe a huge amount.

Abby Parsons at Sphere, who took on an addled author new to her and ploughed through with extraordinary steel and clarity.

Sam Raim at Penguin, who also had to do the same, and brought the same steel and clarity to the unknown. Both of you have my unending gratitude and respect.

The production, design, marketing, publicity and sales teams at both publishers, whose contributions generally go unnoticed by the reader, but who are essential to all books' wellbeing.

All my foreign language publishers, but particularly Aleksandra Saluga and her team at Albatros, who have made me feel so welcome in beautiful Poland.

My friends and neighbours, so many of whom stepped up and checked up and kept an eye: including, but not confined to, BriBri, Charlie, Jane, Claudie, Ariel and Luke, Merri, Ali, Helen, Abbie and Alex, Filipa, Antonia, Venetia, Jo, Marie, Angela and Angie, Sue, Julia. If you're not on this list, that doesn't mean I don't appreciate you, simply that my memory really is dodgy!

Sarah Byrne and Marie Causey for giving me their names.

Erin, to whom this book is dedicated, and who is, as the dedication says, amazing.

Will, Ali, Cathy, David, Lina, Tora, Archie and Geordie, always.

The wonderful Rebecca Davis, whom we lost this year. I shall miss her keen intelligence, her pragmatism, our quiet words behind the scenes, more than I can say.

The beautiful strangers who have become friends on

Facebook, who have provided constant blessed comfort, distraction and entertainment while I was unable to leave the house.

And last but not least, Baloo, who sat guard for a year in a darkened room and only asked for constant tidbits in return. A writer without a cat is like a soldier without Kevlar.